CW00833782

WORKS BY JL VAMPA

The Queen's Keeper
The Ghost Raven
Exquisite Poison Anthology: One Pirouette
Stolen Magick
Exorcism of Faeries, *forthcoming*

The Sisters Solstice Series

Autumn of the Grimoire
Winter of the Wicked
Spring of Ruin
Our Lady of War: a villain origin story
Summer of Sacrifice

Midlerea
Praeval
Helsv
Prilemia
Obur
Drift
Sorscha's
Treehouse
Rive
Eridor
Coronocco
Lyroni
Sudern Isle of Coronocc

Sacrée Mountains
Hiverterre
Lácdelle
Isle of Ballast
Wendolyn's Glacé Manor
Merveille
Forest of Tombs
Mer Row
Mer Noir
Agatha's Cottage
Seagovia
Rochbury
Vorren
Litur
Isle Tiamat
Seleste's Island Hut

Nord
Ouest
Est
Sud

Winter of the Wicked

For more information, address: jlvampa@jlvampa.com.

First edition February 2023

Cover Photography by J.L. Vampa — www.jlvampa.com
Instagram: @jlvampa
Cover design by Franziska Stern — www.coverdungeon.com
Instagram: @coverdungeonrabbit

Hardcover ISBN 979-8-9859261-9-4
Paperback ISBN 979-8-9859261-8-7
Ebook ISBN B0BQ1PN3XW

www.phantomhousepress.com

For all the sacrifices you've made along the way.

And for all the times you thought you couldn't,
but did.

For Kayleigh, my forever and always

Sisters Solstice Playlists

The Sisters Solstice Series is adult gothic literature.

for a full list of trigger warnings, visit jlvampa.com

Winter of the Wicked

PROLOGUE

TWO HUNDRED AND EIGHTY YEARS AGO
BEGINNING OF THE WITCH TRIALS

"What say you to these claims, Magus Proctor?"

The magus ground his teeth together, hands behind his back and shrewd eyes levelled on the council of elders before him.

His council.

The land had descended into madness since the denunciation of sorcery by Grand Magus Delacour. The magi hadn't openly practised in fifty years, sending the common witches and warlocks skittering into hiding. Over the past moon, the elders of his own council had begun trying and hanging anyone they suspected of practising witchcraft.

The Witch Trials had finally come to Hiverterre.

"I say you have all gone mad if you believe Hester Perrault to be the horrid creature you've just described, capable of flaying flesh with sorcery." Jéan slammed a fist down on the table in front of him, a jolt coursing through his defendant and the council of elders, as he'd intended. "Did she not deliver your babes? Nurse your wives and your children back from the brink of death after the plague? Was she not in the fields, bent over with the rest of us at the harvest?" He leaned forward, wood groaning beneath his weight. "Is her door not always open to *anyone* who might need her?"

A hush permeated the dimly lit room after his words, dust swirling lazily in the sun's lone ray through the window. Magus Jéan Proctor craved, not for the first time, an iota of sorcery to discern the thoughts of the men before him. Alas, it was only the woman at his side—the one he stood risking everything for—who possessed magic, and it was none of that kind.

Time dragged on like the perpetual afterlife of a ghost before the new leader of the council bent his head toward the men on either side of him.

Jéan swallowed down a manic laugh. In days not so distant past, he had been the one to whom the council deferred. But that was before they caught Hester in his home. Before they saw her press her palm against his bare chest.

In their attempt to reconcile what they'd seen, the men claimed Jéan's body had been alive with boils until Hester touched it. *Foul beast!* they'd cried, bursting in and seizing her under the charge of performing witchcraft to heal him.

These atrocious excuses for men had no idea what they'd really borne witness to. Though, Hester's punishment for bedding a magus would be only slightly less severe than that for being a witch.

Their land had truly descended into utter delirium.

Jéan shifted on his feet, not daring a look in Hester's direction. He felt her resilience, strong and steadfast, from where she sat next to him in the shabby courtroom of their Nordern coastal town. Hester would not flinch. But Jéan loathed what came next, regardless of the council's ruling.

"We will make our decision by nightfall." The council stood

as one, black robes billowing as they left, sand blowing in amidst their haste. The crowd of their recent friends-turned-foes dispersed, whispering to one another as they glared at the magus and Hester.

Jéan fled silently to his home, the wind off the Sacrée Mountains howling at his back, and the spray of Mer Noir in tumult assaulting his face. It was there in his seaside cottage that she found him, pacing.

"Thank you, Jéan." Her soft voice caressed him from the far side of the room and he closed his eyes.

"I did not lie to them." Jéan faced her, unable to contain the trepidation crawling up his body like wiry arachnids. "Not once."

"I did not accuse you of any such thing."

Her even temper lit fury in him. She should have been terrified. Indignant. But Hester simply stood, immovable as a mountain, arms crossed and one finger tapping against her arm as if she were simply perturbed by a mere inconvenience in her preternaturally long life.

"There is nothing more I can do for you," he spat, knowing his tone was uncalled for. But it would make this easier. "Even if they find you innocent, you will still be a pariah in their sight. You must leave here."

Hurt flashed across her face and he almost took it back. Almost.

"*I* must leave here? Jéan, we're building a life here. If I must go, we go together."

Goddess help him, he wanted to. But it could not be. He was a Magus of The Order of Hespa. "I cannot do that."

Finally, her calm disposition cracked. With it, a tear slid down her cheek. "You would stay here and defend these barbarians? Choose them over *us*?"

"They're not monsters, Hester. They're afraid. They think you're a witch."

Something sinister and wicked slipped down over his Hester like a veil. She took a step forward, her heeled boots thumping ominously against the worn wood of the floor. Long nails trailed over a bottled ship on the sideboard next to him—she'd procured it for him as a gift. Her eyes slid from the long-since pointless trinket up to meet his gaze and Jéan nearly flinched away.

"I *am* a witch, Jéan." The cadence of her voice dripped violence as she took one of her sharp nails and slid it sensually down his cheek. "Or did you forget that?" She stepped back and Jéan blinked. Hester was the perfect picture of graceful ease once more. "These people do not serve Hespa. They are heretics, much as they label me as one. It is the Goddess Three Herself who imbued the witch bloodlines with magic."

"*Magic*," Jéan ground out, "comes from an illicit affair between two wayward gods."

Hester let out a mocking laugh and the air within his cottage instantly fell impossibly cold. Jéan's breath clouded in front of him as she drew closer, the candlelight stretching her shadow into a ghoul along the wall. "I should think you, of all people, know the folly of viewing love from a pious perspective."

Jéan began to shiver, his extremities stiffening with the kind of cold that seeped into his very bones. "*Hester...*"

"*Magic*, poor sourceless magus, comes from the *love* between two gods blessed by their Goddess Three. Lord and Lady Magie de la Nuit. I will not stand here and allow you to blaspheme their love."

"I'm sorry," Jéan breathed, steadying himself with a hand on the sideboard, as a bottle of dark liquor rattled against a glass.

An unidentifiable flash crossed Hester's eyes before the room filled with delicious heat once more. "I think you are correct," she said slowly, deliberately. "I do not belong here." She turned and made her way to the back door leading out to a slice of rocky beach and the Black Sea's raging waters.

"Where will you go?" Jéan reached out, suddenly longing to go with her, but knowing it was foolish.

"I'm not certain." Her hand reached for the doorknob instead of him. "Perhaps I will build a home in the woods, far from this place, where no one will ever find me."

A vicious knock sounded at the front entry, and Jéan instinctually stood between it and Hester, the lovers exchanging glances laced with fear.

"Open up!" a voice shouted, the door splintering with the force of someone ramming it. "We know the witch is in there!"

"*Go*," Jéan whispered. Hester dipped her chin and vanished. His heart fell to its knees, but there was no time to contemplate his pain as the door to his cottage fell in.

CHAPTER ONE

AGATHA

Branches cracked like brittle bones beneath the weight of ice.

Agatha tilted her chin up, basking in the glow of the Reaping Moon. Soon, her Season would be over. She could nearly see the anxious twinkling of the Yule Moon, ready for her grand entrance over the glittering snow falling in a hush. Sister Autumn breathed in the crisp air and took in the fluffed mounds under her oxblood boots. She risked a glance at Grimm where he stood next to her, jaw clenched and gloved hands rubbing furiously together in front of him. She marvelled at how a Marchand de Mort could be so perturbed by the cold.

"Isn't Death colder than snow and ice, reaper?"

Grimm shot her a glare, one perfect snowflake poised on the tip of his nose before it surrendered and melted into his skin. "I'm in this mortal cage, *merci beaucoup*, and it prefers crackling fires and warm drinks."

Mabon poked his fuzzy head out from the breast of Grimm's woollen coat and squeaked his agreement before ducking back in. Agatha let the smile she was slowly growing accustomed to play upon her lips. Grimm's eyes settled on her mouth briefly and she hid her satisfaction.

"Come along, you unfortunate creatures." She took his elbow when he offered it, ever dapper in his fine charcoal coat. His snow-dusted hair was a juxtaposition to his clothing with its wildness, but that was Grimm. Elegant, brilliant, controlled chaos. Agatha smiled up at him, a warmth spreading through her when he returned it.

"I smell mulled wine," she teased as they approached the ivory Glacé Manor. His eyes sparked as he sniffed the air and she laughed.

"Well then"—he gestured forward—"let's meet with your dear Sisters."

Agatha lifted her hand and pounded the owl knocker against the imposing door. Wendolyn had little care for the mundane, average, or modest. Her tastes were… *Lavish* is what Winnie would say. *Pretentious* is what Sorscha would say. *Extravagant* is what Seleste would say. Agatha thought Winnie covered her loneliness with luxury. Her *castle* was certainly a display of that.

"This place rivals the palace," Grimm whispered out the side of his mouth, glancing around to ensure no one overheard. Agatha nearly laughed out loud at his trepidation of her Sister, though she could hardly blame him. "Is it made of ice?" He reached out with curious fingers to touch the door, and it opened beneath his gloved hand.

Winnie's face read annoyance, but she didn't bother to utter a word before turning her back on them in the open doorway, striding quickly into the interior of her home. Agatha vaguely wondered where her Sister's stewardess was if she opened the door herself—so very unlike Winnie—but her curiosity was swiftly drowned out by a greater wonder.

"Where is she going?" Grimm asked, echoing her own

curiosity. "She looks as if she might decapitate someone with her bare hands."

Agatha worried he was right. They rushed to follow in the wake of Winnie's ice-blue gown. Just before they rounded the corner into the main sitting area, they heard a voice shout.

"How many times must I remind you that I am not a witch?" Eleanor flailed at Winnie.

Agatha and Grimm stopped outside the door, exchanging looks before Agatha peered around the corner and beckoned Grimm to follow her in.

"One needn't be a witch to possess a *modicum* of common sense. That's why it's called *common*." Winnie turned sharply to her Sister Autumn, hand splayed at Agatha's former maid. "If I don't kill her, it will be a blessing from the goddess."

"They've been at this for hours." A voice came from across the great room, drawing all their attention.

Agatha smiled wide. "*Vera*." She rushed over and planted a kiss on the old stewardess' head, her snowy white tuft of hair tickling Agatha's nose.

She reached up from where she lounged and clasped Agatha's arm. "I told them both I wasn't doing a damned thing for either one of them until they ceased all their fussing," Vera said under her breath. "A fortnight they've been bickering, and I'm finished." She harrumphed and swatted the air in their direction.

"Ah, that explains Winnie opening her own door like a common peasant, then."

The old woman chortled, returning to her *madeleine*. Wendolyn glared at them both.

"I suppose…" Sorscha drawled, materialising on the lid of a grand piano in front of the window. "That means you won't be making any more *madeleines* for the rest of us, then?"

"Said I wouldn't do a thing for those two fussers." Vera stood with great effort, smacking Agatha's hand away when she moved to assist her. "I'm a hundred years your junior, girl. Don't you dare." Agatha held her hands up in mock surrender, Sorscha snickering next to her.

Grimm stepped forward, presumably to introduce himself to Vera, but the old crone spoke again before he had the chance. "You, on the other hand, are the loveliest thing these old eyes have seen in ages. You'll help me in the kitchen."

Mabon shot out of his coat then, darting to the hearth and hanging in front of it to stretch out his leathery wings.

"I'd be delighted." Grimm held out his arm and Vera wove hers through, her gnarled hand resting in the crook of his elbow.

Sorscha snorted. "Goddess be with you, Grimm."

Vera winked at the Sisters over her shoulder as she led Grimm to her kitchens and most likely heaps of subtle harassment.

As Agatha inched closer to Sorscha, Eleanor and Winnie began to bicker again. "Where's Gaius?"

Sister Spring flung herself down on a chaise, her wine-coloured dress splaying out like blood splattering snow. "He insisted on using the front door."

"He doesn't really have a choice in the matter."

Sorscha shrugged and a strike of the door knocker reverberated down the long marble hallway toward them. Agatha looked back at Sorscha. Clearly, Vera was occupied and Winnie hadn't even heard the sound over her and Eleanor's screeching.

"Don't look at me. He can stand out in the cold for all I care." Sorscha took out her ruby-encrusted dagger and set to filing her nails.

"Are you two arguing as well?" Agatha was nearly ready to string every last one of them up by their toes. It was like herding damned cats and she'd only left them alone less than a moon ago.

"He's very little fun, Aggie."

Agatha exhaled slowly, so as not to maim anyone. "He's not with you to be *fun*, Sorscha. *Please* be serious."

Sorscha rolled her eyes and Agatha stomped to the front door. She flung it open to find Lord Gaius in polite conversation with her Sister Summer. Seleste turned to Agatha, a vision in her marigold cape and muff.

Somehow, she still glowed with the warm sunshine of her isle. Without a word to Gaius, Agatha launched herself at Seleste, her Sister encircling her within her arms, hands trapped in her muff. "It's dreadfully cold, Aggie," Seleste chuckled in her sing-song voice.

Agatha gave her one final squeeze, soaking in her Sister's scent of coconuts and sunflowers. "Come on, then." She gave Gaius a friendly kiss on both cheeks and led the unlikely pair inside.

"Gracious Hespa," Seleste murmured as they strode toward the ensuing chaos that was Eleanor and Wendolyn. "What are they arguing about?"

"Everything."

Agatha turned the corner intrigued to find Grimm sitting at the ivory piano munching on a *madeleine* and a bemused grin plastered to his face as he watched the women bicker.

"Enjoying yourself, are you?" She settled onto the bench next to him.

Eleanor had both arms splayed out, shouting something about Winnie leaving the cabinet doors open. In turn, Wendolyn's rigid stance, with her arms crossed and a haughty look upon her face, seemed to take up the entire space, though she was not the one flailing about.

Grimm flashed his teeth, wolfish. "I am indeed."

Sorscha sauntered over and sat on Agatha's lap. She wrapped her arms around her Sister Spring. "I'm curious which one will combust first."

Seleste came up to lean against the slick side of the piano.

"All of us, if we don't get on with it." She hid her smile behind a steaming cup of tea.

Gaius made it halfway to the group of gossiping wenches before Vera tugged on his arm. "That fine prince of ours helped me with the tea and *madeleines*. Might you assist me with the tarts?" The twinkle in her eye made all three Sisters and Grimm snort in unison.

"Best wishes, milord," Sorscha drawled, wriggling her fingers at Gaius as discomfort slipped onto his face.

"Warmest regards," he bit out over his shoulder, shooting her a dark look.

Winnie's voice hit an obscene pitch, cracking off the walls, and Agatha shot up, spilling Sorscha to the floor. "For the love of the goddess," she snapped. "Cease your squabbling, you *whores*!"

Sorscha cackled from the ground and Seleste spat out her tea. Winnie simply glared, but the colour drained from Eleanor's face. The echoes of Agatha's shout drifted off into silence that descended upon the vast room of white marble and gilded winter. She let it hang there just long enough to centre herself.

Seleste had been correct. They could very well send a mountain down onto Winnie's manor or set it all aflame if they weren't cautious. She glanced at the time dial composed of twisted branches upon the far wall, calculating how long they'd all been near one another.

"The pair of you need to settle your grievances *prior* to our meetings." Agatha was met with two glowering women, one of ice and one of fire. "We have so little time before something terrible could happen. There is none to be spared for solving petty squabbles. In fact, we need to be spending this time figuring out how we *can* be near one another."

Seleste strode forward to stand next to her. "Aggie is correct." She looked kindly at each person in the room, briefly giving them each her full attention. "Dulci is much improved. If we must, our mortal counterparts could simply meet with one of us, in a rotation."

Sorscha stood, chewing on her lower lip. "The mortals can't transport themselves. It would take them ages to convene in a common location. What would be the point? We might as well continue using ravens and scrying mirrors, as we have been these weeks."

Winnie's lips unfurled from their pursed state long enough to speak. "If you're Hespa's favoured, Aggie, why don't you simply ask Her to be rid of this segregation?"

Agatha's eye twitched. She reminded herself that Winnie was just a bitter old hag. "This has nothing to do with Hespa, Sister." She was pleasantly surprised by how diplomatic she sounded. "This is a matter of our magic not being acquainted with another."

It was just a theory, but it held ground.

Agatha reached out a hand toward Sister Spring. "The first time Sorscha and I were together, nothing happened until we used our magic." She gestured toward the air. "Just as nothing has happened this evening. However, even when Sorscha and I did use our magic, we had a fair amount of time together, our powers intertwining and growing familiar with one another before things went amok." She straightened her shoulders. "I'm not certain, but I think if we acquaint our magic with one another—slowly—we might have more time together."

"I don't know, Aggie." Sorscha's mouth quirked to the side. "That seemed to be the case when we worked together rendering the barrels of draught useless, but almost the moment I arrived to see you on the road a few days later, my Estern wind came to battle your own."

"What if—" Eleanor's voice suddenly broke off at Winnie's responding snarl.

"*Why* are you still here?" Winnie snapped, her fingers curled at the maid, with nails as sharp as the talons of her familiar.

"I live here, remember?" Eleanor ground out. "I'm shackled to you for the foreseeable future."

"I meant why are you still in this *room*? We have no need of you here."

Agatha's lips parted to intervene, but great wings pulsed above them as a pristine, white owl swooped down to land on Eleanor's shoulder. The room went utterly quiet. Eleanor simpered, while Winnie shook with rage at her familiar's apparent bond with the maidservant. Yula gave her mistress a soft hoot from Eleanor's shoulder.

"I am *here* to explain my idea to your Sisters," Eleanor spoke with her chin held high.

Wendolyn's face cracked, a fault line in the ice. "Right. Your *idea*," she mocked, fluttering to the chaise. "Do enlighten them with your brilliant thought." Winnie waved a dismissive hand and sat, fluffing out her frosted blue skirts.

Gaius entered from the hall, his pace slowing once he registered the thick hostility in the air, his eyes darting around. "What did I miss?" he asked Sorscha in a whisper before standing sentry near the window.

"Apparently your darling friend Eleanor has a grand idea."

The lord frowned at Sister Spring. Agatha wondered what ill feelings had arisen so quickly between Sorscha and Gaius. They were supposed to all be in this together, but it was turning out to be a bickering nightmare.

Yula flew up into the rafters once more, and Eleanor brushed off her shoulder with distaste. Clearing her throat, she addressed them all. "I've been considering this since we all went our separate ways. I know I'm imprisoned in this ice castle with a lunatic"—she sneered at Winnie, who all but gnashed her teeth in response—"but Merveille is my main concern. It is my home. The draught is the most important obstacle right now. And I think…" She wrung her hands together to the point Agatha thought they'd chafe. "I think Agatha or Prince Grimm should infiltrate The Order."

The room erupted into chaos. Seleste violently shook her head, braids slithering against her shoulders, and at the same moment, Sorscha started spewing curses. Eleanor stood straighter, her jaw tight when Winnie huffed a laugh, eyes haughty, and sipped her tea. Gaius launched forward, one hand chopping the other as he counted every reason he disagreed. Even Vera hobbled back in shouting something.

Only Grimm sat mute and motionless. Agatha blocked out the din and stilled her own mind, reaching out a tendril to explore his coil of their entanglement. He tucked his bottom lip into his teeth and she instantly knew what their bond would tell her. He was analysing every angle of Eleanor's idea.

"Enough." Agatha hardly spoke the word. To her utter shock, every last one of them fell silent and regarded her expectantly. They could at least humour Eleanor. She posed a question to the young woman. "In your estimation, how would we accomplish something like that?"

Evidently, Eleanor hadn't expected to be taken seriously. Her eyes shifted, forehead wrinkling. "I'm not sure. Gain the magus' trust somehow, I presume."

"That's ridiculous," Winnie mocked.

Eleanor opened her mouth to retort, but Agatha beat her to it. "It's at least something to consider."

The wind began to howl more forcefully outside, sleet hammering against the floor-to-ceiling windows. The view of the mountains was suddenly completely obscured, by no fault of the night.

Seleste must have felt it too—the ominous note to air that eerily descended like the lull just before death. "Perhaps it is worth a discussion, but at a later date."

They all turned to the window as a bright flash of lightning illuminated the room.

"We need to at least try. There isn't much time." Agatha held out her hands. "It's now or never." Sorscha and Seleste jumped to each clasp one of her outstretched hands and all three witches looked at Winnie.

She sat, immovable. "This is madness. I'm not *testing* your theories." Winnie pointed at the panes of glass near to shattering beneath the torrent of storm and snow. "You've hardly used magic and look what's happening."

"Winnie, we have to try." The pleading in Seleste's voice knocked Agatha's heart against the cage of her ribs.

"You're on your own." She stood and walked out of the room, Yula following her in a bustle of wings.

"Forget her," Sorscha spat, taking Seleste's empty hand where Winnie should have been. The others looked on, magic crackling between the three Sisters. "We're going to run out of time."

As if the full persnickety nature of their magic were summoned by these words, the ground trembled and a fracture etched itself in the glass of a window. Mabon flew down and pulled at a lock of Agatha's auburn hair with his little teeth. She locked eyes with each of her Sisters. They looked up in unison as a crack shot across Winnie's ceiling, and they severed their connection.

"Time's up," Eleanor said just before Sisters Spring and Summer left in a blink and Agatha had Grimm by the hand in the next breath, Mabon clasped to her chest, transporting them back to Merveille.

CHAPTER TWO

AGATHA

Grimm nipped at Agatha's ear.

"You were uncharacteristically quiet today," she spoke softly, the light of the fire casting their room in a warm glow.

He kissed her neck, the deep rumble that sounded in his chest the only indication of his agreement.

"Care to explain why?" She pulled back, smirking as Grimm scowled at her for removing his temptation. He sat up leaning on one elbow and Agatha's gaze dropped to his lips. The candlelight danced along their edges and she knew all too well their pillowy softness. One corner of his mouth quirked up, and Agatha knew he'd already felt the heat pooling within her down their entanglement. He leaned in and she quickly put a finger to that distracting mouth.

Grimm chuckled. "If you really must know, as much as I loathe the monarchy and wish to see its demise, I shamelessly adore watching you regally command a room like a queen."

Agatha glowered. "I command nothing. We're a council of—"

"Equal parts," he parroted along with her, head lolling from side to side. "Yes, I know."

Agatha crossed her arms, causing the thin sheet to pull tight against her chest and she feared she'd lose Grimm's attention again. She did not for one moment mind that his appetite for her was as voracious as hers was for him, but she felt something niggling at the back of their bond. It had been there since they'd arrived at Winnie's. "Your face reads mischievous flirtation, but I feel your worry. Explain yourself, reaper."

Grimm sighed and sat all the way up. She kept her attention on his face, his anxiety coiling within her. "I simply mean to say that you would make an astounding queen."

"I don't want to be queen." He knew that.

"Nor do I want to be king, but we need to think logically, not hopefully." He pushed a hand through his hair that was already mussed up.

"I thought the goal was to overthrow the monarchy as a whole and give Seagovia to her people."

"Of course, that's our aim, but we need to be realistic and look at facts. At this point, we've not accomplished a great deal. We've rendered one batch of the draught ineffective. That was not a substantial act." He shrugged one bare shoulder. "The draught in our own land only seems to be growing more potent now, and we don't have a clue *why*. We haven't found Empress Amira, nor has your Sister even left to find the mysterious man in the mountain pass Amira sent us after. Let alone the fact that we haven't any idea what information is known by—"

"The traitorous whore?"

Grimm snorted. "Mila. Yes." He brushed a strand of hair away from her cheek and she fought a delicious shiver. "We need to be sensible, little witch."

Agatha took in her husband for a moment. The planes of his

face, the intelligent gleam in his eye. She gazed deeper, behind his tawny skin and into the decrepit creature he truly was. The one she felt such a precious closeness with that it was as if she'd known him an eternity. As if they had always been intertwined and their new bond was simply a manifestation of that truth. "You know," she cooed, "if you speak enough *sense* you might very well lose your mind."

The corners of his lips twitched. "And if you're led solely by your heart, you might very well lose your head." Agatha scowled, but he trudged on. "That is precisely why you and I make an incomparable pair." He reached out and ran his thumb over her bottom lip. "I merely mean to say, if our plans do not succeed, you and I might have to tear down the monarchy by becoming it for a time. *If so*, you will make a wonderful queen who leads with kindness and ferocity, and I will be honoured to stand at your side."

His eyes found her lips again and she snorted. "You're a shameless flirt is what you are."

He shrugged. In the time since their bond had taken root, every flicker of emotion was just another game of three inquiries. Though, most matches were fought within them—separately, yet ever together. Many emotions were so bewildering and complex that there was no choice but to dive deeper. The tangle inside Agatha's consciousness at present was one such occasion. Grimm hadn't been fibbing when he spoke of his concern they would need to truly rule one day—she could discern that much—but there was more. The best Agatha could decipher was that something was bothering him, digging at his logic. A thorn in the recesses of his mind. She wasn't certain *he* even knew the source.

Agatha traced his unshaven jawline with the tip of her pointed nail. "What else is bothering you, Grimm?"

He sat quietly for a moment before heaving a great sigh. "I don't trust Wendolyn."

She had to admit his frankness caught her off guard. "Why is that?"

He scrubbed at his eyes, shifting his weight on the bed. "*Mademoiselle Piety* made no real moves to stop you from burning the Grimoire. After hundreds of years, you give one speech from your heart and she abandons her convictions? Don't you find that a bit odd?"

Agatha twirled a lock of her hair around and around until Grimm reached up and gently took her hand in his, lacing their fingers together.

"It was true, every word that you said. But Wendolyn believing it so easily?" He shook his head, midnight curls swaying. "I don't know. Thus far, she's gone along with our plans, at least for the most part. But *why*?"

"Perhaps she just sees the severity of the situation. Perhaps she actually *did* believe me," Agatha countered. "Or she doesn't wish to abandon her Sisters."

Grimm frowned. "She abandoned her Sisters nearly three hundred years ago, Agatha."

"That was the doing of the Goddess." She knew he could feel her ire shoot through their bond because his eyes softened.

"Was it, though?"

Agatha's frustration pulsed, making her feel trapped. She wrenched herself free of the sheets and stood, not caring that she was naked.

"We were all four trapped by the Grimoire—by the lies we've been fed for centuries. This undoing will take time."

Grimm let out a breath. "That's a beast to slay one day at a time, but it's exactly my point." He held a hand out to her. She scowled at him for a moment before relenting, letting him pull her down next to him again. He nestled her head against his chest before continuing. "I know it's not what you want to hear, but Wendolyn doesn't trust *you*, and yet she's gone along with all of our plans. That worries me."

Agatha couldn't help the stinging truth that sent her heart beating faster. Winnie didn't trust anyone, but she especially did not trust her youngest Sister. The wicked one. The one who spoke heretical things so close to those their mother used to say. The claims that got their coven burned. Logically, Grimm was right. "You think she's harbouring secrets."

"Of course she is." He gently stroked a finger lazily up and down her bare arm, drawing chill bumps in its wake. "You haven't known her—not really—since you were eight years old. That's a lot of time to gather secrets. Malicious or otherwise."

Agatha closed her eyes, letting images of her Sister Winter flit behind her eyelids. The illumination on her young face as one of the first wisps of magic unfurled from Agatha's palm and their Sisters looked on with fascination and glee.

Winnie tucked a strand of hair behind Agatha's ear as she recited a fable about the land of the faeries.

Her heart stuttered as the memories shifted to the hurt in Winnie's eyes as their father shoved his journals into her arms, the younger three Sisters wailing. Smoke was heavy in the air, their cottage burning, and he told Winnie to be strong. The hardness that fell over Winnie in the following days never left.

The day Greta, the previous Sister Winter, came with her Sisters to collect them one by one from Drifthollow when Agatha was only eight years old.

No, Agatha truly did not know her Sister Winter anymore. Another vicious slash against their blind faith in what they'd been taught.

"I've spent an obscenely great portion of my life harbouring secrets and ferreting them out of others like a thief." Agatha grasped the crystals encased at her neck. "I'm afraid we're all four hiding things."

Grimm reclined against the headboard quietly, his even breaths and the steadfastness of his presence within her an astounding comfort. If ever their bond were to be ripped away,

Agatha was certain her ancient soul would fall to ash. It wasn't a need for each other. No, they were entirely whole on their own. It was much deeper than that. They were two tangled souls walking the same road. Two lanterns in the dark trees.

To separate them would be to snuff out the light from them both.

With great effort, Agatha pushed those thoughts away and settled on changing the subject. "You know," she said, "I'm not the only one with brilliant ideas…"

She could feel Grimm smile against her hair. "Eleanor?" Agatha nodded and he toyed with the ends of her hair. "I'll admit, I'm inclined to agree with her."

"How, though? How could we—of all people—possibly gain the magus' trust?"

"Mm. I have some ideas." She sat up and raised an eyebrow at him. He chuckled. "I'll tell you if you won't argue with me."

"Not on your life."

Grimm smiled wryly. "It was worth a shot." He sat up straighter and took a sip of the all-but-forgotten wine next to their bed. When he set the glass back down on the nightstand, she could already feel him bracing for a battle of wills. "I'll take the draught."

Agatha blinked. Once. Twice. "Have you gone quite mad?"

"On the contrary. I think it's an ingenious idea. If I'm truly, *willingly*, on the draught, the magus will eat it right up. He's so cocksure he might just welcome me with open arms."

She pushed her displeasure aside, considering. It would be risky—dangerous. But it could work. Only…

"I'll take it." She lifted her chin.

"Ha! And who's gone mad now? As if I would ever let something happen to yo—"

"I have much more experience with all things magical, and you know it."

"Agatha." He pulled her back to him, her chest colliding with his.

They'd had so few moments like this one, lost in each other's embrace, and Agatha did not wish to see it stripped away again so quickly. They could face the realm and all its iniquities on the morrow. She wouldn't let an argument break out between them. Not yet.

"I cannot believe you're siding with the *help*," she teased after a moment. "Look at you being a revolutionary."

She shifted to look up at him and he gave her a wry grin. "I began this endeavour, if you recall. And I clearly very much enjoy peasants." He slipped a hand up her thigh.

"Face it, you've grown soft, reaper."

He smiled lazily, shifting to press his body fully against hers. "Now *that* is simply not true," he whispered against her lips.

CHAPTER THREE

SORSCHA

For a fortnight she'd had a proper lord under the roof of her treehouse and for a fortnight he'd been so damned *polite*. This was not the jolly ride she'd expected when Aggie threw the Grimoire into the flames and declared Sorscha was partnered with the pretty one.

Sister Spring ran a red-painted nail around the rim of a crystal wine glass, perched quietly at her kitchen island. The first thing Lord Gaius had remarked about her home was how different he'd expected it to be considering Agatha's affinity for black.

Sorscha reached out and silently wound a vine of climbing snapdragons around her wrist, caressing the violet blooms. Ostara slithered across the worn wood of the kitchen island, with her tongue darting out to taste the air. Agatha was the Sister of the night, while Sorscha's only desire to wear black was her snake adorning her arm.

At first, it was endearing, the chivalry of *Lord Gaius Asholm*.

Then, Aggie had said she and Gaius needed to stay put until they could all meet again, and Sorscha had grown bored. With Rosemary gone, what else was there to do but torment a lone wolf? Thus, a game was afoot. She'd tried all of her best seduction tactics, but it was as if the man were made of stone. She even slipped an elixir into his wine two nights ago, but he sniffed it out like some sort of otherworldly hound. *He's an alchemist*, Aggie had said. The following day was spent convincing him she wasn't attempting to poison him. Though, at this point, it would be loads more fun than their current stalemate.

There he stood, idly stirring a steaming cup of tea, his back to her, and he hadn't even noticed she'd walked in moments prior and sat at the island. Cloaked in her silencing magic or not, there was much more to detecting a presence than *sound*, and he needed to pay better attention. What better way to show such a thing than to sneak up on him and scare him senseless?

Still nothing.

Aggie was right. He was indeed a miserable castle dweller. She was going to have to teach this lord a thing or two about using his intuition. That could be a joyous lesson…

"We leave for Eridon tomorrow." Gaius' deep voice jostled Sorscha from her salacious, poisonous fantasies.

He turned to face her and she couldn't help but be impressed. "And here I thought you were unaware I was even in the room," she said as her magic dissipated like fog.

He blinked at her. "Your presence fills the entire treehouse, demoiselle."

Sorscha smiled coquettishly. "I get that a lot."

"Ensure all your belongings are packed by sunrise."

"From debonair to demanding. How delightful you are." He didn't respond and Sorscha tipped the dregs of her drink into her mouth, cracking the glass down onto the wooden island. "You're not still angry about the elixir, are you?"

He pinned her with a stare. At least he was really looking at her now. "I'm not here to play games with you."

"Drat."

The brooding lord shook his head and began to walk away, presumably headed for an early bedtime and effectively rendering Sorscha bored out of her skull. "I've already packed, Your Excellency." He turned back. Reluctantly, but he did turn back, one eyebrow raised. "Everything we need."

"Clothing?"

Sorscha preened and nodded.

Gaius sighed. "Something with more *coverage* than your current ensemble?"

Sorscha's eyes flashed, her grin all teeth. He still didn't glance down, but he'd taken note. "Minimally more coverage, my lord."

"Rations?"

"Some. I can conjure and cook, you know." Never mind that the second part was a fib.

"Two tents?" His jaw was tight and she shoved down a giggle.

Instead, Sorscha feigned a gasp. "Why ever would we need *two* tents? Aren't we posing as an obscenely blissful married couple?"

His mouth formed a flatter line than she thought physically possible. "You embellished the assignment. We could easily pose as brother and sister."

She baulked. "Where is the fun in that? Besides, we don't look similar." She did have to admit his skin was only a shade darker than her own. If white-haired Winnie and glowing-pallor Aggie could be Sisters to her and Seleste, Gaius would be the farthest from suspect. Still, it was *far* less fun.

His countenance not the least bit ruffled by her, Gaius pulled a timepiece from the pocket of his waistcoat, flicking it open. By the time he returned it to his pocket, Sorscha was seething.

Never had anyone—man or woman—rejected her amorous advances for so long. Or with such cool decorum.

"It's no matter in the middle of the woods in the dead of night," he finally said. "We won't come across many people. At least we hope not."

His *indifference* was no matter. The more arduous the hunt, the sweeter the prey. "I only have one tent," she offered, pouting.

"Then please *conjure* another tent," he responded placidly, "or we will purchase one at the nearest town." He retrieved his coat from where it lay on the tufted seat of her bay window, overlooking her lush garden. She'd caught him sitting there, looking out over her grounds of wildflowers and garden vegetables earlier that morning when he was still giving her the silent treatment.

"Good evening," he said, turning to walk away.

Sorscha stood. "Why don't we forget the number of tents," she drew his attention back, "and practise sharing a space?" She took a taunting step closer, her bare feet on the warm floor probably more than he'd ever seen of a woman. "You can sleep in my room tonight." His mouth turned down and she couldn't help the twinkle in her eye. "I'll be a perfect lady." She crossed her heart. "I'll even leave a generous space between us all night long."

"That will not be necessary, nor is it decent, demoiselle."

She hated when he used that goddess-awful proper term. A flash of ire set her blood to boil—so she prowled closer, breaking off just before she reached him, leaning her red silk-swathed hip against the door jamb. He did not budge.

"I would not have expected a traitor to his Crown to be such a stickler for propriety." She could have sworn he was holding her gaze a bit too firmly.

Gaius' eyes narrowed, but his voice was even. "I am no traitor to the Crown. It is my duty to protect it. At present, that just so happens to entail protecting it from itself." He straightened, with his shirt pulling tight across his broad shoulders. "And I am not bothered by propriety. I am a man of respect. You, Mademoiselle Joubert, deserve respect." He smiled knowingly. "And your attempts to rile me are of no consequence."

She'd see about that.

Respect, honour, goodness. Sorscha hadn't corrupted a person like that in *ages,* not since that glorious Spring with a duchess a few lifetimes ago. "Because I'm the fairer sex?" She batted her lashes at him.

A muscle in the lord's jaw flexed. "Because you are a human being."

"Oof." Sorscha pouted. "But I'm not *quite* mortal."

He took one step forward and she nearly took one back for the austere look in his eyes. "Does blood run through your veins?"

"It does."

"Then you deserve respect."

She blinked up at him.

"Good evening, *demoiselle*."

She caught the barest flicker of humour in his eyes before he turned and walked out.

WINNIE

The hinges squeaked as Winnie opened the door of Yula's cage. Her round, golden eyes blinked open blearily and she gave a soft hoot before tucking her head in her wing and returning to slumber. Dusk was only just approaching, and Yula wasn't overly fond of rising until the curtain of night had fallen in a star-speckled hush over the snow.

Winnie was generally a night creature herself. Things were quiet at night. Mortals slumbered, towns sat frozen in tranquillity; even the animals retired to their nests and dens. When the realm was awake, it was intrusive. She couldn't think, couldn't move freely. Every sound, person, and creature compounded until Winnie thought her ears would burst. It was precisely why she'd built her home in the snowy mountains, the drifts too daunting for the common mortal to traverse.

And it was one of the myriad of reasons she was feeling incredibly off-kilter since being shackled to a cantankerous early bird that chirped incessantly.

"Do you know how to forage?" the bird chirped as if on cue.

Winnie stood still, face blank. She knew her preternatural stillness bothered the bird. That was precisely why she froze in place at regular intervals. Eleanor was too busy unloading their overly full cart of belongings to notice right away.

Why be a witch if you have to physically lug all those things around? Sorscha would say. *Do what makes you happy*, Seleste would say. *What are you covering with your need for extravagant indulgence?* Aggie would say. Winnie merely enjoyed her collection of fine items exactly where she could see them.

Apparently, so did Eleanor, the very few she had. It was the *one* thing they agreed upon.

The bird took note of Winnie's silence and halted, snow dusting the crown of her blonde head. "Are you not going to answer me?"

"Why must you fill the peaceful quiet with your prattling?"

Eleanor threw down the knapsack in her hand, snow billowing up. Winnie's blue eyes flashed. Her favourite dress was in that particular bag.

"We have a long, freezing journey ahead of us," Eleanor

ground out. "It would be a lot less miserable if we passed the time with anything other than an argument or shivering silence."

"I'm not shivering." Winnie nestled deeper into her white fur coat. She lifted a hand, her magic sorting what was necessary to unpack and what was not. "And I don't need to get to know you."

Eleanor's jaw clenched and she snatched up the shovel, beginning to clear a space for their tent. After a few moments, she paused and turned to Winnie, one hand on her slender hip and the other gripping the handle of the shovel. "Do you truly hate me so much simply because I'm not a witch? You know Agatha has tirelessly fought to end such bigotry, and here you are."

Ignorant child, insisting she was not a witch when she very well could carry some minute amount of magic in her veins. Not that Winnie wanted her to realise such a thing, but it did reveal a distinct lack of *sense* in the girl. 'Twas best to leave that be.

She cocked her head to the side much like Yula. "Do you actually think Agatha is accomplishing anything? She is not. Things are the way that they are. *People* are the way that they are. End of story."

The bird's face scrunched up and Winnie prepared her ears for the squawk. "*You know what?* I used to think that as well. I used to think Agatha was a hopeless fool for thinking she could change anything. But I was proved so very wrong when I met you. Because you know what I learned when I met you?"

Winnie set down the bag in her hand and crossed her arms.

"I learned the fool is the one who does not even attempt to bring change. The fool is the one who makes no effort to leave this place better than the way they found it. And you know what's worse?" Her weak, mostly mortal lips were turning blue, but still, she pointed the handle of that shovel at Winnie like a sword and spewed her words into the frozen woods. "*You've* been alive for centuries and *you* haven't done a damned thing.

You say you're the hands and feet of Hespa"—she flailed mockingly—"the Bearer of History. But History just endlessly repeats itself until someone has the *guts* to stand up and say enough is enough. And that wasn't you. It was Agatha." Eleanor threw the shovel down at Winnie's feet. "If you want a campsite without snow, shovel it yourself."

She stormed off and Winnie flicked her wrist, the snow instantly evaporating, just to spite her. Eleanor stopped in her tracks, looking down at the dry, brittle grass beneath her feet. She tensed briefly, one hand clenched at her side, and then she stomped into the woods, grumbling.

By the time Eleanor returned, Winnie had the camp set up, except for a fire. Let the petulant bird build her own fire to keep warm.

Eleanor threw a bundle of sticks on the ground at the centre of the camp and Winnie watched as she laid stones in a circle and compiled the fire in the very specific way Agatha had always done. Something about that infuriated Winnie, so she snapped and a lounge chair appeared across from the stacked logs. She lowered herself onto it, relishing when Eleanor's lips pulled back to reveal her teeth.

Far, far too much time passed. The girl was shivering, hardly able to hold her flint and stone any longer. Still, Eleanor tried to light the fire, unsuccessfully. Winnie summoned a book, ignoring her and wrapping herself in deliciously warm magic. When Eleanor's grumbles turned into chattering teeth, Winnie willed a small flame onto the kindling, never raising her eyes from her novel.

Eleanor whooped in celebration and Winnie hid her smirk. The bird's chirps were ringing in her ears, though. Reverberating off the frozen branches and clanging around in her skull. *And that wasn't you. It was Agatha.* But they would all soon see how foolish an endeavour this was. Whoever was truly behind the draught would only find a new way. Whoever took the empress would only find a new pawn. And whoever was in the mountain pass would only tell them what would further his own gain. Mortals, immortals…it was no matter. They were all the same.

As Eleanor unfurled a bedroll next to the fire, so close the flames nearly licked the edges of it, she shrewdly eyed Winnie. Sister Winter did not, however, acknowledge the scathing glances. She kept her gaze firmly planted on the words within her book. There, she was lost in a realm filled with monster slayers. The kind of beasts who did not hide their villainy or parade as anything they were not. Behemoth creatures of horror, with pointed teeth and ghoulish faces. Bodies stretched, torn, terrifying—itching to make a mortal into something similar. Something like them. Then, there was always the white knight, riding in on a white steed to rescue the fair maiden.

It was the white knight whom Winnie found to be the true monster.

The villains…the villains know what they are. Their ambition might be sullied and misguided, but they are what they are. Knights pride themselves in saving, while the true conqueror would prepare his people to save themselves. Like their father had, spending evening after evening teaching his daughters to wield knives, perform protection spells, and use their fists to fight back.

Oh, yes. A damsel with her own dagger is worth far more than a white knight.

Perhaps that very ideology was what perturbed Wendolyn about Aggie. She would accomplish nothing until she let the people fight for themselves.

"Why did you come, then?" Eleanor finally squawked, perched at her warm slice of the camp. "If you don't believe any of this will change anything?"

Eyes still on the page before her, Winnie kept her face blank. "That is a question I do not feel inclined to answer." Nor did she *know* the answer.

Eleanor huffed. "She trusts you, you know. Agatha."

Winnie closed her book at that, folding her hands over it elegantly. "Young maid, by the time you were born, I had already haunted this realm for nearly three centuries. I have seen things, *done* things"—she let the Winter wind slip into the fire then, flames guttering—"that would cause your blood to curdle until your viscera shrivelled up into empty husks within your very mortal body. You cannot, even minutely, understand the depths of me." When Eleanor shivered from more than the low temperature, Winnie went on. "I am here, in what must be the frigid crevice of the Underworld, with *you,* searching for a man shrouded in obscurity *because* my Sister trusts me." She reopened her book. "Now, I don't wish to discuss anything further with an infant."

"At least I know you can string together more than four words when it isn't berating me over which shoes I wear on your precious white floors."

Winnie blinked at her. "*Ivory-marbled* floors."

"Gods, no one cares!" the girl snapped, shifting away from Winnie. After several moments of blessed silence, she could feel the bird's eyes on her again. "Just… Please don't hurt Agatha," she chirped.

Winnie's fingers gripped the edges of her book tighter. "Aggie is the last person in all the realms I would intentionally harm." Even if she was diametrically opposed to absolutely everything she did.

Eleanor's shoulders lost their tension and a pang of guilt shot through Winnie. She'd lost count of how many times she'd hurt Aggie inadvertently. Three centuries of that took its toll. She shook her head and focused her attention back on her book.

CHAPTER FOUR

GRIMM

Augustus threw a fist, narrowly missing Grimm's jaw. The prince growled deep in his chest and adjusted his stance, hardly able to resist the cold any longer.

"You're distracted." Augustus had always been a bit curt during training, but he was more sure of himself in Grimm's presence as of late and it was a nice change of pace.

"Agatha and I are at a bit of an impasse."

"Shocking."

Grimm snorted, using the distraction to shoot forward, landing a swift jab to the guard's ribs.

He grunted from the impact and chuckled. "Not bad. Use your wit and speed."

Where Augustus was a corded, muscular brute—with the soul of a lap dog—Grimm was lithe; quick and nimble. Sure, he'd packed on some muscle in the time Gaius and Augustus had trained him in hand-to-hand combat and swordsmanship, but he would never be the hulking one. His strength definitely resided within his mind. Oh, and his ability to rip a soul from the flesh. That didn't hurt matters.

He'd spent the weeks since he was stabbed, and Amira was taken, grappling with the idea of taking off the limits from himself. He didn't wish to anger Lady Death or create mayhem, but he worried there was a day swiftly approaching when he would need his Marchand de Mort abilities to be unbridled—unbound from the confines of life and death, collection, and the Book of the Dead. The more he considered the possibilities, the more ludicrous it seemed that he was fettered to a strict set of rules. Of course, Lady Death had always been enamoured with him, loving and compassionate, not a tyrant queen resolved to entrap him. However…he could not shake the notion that he was more. Capable of more.

Perhaps it was part of the reason The Order had sent Pierre in an attempt to assassinate him if that was even true. Mila had muddled everything up. After her betrayal, as much as he understood her lack of fulfilment and potential reasons for what she'd done, Grimm could no longer take anything she'd said as truth.

Alas, what transpired had done so, and the only trajectory was forward. Their plans were falling into place and the waiting game was underway. With Wendolyn and Eleanor headed for the mountains while Sorscha and Gaius searched for Amira or the truth behind the peculiar death of the young mage, Grimm and Agatha were biding their time, sifting out secrets and deciding what to do about Merveille's draught stores. Though waiting was a strong suit of his, he did not favour it. Auspiciously, it provided ample time to delve into his store of power—researching, experimenting, cultivating.

He'd first attempted to enact what he suspected he was capable of with a mouse, days prior. A tiny thing he'd found scuttling around the lighthouse one night after he and Agatha had ravaged the place and she'd whisked herself back to their bed, spent. Grimm, however, had lingered to mull over too many things to count. He'd been toying with the idea of what more his power could do when he bent down to retrieve a notebook amidst the mess they'd made. A mouse ran across his boot and Grimm scooped it up without thinking.

Most found mice irritating at best and diseased at worst. He'd run a finger over the little creature's head, marvelling at how still it sat, whiskers twitching. Grimm held the mouse up in his palm, nose to nose, wondering if he could really do it. Could he snatch any soul he desired? He'd done it with Pierre. The man was not appointed yet to die, and still, Grimm had ripped his essence out by the ruff. And then he'd put it back. The mouse gave a little squeak and Grimm shushed it. "There, there. This might hurt a moment. But I'll put you back right as rain." At least he'd hoped so. He didn't relish hurting the innocent.

With one finger in between the mouse's ears, Grimm closed his eyes and focused. He felt his mortal body shift in tandem with his reaper form. With it, he could feel the mouse's soul flickering in and out of his grasp. The mouse squeaked painfully and Grimm pulled back, dropping it to the floor. He'd cursed as it scampered quickly away into a hole in the wall, shaken that he'd almost hurt something so frail and harmless.

Grimm chewed on his lip as he and Augustus walked to the side of the practice field, pushing the mouse debacle out of his mind. He tossed a waterskin to his friend. "Does your sister still work in the kitchens?"

Augustus swallowed his gulp of water and ran the back of his hand across his mouth. "Of course. Lilah would never do anything to lose that position. Those don't come around often for someone from the slums. She's so grateful you arranged it for her."

Grimm nodded tersely. He wasn't fond of the *thanks* that

came with just being a decent person. "Can Delilah keep a secret?"

Augustus stopped dead in his tracks, his close-cropped black hair shining with a sheen of sweat, despite the frigid temperatures. "Why..."

There was no use dancing around the truth. "We need an informant in the kitchens. One we can trust now that Gaius is gone and I need you elsewhere." He nearly snorted when Augustus paled. He was going to have to get used to Grimm's antics or find someone else to guard.

"*Why*?" he asked again slowly, like the word was gumming up his mouth.

"Because I'm going to take the draught, and I don't want it in my wife's food." He shoved his hands in his pockets and strolled off.

When Augustus shook off his stupor, he jogged to catch up. "Princess Agatha agreed to this?"

Grimm set his jaw. "She will."

"Like Hades," Augustus mumbled, veering off toward the barracks. "I'll have a talk with Lilah. But if anything happens to her—"

The prince held up a hand. "It won't." Augustus grimaced and strode away.

Grimm ambled toward the stone castle. The day was uncharacteristically sunny, the snow shimmering in its light. He inhaled the cold air, wishing it would cool his roiling anxiety.

Eleanor's idea to infiltrate The Order was not without its difficulties, however, it was something he knew in his gut needed to be done. But...ever the focal point he'd never expected to have, Agatha gave him pause.

He never paused before her.

Before Agatha, logic and principle guided his every step. But from the moment she'd spat contentious words at him in the throne room the day they officially met—*Hades*, from the day she'd spat contentious words at him at an inn in Rochbury without knowledge of who he was—she'd been the axis he based everything on.

Before Agatha, he would have downed the draught days ago and wormed his way into the magus' bosom. The only way to glean secrets was to gain trust and enter into The Order. He'd far and away ruined every chance of that by being a royal arse to the magus since he was fifteen. The draught, however, provided a way to mend all that. Logic stated any chance of success hinged on this entrance. Principle stated it had to be him—his kingdom, his responsibility.

Alas, terror now had her grip firmly on his throat whispering *Agatha.* While she, herself, was in his ear whispering that it should be her.

He'd turned it over in his mind a thousand times. She was strong, capable, and intelligent—a damned *witch* for goddess' sake. But, if she were under the influence of the draught, *he* had no means to protect her. Not without harnessing the scope of his power, and he was really no closer to doing so. If *he* took the draught, Agatha would have her wits about her—her magic, her mind. She would be safe, able to protect herself, and their comrades.

He saw no other way.

Achieving something as grievous as getting his wife to see *reason* was another matter entirely. At present, she vehemently refused the plan, and he worried she would take the draught any day just to spite him. He suppressed a smirk. He did enjoy her stubbornness, but he much preferred when it was directed elsewhere. Usually. A rush of heat coursed through him at the memory of some more enjoyable moments of her obstinance and he quickly shoved all thoughts of his little witch away before she brought trouble down on his head without even being present.

The temperature shift from the chilling grounds into the warm castle was divine. The sweat from their training session had nearly frozen onto his skin and Grimm couldn't wait to sink into a warm bath and soak his sore muscles.

To his immense delight, he made it halfway to his rooms without being seen by a soul. The castle hadn't exactly been devoid of courtiers, but there was less milling about as they were preoccupied with the coming Thirteen Days of Hearthmas celebrations that would commence soon. Boughs of holly were being strung and candles littered the peaceful corridors. He did not relish being caught out in the snow, but watching it fall out over Mer Noir was a delight Grimm never thought he'd tire of year after year. Life after life.

Just as he was beginning to marvel at the towering evergreen someone had brought in to decorate the foyer leading to his wing of the castle, the Grand Magus rounded a corner, bringing them face to face. Every ounce of jovial Hearthmas bliss caved in like the sunken chest cavity of a corpse.

"Ah, just the man I was looking for," Magus von Fuchs uttered.

Wiping his countenance clean of emotion, Grimm nodded. "What can I do for you, Grand Magus?"

Von Fuchs' eyes sparked at the use of his title, something Grimm hadn't properly used in many, many years. If he was going to take the damned draught, he wanted the snivelling bastard thinking he was already on it via the food he incessantly tampered with. Not to mention leading him to believe the new potency level was doing its work before he tried upping it again and making things worse. Granted, Grimm wasn't certain von Fuchs had much of a say over anything—or whomever he was working with—but he was decidedly against taking any chances with him.

"I received word from Lord Gaius this morning." Grimm's shoulders stiffened at the magus' snide words. "He's informed me that he'll be away quite a lot longer and it is unclear when he will return." His thick brows furrowed, pale lips puckering until

Grimm wanted to launch a fist into his teeth. "And yet, he still hasn't mentioned *where* exactly he's run off to."

Grimm's hand clenched at his side as he shoved his irritation down before it could show itself along his tense jawline. Why did the Grand Magus need to know where a simple lord had run off to so badly? He kept his voice as even as possible. "I do believe he's gone to stay with distant relatives in Prilemia." He hoped to Hades that Gaius and Sorscha had made it near Eridon's borders already, in case the magus sent scouts to test the information.

Von Fuchs' paper-thin lips made a small, wet smacking sound as he opened his mouth and Grimm's stomach roiled. "I thought all of Lord Gaius' family had perished."

The prince failed to keep the fury from flashing across his eyes. Grimm had long suspected the magus had something foul to do with the darling excursion Lord Rupert and Lady Manu Asholm had never returned from. One that their relatives were all to convene at in the countryside. Gaius had fallen ill and not gone, thank the blessed goddess. It was something Grimm had never untangled, but the suspicion resurfaced once more.

"It would appear not"—Grimm bowed slightly to cover his outrage—"Grand Magus." He straightened and stepped to the side. "Now, if you'll excuse me."

He could feel the magus' eyes on him until he turned a corner toward his and Agatha's rooms.

WINNIE

The aged binding of her Sacred Text of Hespa creaked as she shut the holy book. Winnie still read the scriptures daily and had half a mind to write her Sisters to ensure they were doing the same. They insisted on using inappropriate means of conversing, going to one another in mirrors and other such forbidden things.

Just because Aggie had a vision in the woods, or however it had occurred and sent the Grimoire into the flames, that did not mean they turned their back on their Goddess Three or the rules. There was a place for order, for obedience. Just as there was a time for taking a stand. If the Grand Magus was as dastardly as Aggie claimed, it was reasonable to set his demise in motion. Defying their Goddess Three, on the other hand, was inexcusable.

Something strange had fallen over Winnie, though, when the Grimoire succumbed to the fire that night. No, it wasn't something that had fallen over her, per se. It was more like something that had fallen *off*. Winnie looked down at the dusting of fresh snow coating the holy book and brushed it off gingerly. Yes, it was something like that. A blanket of snow brushed away. Or a veil lifting to reveal a bride. Winnie let her eyelids flutter shut, suddenly feeling immensely heavy. A veil that had been lifted to reveal a rotted bride.

She should've taken a stand all those years ago when she'd had the chance. Alas, she had not. And therefore resigned herself to a life of dancing with her ghosts.

Winnie opened her eyes, lashes coated in snowflakes, at the sound of chirping. The night had well and truly ended. The sky beyond the weighted trees began to turn from velvet black to a dusky grey. Red birds hopped at her feet, little cheerful drops of blood in the snow. Soon, the other bird would awaken and chitter at her like these.

These birds she knew how to silence. Rustling in the pocket of her elegant coat, Winnie pulled out a small ration of stale bread. Within moments of the crumbs hitting the snow, they were gobbled up, and the chirping began again, with renewed vigour.

Sister Winter's lips tipped up in a mournful smile that didn't reach her eyes. These creatures would lose out to the harsh course of this realm just like all the others, eventually. She conjured a hot loaf of bread, inhaling the scent before breaking it apart for the birds.

She felt the snow behind her suddenly shift. Ah, the irritating bird had risen.

"Did you even come in the tent last night?"

Winnie didn't know why she cared. "No."

Eleanor put a hand on her hip and Winnie vaguely wondered if she knew a spell for convincing birds to turn murderous. Perhaps the correct method would be to simply turn Eleanor into a worm...

"We have a long travel day ahead of us. I don't exactly want to be sleeping in the freezing woods again. We need to make it to a village."

When Winnie didn't reply but kept pinching off bits of bread for the growing number of birds, Eleanor huffed.

"You're going to fall asleep on your horse and I don't know where to go."

"Did you just admit a weakness, all-knowing maid?"

Eleanor's lip pulled back in a sneer.

"I don't sleep often." Winnie dusted the crumbs off her hands and summoned a steaming tin cup, holding it out to Eleanor. "Try this."

She reluctantly took the cup, her face instantly going slack with an appreciation for the warmth that no doubt seeped into her frigid hands. She sniffed it, her face scrunching up. "It's coffee. That's not exactly a revelation."

"It's spelled, you half-wit."

Eleanor spewed her sip into the snow. A drop landed on Winnie's white coat and she took three steady breaths so as not to reach into the bird's chest and rip her heart clean out.

"Spelled with what?"

"Every utterance from a witch's mouth is a spell." One of the birds–a robin–landed on her knee and she rewarded him with a large chunk of bread for his boldness. "That particular enchantment is something I perfected long ago." She rose, fluffing her coat and skirts. "You could say it's spelled with…vitality."

With one step forward, all the birds rushed into the air, a flurry of wings headed for the treetops.

"Do birds always flock to you like that?"

Winnie's eyes slid to her, sardonic. "Yes." She summoned her own cup of spelled coffee and took a sip. "Come on, then. Sterdon is nothing to write home about, but there is an inn there that will be warm."

When they were all packed—Winnie let Eleanor handle it the mortal way, of course—the horses were stamping their hooves. The great white beasts must have grown as anxious to find a stable as Winnie had to sink into a bath. Eleanor mounted her steed, and Winnie made to do the same, but a thought struck her.

"What is it?"

Winnie's eyes narrowed at her astute observance. "I'll be back shortly."

She glided through the snow, careful to be swift, lest Eleanor attempt to follow her. Within the frosted tree line, Winnie looked over her shoulder to ensure that she was alone and wrapped a blanket of invisibility around herself just to be safe.

Satisfied Eleanor would not be able to find her, Winnie wound her white-blonde hair around, laying it over her shoulder, and removed a glove. She rested her hand against the trunk of a naked tree, its branches heavy with frost.

"*Évider.*"

The wood beneath her hand groaned, bark snapping and a deep wound chiselling itself into the tree. When the hollow was wide enough, Winnie issued a four-note whistle into the frosted air.

A finch fluttered past her ear, flying into the tree trunk.

"*Soyez toujours en sécurité.*"

The finch chirped happily and Winnie hollowed out several more tree trunks before she brushed the many wood shavings from her skirt and donned her glove.

Warm, safe abodes for her birdlings. *There*. She'd left their camp better than she'd found it.

CHAPTER FIVE

AGATHA

"One more stitch and you'll be squared away, darling."

Agatha nodded mutely, entirely unable to tear her eyes from the intricate lacework created by Tindle's deft hands. As a welcome home, he'd called on her to select fabrics for thirteen new items of clothing. She had, and he'd finally finished the first exquisite piece. Soft fabric of the deepest black cascaded down her body, concealing her every ample curve in a formless dress of immense beauty. Her arms were left bare, but over the top of the gown, champagne tulle fell in a delicate wave. The tulle sleeves cinched at her wrists, and intricate, black lace dahlias crawled up her arms, drawing the eye to the only visible skin.

It was breathtaking. And comfortable. Extra points for comfort.

Tindle spoke around a mouthful of needle and thread, inspecting his handiwork. "I still can't believe you finagled me into your private *rooms*, you scandalous thing." He cut away the last bit of dangling thread. "There you have it."

"I'm done playing by the rules."

Tindle scoffed, scanning Agatha and Grimm's personal chambers. "You never did follow the rules, my dear." He walked over to smell the fresh flowers in the sitting area—dahlias Grimm had stolen right out of the queen's private arboretum. That, of course, was more delightful than the flowers themselves.

Agatha returned her attention to the mirror, marvelling at the lovely gown. "You said there are twelve more pieces coming?"

Tindle plucked a piece of cheese off the charcuterie board and nodded. "Isn't thirteen significant to witches?" He popped it into his mouth.

Agatha turned and glared at him. "That's a myth."

"*You're* a myth, darling."

Grimm had not been on board for telling Tindle her little secret, and he still wasn't thrilled she had. Nor had he revealed his own dark identity. But, with Dulci and Eleanor both away, Tindle needed all the way in. This was a start. Now, if he'd just stop teasing her relentlessly and spouting the protected secret like a gossiping hen. She opened her mouth to say as much and Tindle's eyes glittered as he mimed sealing his lips and locking them with a key. A knock sounded at the door and Tindle went to answer it.

Agatha had recently demanded she not have servants or lady's maids any longer. She was tired of standing for equality and then relying on a person to wait on her hand and foot. It was deplorable. They couldn't *make* her keep servants.

It had rendered things…interesting. Grimm making a bed and folding laundry was at the top of her most amusing sights in her three hundred years. She'd thought he'd grumble, and sometimes he did, but his emotions read contentment within their bond. It turned out the spoiled princeling found great comfort in a more normal life. And it made her love him all the more.

Anne, however, continually snuck in to clean their rooms and bring their food. The latter had more to do with the magus still trying to sneak the draught into Grimm's meals. They hadn't yet discovered whom he had employed to do such a thing, but Anne threw every meal away, replacing it with plates she'd served herself.

Tindle's shoulders tensed at the door, and Agatha watched as he went straight as an arrow before lowering into a deep bow.

Merde.

Queen Fleurina floated into the room followed by three stoic guards and a fluttering lady-in-waiting. The courtier had a striking resemblance to Mila, and Agatha suppressed a growl. There hadn't been a sign of the damned traitor since she'd taken Amira. To keep someone hostage, she had to be in a solid form sometimes, and that gave Agatha hope that Sorscha and Gaius would find her. Hopefully, they would show her very little mercy.

"Queen Fleurina." Agatha dipped into a curtsy. "What have I done to deserve your presence in my chambers?" She half expected the monarch to have the guards arrest her for something, truthfully. Her magic silently added an extra ward around her father's journals and the several tomes she'd collected regarding sorcery and other such folklore.

The queen primly folded her hands in front of her, nearly lost within the fabric of her voluminous blush skirts. "It has come to my attention, all thanks to my nosy courtiers, that I did not bestow upon you a proper wedding gift." Her jaw tightened minimally, but there was a cunning gleam in her eye as well. Agatha wasn't certain if what was happening was a trap or a game. She'd learned over the last moons that Queen Fleurina's every move was as one on a chessboard.

"Oh, there's really no need for gifts." Agatha let a syrupy smile play on her lips. If the queen wanted to play games, so be it. "You've truly done enough." She gestured to the lavish room around them. "You've welcomed me into your home and your family."

The queen's eyes followed the sweep of Agatha's hand, landing hard on the stolen dahlias. Her lips pursed. "Yes, well, a gift is customary. And, as such…" She motioned to the lady-in-waiting behind her, who handed over a small, beautifully wrapped box. The queen, in turn, gave it to Agatha.

Sister Autumn bit back her annoyance that the queen couldn't even be bothered to carry her own gifts. She lifted open the golden-wrapped lid, her brow furrowed as she reached in and took up the gift between her fingers. "A key?"

"Yes. To your own drawing room." Still, Queen Fleurina's face read nothing. "So you can host your own visitors." She let her gaze slide to where Tindle stood examining a lampshade too closely, and back to Agatha. "Properly."

While Agatha fought back a blush of rage and embarrassment, the queen walked over to the hearth and ran her finger along the dust on the mantle. Her brows drew together as she rubbed her thumb and forefinger together. "I'd heard you dismissed all your maids." Her ice-blue eyes shifted to Agatha's. "Intriguing choice."

Her curious display evaporated and she stood regally. "To apologise for such an oversight as the one I have made, I'd like to gift you with something of your own choosing as well." Agatha opened her mouth to speak, but the queen held up a delicate hand. "This gift should mean something to you." Again that intensity in her eyes. "Think it over, Agatha." She moved toward the door, skirts swishing, but turned back. "And I suggest you choose *very* wisely. There will be a court dinner in celebration of our ballroom being restored to its former glory in two days' time. Decide before then."

Agatha bit back a retort that perhaps if they'd spent as much manpower and coin on finding the ones *responsible* for destroying the palace ballroom in the first place as they had in repairing it, perhaps they'd be having a better celebratory dinner. Alas, she only nodded. "Of course, Your Majesty."

The queen's attention remained locked on Agatha momentarily before she abruptly turned and nodded to Tindle. "Monsieur Tindle."

He dipped into a low bow. "Your Majesty."

"Think, Agatha." And she moved toward the door once more.

Agatha curtsied, the queen's words clinging to her skin in Winnie's voice. *Think, Aggie.*

The queen and her entourage left, the door clicking softly closed, and Tindle melted into a chair. "That woman is terrifying."

Agatha stalked over to her armoire and retrieved her cloak. "She is, but it's because I can't seem to get into her head. One moment she's courtly and the next I would swear she's playing some mental match with me."

Tindle crossed one leg over the other, bouncing his foot. "Oh, it's definitely a game. Are you going somewhere?"

"*We* are getting out of the castle."

Tindle raised an eyebrow at her but stood to don his hat and austere, woollen coat. "What do you have in mind?"

Agatha handed him his scarf. "There is a new tea house on the Row, is there not?"

"And you plan to simply walk out of the castle on my arm without guards?"

She straightened his scarf and patted the cashmere where it tucked into his coat. "You will, by all appearances, be leaving here alone."

Safely in a guardless carriage destined for Mer Row, Tindle pulled down the shades over the windows and Agatha lifted her invisibility. "Sly girl," he whispered.

When the din of horse hooves against cold cobblestones and the ruckus of Hearthmas shoppers grew loud enough to drown out the driver's ability to hear them, Agatha finally spoke.

"What do you really know about Fleurina and the king? Dulci told me they were betrothed in a strange manner."

"*Goddess*." Tindle clapped his hands together. "Finally you're ready to gossip with me."

Agatha frowned. "I need facts, Tindle, not gossip."

The stately dressmaker's lips puckered. "Darling, I collect secrets, not rumours." Agatha waved her hand dramatically, and he began. "King Frederic was just a boy when he inherited the kingdom after his parents died. The circumstances of their death are something I've always personally found suspect, but no one speaks of it. He was so very young that Seagovia was truly run by his advisors for quite some time. When he came of age, I was only a little older than him and studying under the castle seamstress.

"That Summer, he went with his advisors to meet the royal family of Coronocco." He moved his hands erratically as he spoke. "Something about a lack of proper cultural aptitude. Personally, I've always thought it was their ploy to make a kind boy believe he was superior to other races. But it backfired. There, he fell in love with a girl. She wasn't royal, but she wasn't quite a commoner, either. A countess, I believe. He secretly proposed marriage to her and planned to bring her to Seagovia. When his advisors discovered this, they whisked him back to Merveille and Grand Magus von Fuchs arrived soon after. No one knows where he came from or how the king's advisors even knew of him. He just"—Tindle flourished his hands—"appeared."

Agatha twirled a lock of her hair, brow pulled low as the carriage jostled her. "Who were the king's advisors?"

"He didn't have any family left, aside from a mad cousin and his maternal uncle. The uncle stood as one advisor and I can't recall who the others were. It wasn't of much interest to me then.

I was much more concerned with fabrics and who kissed who behind Tessa Carnegie's barn."

Agatha considered Tindle's words silently for the rest of the ride. When the carriage pulled to a stop, she suddenly vanished.

"How do you plan to have tea time with me?" Tindle whispered to where she'd been sitting.

She did not answer and the door to the carriage opened. Tindle made a fuss over his scarf, presumably to give her time to exit the carriage before him. It wasn't necessary, but he didn't need to know that. Silently, Agatha followed him out of the cold and into the lush *Madame Mauve's Tea House.*

She had to admit that it was magnificent. Smaller and less refined than the tea shops on Gemme Road, but that made it all the more appealing with its mismatched chandeliers, eclectic furnishings, and feel of Coronoccan luxury.

Tindle inquired politely for a table for two and Agatha made her way to the lavatory to re-emerge in the flesh. Hat pulled low, she manoeuvred her way through the establishment and took the chair facing Tindle and the lavender damask-papered wall.

"This is bold," he censured, eyes darting around as she sat down.

Agatha waved him off, eyeing the tea service that had been delivered in her absence. "No one will think twice about me if I have no guards or a chaperone. There are seven other ladies in here with this hat on, anyway." She lifted a deep teal and gold teacup in front of her to her cold lips.

Tindle lifted his chin. "I make excellent hats."

Agatha snorted. "You do, indeed." She went on without missing a beat. "Where are the king's former advisors now?"

Tindle shrugged, stirring a cube of sugar into his own tea. "Another mystery. Von Fuchs arrived and was granted the title of Grand Magus, while the former one was sent away somewhere. Von Fuchs' first order of business was to travel to Eridon." He fidgeted in his seat and leaned forward. "You see, Eridon is the infant land of this continent."

Agatha knew this bit of information very well. It was she who'd set the house of cards tipping in order to give Eridon her kingly line. Another Order steeped in blood.

"They're only a little over a century old," he went on. "But their army is…" He blew out a breath. "Incredible. Nearly invincible. Thirty-five years ago, there were whispered tales that Eridon would invade Seagovia to take ownership of half the continent. Von Fuchs brokered peace, and the youngest princess of Eridon returned with him to wed the young King Frederic."

Agatha chewed on his words, worrying her lip between her teeth as a three-tiered stand of *macarons*, *tuiles aux amandes*, and *tartes tatin* was placed in front of them on a doily. "I wonder if the queen is happy," she mused, reaching for a *macaron*.

Tindle sipped some of his tea, inspecting the cerulean teacup adorned with peacocks. "Goddess, Agatha, are there *birds* adorning your china, as well?"

"Tulips." She held it up for him to see. "I'd think you'd like peacocks best of all the birds since you are one."

His lofty sneer melted into an impressed frown as he inspected the cup again. "They're actually rather stunning…" He shook his rambling thoughts away. "Fleurina never would have ruled Eridon with two elder brothers and an elder sister. This way she gained a crown." He took a sip and swallowed, pointing a finger at Agatha from around the teacup. "But you and I both know that a crown does not equate to happiness."

Agatha murmured her agreement, the sounds of *tinking* china and quiet conversation filling her ears.

"Truth be told, I think von Fuchs is still wary of Eridon. They're small, but they're the kingdom right at the heart of Midlerea that we all skirt around as if it's full of the undead or some other malevolence. I think von Fuchs is afraid of them."

Agatha hummed, chewing a *tarte*. "The draught would have fixed that problem."

Tindle stabbed his finger out again. "Precisely. So why didn't he have it sent there, too? Surely Fleurina could convince her own brother."

"He didn't have it sent to Prilemia, either. Not yet."

Tindle set his teacup down, reclining pompously, hands folded over his abdomen. "Ah." He grinned. "Rumour has it, the Prince of Prilemia has recently begun courting the youngest daughter of the Duke of Larosche, Lord Bonham. His is the largest estate in Eridon."

A kind woman who worked at *Mauve's* stopped by their table to set down a tray of tiny sandwiches and gush over Tindle's latest creations she'd been admiring in his shop window. Agatha kept her head down, willing the woman to not recognise her, and mulling over the conversation in her mind.

When the woman finally scampered off to assist another patron, Agatha's thoughts snagged on something Tindle had said earlier. "You studied under the royal seamstress?"

He nodded behind his cucumber sandwich. "I did. I was her apprentice, actually."

"How did you land something like that?"

"My parents migrated from Coronocco to Seagovia before I was born. My mother always had it easier than my father, she was fairer skinned and had never met a stranger in her life." Tindle smiled fondly, eyes far off. "She made friends everywhere she went. She was also a terrific saleswoman. My mother knew what you needed before you did.

"When I was still just a babe, I already had an eye for fashion. My mother noticed it, and one day when she was delivering a shipment of silk to a modiste on Gemme Road, she began asking around for the name of the royal seamstress. When she learned it—and because she could always sniff out a person

—she walked right up to the woman's shop and made her a deal she couldn't refuse."

Agatha couldn't help but smile. "Which was?"

"Me." He beamed. "For free. As long as she taught me everything she knew." He chuckled. "Hardest work of my life, but Rion kept her word to my mother, goddess rest her soul. She even planned for me to take over her duties one day. But, I wanted my own legacy on Gemme Road, not just serving the royals." His face abruptly fell, jarring Agatha.

"What happened, Tindle?" He'd never talked about it, no one seemed to even know... "How did you lose it all and end up Blacklisted?"

He sat silently, so she leaned forward and reached out to grasp his hand across the table, one of the teacups clinking against his plate as she knocked into it. She didn't want to pressure him, but there comes a time when one's ghosts need to be set free. The longer they roam the soul, the more havoc they wreak. Agatha would shoulder Tindle's spectres without question if she must.

When he looked up from his *tarte*, his eyes were misty. "I fell in love. With one of von Fuchs' guardsmen."

Agatha closed her eyes against the impact of his words. She suddenly knew precisely what she desired her gift from the queen to be. Let the games play on.

CHAPTER SIX

ELEANOR

"How did you receive a letter?"

Eleanor jumped at the sound of Wendolyn's voice, startled into crumpling up the parchment and shoving it into her satchel. They'd only been at the inn long enough to procure a room with two small beds and a window offering a picturesque view of the Sacrée Mountains off in the distance. The snow was much lovelier when one wasn't standing in it.

"We've hardly set our bags down and you've already received post," Wendolyn pressed, a haughty glint in her eye. "How?"

"For an ancient witch, you're awfully dense at times." Eleanor did not wait to see the effect of her words on Wendolyn's face—there would be none. She would stand there, icily stoic as ever, and glare.

Eleanor took off her sopping boots and set them by the blissfully warm hearth before unbuttoning her coat. She felt the

Winter witch's condescending eyes track her movements as she moved to discard her dress, neither of them uttering a word, and Wendolyn turned to sit with her back to Eleanor.

There was no way in Hades she was taking a bath second. Wendolyn could conjure her own damned tub and heated water if she needed to. Eleanor was done being seen as the servant in this endeavour. Or ever. No one should have to serve unless they wanted to, and even then, it should never be servitude, but a respectable profession with proper wages.

Eleanor had begun in the castle as a serving wench at dinners and balls. She worked her way to the laundry, and then, one day, she'd been asked to attend the queen's tea party. From then on, her duties were…more tolerable. When Agatha showed up at the castle, the queen frantically pointed out two maids she could spare to attend to the prince's betrothed. At the time, it had felt like an honour. Once she learned Agatha's origin, it felt like a demotion. And Eleanor had grown tired of chains. She was worth something. More than servitude. More than assistance. She might fault Agatha for…a lot, but she could credit her one thing: she fought for equality. And Eleanor would fight for it, too.

Sometimes, Eleanor thought perhaps she'd been horribly mistaken for getting herself willingly mixed up in the whole charade. She could have simply left the castle and worked with her gran to provide a more tolerable life for those in the slums.

When she'd begun to suspect Agatha was a witch, she could have just kept her head down; kept moving. But she hadn't. When she saw Grimm's eyes begin to linger on Agatha and how the spark between them turn into an inferno, Eleanor should have just ignored it. When they began sneaking out at strange hours and going to peculiar places, she should have just assumed she'd find them naked and in the throes of passion.

But she'd known better. And that was all she wrote. The decline of normalcy for Eleanor Moreau.

Alas, her gift of curiosity—as Gran called it—led her into a den of trouble and on a chilling path with a frigid witch.

Deep down, Eleanor knew her task could help save Merveille—help save Seagovia and all Midlerea. She knew there was more to this man in the mountain pass than a petty errand from a superstitious empress. Either way, Eleanor regretted her moment of stubborn independence that night in the woods surrounded by witches lit by the power of the moon. She should have just gone with Gaius. Their friendship was casual at best, but he wouldn't have driven her mad and she could have fought for freedom without a needle in her spine named *Wendolyn*.

Winnie looked up from the book she'd opened in her lap. "Why am I so daft, witty maid?"

Eleanor fought a snort. She hadn't expected *Her Highness* to respond at all. Perhaps she'd gotten under her skin. *Good.* "People do not only look at parchment if it is a letter. And if it is a letter, it does not have to be one sent by post or one received right at that moment." She smiled smugly and slipped into the deliciously warm bath water. One day when she was filthy rich, she would send a hefty sum to whoever drew this bath up for her.

As the water soaked into her tired muscles and worn soul, Wendolyn stared ruefully. Ruining everything. Her countenance bordered on cold confusion as she spoke again.

"It is sentimental, then?"

As if the thought of sentiment had never even crossed the witch's mind before. Eleanor positioned her neck against the cool lip of the copper tub, letting it press against the tension there, and closed her eyes. The steam rose off the water, climbing up her chest and moulding to her cheeks. Perhaps it would draw the dark circles from underneath her eyes. She'd not looked in a mirror since before they left Wendolyn's icy manor, but she was certain her countenance was abysmal. Between restless, shivering sleep on the road and the crime against nature that was Wendolyn's coffee, Eleanor hadn't seen rest in far too long.

"It's really none of your business," she murmured, lost in her small corner of momentary bliss.

"It is if it was a letter from one of my Sisters."

Eleanor opened one eye, without so much as moving another muscle. "Why would a letter from any of your Sisters reside in my bag as *sentimental*?"

"I mean," Wendolyn ground out, "if Agatha has sent any more information, I deserve to know."

Eleanor lifted her head, angling it toward the Winter Witch. "And precisely why would that information come to me, hm?" She rolled her eyes before closing them and returning to her relaxed state.

Wendolyn huffed, returning her attention to her book. Three breaths later, she stood and stormed for the door, tossing the tome onto the bed.

"Where are you going?" Eleanor asked. "To get us some stew?"

Wendolyn reared back like she'd been slapped. "Do I look like a servant to you? I must go tell them to draw another bath because I will not tolerate tepid or *used* bath water."

Spoken like a true witch with ne'er a sordid day in her life. "Does that mean you expect *me* to retrieve supper for us, then?"

Wendolyn did not miss the challenge in Eleanor's eyes, her own narrowing in response. Eleanor was done playing the servant. She did not weasel her way into the castle kitchens and claw her way up to attending the princess to be reduced to a scullery maid by someone she hardly knew. She raised her chin. "I can do more than collect supper and firewood, you know. I'm here because Grimm and Agatha saw value in my coming along."

Wendolyn snorted derisively and opened the door.

Water sloshed over the sides of the tub as Eleanor sat up. "If you'd just tell me the plan, I could *help*."

The peeling papered walls rattled with the force of Wendolyn slamming the door behind her, leaving Eleanor alone and fuming. *Fine.* If Wendolyn wanted to keep her in the dark, she'd figure out the secret plan herself.

She rose from the tub, loath to find there was nothing by way of a towel nearby. Grinding her teeth, she used her sodden dress to wrap around herself and drip over to where the *one* towel was folded over a chair across the room. Eleanor wrapped it around herself and headed straight for Wendolyn's pack. Prepared to rifle through it and memorise its contents to put them back in order, she reached to untie it. The moment she touched the strings at the opening, a zap of static shot through her hand with such force it felt like a bolt of lightning coursing all the way up her arm. Clutching her shoulder where it radiated with pain from the enchanted bolt, she shuffled back to her side of the small room and dressed in simple wool stockings and a dark grey woollen dress.

Methodically, she plaited her golden hair into two braids and wove them together on top of her head. Despite the fire in the hearth, the room still had a draft. Eleanor considered sitting by the fire, but she knew once she moved away from it, she'd only be colder than before. It was best to snuggle up under the covers of the disgusting bed until her hair dried. She might have grown up in the slums with her gran, but she would never again sleep in sheets any less than crisply clean after this endeavour was over.

Face scrunched in disgust, Eleanor took the corner of the blanket between her thumb and forefinger, pulling it back. She suppressed a shiver as she climbed in. The mattress was more comfortable than the ground—she could grant the inn that much. Who was to say how the food would taste, though. At the thought, her stomach rumbled.

She had not been fibbing. Eleanor refused to go in search of their meal and would rather starve or eat hard cheese until they reached Merveille—*home*—once more, than go fetch supper for the witch. Resignation settling into her stiff shoulders, Eleanor took out her Sacred Text of Hespa and opened to where she'd last left off.

Not three lines in, Wendolyn flung the door open and walked in, slamming it shut again. She kept walking, her pale boots and snow-soaked skirts stark against the dark wood floor. Stopping next to Eleanor's bed, she slowly lifted her eyes to meet Wendolyn's. Blue and icy as the cold witch's heart.

Momentarily, her sharp gaze dropped to the book in Eleanor's lap, attention faltering. "You read the Sacred Texts?"

"Every day," Eleanor confirmed. Though, she was struggling with it more every day, too.

"Good." Wendolyn nodded once and turned away.

"Just tell me the plan, Wendolyn." She watched as her words made the witch's face pinch.

"My Sister might trust you, but I do not." She strode back to her bed and sat on the edge of it.

Eleanor shifted under the covers to sit up further. "I can help. I know I can. You just have to tell me what we're really doing out here."

Wendolyn set to rubbing her temples.

"How do we find this man?"

"I don't know!" she snapped, hands coming down hard on her knees. "I don't have a plan, alright? Does that make you feel better? I don't know anything about this man and the Sacrée Mountains are formidable."

Eleanor pinched the bridge of her nose with her fingers. "Do you mean to tell me we're just traipsing through the frozen mountains until we stumble upon a hidden hut somewhere?"

"No."

Eleanor threw her hands up in the air. "Then, *what*?"

Many moments ticked by of Wendolyn looking at the

floorboards, sitting still as a marble statue. So many moments passed that Eleanor returned to her reading. Until Wendolyn spoke again. "There is a clan of Druids you probably know as *Barroque's Bazaar of the Peculiar.*"

Eleanor baulked. "The *cirque troupe* that travels around performing plays and carnival tricks?

"Yes."

"They're *Druids*?"

"Yes."

Eleanor gaped. "Druids are real?"

"Yes."

"Aren't they fabled to be descendants of Elves?"

Wendolyn blinked. "Yes."

"Then why are they so…"

"Disfigured?" She gave a small sigh. "Druids have Elven magic in their veins, but when they use it, it distorts them, making them deformed. Some have been known to barter for more magic, in order to wear a glamour liken to their former Elven beauty, but it doesn't hold." Winnie looked away, out the window at the snow drift beyond. "It isn't real."

Eleanor blew out a breath, shaking her head. "And why do we need the Druids?"

"Because of their constant travel throughout this side of Midlerea—and the nature of their performances—the Druids are privy to a lot of information."

Eleanor leaned forward, hopeful for the first time in a fortnight. "They might know of the man in the mountain pass."

"Yes."

"That sounds like a plan to me." Eleanor frowned.

Wendolyn glowered. "It is not. We are merely traipsing around the frozen mountains trying to locate *them*."

Eleanor scoffed. "Well, that's easy enough." Wendolyn perked, her head cocked to one side. "Their next bazaar is in Vorren."

With eerie slowness, Wendolyn stood. "Back in the other direction?" she asked. "Past Merveille?"

"Yes, that's where Vorren is."

"How do you know this?" she asked, her tone dipping low into accusatory.

"I saw a posted notice when we rode into town." Eleanor crossed her arms. "If you would have *told* me what we were doing, I could have let you know."

Wendolyn started to walk toward Eleanor's bed, but she halted when her elegant boot slipped forward. Cringing, she watched as Wendolyn's eyes tracked across the floor from her bed to the tub of cold water. Her gaze lifted to Eleanor's face. "*Why* is there a trail of puddles from the bathtub to my *bed*?"

"I got lost."

Wendolyn's jaw tightened, but she let it go. "Take me to this notice about the troupe," she demanded.

"But I just got warm!"

Wendolyn surged forward and snatched Eleanor's arm, hauling her from the bed. "You said you wanted to help. Now *help*."

Once the notice had been located and Wendolyn had torn it down to bring back to their room for the night, Eleanor wasted no time climbing up the stairs and sinking back into the warmth of the vile bed.

Several moments later, Wendolyn came up. She stalked to Eleanor's bed and slammed a bowl down onto the side table. "Your stew," she muttered, moving to her own bed and lying down—or, rather, *hovering*—with her back to Eleanor.

WINNIE

"Get up." Winnie smacked Eleanor's foot—again. If the snoring twit didn't rise from her slumber this time, she was going to summon a bucket of snow and dump it on her pretty head. The thought drew a smile out of Sister Winter. That is, until Yula spread her great wings and flew to land on Eleanor's headboard, talons scraping against the unpolished wood. Yula gave her a low hoot and Winnie's eyes narrowed. "Who's familiar are you? You ungrateful bird."

Eleanor began to stir, a drip of disappointment sliding down Winnie's spine at the realisation she would not have reason to douse her in frigid ice. "*Get up.*"

"I used to think I was grouchy." Eleanor rubbed at her bleary eyes, sitting up and scowling at Yula. "But I'm a right ray of sunshine compared to your crotchety arse." She shot Yula another dark look. Winnie's familiar might have decided to adore the maid, but her affections for the owl were selective at best—usually only when Yula chose her over Winnie during an argument.

"We can't all be cheery, or nothing would ever be accomplished." Winnie strode purposefully to the window and flung open the curtains, eliciting a hiss from Eleanor. The curtains were coarse and gritty between her fingers and Winnie suppressed a shudder. The entire night, she'd levitated above her bed to sleep. There was simply no way she would disgrace her body by touching tarnished sheets crawling with Goddess knew what. She'd wager half of Glacé Manor that they hadn't been cleaned since *several* guests ago.

For the last three hundred and eight years, Wendolyn had been sent to countless places by three hundred and eight Orders. For the last two hundred and eighty, no matter what reaches of the realm she was sent to, Winnie always transported herself back to her luxurious bed when the stars arose from their slumber. Occasionally, she had to suffer through a night in an inn, or a dusty cottage, but even then, if her Order had not commanded her presence in the moonlight hours, Wendolyn went home. Though *home* had been unconventional for most of that time, it was home nonetheless. Or, it used to be.

The presence of this blonde bird made it impossible to go anywhere by magic.

The absence of the Grimoire made the future seem impossible as well. In a fortnight, on the shortest eve of the year —her Solstice—Winnie would receive no Order. She would be given no direction; no purpose. It would be a day like any other. They would all be days like any other, now. Another unwelcome shift in the paradigm of her lengthy existence.

Winnie shook her thoughts loose. "The buxom woman downstairs. The one with the moustache—"

"Roberta," Eleanor grumbled.

Winnie waved her off. "She informed me that *Barroque's Bazaar* passed through here three nights ago. If we leave soon, we can intercept them before Vorren and save ourselves an extended trip back in this direction later."

Eleanor had a glint in her eye that unnerved Sister Winter. "Did you know your neck turns pink every time you mention the Druids? And you look out the window."

Observant little wench. Winnie should like to string Aggie up by her toes for a decade after partnering her with this atrocious girl. "Did you know that you snore?"

Eleanor blanched.

Winnie muttered and all of their belongings lined up within their bags. "Come along."

CHAPTER SEVEN

AGATHA

Agatha blinked against the light. She hadn't seen the sun in several days, what with the heaviness of Winter's approach cloaking Merveille in ceaseless gloom.

Judging by the sunlight and slightly warmer temperature, the beacon of magic that located her Sister Spring had brought her to Eridon. A land of rolling countryside and sprawling vineyards, the Sud of Eridon was a place many spent Yule to have a brief respite from the harsh Winter in Merveille.

Oddly, Agatha saw no sign of Sorscha or even Gaius where she stood at the crest of a hill, a small vineyard inn below. Their location magic had never delivered any one of them even a fraction off target.

To be fair, it was generally alarmingly accurate—placing them in startling proximity more often than not.

Since the burning of the Grimoire, their struggles as Sisters had only compounded. They still couldn't be together or their magic would cause mayhem, and their own journeys toward their common goals left them each alone to deal with the fallout of the Grimoire's loss.

The longer they waited, the deeper in the trenches they each were with the problems of the continent, and the harder it would be to acquaint their magic.

After several moments, Sorscha was still nowhere to be seen. Cursing, Agatha decided to make her way toward the inn, presuming the location magic was as garbled as everything else.

"*Boo*."

Agatha jumped out of her skin, turning to find Sorscha cackling behind her.

"It's unsettling to be peeped on, isn't it?"

"Have you been watching me since I arrived?"

Sorscha shrugged. "No, I was off in the trees relieving myself and letting the horse graze, thank you very much."

Her horse, Carmine, came out of the brush then, and Agatha rubbed his muzzle. "Where is Gaius?"

"Right there." She pointed to the bottom of the hill behind Agatha, a horse coming into view as she climbed onto her own. "He had post sent to that inn down the way and he said my attire was not appropriate enough to join him." She rolled her eyes and Agatha snorted. Her Sister's dress was indeed a bit too flashy for a proper Eridonian establishment.

"Do you have any news of Amira?" Agatha asked Gaius as soon as his horse was within earshot.

"Hello, Gaius. How are you, Gaius? I'm well, Agatha, how are you?"

Agatha frowned up at him. "Come off it. Why are you so crabby?"

Gaius looked between the two witches. "You Joubert women are insufferable. Do you know that?" Sorscha snickered and jumped from her horse onto the back of his, and Gaius growled. "Get off my horse, S—" He cut himself off and Sorscha's face broke into a manic grin.

"You almost slipped and said it!" she howled, then cackled into the sky.

He turned back to Agatha sardonically. "Please tell us what you need so your Sister will get off my horse."

Agatha couldn't help but smile. They were the strangest pair to have mashed together, but it was amusing to watch. To everyone except Gaius.

Sorscha preened. "Has something happened, or you're here to—"

Seleste appeared in the middle of Sorscha's sentence.

"Alright." Sister Spring leapt off Gaius' horse, flicking her wrist as red flames danced at her fingertips. "Let's do this before Lord Fancy Pants has a coronary."

"You're driving him mad, aren't you, Sister?" Seleste asked with a warm smile.

"It's mutual," Sorscha retorted, waving her Sisters on to let their magic twine with hers. "He's too damned proper."

"He's *what*?" Agatha said through a laugh, eyeing Gaius. "He's just trying to get under your skin."

"Because she's insufferable," he grumbled.

"You said that already," Sorscha snapped.

Gaius mumbled curses and kicked his horse into a trot back down the hill.

"Wait," Aggie interjected as she watched him leave. "You truly have no news of Amira?"

Sorscha deflated, her crimson sparks disintegrating. "None. Not a word. Have you heard anything, Seleste?"

Sister Summer shook her head. "Dulci even sent word to every person she still knows in Coronocco and no one seems to even know she's gone."

"How does the whole of Midlerea lose an empress and no one realises it?" Sorscha murmured.

Agatha shrugged. "Coronocco believes she is in Seagovia, and Seagovia believes she's returned to Coronocco, I presume."

"Perhaps," Seleste added. "Though, it doesn't explain her guards' disappearance."

"Gone, just like her."

Scoffing, Sorscha pulled her magic from her palm once more. "It's likely she was in on it with Mila and the magus in the first place."

Seleste considered Sister Spring's words, Aggie watching her carefully. "I don't believe so. It wouldn't fit the evidence we have to the contrary, little may it be." Shimmering gold flowers bloomed in her open palm. "Where is Winnie?"

Agatha chewed on her cheek, anxiety crawling up her chest. "I summoned her, too…" They all three looked around, the wind already beginning to pick up, swirling around them in various temperatures not likely to combine harmoniously.

"Can we ignore summons?" Sorscha shouted over the wind.

Agatha didn't know, but she wouldn't put it past Winnie to figure out how.

"What if she's hurt?" Seleste pulled her magic back.

"I received a raven from Eleanor two days ago," Agatha said. "They're still travelling, but fine."

A crease drew Seleste's brows together. "Anything could happen in two days' time. I'm going to check on her."

Sorscha looked up at the darkening sky, thick, ominous clouds rolling in far too quickly to block the sun. "Time's up, anyway, Sisters."

WINNIE

Like a goddess come to earth, Seleste appeared next to Winnie where she sat in a small inn, feeding Yula a mouse.

Her Sister Summer's head tilted to the side and she came forward to stroke Yula's wing. "Is she ill?" Seleste's worried attention moved to Winnie. "She's always hunted her own rodents."

Leave it to Seleste to notice such a thing. "She's fine." Admitting she was bribing her familiar with treats would be admitting Yula was truly forming an attachment to the maid. "I take it you're here because I ignored your summons."

"Aggie's," Seleste clarified, her voice even and amiable as always.

"We shouldn't be together. It doesn't matter who does the summoning." Winnie let Yula consume the mouse and moved to wipe her hands with a linen.

"What if it had been important?"

"You're all fond of using scrying mirrors. Why not use that?"

Her Sister studied her face. "You knew it was to practise being with one another without destruction."

"There's more to our magic's inability to be together than a simple lack of acquaintance." And she couldn't very well leave an incompetent Eleanor alone in the frigid woods.

"Do you have a better idea?" Seleste asked evenly.

When Winnie didn't deign to respond, Sister Summer's gaze roved over her face, her limpid eyes giving away none of her cunning. Winnie wasn't sure Aggie and Sorscha even knew their Sister Summer had that distinct gift of noticing what others could not.

She must have seen something there in Winnie, because her demeanour softened even further and she let the subject go. "I only wanted to ensure that you're all right."

The floor hardly creaked under Seleste's nimble steps. She glided about the small room like an umber ghost, most likely observing things until she deduced where Winnie was. Her gaze moved from Eleanor's empty, made bed, to the sodden boots by the hearth. With a delicate hand, she reached to run her fingers down Eleanor's discarded coat. When she turned back to Winnie, Seleste's brow was furrowed. "You're headed back toward Merveille."

"Yes."

Seleste smiled sincerely. "I shall see you soon then, Sister. I must return to Dulci. I left her behind at a camp just Sud of Merveille."

AGATHA

The last pewter button tucked through its opening, Agatha laced her boots and grabbed her forest green overcoat. Rushing through the front entry of her rooms she skidded to a stop just before colliding with Anne.

The young maid clutched her chest from the near-collision and Agatha sighed. "Anne, Tindle has made all my dresses so that I can put them on *myself.* Grimm lights the fire in the mornings and there is simply nothing else for you to do. How many times must I remind you?" she chastised, admiring a brown curl resting on her friend's shoulder. She wasn't in her maidservant's uniform, but a pretty blue dress the colour of her cornflower eyes.

"I know that." Anne's face dimpled. "I've more free time now, and I came to ask if we could spend the morning together."

Of all the things she could choose to do with her time, Anne was seeking the thing she'd been given freedom from—Agatha. But she came back as a friend, not a maid. "I would be *delighted.*"

She gave a little hop. "Splendid!" Looping her arm through

Agatha's, they ventured out into the corridor. "What were you off in such a rush to do?"

Agatha's step faltered. She wanted nothing more than to confide in her friend. Along with Tindle, Agatha felt Anne needed to know exactly what was happening. However, Grimm had been correct in his declaration that the more people they told, the further they put those very people at risk. It was not a chance either one of them was willing to take. Not yet. And definitely not with Anne.

"Grimm and I are in a bit of a debate." They wandered down the corridors dripping with garland and berries, the scent of fir and frost dancing in the air like sugar plum faeries. "He claims to know more about folklore than I do. I plan to find every bit of literature I can on the subject and prove to him just how wrong he is." She didn't relish fibbing to her friend, but it was partially true.

If Grimm was bent on honing his abilities outside of commanded soul-collections, she wanted to be thorough in their research. Half of his time was still divided with frivolous court matters and heavy correspondence with Gaius, as well as with his other men stationed throughout Midlerea. If Agatha could locate the necessary materials, she could comb through them and eliminate anything that would be a waste of time. She could also learn more than him, or find the answers herself, and then gloat for ages.

Anne giggled. "That sounds like a nice lull from your"—she leaned in close—"draught activities."

Alright, so Agatha had told her *some* things. She and Augustus had gone to Grimm together and twisted his arm. He couldn't possibly expect them to keep it all a secret from Anne. It had been one of their less explosive arguments, at least.

"That's on a bit of a hiatus." Another lie for the checklist at the pebbled gates of Hades. As they spoke, Grimm was off with Augustus in the lighthouse, examining the draught's potency levels using Gaius' alchemical notes and what little literature they'd found on the subject. Before either of them could begin taking it, they needed to know the risks.

Grimm had been on edge and more than a little furious every time she broached the subject. He wouldn't even entertain the damned discussion until he had a better handle on his abilities as a Marchand.

We must be cautious and level-headed, he'd said. But he held her a little tighter as of late, a knot of worry tangled amongst his logic and resolve.

"Good." Anne said, drawing her attention back, and Agatha regarded her quizzically. "I just mean, what you're doing is wonderful, the two of you—"

"And you and Augustus," Agatha interrupted.

Anne looked at her feet. "*But*, you can't save all of Midlerea in a day and it would be nice for you to take a break." She paused and smiled wide. "And argue over something a fair bit less dramatic."

Agatha forced a smile. "Right you are."

Alas, there was no time for frivolous study and fanciful games. If the expansion of Grimm's powers—and the knowledge therein—would bring them a step closer to infiltrating The Order, she would not sleep until it was accomplished.

GRIMM

Grimm jerked back as an ominous stack of tomes fell out of thin air onto the desk in front of him, nearly smashing his hand. A breath later, Agatha appeared on top of the other desk, Mabon on her shoulder.

Despite the minor fright she'd just given him, he couldn't help but think she was a lovely, macabre vision in her latest ensemble. They were due at a royal dinner very soon, and her gown was fit for a ball in Lady Death's Court of Achlys.

The obsidian gown hugged every curve, spilling out below her hips into a wraith-like swath pooling at her feet. Her sleeves reached down to her wrists where cobwebs of lace fell over her hands, only the tips of her sharp fingernails visible. The neckline, though, had Grimm sucking in his bottom lip to stave off his craving. No one in all of Merveille let their neckline plunge like that. He rose and rounded the desk, moving toward her.

His face was generally unreadable to most, but not Agatha. Not anymore. Even without their entanglement, she could read him like a book. One side of her mouth tipped up in confirmation of his suspicion. "I know that look, reaper."

Mabon sighed through his snout, falling from her shoulder into flight. "There's an ear of corn by the window," Grimm muttered to the bat as he looked down into Agatha's honey eyes. He snaked one arm around her waist, surprised to find the fabric of her gown was soft velvet. Tentatively, he ran one finger from her décolletage up to the hollow of her throat, just to feel her pulse quicken under his touch. To his delight, chill bumps rose to meet his caress, the first sign he was riling her. "You're going to cause several fatalities tonight, I'm afraid."

"Hm. Keep your Book close, then."

He chuckled. "I've never seen the Book of Death catalogue Death by Lust."

Her plum-painted lips turned up at the corners and he bent down to kiss her but she *tsked* and pulled back. "Don't you dare smudge this lip stain."

Grimm moved closer at the challenge in her tone, his mouth a whisper from hers. "You tantalise me with that dress and then think I won't smudge your lip stain?" Her gaze dropped to his mouth and he smiled with satisfaction. "Teasing isn't very nice, is it?" He kissed her cheek before walking to the stack of books she'd nearly assaulted him with. "What have you found?" he asked, flipping one open to thumb through it.

"Looking through all those books about The Primordial yesterday, I remembered a bit of lore that suddenly seemed like it could be more than a hearth tale."

At this point, Grimm thought they should just assume it was all true to some degree. It's the reason they'd begun looking into such things as fairy tales and nursery rhymes in the first place. Grimm stopped on a page with a drawing of a centaur and gave Agatha his full attention.

"The Primordial is known for being the first, the original of the gods. But, the specific basis for this is his ability to breathe life into anything, giving it a spark of his own life force."

Grimm furrowed his brow, considering where she was going with that. With one leg crossed over the other, she leaned back on her hands from the desktop.

"A thousand years or so ago, a woman from another realm fell into ours by accident, claiming she hailed from the Void and came on the behalf of The Primordial. Because of the differences in our realms and the differing functionalities of magic, she was stranded here. Legend has it she is the one who opened the archaic Academy of Alchemy."

Grimm folded his arms across his chest and leaned against the edge of his own desk. "Morgana the Arcane. All the greats supposedly studied under her before the Academy fell into the hands of the Crown, limiting what was allowed to be studied."

Agatha nodded. "Exactly. And that had me curious as to what precisely the Crown had taken out of the Academy's curriculum. What was it the students weren't allowed to study?" She stood and walked back and forth in front of the fire, its light glinting off the onyx stones dangling from her ears. "Magic, of course, a few hundred years ago. But the Academy dates back much farther than that, almost exactly to the time Morgana the Arcane is said to have arrived here from the Void. So, what did the Crown know, and what else did they forbid at that time?" She stopped abruptly and turned to him, a gleam in her eye he knew all too well.

"What did you discover?"

"One of the pages had a scribbled note that some of their practices had recently been forbidden and most of the associated texts had been burned."

Grimm took the bait. "*Most*?"

She grinned. "Exactly. I had my magic search out all the books in the library with the Academy mentioned in them." Agatha pointed at the stack of texts next to Grimm. "That's what a few of those are. But…one of them in particular had a mention of the Academy teaching necromancy."

One of Grimm's brows shot up. "Intriguing."

"It is indeed."

She wound a lock of hair around and around her finger. Grimm focused on the tether between them and found precisely what her hair-twirling habit already told him. She was nervous about something. "Agatha…"

But she'd picked up on his suspicion. "I had my magic search for necromancy books as well. There was one in the library with very little mention and…the other two were in the magus' hidden study."

Grimm's mouth formed a flat line. "He's going to notice if you continue to steal books from there."

"I have decoys in place." She lifted her chin.

"And if he decides he wants to read these two exactly?"

She smoothed her hands down her curvaceous hips. "I suppose you should read quickly then."

"We have a court dinner to get to. You need to return these and we can get them later."

A coy smile curved her lips and he felt her mischief crawl

down his chest like her fingernails. "It appears you're feeling dreadfully ill." Her eyes blinked into innocent doe eyes. "You won't be able to make it to the dinner, unfortunately, and Tindle will take your place as my honoured guest."

Grimm blinked at her. His little witch and her schemes. It was becoming increasingly difficult to be angry with her when each one was more impressive than the last. "Why do I get the feeling you've had this planned for some time?"

Agatha prowled closer to him, her smile all the more wicked for that dark lip stain he wanted nothing more than to taste. "It's as if you've met me before, it would seem."

She approached and kissed his lips softly. "Read swiftly, reaper," she whispered before disappearing.

CHAPTER EIGHT

WINNIE

They'd made it within a week's ride of Merveille. Even if they rode through the nights, they would never catch up with the Druids before the Solstice.

If she were kind, Wendolyn would veer their horses and wagon off the king's road and into the Forest of Tombs toward where she knew Agatha's cabin sat vacant. It would be more comfortable for Eleanor than the frozen woods.

But she was not kind.

Of all the places she'd ever set her polished boots, Aggie's home was her least favourite.

No, they would cross the river and venture on until Eleanor could no longer sit atop her steed. Then, they would camp in the snow. Again.

"Pleasant eve!" a gravelly voice jolted Winnie from her thoughts.

She turned in her saddle to find an amiable-looking man on the road behind them, dressed in the average garb of peasants in the area, leading two old mares pulling a rickety cart. They hadn't passed another cart since early morning and she never would have missed one coming up behind them.

Winnie's attention darted to tracks leading off into the snowy woods.

His voice was still ringing in her ears. It was off. Raw.

By the time his mouth opened again, she had her dagger unsheathed.

"I've some wares you might be in want of," he continued pleasantly.

Eleanor peeked behind him at the covered wagon.

"Got hot cider, too." He winked.

The young maid dismounted at that, but Winnie watched his teeth as he smiled. The twitch in his forefinger. The sallow, gaunt cheeks. There were no well-travelled roads in the area, nor any towns for over a day's ride in the Spring, let alone in the height of snowfall.

"Peddler," Winnie called out, just before Eleanor followed him around toward the back of his wagon. The man looked over his shoulder at her, and Winnie threw her spelled dagger, the blade sinking into one wide eye, all the way to the opal hilt. He dropped to his knees, tumbling forward and sending the blade deeper into his skull.

Eleanor screamed.

Winnie's lips pursed and she magnified the sound-muffling power of the snow drifts to hover around the dramatic maid. Whilst she waited for her to calm, Winnie whispered to the snow to let the blood pass through, nourishing the ground beneath and returning the snowflakes to their glimmering brilliance. By the time Winnie had the ice melted and the soil parting to make way for the body, Eleanor had finally stopped screaming.

She was still as pale as a cadaver, but she was lucid enough. "Do you cease caring about lives after a hundred or so years?" she spat.

Winnie stalked forward and kicked the deceased over. One

foot on his chest, she pulled her knife free with a yank and spray of blood that dissipated in the air at her command.

"It isn't a lack of care for life." She waved a hand over her gory blade and the man's lifeblood evaporated, reflecting her prim face back at her. "It's about knowing when your own life is being threatened."

She waved Eleanor forward with her dagger, beckoning her to follow. They rounded the corner of the wagon and Winnie flicked her wrist. A large blanket ripped free of its confines, revealing a torture device and chains. A ghastly contraption made up of a wooden chair fitted with leather binds, metal spikes, and a pulley and lever system cranked to put those spikes in many tender, horrifying places. Eleanor gasped at the sight, clasping a hand over her mouth.

"He's a flesh trader," Winnie explained and Eleanor paled further. "And addicted to Sugar."

Eyes still wide and a tremble in her hands, Eleanor made a face. "Most everyone likes sugar…"

"Not that kind. The opioid." Winnie strode over and stooped down next to the corpse. "Come look." She used the tip of her dagger to lift up his top lip to reveal unnaturally white teeth. "Confections rot your teeth. The drug leeches the colour from them." She let his filthy lip flop back down and stood. "It's essentially like drinking a wound disinfectant."

"Why do they call it Sugar?"

"Because it's in an elixir that tastes like sugar. Better, even." Winnie kicked his boot hard, his limp leg rotating. "And Sugar Eaters will do anything for it." She locked eyes with Eleanor. "Including stealing and selling you."

The maid blanched, but recovered quickly, turning haughty. "He would steal me, but not you?" She crossed her arms across her chest.

Winnie frowned. "No, not me."

"So, you would have just let him go, then, if I weren't here?"

And let him hurt some other poor soul? Never. If she were feeling benevolent, she might have merely cut off his hands and manhood as a lovely warning. He'd received a *merciful* death because Eleanor was present. There was a time for order, and there was a time to stand up and restore it.

"Maybe," she said instead. When Eleanor's face contorted with disgust, Winnie moved to unbridle the dead man's horse. She sent it off into the forest, hopefully to a life of freedom and not danger. Whispering a complicated incantation, the man's body lifted and slid into the soil that would consume him. *Drink your fill,* she thought. *Let the land feast.*

Winnie was halfway to her horse—Eleanor staring daggers at her back—when she recalled the torture devices. She strode over, licking the pad of her finger from the first joint up to the tip of her nail, and touched it to all the contents of the wagon, turning them to ice.

"*Briser.*"

With a deafening crack, it all shattered into shards skittering across the wagon.

A chill that had nothing to do with the snow had descended upon her the moment she heard that man's voice and it would not lift. His vocal cords had been marked by the acidic drug, but his accent was refined. Too refined for a peddler. And no flesh trader had devices quite so devious as to permanently maim his source of coin. Perhaps he'd simply been a depraved monster. But similar men had followed Agatha and Eleanor in Autumn. And she'd seen the mark on the inside of his wrist—one Grimm had implored them all to search for.

Winnie wrapped herself and Eleanor in cloaking magic. "Come along, maid. We've a frigid river to cross before nightfall."

AGATHA

"I can't tell if Lord Wellington is staring at your décolletage or he thinks you're going to suck his blood."

Agatha snorted at Tindle's comment, her arm looping through his as they walked into the crowded dining hall. "My estimation is both."

"Yes, well. I despise it." Tindle shivered, dashing in his exquisite coat of black velvet trimmed with gold filigree—all to compliment Agatha's gown, of course. He was easily the best dressed in the room. That was, aside from the towering fir tree situated in the corner.

Merveille royalty took Yuletide very seriously. *Hearthmas*, they'd called it since magic had been banished and the witches were strung up in trees like the dangling pastries on spruce. Agatha always found it comical that the people still kept the same traditions begun by Hespa's witches of old, merely changing the name of the holidays. Mortals rarely knew where their traditions originated. It seemed the ability to think critically, or to make up one's own mind, slipped further away the longer time stretched on.

The room suddenly went eerily quiet—all eyes on them—both their steps echoing off the white walls strewn with holly and garland. The light wood floor was so polished Agatha feared she'd slip, giving the aristocracy more to gossip about than the man at her side and the revealing bodice of her dress. Tindle's arm was tense beneath her hand and she squeezed it lightly to comfort him. The dressmaker had not stepped foot in the castle's dining hall for over twenty years. Even then, it was never as a guest or member of the court.

As Agatha and Tindle approached their seats at the table, Queen Fleurina cleared her throat daintily. The conversation and din of utensils scraping across plates picked up once more. Lord Wellington, seated right across from them, kept his attention firmly on Agatha. She refused to squirm beneath his scrutiny or gawking—whichever it may be. Instead, she focused on placing the linen napkin in her lap and shifting so one of the many centrepieces of juniper, spruce, and spiced pine cones would obscure his view. Taking a sip from her goblet of wine, she positioned it next to a thick, silver candelabra and Wellington nearly disappeared from her evening.

Until he reached out and snatched the sleeve of a servant, causing her to spill some of the onion soup onto her tray. "Remove this candelabra." He sneered, gesturing broadly at the table in front of him. "I cannot speak with the guests across from me."

The servant mumbled something feverishly before gingerly picking up the candelabra and balancing it on her tray with the soups.

Tindle leaned in as the poor woman walked away and whispered, "If that disgusting excuse for a human looks at your breasts one more time I'm going to shove my napkin in your bodice."

"Ah," Lord Wellington crooned, looking at Agatha. "Much better."

Agatha clenched her teeth to keep her lip from curling and turned to Tindle, ignoring Wellington entirely. "You made this dress."

He scoffed and spoke under his breath. "Darling, I made this one for *Grimm*, not you. I didn't expect you to wear it to *dinner*."

Agatha smiled. Sorscha would be so proud.

Her smile melted into disgust when her eye caught Lord Wellington's again.

"You look truly ravishing tonight, Princess Agatha," he

murmured. "And where might our beloved prince be this evening? Surely he doesn't relish missing the First Day of Hearthmas."

With any luck, their *beloved prince* was eyebrows deep in necromancy texts and one step closer to honing his reaper powers outside of collecting. Perhaps she could convince him to reap Wellington first.

"His Highness was feeling under the weather this evening, I'm afraid."

The door creaked open then, a hush permeating the hall once more. Magus von Fuchs strode in, his usual golden robes replaced with those of bright red that billowed behind him. Musicians situated in one corner of the room began to play a melody attributed to Hearthmas, but it was much, much older. Agatha would venture to say no one in the room had any idea of its true origin.

Night of serenity, bright as the dawn

Light of life given to each one

Written by the first witch coven long, long ago, it was their anthem of thanks to Hespa for restoring peace. A mage had been attacked and her husband was slaughtered by a clan of Druids. Widowed and so very weak as a *frail, useless woman*, the mage sought a new husband. The true valour displayed by the Druid clan's leader stole her heart. She married him, a perfect bride.

And then she ripped his throat out on their marriage bed.

Chaos ensued between the Druids and the coven yet again. That was, until one Winter's night, Hespa divinely halted their bloodshed and bid them peace forevermore.

Of course, all such things were but hearth tales now. The song of great triumph and Hespa's great power had been reduced to a Hearthmas carol sung around tables laden with food.

History is always so easily forgotten until it begins to repeat.

Guests watched as the Grand Magus lit the first of thirteen flames, situated in a crescent shape of red and white candlesticks. Another tradition the fools did not understand. Thirteen flames for the thirteen lords and ladies born of Hespa's likeness. For several generations, the flames had merely represented the thirteen days before Hearthmas. Nights when magi all over Seagovia would light candles, sing carols, and speak out of context from the Sacred Texts of Hespa, demanding such things as devotion to the Hallowed Church, the giving of oneself and resources to the Church until coffers ran dry, and—Agatha's favourite—how truly wretched the Hollow were.

This particular subject was precisely where Magus von Fuchs settled and began speaking about as the guests nibbled their *coq au vin*.

It never made sense to Agatha, the horrible line drawn between souls—Hallowed or Hollow. Especially when the point of the Hallowed Church dictated by Hespa was to gather *every* soul. Sybil used to whip her with a switch every time she brought such things up as if comprehension was immoral and blind obedience righteous.

"The Order selects their magi for good reason. They are the hands and feet of Hespa as much as we are the hands and feet of Her History," she used to say.

With the Grimoire gone and Hespa's audible voice still ringing in her ears, Sybil's words, as well as the Grand Magus', all sounded like a self-serving crock of waste.

The magus finished his prattling, setting the worn Sacred Text down on an altar strung with holly berry, and the guests all murmured in unison, "*Convenu*." Agatha stifled a snort and Tindle shot her a glare, eyes bulging at her heresy.

The music picked up again and chatter filled the hall alongside it. Magus von Fuchs moved to sit in his position next to the king and queen, but he caught Agatha's eye just as he was hovering over his chair. He straightened, muttering something to those around him, and headed straight for her.

"Blessed Hearthmas," he said, pasting on an eerie smile.

"Blessed Hearthmas," she parroted, pasting on a sickly sweet smile of her own.

The magus' eyes narrowed and he placed his hand on the back of Tindle's chair, turning his attention toward him. "Monsieur Tindle. It has been such a long time. To what do we owe the pleasure of your presence here?"

"Haven't you heard?" Agatha drew his slick attention back to her, catching the gleam in the queen's eye from across the room as she did so. "Monsieur Tindle has been cleared of all charges against him." The magus stiffened, and it took every ounce of effort for satisfaction not to show on Agatha's face, though Tindle's was set in a precarious smile. "He is no longer Blacklisted."

"How marvellous," the magus bit out.

"*Isn't it?*"

Fury swelled behind his grey irises as she looked up at him and he held her stare. He broke away first, dipping his chin to Wellington across the table. "Lord Wellington"—he leaned in, his robes brushing Agatha's arm—"I've been meaning to drop by your estate. It has come to my attention that you're in need of another scullery maid, and it just so happens Princess Agatha has recently relieved herself of hers."

Filthy fucking maggot. She ought to crush his insides with her magic until his viscera pulverised and oozed out his eye sockets, right there in front of the dinner guests.

Wellington ran a gloved hand up the stem of his wine glass. "That would be divine."

Both of them.

Von Fuchs glanced sidelong at Agatha, triumph smeared across his withered face. "Anne should be of great use to you, my lord."

"Yes, absolutely, Grand Magus. It's been terribly difficult keeping things tidy without Miriam of sound mind."

What in the seven realms? Her palms were beginning to

overheat. Tindle reached under the table and squeezed her hand in warning.

"We will get it all sorted out. Don't you worry, my lord." Von Fuchs, still leaning over Agatha's seat, bent his head toward her ear. "Your move," he whispered before returning to his seat near the head of the table.

A jolt shot through her, a blinding fury heating her skull until everything through her eyes was tinged red.

She felt a hand on her arm, grounding her, and Tindle was saying something under his breath. Agatha shoved her chair backwards, the wood screeching across the floor until everyone was, once again, staring at her.

Ah, ah. Take your emotions captive, Winnie would say. *Never let a man rile you*, Sorscha would say. *An outburst here will not save Anne*, Seleste would say.

Damn them all for being correct.

CHAPTER NINE

GRIMM

Blinding light assaulted Grimm from behind his eyelids. Before he could manage to open them, something crinkled as it was shoved against his chest.

"Here."

Grimm grasped whatever it was and sat up, blinking against the sunlight rendered doubly intrusive for reflecting off the fresh snow outside the window.

"What is this?" He looked from his wife, indignation dripping off her in waves, down to the crumpled parchment in his hands. Agatha's impulsive, almost violent penmanship scrawled down the page in a list. He'd come to learn *lists* were the equivalent of holy doctrine to her.

"You wanted logic." She pointed a sharp, black fingernail at the paper. "There are thirteen reasons *I* should be the one to take the draught instead of you. One for every damned candle the magus lights this fortnight." Agatha crossed her arms as if that would solve the argument expeditiously.

Grimm blinked several times, letting his bleary eyes adjust to better read the list.

"Agatha..." He frowned, shaking his head. By number seven he couldn't help but snort. He held up the wrinkled parchment. "Six of these are just you granting yourself permission to gruesomely slaughter the magus when all is said and done."

"And?" Somehow, her vexation was amplified by the inky swath of silk that was her nightgown.

He folded the list and set it on the nightstand. "I take it dinner did not go as well as you thought it would last night."

"That bag of bones has done something to Miriam and he wants to transfer *Anne* to Lord Wellington's estate. *Anne*, Grimm!" She paused, and he grimaced. "All because Tindle is off the Blacklist."

"Tindle is off the Blacklist? How did you… Never mind." He scrubbed a hand over his face. "None of this means you need to be the one who takes the draught. We've been over th—"

"I'm more experienced with magic than you are." She put her fists on her hips.

"Obviously." He extracted himself from the warmth of the blankets, facing her bare-chested. "That is why I need you to be of sound mind and I need to know the scope of my *own* abilities first."

"We don't have time for that. I need to start taking it *now*."

"I found some interesting literature last night, stemming from necromancy. I can start taking it soon, I just need to learn a bit more about this subject of animancy."

"Grimm, I'm telling you we do not have time for that anymore."

"It's an interesting subject and one I think is very promising—"

"You're not listening!" she shouted.

"*Dammit*, Agatha!" Grimm threw his arm out wide. "You cannot possibly expect me to sit idly by and watch the one I love most in the world put herself in harm's way!" His voice echoed off the walls and Agatha staggered back a step as the reverberated fervour of his words coursed through their bond.

All the fire had gone out in her eyes and she almost looked stricken. As if she never expected anyone to feel such a way for her and somehow hadn't entertained the idea that he did.

"Isn't it painfully obvious by now?" Grimm came forward and took her hips in his hands, pulling her closer. She looked up at him with enough tenderness to set his decrepit soul aflame. "You, Agatha Peridot"—*goddess*, he loved that she carried his name—"are everything I never knew was lost from me." Her eyes were misty and his heart constricted. "If all else in the world faded away, but you remained, I would stand firm. If the opposite were true, I'd burn the world down for your loss."

"You'd do away with everything—all your people; yourself—just to keep me safe?"

He spoke without hesitation. "Yes."

She huffed a laugh. "That's terribly romantic, reaper, but it would make for a very poor king."

"I already told you I have no desire to be king."

"And yet you said you might need to be for a time."

"My *point* is…I will not risk you. Not now, not ever. And certainly not with The Fucking Order." He tightened his grip on her waist. "You are more than capable of protecting yourself if your mind and your powers are *your own,* not in the hands of some sadistic, wayward mages."

She looked up at him silently for a moment, and Grimm let the rush of her emotions bleed into him before Agatha reached up to twirl one of his black curls around her finger.

"Alright," she said softly.

"Alright?" He couldn't help the pang of triumph within him.

"But I would caution you against getting used to winning arguments."

Grimm chuckled and bent down to kiss her gently, but her

lips parted and she deepened the kiss. He lifted her up by the waist, her legs wrapping around his hips. A rush of heat bursting through him, he pushed her up against the edge of the table until she perched there on the corner, his hand tangled in her hair and dishes clinking together. Grimm pulled back, deeply satisfied to find her breathless, looking at him with heavy-lidded eyes laden with desire. Watching her reaction, he knelt before her, sliding his hands slowly up her legs beneath her nightgown. A wicked look crossed her face and he sucked in a breath when he discovered the reason why. She was entirely bare beneath the thin silk and *very* ready for him.

Grimm smirked up at her, gently urging her knees apart. He teased her, brushing his lips against the sensitive skin on the inside of her thighs. When she leaned back on her hands, face tilted to the ceiling in abandon, he could feel her anticipation. He slipped his tongue into the silken warmth between her legs, gripping her backside, and a moan escaped her lips.

As his stroking tongue found the place he knew brought her the most pleasure, Agatha gasped. Leaning further back, her hand pushed the breakfast platter off, dishes filled with porridge, fruit, and eggs clattering to the floor. Undeterred, Grimm continued the methodical movement of his tongue, the taste of her driving him to near madness. Every breath from her was growing shorter and more desperate, and Grimm groaned in response, one hand coming up to feel her peaked nipple beneath the silk. She writhed underneath him, her body tightening until a knock sounded at the door.

"Your Highness," Augustus called from the corridor. "We're due to meet with Dubois in five minutes."

Grimm pulled back and looked up at Agatha. "Say you wish me to go and I will," he said wryly.

"Don't you *dare*."

He bit his lip. "Inform Dubois I will be late," he called.

AGATHA

If she read the words one more time, she was going to scream. They'd revealed no more information than they had the first time she read them five days ago.

"Well?" Grimm had one arm tucked around his chest, holding the other up while he scratched at his short beard.

Agatha groaned, bending forward to rest her forehead on the dusty tome. "It still says the same damn thing it's said, Grimm."

"We have to be missing something."

Without lifting her head, she gestured toward the spider encased in glass upon the chaise. "By all means, try it again."

"Maybe it's not working because the arachnid isn't a mortal."

Agatha banged her head against the book three times before lifting it to stare at him sardonically. "We've been over this four hundred times, reaper. This"—she gestured to the open page—"is a spell. It's written like a spell. It has the cadence of a spell. It's *a spell*. Nowhere is it mentioned that it only works on mortals. And I'd like to take this opportunity to say, *again*—"

"My powers are separate from spellwork. I *know*."

No matter how many times Grimm recited a spell, even to perfection, it simply didn't do…anything. There was no magic in his veins. His power had another source entirely and they were no closer to discovering it than they had been at the start.

"Grimm, it's not going to work, anyway. It says here that this spell was used by mages at Morgana's academy to reach into dormant bodies and wake the soul. A raising of the dead."

"Animancy," he recited studiously. Since discovering the subject in one of the tomes stolen from the magus' hidden study,

Grimm had thought of little else. He had three journals filled with notes and he hadn't been sleeping for attempting to unlock the hidden knowledge behind it all. His theory was that if he could master animancy, he could reverse it, too. But Agatha didn't think it had to do with anything more than an unfettering of his abilities. No magic needed. He could already commune with the dead once he was sent to collect a soul, just as he could retrieve it from the body. If he had the innate power of necromancy, why wouldn't he have the innate power of animancy and its counterpart—whatever that was?

They both looked at the spider elegantly spinning a web, spindly legs busy and purposeful. "There is nothing dormant about him."

"Her." Grimm moved toward the window, Agatha staring after him.

"Pardon?"

"The spider is female," he answered, his back to her.

"Does she have some sort of marking?" She reached for the glass, tapping on it gently, trying to get a better look.

"No. I can see her essence." He stared out over Mer Noir, hands shoved in his pockets while Agatha studied him. "Only female spiders spin webs as well." He smirked at her over his shoulder.

Agatha scowled at him and he snorted. "Is this something you can do with all creatures? See their essence?"

He shrugged and turned back to face her. "More or less if I focus. Since I've been toying with my powers, it's gotten stronger."

Thoughts skittered across her mind like the busy spider, weaving something she couldn't quite yet grasp.

Grimm's head tilted to one side. "What is it?"

She held up a finger to silence him, letting the tangle of a notion form more fully. "I have an idea," she finally said, jumping up from where she'd crouched in front of their little friend. Dashing to the table, she shuffled through the many books, landing on one in particular. She flipped through the pages feverishly, then held it up with gusto.

"It says here that the Academy was forbidden from dabbling in necromancy after two mages somehow managed to reanimate a corpse."

"Right." He looked unimpressed. "*Animancy*."

The threads were still disjointed in her mind, but they were slowly coming together. "It was the wrong soul, though."

"How do you know that?"

Agatha picked up another book and flipped through it. "This note scribbled in the margin here."

She pointed and Grimm came over to read it aloud. "*Last known case of animancy: two mages misplace a soul.*" He looked up from the book to Agatha. "Misplaced? So these two mages *lost* a soul when they were attempting to commune with it and tried to put it back in?"

"That's what it sounds like."

"There was a different soul just floating around nearby and they put it in a vacant body?"

Agatha shook her head. "I don't know. But doesn't that make it seem like they took the soul out, even by accident?"

Grimm worked his bottom lip between his teeth. "It could be. How, though? How do mages studying at the Academy achieve something like that without some form of malevolent blood magic?"

"What if one of them was a reaper—"

"Marchand," he interrupted, and she glared.

"What if one of them was a *Marchand*, or had the same power you do, in some manner." His eyes unfocused, in that far-off way that meant he was in the midst of deep consideration, and the rest of her web of thoughts coalesced. "I think your power comes from your reincarnated *soul*, not any body you've had."

Grimm inclined his head toward her, brows furrowed and

wheels spinning. She could almost hear the cogs turning. "I take it you have wards up?"

Agatha nodded.

"*Thanasim.*"

Decrepit bone and gloom enveloped Grimm, inky black smog billowing around the edges of his reaper form. Though she'd seen him as such before, it never lost its magnificence. She watched in wonder as he stalked over to the spider's makeshift home, a shadow creature and his kindred beast.

Grimm knelt down, the fog sweeping behind him like a dark cape. Slowly, he lifted the glass encasing the spider and set it aside. With great care to be gentle, he slid his skeletal hand forward, letting it rest just next to the arachnid. Within a breath, the creature's spindly legs found Grimm's finger, climbing upon the bone like she'd belonged there from the start.

"Hello, you."

His voice was the same as in his princely form and it left Agatha's heart feeling swollen and tender. A thought struck her because of it, but before she could speak, Grimm was already pulling at the creature's soul.

"I'll put you back, don't you worry," he cooed. Though Agatha knew there was no guarantee of that. After a moment, the spider twitched in his cadaverous palm, only to right herself and explore the curves and fissures of his bones once more. Grimm growled and set her back down.

The glass tinked against the dish her branch rested on and Agatha spoke. "I don't think your reaper form is indicative of your soul, either."

He looked at her, his decayed face shrouded in darkness like a hood, but she could feel his frustration even without their bond. "And how in the seven realms am I to dislodge my own soul from either form without dying?"

"Well, I don't kno—"

"For the love of the *goddess*." Sorscha materialised next to Agatha. "I've been trying for ages to get in here."

"Excuse me for having strong wards," Agatha bit out.

Sorscha glanced away from her Sister, gaze landing on Grimm. Her eyes grew wide and her mouth fell open. "Oh, my…" She stepped forward slowly, exhaling a shocked, breathy laugh. "You're exquisite… Aggie, do you see him?"

"No, I've gone blind," she said drily.

One hand reaching out to touch him, Sorscha smiled and Grimm stepped back.

"If you're quite done gawking." He crossed his arms, bone and deteriorated sinew bathed in candlelight. "What are you doing here, Sorscha?"

"You're awfully glum in your Marchand form, aren't you?"

"We were in the middle of something."

"Oh, dear." She beamed, looking between them. "Now that would be something, wouldn't it?"

"Not *that*," Agatha snapped. "What is it you need?"

Sorscha sidled up to her youngest Sister. "I thought perhaps now would be a good time to head to the Isle and let our magic spend some time together."

Agatha's face contorted. "I don't know, we have a lot going on here."

"Just go," Grimm said. "We can't move on the draught just yet and I'll only be here doing this." He gestured toward the little spider, happily spinning her web once more.

"Alright, I—" Agatha opened her eyes to black sand under her toes and the scent of the sea filling her senses. It had been ages since she'd been to the Isle of her exile. Sombre clouds clustered above the dark waters of Mer Noir and the tepid wind blew her hair back. She looked at her Sister and Sorscha giggled.

Agatha removed her boots and they walked a bit further up the beach, the waves beckoning them both.

"Ah." Sorscha threw her head back, breathing it all in. The

clouds obscured the sun almost constantly on the Isle of Ballast, but it was never too hot, nor too cold. "If your Season and mine came together," Sorscha mused, "this would be it."

Agatha huffed a small laugh. She was right. "Do you remember this spot?"

Sorscha dropped her head back down and her face darkened. "Do you mean to ask if I remember pulling your corpse from the damned sea because you jumped off that cliff?" She shook her head. "No. I only remember throwing ancestral dirt over you until you rose from the grave." She gave Agatha a weak smile and moved to sit in the sand.

"Wait a moment." Agatha froze, hovering over her. "What is it about the ancestral dirt of Helsvar that resurrects us?"

"It's something to do with *from the soil we arise, to it we return.*"

"There's no extraordinary power to it?"

Sorscha mocked an exaggerated frown, thinking. "That would be a question for Winnie, but I believe it's more to do with our blood."

Agatha sagged. That was a dead end. And they had absolutely no idea what Grimm's original body had been named, let alone where it was buried. She slumped down next to Sorscha in the sand.

"Well then"—Sorscha laid her head on Agatha's shoulder—"won't you let your magic come out and play with mine?"

Agatha nudged her playfully and sent a tendril of her magic out into the air. To the mortal, or even a mage, witch, or magical creature not born of Joubert blood, there would be nothing much to see. Perhaps, if their cunning were strong or their own power formidable, they would see a ripple in the air; a bend in colour like heat waves above Coronoccan sand. To a Joubert witch, a brilliant onyx thread reached out like a climbing vine to playfully grasp the glowing scarlet tendril awaiting it. They wound around one another, sweetly pulling and embracing as if they'd missed one another.

When the sea remained calm and the wind steady, Sorscha spoke. "What were the two of you doing, anyway?"

Agatha watched Sorscha's magic bounce off of hers, jumping back to wrap around it in some form of a game. "We have a working theory that Grimm can use his power outside of collecting souls."

Sorscha looked impressed. "Wouldn't that be handy? I can think of several people I'd love to rip the souls out of."

Agatha made a sound of agreement in her chest. "He insists on harnessing this ability before he takes the draught."

One of Sorscha's brows rose. "You finally came to an agreement, then?"

Nose wrinkled, Agatha brushed her hair out of her eyes, noting the uptick in the wind. "How are things going for you and Gaius?"

With a shrug, Sister Spring sighed. "Dull. Bland. We plan to attend the Duke of Larosche's Hearthmas Ball just before I return to Merveille for the Solstice. I thought since Tindle said his youngest daughter was betrothed to the Prince of Prilemia, that could play into the reason no draught was sent there. Gaius thinks, perhaps, he could even be linked to Mila and that could put us closer to finding Empress Amira."

Agatha watched the sea for any sign that it would revolt at the Sisters' proximity to one another. "It's not a bad plan."

Sorscha shook her head, eyes on their magic. "Gaius is hoping to find anything indicating the duke is in bed with Mila, or that she's even in bed with the magus, but I'm not sure he's going to find the connection he wants there. Not at a Hearthmas ball at least."

Agatha tilted her head to one side, another onslaught of thought assaulting her. "Wait. Mila can't be in bed with the magus…" For the first time, she had an inkling of *why* Mila had betrayed them—a reason she never would have thought possible before Grimm's interest in animancy.

Sorscha snorted. "That's just a turn of phrase, Aggie."

"No, no. She *can't*." Agatha shifted in the sand to face Sorscha. "She's a wraith. She can't feel or taste or…"

Sorscha's lips parted. "Experience any of the joys of this life," she finished for her.

"She can solidify to a certain extent only because of what Lady Death has bestowed upon her." Agatha twirled a lock of hair around her finger. "What does a ghost want?"

Sorscha blew out a breath. "Goddess, if it were me, I'd want a body so I could feel again."

"Exactly." Agatha grinned.

"Fine," Sorscha said cautiously, "*if* you're right…who could manage that?"

Agatha's attention was momentarily drawn back to the sea, its waves crashing onto the shore harder than before. Their magic had intertwined to make a glowing oxblood orb she worried even a mortal could see, its power violent and glorious.

"Should the tide be coming in?"

"No," Agatha said. "That shouldn't happen for a while yet." Despondent, they detangled their magic and pulled it in. "Anyone with the ability to commune with ghosts could potentially help Mila get a body."

"Necromancy?" They both stood, dusting the sand off their dresses. "Aggie, that's archaic and dodgy at best."

"It's archaic, but it's not unlike what Grimm can do."

Sorscha put a hand on her crimson-swathed hip. "He's a *reaper*. How many times did the spirits of Mum and Father come to your Eve of Hallows in the woods when you called?"

"Never. But what about a group of mages poisoning an entire continent? Surely someone in that circle could manage it."

"The Order? I don't know, Aggie…" She toyed with the ends of her hair. "I don't know what The Order is involved in, or really anything about them. Helda was very close-lipped about it. Was Sybil?"

Agatha nodded mutely.

Sorscha looked at the sea again, the wind lifting their hair. "We need to part, sweet."

"Whoever it is," Agatha spoke quickly, "an abducted empress might be a high enough payday to gain a body for a ghost."

"Perhaps you're right." Sorscha winked and was gone.

CHAPTER TEN

SORSCHA

At the sound of glass shattering across the wood floor, Sorscha spun around. Concerned with yanking her dagger out of its thigh holster, the slip she'd been donning pooled at her feet.

"What in all the realms?" she snapped, realising Gaius had been the source of the crash.

He averted his eyes from her, bending down to pick up the shards of glass. "Could you please put some clothing on?"

Sorscha snorted. "That's what I was trying to do before you broke a teacup on the floor."

"I apologise." He still didn't look at her—not even her feet. "I'm not exactly used to living with a strange woman."

Bending down, she took up the slip and slid it up and over her curves, setting the straps in place. "Strange?" She smiled coyly, but Gaius missed it, still avoiding her.

His jaw tightened and he stood, brushing off his pants before he finally looked at her face. "A woman I'm not familiar with."

"Then familiarise yourself, Lord Gaius." He frowned and she rolled her eyes, a hand on her slender hip. "It's been weeks."

"Can't you at least dress in the lavatory? And wear proper attire? I realise that is difficult in such close living quarters, but I implore you."

She tapped a long fingernail to her chin dramatically, walking a small circle around him. "I will wear *some* clothing in your presence if you will cease calling me *demoiselle*." She drew out the last word with as much mocking as she could muster.

"No." His eyes flashed.

Sorscha crossed her arms. "You don't call Aggie *Your Highness*."

"In public I do."

"Well, *in public* we're using false names, anyway. I don't recall Aggie saying that you ever had this strong sense of formality with her." A sly grin lit her face. "In fact"—she popped her lips—"it was quite the opposite, from what I've gathered."

Gaius stiffened. "That was different."

Sorscha sat at the small table in their room, leaning forward on one elbow. "Was it, really?"

"Yes. The mission required that your Sister trust me very quickly."

"So, you tricked her?"

"I don't believe it's possible for Agatha to be tricked."

Sorscha let out a long breath. "Do you hear how easily you say her name?" Gaius kept his gaze trained on her face, lifting his chin. "It slips off your tongue like the sweetest honey." Eyes narrowed, her gaze bore into him until she almost thought he'd flinch. "Do you hold unrequited love for my Sister, my lord?"

"Your Sister is married," he ground out, posture rigid.

Sorscha lifted a tanned shoulder. "That doesn't render you *immune* to feelings, now does it? Do you love her?"

"No."

"*Liar*."

A muscle in Gaius' jaw twitched. "Would you like the honest answer?"

"No, I want you to lie to me wickedly. Alas, I know you will not, so..." She flipped a hand back and forth impatiently.

After clearing his throat, Gaius said, "I *contemplated* feelings for Agatha. But then Grimm tripped over his own scheme and truly fell for her. And I let it go. Agatha is a *very* dear friend to me and my Crown Princess. Nothing more."

Sorscha smiled. "Easy as that?"

"I wouldn't say it was easy. But it is done."

"You're certain?" she pressed, one arm draped over the back of her chair.

A spark shot across his eyes as they bore into her. "*Very* certain, demoiselle."

Sorscha's toes curled into the floorboards under the table at his tone.

"I am no longer a young man who can't control himself or his feelings."

She grinned, leaning back in her chair and bringing her legs up to rest on the tabletop, ankles crossed and slip-sliding down her thighs. "I hate to break it to you, Gaius, but compared to me, you are still a young man." She ran her tongue over her strawberry-red lips. "And you cannot *control* your feelings. Only the subsequent actions that stem from them."

Gaius' brows rose, his green eyes sparkling. She might be an old crone who cared not which mortal form her lovers took—male or female—but she most assuredly still had a weakness for the strong and dark of either.

"Wise words," he finally said. "Wise indeed."

"You seem surprised. I can certainly show you things that will shock you even further."

Gaius snorted. "As tantalising as that offer sounds, I believe I'll decline."

She brought one shoulder forward coyly. "At least we can agree for you to call me by my given name?"

"No." She swore a smirk lifted his lips briefly. "I will not tarnish your reputation."

Sorscha's eyes fluttered shut. When she opened them, she began to fan herself, sucking her bottom lip between her teeth. "You are a yummy scrummy thing with your debonair chivalry. However, my *reputation* has a life force all its own." She let her feet drop back to the ground and reached for a peach, biting into it. Gaius looked away. "You are a right gallant gentleman, so you have yourself a deal."

He looked back at her, one eyebrow raised. "And what deal is that?"

Sorscha spoke around a mouthful, "I'll wear more clothing and dress in the lavatory." He started to nod appreciatively, but she wasn't done. "Until the day you slip and call me *Sorscha*." She tipped her head back and laughed at the look upon his face. "Would you just look at that reaction? Better than I could have imagined."

Gaius sighed. "Please get dressed, *demoiselle*. We need to get to the duke's Hearthmas ball and see what we can find out."

For a lord tucked up in a castle all of his life, Gaius had quite the hulking muscle hidden beneath his fancy overcoats. Sorscha held onto his arm as they walked the steep pathway leading to the duke's estate. She squeezed his bicep just to see him glare at her. He did and she giggled.

"Please behave yourself," he whispered out the side of his perfect mouth.

"On my honour"—Sorscha crossed her heart—"I will not."

Gaius shook his head, lamplight dancing in his eyes as they approached the mansion. "I worry you'll be the death of me."

"You might be right about that, my dear Lord Gaius Asholm." He glanced sidelong at her and she smirked.

Gaius yanked them to a stop and looked down into her face. "One more step and you cannot refer to me as that until we are safely back at the inn. Understood?"

"Yes, Lord Gaius Asholm." She fought the giggle bubbling up in her throat. Two could play the High Society Titles game.

He blinked at her. "Is it out of your system now?"

"I am a woman of leisure and delight, Lord Gaius Asholm, but I do know when duty calls." She took one exaggerated step forward and looked back over her shoulder. "Well, are you coming, Lord *de Montagu*?"

Gaius' chest heaved with his sigh, stepping up to her side and resuming their promenade toward the massive estate before them.

"This place is…"

"A bit much," he murmured.

Sorscha scoffed. "Says the lord living in a castle."

He shrugged. "That's never suited me, either. Give me trees and wildlife any day."

Sister Spring considered him as they walked through the door that ensured their masks must be set firmly in place. Tonight, they were Lord and Lady de Montagu of Beralone—a villa estate outside an obscure village in Estern Seagovia. To her immense surprise, Gaius had used his vast knowledge of inner court workings to procure legitimate invitations to what was known in Eridon as *the* Hearthmas gathering. It just so happened Lord Bonham's youngest daughter was also recently betrothed to the prince of Prilemia, whom Agatha had concerns might be in the magus' inner circle.

Once they were over the threshold and ushered into the ballroom of gaudy proportions, Sorscha watched as Gaius scanned the room. His eyes were creased at the corners and his jaw was set. She'd come to learn over the past moon that meant he was assessing, plotting.

Sorscha just wanted a drink. She turned away without a word and slipped into the crowd of voluminous dresses, a table of mulled wine and champagne beckoning her. Her eager fingers had just closed around a chilled flute of bubbly when a presence shifted behind her. Sorscha tucked her frown away and turned with a smile, bringing the flute to her lips. She took a sip slowly while he watched.

"My lady." A posh, milquetoast gentleman folded into a shallow bow and Sorscha dipped her chin, hiding her hand in her skirts. The one that held a simple gold band matching the one on Gaius' finger. She glanced in his direction to find he had that hand shoved into his coat pocket. Apparently, they both had a similar train of thought at present. They'd never *quite* landed on spouses or siblings.

"My lord," Sorscha drawled.

"I would be delighted if you would honour me with a dance this fine evening."

Despite the general distaste he was drawing in her with his too-slick hair and the soft hands of a dandy, Sorscha opened her mouth to accept. Abruptly, she was cut off by a staggeringly beautiful woman stepping up next to her.

Looping her arm through Sorscha's, she addressed the man. "Lord Kensington." The mysterious woman gave him an austere smile as he raked his eyes over her dismissively.

"Lady Bonham," he finally bit out.

"Tell me," Lady Bonham spoke quietly, "did you, once again, *accidentally* forget to speak with a lady's escort before botherin– I mean, approaching her?"

Sorscha hardly kept her snort from escaping, or her shock from showing on her face. This bold, mystifying woman of unimaginable beauty was the Duke of Larosche's illusive, rebellious eldest *daughter*. Gaius had mentioned his eldest daughter was a societal spinster—having reached her thirties without accepting any of her four proposals.

Standing next to her, arm in arm, Sorscha was willing to stake her life it was all by Lady Bonham's—wise—choice.

The lord's jaw clenched and Lady Bonham smiled. "I do believe the gentleman you're looking for is over there." She pointed across the ballroom to Gaius where he stood speaking with a new set of well-to-do men, with that hand still in his pocket. Lord Kensington muttered something under his breath and headed in the opposite direction. Lady Bonham dropped her arm and Sorscha swiftly pulled off the gold band around her finger and tucked it into her bodice.

"Elizabeth," the beautiful woman introduced herself. "I saw you come in. You are"—she looked into Sorscha's eyes, a flush of pink running up her neck and landing on her cheeks—"difficult to miss."

Sorscha pulled the tip of her tongue between her teeth behind her lips. Oh, yes. It was definitely Lady Elizabeth Bonham's choice not to marry. "Lorelai."

"What a beautiful name," Elizabeth mused.

"Thank you, it was my mother's." Sorscha reached out and gently touched her arm, just one lady being kind to another, and let warmth bleed into her tone. "How can I ever repay you?"

Elizabeth's eyes sparkled. "Take a walk with me?"

"But, of course. I'd be delighted." The two women glided through the ballroom toward a door that would lead down the hall and into the interior of the grand estate. When they neared Gaius, Sorscha hardly broke her step, leaning in close to his ear. "*I'm your sister*," she whispered, "*not wife*." Gaius nodded curtly, and she almost thought his shoulders stiffened. But she was already following a sinfully beautiful creature out into the gilded corridor.

They walked aimlessly, dodging party-goers and enjoying the

eccentric display of Yule decor. *Hearthmas* all the moronic mortals called it.

Elizabeth spoke of trivial things and Sorscha attempted to keep up, but her eyes were scanning, ears listening. They'd come to see just how close the Duke of Larosche was to the magus. To see if anyone knew of a woman named Mila from Merveille or anything about a mage that had gone missing in Prilemia. The latter was a long shot and the former wasn't a subject that would naturally come up, but Sorscha could dig. She was very good at getting what she wanted. At present, the best source she had also happened to be rather easy on the eyes. The sugar on top, if she could learn something.

"Don't you find all these events droll?" Elizabeth's candied voice pulled Sorscha back into the present.

"Mm. I would say that depends entirely on whom you choose to keep company with at events such as these." Sorscha smiled at her sidelong and she saw Elizabeth's throat bob as she swallowed hard. So young and beautiful. "I used to have a friend. A lovely woman in the Court of Merveille." The lies slipped easily off her tongue. "We used to fill our plates with delicacies and our dance cards with faux names, and then escape to the gardens until it was over." They passed a couple of guards and bustling ladies, before rounding a corner into an unlit hallway. "Her name was Mila." Sorscha stopped walking and Elizabeth followed, leaning up against the wall, back slightly arched. "Perhaps you have met her in your own court dealings."

Elizabeth bit her lush bottom lip and Sorscha made herself look away. She needed information, not a clandestine moment with the heir to a duchy, but she was begging for it. And *goddess*, it sounded divine. "I don't believe I've ever met anyone by that name."

"Have you travelled often to Merveille? Or had many dignitaries visit you here?"

"There you go making the droll conversation I was trying to avoid." Elizabeth smiled coyly.

"Apologies, my lady." Sorscha licked her lips. "What would you like to discuss?"

Elizabeth's head lolled back and forth, lips puckered in thought. "Why don't you tell me whether you intend to marry one of those pigs in there?"

"Marriage is not for me, my lady."

Eyes glittering, Elizabeth stepped closer. "Nor for me. But you knew that already, did you not?" Sorscha's pulse kicked up. "I am an old spinster, after all."

"You're no older than I," Sorscha crooned.

"Thankfully, my father simply thinks me headstrong." She shrugged and walked forward slowly.

Sorscha did not respond right away. She should have known the duke's unconventional heir would not hold any information. Perhaps she could lead her to it, though…

"Hmm." Sorscha tapped a fingernail to her chin. "Rebellious heir?" She only meant to prod her.

It worked. Elizabeth's pink mouth tipped up seductively at its lovely edges. "No, no." She came closer, a mere handbreadth away, candlelight from the adjacent hall lighting her face in the darkness. "I simply know what I like."

Before Sorscha could formulate a response, Elizabeth had a hand on her hip, pushing her back against the wall. Sorscha grabbed Elizabeth's skirts and pulled her flush against her body, breast to breast. Elizabeth's breath hitched and Sorscha claimed her mouth. Her lips were pillow soft, the delicate sweetness of Summer fruit. Elizabeth's tongue slipped into her mouth and Sorscha clutched at her waist.

Lady Bonham pressed against Sorscha harder, her lips insistent and tasting of champagne. She left her mouth to find her neck, hands frantically lifting up Sorscha's skirts. Chest heaving and a wet ache building between her legs,

Sorscha let her hands rove over the bodice of Elizabeth's dress.

"Perhaps," she breathed against Lady Bonham's neck, "we could find a place more private."

Elizabeth pulled back, painted lips smudged.

"A study or office?" Sorscha suggested.

She took her hand, leading her a couple of doors down and pulling out a key ring. Door unlocked, she shoved Sorscha inside and threw the bolt.

With a smile as sweet and sinister as sin, Elizabeth led her to a chair in front of the cold fireplace and pushed Sorscha onto it. The only illumination in the room was the moon through the window, but there was plenty of light to see Elizabeth's breasts heaving, her lips parted and eyes hungry.

Suddenly feeling wild and desperate, Sorscha reached for Elizabeth and pulled her on top of her, hands clutching at her bodice as she kissed the tops of her breasts, aching to taste more of her. Hands grasping, needy, Elizabeth fought with Sorscha's skirts, lifting them, her bare hand grasping Sorscha's thigh.

It was not supposed to have gone this far.

She hadn't been with anyone since Rosemary.

And with that thought, an ice-cold bucket of water drenched Sorscha's insides.

She pulled back, reality sinking in. She didn't know this woman at all. Which was not something that ever would have bothered her before. Damn Gaius for rubbing off on her.

And Rosemary.

Grief could not make her weak.

Sorscha startled backwards. "Champagne," she breathed. The only thing she could think to say.

Elizabeth's brow furrowed, beautiful mouth swollen and lip stain smudged in the most endearing way.

"We need more champagne."

Lady Bonham stood and adjusted her bodice and skirts.

Sorscha cursed herself. "Brilliant idea. I will return momentarily."

The door clicked shut and Sorscha ran for the desk.

"*Lumière*."

She rummaged through it, muttering oaths to Hespa. She needed *something*. Anything about Mila or Amira. But there wasn't time. She slammed her hand on the desk and cursed again.

They needed to get out. She couldn't face this woman again. Snatching a quill, she scrawled out a short letter with her regrets and a few well-placed, yet veiled sweet nothings.

Fluffing her hair and placing her nearly exposed breast back in place, she exited the room, scurrying down the dark hallway toward the ballroom.

"For Lady Elizabeth Bonham," she instructed the nearest servant, handing him the hurried note, eyes searching for Gaius.

When she found him speaking with a pretty young woman, rage bubbled up where her shame and grief were already boiling. Stalking over, she grabbed him by the arm and yanked. "Time to go."

Gaius looked as if she'd slapped him, but made no attempt to give his excuses to the young woman. Instead, his brows pulled down as he searched Sorscha's face.

"Are you all right?" he whispered as they shoved past dancers and eavesdroppers, headed for the door.

The icy air hit her in the chest. "I'm fine."

"Your lipstick is smudged." He pulled her to a stop under the stars, his face etched with concern. "Did someone hurt you?"

A lump crowded the back of her throat at his tone. "No. Only myself."

CHAPTER ELEVEN

WINNIE

"You are a lovely thing, you know that?" Yula hooted softly and leaned into her witch's tender touch. Winnie sighed at the sound of snow crunching behind her, interrupting her tranquil moment. "I might as well travel with a whole herd of oxen."

"Just because you have the gait of a ghost doesn't mean there's anything wrong with mine." Eleanor stepped up next to her and ran her hand down Yula's wing. "Why an owl?"

Prattle, prattle. She rolled her eyes. "Witches are chosen, not familiars."

The maid's face scrunched up. "The familiar chooses the witch?"

Winnie didn't even bother with a nod. If she couldn't piece that together she was three shades duller than Winnie had originally assessed.

"All witches?"

Her face was going to freeze that way if she wasn't careful.

"But my gran doesn't have a familiar."

Winnie snorted. "Yes, she does." Mercy, that face was worse.

"I lived with my gran for twenty years, I think I would notice if she had an animal watching over her."

"Perhaps she simply hid it well." Ah, so the answer to silencing the bird was to hand her a riddle. Winnie stored that information for later, while Eleanor's brows scrunched up as she thought too hard.

Satisfied she'd shut her up, Winnie left her standing there with Yula and trudged off to retrieve her bow and quiver. By the time she'd done so, Eleanor was still standing with her face askew. "Come along. We're hunting supper tonight. I'm bored." The girl made no move to follow, nor did her face even register that Winnie had said anything at all. "Eleanor."

The girl still didn't move, so Winnie walked back toward her, stopping right in front of her vacant eyes. "Are you broken, maid?"

"Magpies," she said in a low voice.

"Magpies," Winnie repeated, looking around them. There were no magpies.

"My gran," Eleanor explained, eyes clearing. "She has a ridiculous habit of giving everyone and everything a peculiar name." She tossed her hands around as she spoke. "A goat on the road named Magdeleine, a mop bucket she named Pete…things like that. But the magpies were all named Stolis." She met Winnie's eyes, her brow still bunched up. "What if it was the *same* magpie?"

Winnie *hmmphed*. "A magpie named Stolis. I told you she had a familiar." She slung the bow across her back and entered the woods, Eleanor close at her heels.

"Familiars select the witch, you say? How does that work?"

Winnie had never truly considered the *how* of it, she only knew that they did. "When a witch or warlock comes of age, their magic begins to strengthen. If they are full-blooded, the power can no longer be ignored and it calls out to its maker. This is largely debated in our realm. Some say the power calls out to the Void or the Primordial. Others say Hespa because it was Her that imbued witch lines with magic at all."

Eleanor nodded along, her cheeks pink and chapped from the cold. "And what do you believe?"

They went five more paces before Winnie settled on an answer. "I don't know anymore."

"I think that's okay." Eleanor's words were soft, but they pierced a deep part of Winnie.

"Regardless, the magic calls out, and a familiar answers the call."

"They just show up one day?"

Winnie dipped her chin. "Pretty much. Once the familiar shows up, a witch or warlock's first true test of their power is to seek out the familiar's name within its essence and declare it."

"And mages do not have this experience? I'd always thought mages were simply lesser witches and warlocks."

"No." Winnie's hood fell back with a shake of her head. "Mages are nothing like us. Their power, if they have any at all, is different." She swallowed hard. "I no longer understand that, either." If she ever truly had. "Now hush, or you'll scare off our supper."

AGATHA

"Goddess' *teeth*!" Agatha shouted, startling backwards from a falling steamer trunk as a form materialised within her rooms. "What in all the realms, Vera?" she snapped.

The old witch cackled while Agatha calmed her breathing.

"You wrote me and asked for all this junk." Four more large trunks slammed to the floor with four massive *thuds*.

Eyes wide and teeth nearly bared, Agatha eyed her Sister Winter's stewardess where she stood very pleased with herself. "That was enough commotion to cause panic from the guards. They'll come charging in at any moment."

Vera held a gnarled hand to her ear dramatically and made an over-exaggerated show of listening. "Hear that?" She grinned maniacally. "*Silence*." Vera straightened and smiled innocently. "Joubert witches keep wards up, do they not?"

"Any good witch does."

Though Winnie must have excluded her stewardess from Agatha's, it would seem.

Vera made a clicking sound with her tongue and winked. "Exactly." She moved around Agatha and Grimm's rooms, gaping at and touching *everything*.

Agatha ran a hand across the domed top of a trunk, enjoying the feel of leather and embossed metal. Winnie would have only the best trunks in all the land. Rounded on top so they'd never have another trunk or pile of clutter stacked atop them. "*Did* I ask for all this?"

The old woman had a crystal decanter of dark liquor poised above her head, squinting up at it. Without responding, she took out the stopper and sniffed. "This here's older than me. Good stuff, I reckon."

It was, in fact, delicious.

"Vera, this is too much. I didn't ask for all this. What am I going to do with it?"

She set the decanter down and hobbled over to the window. "Are you a ninny now that you bear a title and live in a castle?"

Agatha frowned.

"'Cause I've been here all of a shake of a lamb's leg and you've thrice"—she held up three twisted fingers—"asked a stupid question." She waved her hand dismissively and looked out over the dark waters of Mer Noir. "Spell it into hiding if you must, but you did ask for all this. Your raven said you needed anything Winnie had on the Academy of Alchemy."

Agatha chewed the inside of her cheek. "Winnie had all this about the Academy?" There were hardly any books about it in the royal library of Castle Merveille. How did Winnie end up with so many?

She watched as Vera shuffled over to the bed and lay down. "How should I know?" She shrugged and pulled the covers up to her chin, white hair splayed across the black silk pillow. "Winnie keeps it all pretty and organised." She snuggled further into the blankets. "Once I found one book about the Academy, I simply packed all the shelves around it." Vera closed her eyes and within a blink was softly snoring.

Agatha snorted and shook her head.

"*Ouvrir*."

The lid of the trunk nearest her flew open, knocking into a side table. Agatha cursed. She was clearly more high-strung than she'd realised, for her magic to be so violent and wily. If one of them didn't take the draught soon, she was going to lose her mind. *Grimm*. If Grimm didn't take the draught soon, she was going to lose her mind. Agatha rolled her eyes, still perturbed she'd let him sweet talk her into winning that argument.

Nevertheless, she was itching to sift through all the knowledge at her fingertips. She selected a tome at random and opened it.

Areas of study were printed in stately script across the top of each page, followed by columns separated by dashed dates, presumably to commemorate an academic year. Beneath each column there were listed two or three names—professors presiding over that area of academic study.

Every few years the names changed, only a scattering of a few listed for decades at a time.

Orrin Pollock

Chresedia Gauthier
Nadja Rashad
Achilles Zivai

Representatives from multiple lands across Midlerea when segregation had been rampant were intriguing, but there wasn't much else to glean from that book. Agatha closed it, reaching for another when the door opened and Grimm strolled in.

He paused mid-stride, hands in his pockets, and whistled at the sight of all the steamer trunks. "Vera received your raven, it would appear." He nodded to where the old woman snored loudly on their bed and chuckled.

"I'd like to say she was being thorough." Agatha gestured around them. "But she admitted it was sheer apathy."

Grimm rubbed his hands together and set to rolling up his shirt sleeves to the elbow, the pursuit of knowledge his favourite delicacy. "Let us dig in, then."

After a few less-than-helpful texts, Agatha slammed one closed and tossed it aside. "Grimm, what if we don't discover anything more about your powers? We can't keep waiting."

"Give me two more days." He turned over the tome he was sifting through and laid it, open, across his knee. "If I can at least understand my powers more, I might be able to figure out what it is they wanted with me when they sent Pierre. That information could lead this investigation in the correct direction."

"If your experiments last Autumn were any indication, you won't have any idea what's going on while you're on the draught. What you discover about your powers now could be useless while you're on it."

"Not useless for *you*."

Agatha stretched her sore neck. Patience was not a gift of hers and the ominous feeling in the air only thickened with each passing day.

"I feel that foreboding, too," Grimm said quietly. "But rushing will not help us."

Part of her was relieved by every second Grimm remained unsullied by the vile drug, but the other portion of her was sick with worry for the entire continent. Leading a revolution was much more than black and white, it was so full of grey that she feared nothing would ever be simple again.

"I'm to meet Anne soon. She's being sent to Lord Wellington's in the morning." Agatha stood and rubbed the weariness from her eyes. She bent to kiss Grimm's cheek and he caught her wrist, rubbing small circles on the back of her hand with his thumb.

"Two days, love. I can't leave you without the knowledge you need."

She cupped his face with her hand, his beard tickling her palm, and leaned in to brush her lips against his. "Two days."

GRIMM

A very unladylike snort issued through the bedchamber and Grimm smirked, looking up from the book poised on his outstretched legs. He brought his feet down from the table to the floor and pivoted in his chair just as Vera sat up bleary-eyed, white hair in a manic state.

"Good morning, Slumbering Beauty," he drawled.

"Morning?" she grumbled. "How long have I been asleep?"

"Oh, a few hours. It's actually closer to teatime." Her eyes lit and he chuckled, standing to pour her a cup.

When her wrinkled hands wrapped around the teacup, she looked up at him with doe eyes. "Someone serving me for a change. I like that."

Unease crawled up his spine. His trust in Wendolyn was

minimal at best, but it foolishly hadn't occurred to him that she would differ from her Sister so very much as to truly break the back of her help. Perhaps he was merely reading too much into Vera's comment. "Wendolyn knows how fortunate she is to have you, I'm sure," he said instead of what he wanted to say.

Grimm handed Vera an orange scone and she bit into it with fervour, still reclined in his bed. His lips twitched at her carefree manner. There was a certain freedom that came with old age and a lack of regard for the opinions of the populace at large. That was, unless you were ancient and yet appeared young...

"Winnie's all bark and no bite," Vera said around a mouthful. "She keeps a tight ship, though."

Grimm strode over to the platter of food he'd collected from the kitchens and filled a plate for Vera. He'd found that he enjoyed such menial tasks as obtaining their own food and laundry. There was something peaceful and charming about the idea of a simple life—out in the forest in Agatha's cottage, tending their own land and preparing their own food.

It hadn't taken long to realise just how independent Agatha was, but he'd since learned *de*pendency was possibly her greatest fear. Though Grimm wasn't certain Agatha even knew it.

If he could grasp the scope of his powers, infiltrate The Order, and tear the whole thing down...perhaps he could finally offer her the life she craved. As it turned out, *his* greatest fear was that he'd trapped her that day at the altar. Killing any chance she had of the simple life of independence she craved. Worse, his fear was compounded by the thought of digging her deeper into a hole she could never escape from unscathed.

"Vera"—he handed her the plate—"how did you come to work for Wendolyn? She's been a relative recluse for centuries, yes?"

The old witch popped a grape into her mouth, shaking her head. "*Relative* recluse. I don't know what she did before I came around about fifty years ago, but I don't think she'd ever had nobody serve her before the likes of me." She bit into an apple slice, the crisp *snap* of it enough to make anyone want a bite. "Had to train her how to manage Glacé Manor and a stewardess myself."

Grimm's head cocked to the side. Why have a stewardess at all, after two hundred and fifty-some-odd years, then?

"That manor of hers is a right menace," Vera went on as if he'd asked the question aloud. "What she did before I came along definitely didn't have nothing to do with lavish estates, that's for sure."

"How did you come into her employ, then? How did she find you?"

With an ungraceful swallow, Vera held out her hand impatiently, waiting for Grimm to help her up. He did. "The Witch Trials did away with most of us, but not all. We have a way of communicatin'. I reckon she figured that out 'cause she put an advert right there in our paper."

The notion struck him as amusing. "Witches have a paper? As in a news source all their own?"

"Right you are. Society paper included. Witches enjoy gossip, too." She sniggered. "Aggie would know that if she didn't live like a black widow tucked up under a rock. Love that girl like a daughter but she never sticks around with us long."

Because she couldn't. Surely Vera knew that much. "This is commonplace knowledge amongst witches? Agatha aside?"

Vera nodded, adjusting her wayward bosom as Grimm looked away awkwardly. "If you're in communion with other witches, you know about *The Spectre*." She hobbled a step toward her discarded teacup and drained it. "Hades, more'n just witches use it, really. Easy way to keep messages from mortals and other creatures—cyphers 'n' whatnot."

Grimm could think of at least a dozen more questions for the old witch, but she patted him on the cheek and said, "You've been a right peach, Your Highness, but I best be goin'.

Glacé Manor's ice can be crotchety when her mistress i'n't home."

With a theatrical wink, Vera vanished.

Two days. They'd agreed upon two days. He should've bargained for four. But their plan was already hanging by a thread. Grimm turned a small circle in their rooms, books littering every surface. It was a damned good thing they'd dismissed all their servants a moon ago.

He ran a hand through his hair and let out a breath. They hadn't found one useful piece of information since Vera brought the trunks of books the day before and Grimm hadn't slept a wink.

Agatha lay slumped onto what must have been a particularly boring text, eyes closed and breathing deeply. The sight sent his heart plummeting. He'd not said as much to her, but he was more than a little uneasy about taking the draught. The entire reason he'd been a bastard to her when she arrived, pushing her away and attempting to find a way to end their betrothal, had been to keep her safe. Even before he knew he loved her, the thought of an innocent falling because of him was sickening. Then, it happened with Alestair and Professor Ludwig… Who else, of his men, of his faction would he have to collect the souls of? By his own damned failing?

Grimm shook his head. The Order knew how to hit him where it hurt and his adoration of Agatha was no longer rumour and something they kept secret, but nauseatingly obvious.

Still, she was powerful and cunning. Headstrong and strategic. Agatha could care for herself, with or without Grimm. But he…he could not stop anything coming against her, were she on the draught and incapable of protecting herself. Not as it stood, his full scope of power and how to harness it was a mystery to him. In all reality, she was far stronger than him outside of his Marchand form. Hades, she was most likely stronger than even his reaper.

Running his fingers down his bearded jawline, Grimm let himself consider that his relentless search for animancy was steeped in his fear that Agatha would still end up in danger and he would be powerless to protect her.

Pushing all of those thoughts away, he approached the last two stacks of books set against the far wall near Agatha's closet. The titles were innocuous and they'd shoved them to the back in hopes they would find the answer before having to waste time on the likes of these.

Alas, here he was, his last-ditch effort hinging on—he leaned in to read the title of the third from the top—*Botany: A Mage's Guide*. Grimm groaned and pulled the book out of the stack. As he did so, the one underneath tumbled to the ground. He turned to ensure it hadn't disturbed Agatha's adorable slumber and bent to pick it up. One of its pages rose askew from the top. It struck Grimm as strange, considering the pristine condition of all the other tomes, and of Wendolyn herself.

He flipped open the volume, thumbing through the pages until he reached the one protruding. To his surprise, it was not a page accidentally bent out of place, but a loose page that fell to the floor. Upon further inspection, it was not a page out of the book at all, but a piece of parchment entirely its own. A letter.

Grimm let the book fall on top of a nearby stack and he sat hard onto a wingback chair near the window. No. Not a letter per se. It was too smudged to make out all of it, but it was almost like a diary entry, only more formal. Perhaps the recounting of some event, not meant for the eyes of a friend, but someone else. Someone unfamiliar.

He flipped the letter over, inspecting it from every angle. The ink was smudged but all on one side and in the same pattern. A handwritten account would have smudges here or there sporadically, but the prior lines of text would have had time to dry, never having smudged in the exact same pattern. Unless…

Grimm bent forward, blinking to clear his fatigued eyes. Unless it was a copy.

Most common folk did not have need for copy paper because they had no need for more than one copy of a letter or document. Grimm, however, had used the copying system on more than one occasion for court—and rebellion—matters. One merely had to pen the letter over copy paper, where the strokes of the quill would make indentations, then use the copy paper and an ink press to transfer the text onto fresh parchment many times over.

But what kind of personal account needed to be copied a multitude of times? And why had Wendolyn received a copy?

Grimm moved to the table and set to work in his notebook, copying what he could make out and piecing together enough to get some semblance of the gist. By the time he set his quill down, Agatha was stirring.

"What have you found over there, reaper, hunched in the corner like a ghoul?"

Grimm thought of Vera's comment likening Agatha to a black widow and he snorted. The perfect macabre pair. "I'm not sure," he responded over his shoulder.

Agatha padded over and leaned her chest against his back, wrapping her arms around him, her chin on his shoulder. He'd pieced together two names thus far, and they'd sent him into a frenzy. They were common enough names, but he'd seen them paired importantly. In fact, that they were paired in this instance was unsettling, because no one was to know of the story of those two ill-fated lovers.

Grimm's garbled notes came into focus on a surname and he would have leapt out of his seat if not for Agatha's arms around him. She kissed his cheek and moved to sit opposite him.

"Does the name Jéan Proctor mean anything to you?" he asked, trying to keep furore out of his voice.

Her face scrunched up in thought, freckles colliding. "No, not that I can recall. Why?"

He tapped his journal with the pad of his finger. "Jéan Proctor was killed during the Witch Trials. One of the first in the far Nord, up in Hiverterre."

"Oh, he was a warlock? Or suspected of being one?"

Grimm shook his head, adjusting his shirt sleeves and rolling them up his forearms. "No, he was a magus actually."

Agatha inclined her head, setting down the teapot she'd begun pouring from.

"Have you heard of Hester Perrault, then?" She shook her head again. But she wouldn't have. No one had. Yet, here in front of him sat a *copied* account of what happened to them, nearly word for word what Professor Ludwig had learned.

Grimm stood, shoving his hands into his pockets, and leaned up against the table laden with open books. "Over two and a half centuries ago, near the beginning of the Trials, a woman named Hester Perrault was accused of being a witch after she was seen healing the town's magus, Jéan Proctor. The magus defended her in court himself, but the council found her guilty.

"When they came to take her to be hanged, they found only Jéan. Hester had vanished. Magus Proctor refused to give up her location and told them he would die in her place. That it was he who possessed magic, not her. They hanged him, in her place, but the council struck them both from records soon after the hanging.

"They'd discovered the two of them had been lovers and came to the conclusion the magus had lied to protect her. The council hoped one day Hester would return to find her lover and they could capture her, too. But, she never did. That we know of."

Agatha leaned back in her chair. "How do you know this story if it was stricken from record?"

"Professor Ludwig had a knack for uncovering forbidden literature and other private documents, as well as procuring it. He recounted it to me, saying he'd discovered a letter during one of his informational conquests."

He could feel Agatha's trepidation and unease as he watched her ponder what he'd told her, knowing he was not simply telling her a romantic legend.

"And why bring this up?" she finally asked.

Grimm withdrew the copied letter and his notebook and held them out to her. "I just found this stuffed in a book of Wendolyn's."

Agatha snatched them, eyes roving over his scrawled assessment. She finally looked at him, stricken. "Why would my Sister have this?"

Grimm shrugged. "I'm wondering the same thing. Perhaps it was merely in the book when it became hers."

Their bond confirmed that she agreed with him concerning the unlikelihood of that scenario.

"You think she had something to do with this? She was there?"

"Agatha, think about it. The four of you have seen each other a few hours, four times a year since you were eight years old. There is much you don't know about one another."

"She would have told us something that terrible… If she'd been that close to another Witch Trial."

"Perhaps not." It was bothering him that she had a *copy* of the story. A smudged one that had barely had time to dry, as if she had been the one to press it. "What if she used it as blackmail?"

Agatha shook her head again and handed the letter back to Grimm. "No. Absolutely not. Winnie must have been the one who wrote their story and sent it out, thinking those souls deserved to be remembered."

Grimm hoped to Hades that Agatha was right about her Sister.

A knock sounded at the door, and Tindle's voice drifted in from the entryway. "Are you decent?"

"Depends what you deem decent," Grimm called back and Agatha smacked him.

Tindle bustled in and snatched Grimm by the sleeve. "Come quickly."

"MOTHER." He'd addressed her three times already. Tindle cut him a worried glance and Grimm shifted in his seat. "Mother, Tindle has brought you three gowns to select from, for the Hearthmas Eve dinner."

Queen Fleurina blinked, the rest of her body remaining eerily still. The dressmaker had summoned him, claiming the queen seemed ill, but *ill* no longer seemed accurate. Grimm leaned forward and put a hand on her arm. She startled backwards as if a serpent had latched onto her instead of her son's hand.

"Oh, Grimm." She put her gloved fingers to her chest. "You frightened me. Your hand looked almost…" She drifted off into another realm again.

A cold sweat slithered down his spine as he watched her. The glaze over her eyes did not look feverish. Tindle's forehead wrinkled with worry and he fussed over the dresses hanging on the armoire.

Grimm pulled his hand back, dread beginning to wash over him. "Mother, the dresses."

Too slowly, her head shifted to face him, eyes finally focusing a moment later. "Oh, hello dear. Did you need something?"

Grimm ground his teeth so hard he thought they might crush into powder. His astute, resplendent mother sounded like a fanciful dolt. "Tindle has brought some dresses for you to choose from," he repeated, looking pointedly at Tindle, who rushed over.

"How lovely." Her voice was too far off. Too high. Too dreamy. Almost like she was…

Oh, gods.

Panic gripped him and Grimm stood too quickly, his chair sliding back, grating across the wooden floorboards, jarring them all. "Tindle. Mother." He nodded to each of them and rushed out of the room, Tindle gaping after him.

Someone said something to him in the corridor but it was muffled by the ringing in his ears. He nearly collided with a maidservant carrying boughs of holly up the grand staircase in his hasty descent. So long as he didn't run into the magus, he didn't care. The mental fortitude it would take to feign complacency whilst his blood boiled over his mother—the gods damned *queen*—being toyed with… It would take much more self-control than Grimm possessed to not rip his sagging skin from his skull on sight.

Mercifully without incident, he made it out of doors, stepping into shin-height snow he'd failed to realise even coated the grounds. Too many days he'd spent holed up in their rooms. Perhaps, if he'd left long enough to visit his mother, he would have realised something was amiss in time.

Huddled in his cloak against the chill, he found his little witch taunting Augustus on the practice field, swinging her sword around like she'd held one in her hand since birth. Agatha had told him time and again that she knew her way around a foe without magic, but seeing her with his own eyes was another thing altogether. She was rusty at first when she'd begun training with Augustus, but a hundred years as a recluse would do that to a witch.

Grimm caught his lips tipping up as he watched her parry and strike through the snow drifts, spewing unladylike insults and making Augustus laugh. He'd have to abandon his quest for knowledge about his powers and animancy for a moment to take her on himself, just to hear what filthy ways she'd come up with to provoke him. Alas, there were more pressing matters at hand.

Augustus shot forward, Agatha barely spinning out of reach of his sword tip, snow spraying up around her like a ball gown. Mid-twirl, she caught Grimm's eye and halted. He watched as her tender smile slipped down into concern that furrowed her brow and coursed through their bond. Without a word to Augustus, she left the practice field and strode purposefully toward him. He considered walking to meet her halfway, but their conversation was less likely to be overheard in the alcove of the guard's outbuilding where he stood observing. There was no way he could thwart her questions long enough to get to somewhere else more private.

"What is it?" she whispered, voice edged with concern. "What's happened?"

"It's my mother. She's acting strange. The magus has her on the draught, I'm sure of it."

Agatha shook her head. "Why? Because she absolved Tindle?"

"That would be my estimation." He ran a hand down his face and Agatha reached for his belt, pulling him close to her.

"We'll figure it out." She looked up into his eyes. "I'll go in and render her stores useless. She'll be back to normal in no time."

He took the tip of her braid in between his fingers, the other hand coming up to cup her face. "This has to end. All of it. You were right, we can't wait any longer."

Her resolve faded within their bond and he pushed back against the sway of his nerves because of it.

"It's time," he said. "Let's gather everyone together."

CHAPTER TWELVE

WINNIE

The girl reached out and snatched the dagger right from Winnie's hand. Once she'd seen the maid's hand shoot toward her, curiosity got the better of her and Winnie simply let it happen. She watched with bored intrigue as Eleanor thoughtlessly launched the dagger away from her, oblivious to the blade tip sinking into a tree trunk just before it tumbled down into a drift of snow.

"It makes a goddess-awful sound, when you file your nails on that damned knife."

"Dagger."

Eleanor growled and stomped off.

"We won't make it to the Druids in time." The maid turned back, lips tight and face wary. "We need to be in Merveille in only a couple of days for the Solstice and the Druids are at least three ahead of us."

"What does the Solstice matter, if you don't have the Grimoire anymore?"

It mattered that Winnie wasn't ready to give up their

tradition. It mattered that it was the only time she didn't feel guilty about seeing her Sisters. It mattered that it was her day of birth. Her three hundred and sixteenth year.

"It's when we need to convene, all of us. But we cannot be together until the Solstice begins," she said instead. Aggie and Sorscha might play with fire, allowing their magic to mingle, but Winnie was still not convinced it was wise.

"How far are we from Merveille?" Eleanor looked around the woods as if she knew anything about them.

"It's just over that hill." Winnie pointed in the opposite direction of Eleanor's attention.

She squinted toward the hill. Her shoulders slumped forward and she sighed. "We can stay with my gran."

"In her hovel?" Winnie scoffed.

"My apologies, Ice Queen, but it's better than a tent."

When they arrived, it turned out it was not much better than a tent. Shanty was a more accurate term even than *hovel.* The entire dilapidated building was hardly the size of Winnie's kitchen. Granted, her kitchen was fit for a royal family's staff of plenty, but Winnie had developed a delicate, refined taste over the last fifty-some-odd years and didn't feel shoving Vera—stewardess or not—into a cramped kitchen was right, at any rate.

Still, the entirety of the weather-worn cottage in front of her could have fit within one room of Glacé Manor. Not only that, but it looked as if a hurricane had taken it captive, lifting it off its foundation and setting it back down crookedly on a grassy knoll now laden with snow.

Too much snow.

Winnie looked up at the heavy grey clouds, feeling their weight upon her shoulders.

Too close. She was too close to Aggie.

Being in Merveille so early was a mistake, but she hadn't another course of action to take, aside from setting foot in squalor. Winnie held out a hand, directing Eleanor to lead the way forward. How such a petulant bird could have hailed from a rotted cottage was beyond her. Perhaps she'd been able to see the sunrise through a crack in her bedchamber wall and foolishly counted it a blessing.

Winnie shook her head and ascended the creaking steps after Eleanor, worried her heeled boots would sink straight through the wood. A shiver went down her spine as she considered the plethora of contagions that she could encounter once over the threshold.

The door flung open to reveal a stern-looking woman well on in years. As soon as she laid eyes on Eleanor, the woman's features softened and she rushed forward, folding her granddaughter in an embrace the likes of which Winnie hadn't experienced in far, far too long.

She sent the thought up into the weighted clouds to slumber amongst her ice and snow.

The old witch shot Winnie a cursory glare and beckoned them both inside, out of the weather. To be fair, the warmth coming from inside the hovel did hold the illusion of invitation.

An illusion that quickly faded once inside. The home was so cramped that the fire could have engulfed any number of comely trinkets littered about. The walls so close together they were suffocating and far from the smooth, clean surfaces Winnie had grown accustomed to the last half-century.

Eleanor watched Winnie with caution. "I'll help you with the tea, Gran," she spoke, eyes still pinned on Winnie, as they headed for an even smaller interior room.

They disappeared from view, but their hushed conversation drifted to Winnie's ears as if they were still in the room with her. The old witch was none too pleased her granddaughter had brought a stranger in to her midst.

Her chest beginning to feel entirely too tight, Winnie paced in front of the hearth, setting down her luggage and stripping off her fur coat. The floor even lilted to one side so badly that one of her bags fell over and the crystal ball within it rolled out and down to the other side of the room like a boulder down a mountainside.

Winnie stood staring at the crystal where it landed against the cobwebbed baseboard.

Three Hundred Years Ago

Everyone was fussy. Winnie most of all.

Agatha was crying because her dahlias had scorched in the sun. She sat on the floor, legs outstretched and a wilted blossom in her fist.

"You're not an infant, Aggie, for goddess' sake," Winnie snapped. The little girl's lip wobbled and Winnie relented. She knelt down beside her, running a hand over her wild auburn locks.

It wasn't about the flower.

"I'm sorry. We'll plant new seeds come Autumn." The girl smiled shakily and Winnie tapped the tip of her freckled nose.

Sorscha was cursing up a storm across the room, her newly planted lavender shrivelled on the windowsill.

"Mind your tongue," Winnie censured.

"I told you it was too late in the Season for me to plant," Sorscha growled at her. The withering flowers crunched in her fist as she squashed them, letting the dried petals drift to the floor.

"There was nothing for us to do about that, Sorscha." There was nothing for any of them to do about not having a home during her Season. They were all displaced, but Sorscha had taken it the hardest. She never knew what to do with her hands if she couldn't cultivate plant life or create tinctures with her beloved botanicals.

"Aggie can't sleep," Sorscha whispered harshly, both of them darting their attention over to the child in the corner, still marvelling at the dead thing in her hand. "How am I to help her if I can't grow any damned lavender?"

"*Mind your tongue,* I said." Winnie winced at her own words. She sounded like their mother.

"I just need the lavender." Sorscha's face was maturing, no longer that of a child, but it was made of stone these days.

It wasn't about the lavender.

"We'll figure it out, Sister." Winnie picked up Sorscha's discarded botany book from a chair and held it out to her. "I'll help you look after supper."

She smiled weakly at her Sister and moved toward the kitchen of their small cottage. Winnie was not a witch of great power, but she hoped one day to be. It had taken three moons, but she'd gotten her Sisters out of the wilderness. Out of hiding. No more caves, or lean-tos in the Spring rains. Every day, Winnie used their father's journals and the one spellbook she'd had time to snatch from the flames, to build her Sisters a home. It wasn't much. The logs creaked during strong wind, the floor was uneven, and she'd only had enough power for one bedroom, but they were together. They were safe in the woodlands of Drifthollow, far from the fire of Helsvar. But the heat of Summer made it feel like the flames were yet chasing them down.

Even Seleste was fussy. Winnie had never seen her blissful, ten-year-old Sister Summer with a crease of distress between her brows, but it showed itself often these last moons. She huddled over a tray of meagre lemon tea cakes, their frosting melting, dripping plump dots of glaze onto the crooked table. Seleste glanced over to find Winnie hovering in the doorway. "The frosting won't stay on. It's too hot."

Winnie strode over and swiped a dot of frosting off the table, bringing it to her tongue. "Mmm. It's delicious, though."

Seleste's face crumpled and she wilted into a chair, dropping her frosting knife onto the tabletop with a clunk.

It wasn't about the frosting.

"We'll try again after nightfall. It'll be cooler then."

Seleste nodded, but it was half-hearted.

It wasn't about the heat.

"Come." Winnie took her Sister by the hands and pulled her up. "It's too hot to cook. I'll conjure us some lemon-herb chicken and potatoes." Seleste's face brightened. She loved anything lemon. Sorscha loved chicken, and Aggie loved potatoes. "Perhaps I can frost over some lemonade as well." Seleste smiled wide and Winnie swallowed the lump in her throat. Their smiles were so very rare these days, but she was doing everything in her power to bring them back.

Despite her worry that her magic was not honed enough to mimic the recipe, Winnie found success. As the sun dipped and the stifling air finally began to release its grip, the Sisters sat down for the best meal they'd had in what felt like ages.

"This tastes like Mummy's chicken." Aggie dangled a sliver of herbed skin over her outstretched tongue.

A pang of grief shot through Winnie. Their mother the heretic. Their mother, the reason they now suffered. Their mother, the one who failed to tell Winnie the truth until it was too late. Until their coven was already burning.

Now, Winnie didn't know how long they had left.

She watched her Sisters, sitting around the table, looking like *themselves* for once. The sight prodded at the tender ache in her chest. She watched a bead of condensation slide down her glass of lemonade instead.

A small thud sounded from the living room and Winnie shot out of her chair. "*Stay here.*" Her pulse thundered in her ears. Surely it was just a rabbit or one of Aggie's books toppling off the shelf. They'd encountered some feral animals in their time living out of doors, and she'd conjured a dagger for each of them. Their father had trained them to wield knives and swords, something Winnie had relentlessly forced her Sisters to continue practising.

Slinking through the shadowed cottage, she chastised herself for not making them keep their daggers on their person. Father had always warned them they needed a knife on them at all times. That they needed to know protection spells by heart. None of it seemed necessary until screams broke out that fateful night. She'd been a fool not to heed the warnings still. Winnie grabbed a heavy candlestick holder, gripping it with all the force of her compounding fear. She told herself again it was just a mouse, or a rabbit, or the sounds of the house. If it was more, she would use her small store of magic to summon the knife. It was just a mouse. Just a mouse.

She heard a whisper and knew she was wrong.

Rounding the corner, Winnie witnessed four women, advanced in years, standing in a small circle. Her breath caught in her throat and she dropped the candlestick to the ground. The *thunk* as it hit the floor drew all their attention toward her. The eldest of them softened when her gaze landed on Winnie. Another offered her a smile, but it was bleak and edged with bitterness. The third stood stoically. The fourth stepped forward. "Do you know who we are?"

Winnie nodded. "The Sisters Solstice." It was time, then.

"Good." She brushed her hands together as if she'd just avoided a troublesome introduction. "You needn't collect but a few belongings. We have plenty enough for each of you."

Hands trembling, Winnie opened her mouth to speak, but she heard the floor creak behind her. She rounded on her wide-eyed Sisters. "To bed," she hissed. "*Now*."

They skittered away like frightened mice.

"Please, give me one more day with my Sisters. I– We just

lost our parents, and I haven't had the heart to tell Agatha what is coming." She moved closer to the elder witches, sensing Sorscha lingering in the hall.

The shrewd one cackled, a severe laugh that ended as abruptly as it had begun. "We haven't room for weakness amongst the Sisters. It is time for her to come with me."

Winnie's pulse beat furiously against her ribs. This woman could not take Agatha. Not her sweet Aggie. But what could be done? The Goddess Three demanded it.

"Sorscha," she spat over her shoulder. "Go and lie down immediately." Winnie felt more than saw her Sister finally retreat. "Please," Winnie begged, turning back to the Sisters. "She's only eight years old—"

"That's how this works," the first witch cut her off, the coarse one muttering her agreement.

"Let them have a day, Greta," the eldest spoke up.

"*Tonight* is the Solstice, Helda." She splayed a hand out toward Winnie. "I only have moons to train her as it is."

The stoic one broke in, "Greta, you were the youngest, as well, when you were retrieved. Certainly, you can empathise with this request."

Greta frowned, the creases in her face deepening. She looked to the harsh Sister. "Sybil?"

"It's only a day, I suppose."

"Prue?"

The quiet one nodded her agreement.

Helda smiled kindly at Winnie then turned to Greta, Sybil, and Prue. "What's one day?"

Greta sighed. "Fine. We will return separately on the morrow to take each of you."

"Take me last." Winnie fought the tears building hot behind her eyes.

"You're not in the position to make any more demands. It is risky enough, as it is, to not do this on the Solstice."

Winnie gritted her teeth. "I will be with them until the last possible moment," she ground out.

The two Winter Witches mirrored one another, chins raised and arms crossed. Something glinted across Greta's eyes as she stared down her successor. Winnie caught a small smile from Helda just before Greta deflated. "Fine. I will return last. Be prepared."

The witches disappeared and Winnie stepped backwards, sagging into a chair.

A small voice sounded from the shadows. "It's time, then?"

Winnie held out her hand and beckoned Sorscha to come to sit on her lap. "I'm afraid so, Sister." Sister Spring wrapped her arms around her elder Sister's neck. "I bought us a day," she whispered against Sorscha's hair.

"Does Aggie know yet?"

"No. I couldn't bring myself to tell her. Now it's too late."

Sorscha pulled back. "It's not too late. We have a day. We'll make it memorable."

Winnie swallowed hard, eyes misty, and nodded. "I think Aggie and Seleste would like the new bazaar. It's a fanciful cirque. Have you heard of it? It arrived in Drifthollow last night."

Sorscha nodded. "One more day."

"One more day," Winnie echoed. With the words, a perilous idea took root in the recesses of her mind.

GRIMM

Tindle straightened Grimm's cravat, whispering low enough that the others could not overhear. "You do realise this is a phenomenally dreadful idea"—the old dressmaker pulled back, eyes fiery and lips pinched—"*Your Highness*."

Grimm snorted at his comrade's derisiveness and swatted his hand away, pulling at the cravat to loosen it once more. Fine clothing was something he had a great taste for, its restriction and arrangement less so. "We have little choice."

"Any option is better than this," Tindle hissed, worry flashing across his bold features.

"Our only other option is a possibly fictitious man in a snow-covered mountain pass being hunted down by someone I'm not inclined to trust."

Tindle straightened. "If Agatha trusts Wendolyn, so do I."

Running his tongue over his teeth, Grimm took a breath. "I'm not quite there yet," he bit out.

"Fine, but this is madness."

"We need to infiltrate The Order, Tindle."

"There is *surely* another way," he pressed.

Grimm glanced across the parlour to where Agatha stood in conversation with Augustus and his sister Delilah, as well as Tindle's valet, Demitri. The moon shone through the curtains of Tindle's home, nearly full with the approaching Winter Solstice. The sconces along the damask-papered walls flickered in time with Agatha's unease coursing through their bond. He shook his head, black curls bouncing, trying to dislodge his guilt. His trepidation and fear. But Tindle's face only reflected it back at him.

He'd almost told Tindle the full truth. Almost. But, in the end, he'd promised himself to have that conversation *when* this infiltration was over. Another lifeline laid out to keep him putting one foot in front of the other.

Demitri cut a worried glance in their direction, but it only landed on the dressmaker, a tenderness there that Grimm hadn't seen before. Perhaps he'd simply never paid enough attention.

He blinked and held his eyes closed for the length of a

breath. If he caused these that he loved harm, even for a moment, he would beg Lady Death to obliterate him once and for all.

Grimm shook his head again. It was too much. But that weight was his to bear. His alone.

He turned back to Tindle and rested a hand on his shoulder, the texture of the dressmaker's fine olive coat an unexpected comfort beneath his unsteady fingers. "I'll be all right, Tindle." He did his best to smile, though he knew it was lopsided.

Tindle knocked his arm away, eyes glistening in the firelight. "As if *that* is what I'm concerned about." He turned away, hiding his sniffle with a snort and Grimm swallowed hard before shoving his hands in his pockets and ambling toward the others.

At his approach, their conversation died on their lips, the silence heavy. It settled there on his chest with his worry and fear, reflected in Agatha's thread of their bond. Her anxious eyes met his and he twirled the vial within his pocket between his fingertips.

Fuck, he wished Gaius were here.

With Agatha looking at him like that, he feared he would lose his nerve.

It did have to be done. *For* Agatha. For his mother and Tindle and the rest of blasted Merveille; Seagovia; Midlerea. And the only one he was willing to risk was himself.

He cleared his throat and began. "I will take a full dosage of the draught now, before you all." Every last one of them looked away from him. "You are to let my food come as it will. Until the magus is certain I am truly under the effects of the draught, he will continue to lace my food with it and we need it to reach me, even if that means I ingest extra."

Tindle cursed under his breath in Coronnocan, but Grimm ignored him.

"Agatha's food, however," Grimm continued, "will be watched like a hawk." He looked pointedly toward Delilah. "I *will not* have my wife's food tampered with."

"I'll retrieve it myself, Delilah," Agatha broke in, and Grimm glanced at her, jaw tight, before addressing Delilah again.

"It doesn't matter who picks up the tray of food, it is your duty to watch it. Understood?" Delilah nodded sharply. He despised being the forceful brute, but he would not take chances with Agatha's safety.

They were all looking at their feet, forlorn, and Grimm blinked away the beginnings of a migraine. "It's not a fool-proof plan," he spoke, his voice a fraction of what it had been a mere breath ago. "It could all be for nought, but we must try."

Tindle swiped at his eyes, his other hand in a fist as he fixed his attention on Grimm. "We don't know how they issue demands. What if Augustus is given a command and he doesn't obey because he didn't know it happened? They'll know he's not truly on the draught and you'll be found out, too."

Agatha answered before he could respond. "It's a risk we have to take, Tindle." She spoke kindly, with confidence, but none of her usual obstinance. She truly would make a fine queen… "Augustus will blend in. He will be as innocuous as possible—just another guard and minion. That will allow him to go unnoticed and give him ample opportunity to get close enough for the spelled brooch to feed us information."

Tindle cursed again and Grimm watched Demitri subtly squeeze his hand in comfort. "And what if The Order senses this brooch, hm?"

"It's our only option." Her voice was suddenly too quiet. Grimm pushed back against her fear pulsing at him through the bond. He couldn't back out now.

She was right. It was their only option and her bat brooches had been replicated by no less than seven shops on both the Row and Gemme Road. The people were bucking against the magus and the Crown. Many of von Fuchs' minions had begun wearing his sigil in response—at his command, of course. He wouldn't think twice about a draught-soaked guard wearing one.

The clock struck midnight—the Witching Hour, his little witch would say—and they all looked at him.

Grimm walked forward and tangled his fingers in Agatha's hair at the nape of her neck, his other hand snaking around her waist. He kissed her hard, memorising the feel of her, their shared trepidation nearly intoxicating. He pulled back, uncaring of what the others thought or saw, and rested his forehead against hers. "Look at me," he whispered. Her eyelids fluttered open. "I will always find you. Tell me you know that."

Agatha swallowed audibly and nodded, resting her cheek in his palm as he moved to cradle her face in his hands.

"Always," Grimm repeated.

He kissed her forehead gently and stepped back, pulling the amber vial from his pocket. He held it up to the lamplight, its contents glistening in false serenity. Grimm pulled the cork, the room so devoid of sound that the stopper's squeak sounded too loud in his ears.

"Bottom's up." He smirked and drained the vial.

AGATHA

She watched as the golden liquid passed Grimm's lips, the last drop sliding down the vial into his mouth. Her heart thudded against her ribs, dread coating her veins. She watched as he pulled the vial away from his mouth and met her gaze, a casual smirk playing at his lips as he silently tried to tell her it would all be okay. That *she* would be okay.

But then she watched the light leave him. Watched his face go slack. Watched vacancy cloud his eyes.

CHAPTER THIRTEEN

AGATHA

Anne gasped. "*What are you doing here*?" She rushed out the back door to the kitchens and snatched Agatha's hand, dragging her through the dark gardens at the back of Lord Wellington's estate. She pulled her down under the cover of a bush. "Princess Agatha…" She shook her head, eyes wide in the dim moonlight. "You shouldn't be here."

Agatha reached to pull back her hood but Anne stilled her hand with a shake of her head. "I needed to make sure you're all right."

Anne's lips pursed, her brows knitting in the middle. "Lord Wellington is rarely here. Everyone else is…fine."

"Miriam?" Agatha couldn't help but ask about the servant brutalised by Wellington and most likely the magus as well, not after their off-hand comments about her being *not of sound mind.*

Anne looked away briefly, beginning to shiver in the cold. "She is Wellington's favoured."

The tone of her voice made Agatha's skin crawl. "Why do I get the feeling that's a terrible, horrible thing?"

"Because it is. When he's here, he uses her up until she's nothing but a husk. Her skin is sallow and her eyes sunken… I'm certain there are bruises we can't see."

Agatha's stomach churned. She felt it was her fault, in part, after the way the magus used her to rein in Agatha's rebellion last Autumn. "But he's not here now?"

"No. He's been away for several days now. The magus arrived with a hooded man who required his accompaniment somewhere."

"A man in a hood, or a man in robes?"

Anne's head cocked to the side. "They did look more like robes, now that you mention it, but not the golden ones of the magi." Her sweet face contorted. "Who else wears robes?"

"Black?" Anne nodded. "Did you happen to see a"—Agatha moved her hand about, thinking of the word—"a marking of any kind?"

"No…" Anne regarded her with suspicion. "Nothing like that. He was only here a moment and never left the foyer." She frowned. "Agatha, what's going on?"

"You're freezing, Anne. Can we go somewhere else? Your rooms perhaps?"

Anne blanched. "Of course not! I won't risk you being found here."

"You said Wellington is away. Can I not simply pass as a friend here for a visit?"

Anne blinked innocent blue eyes at her. "But you're the Royal Princess…"

"And exactly how many of these servants have made it all the way to Castle Merveille to have laid eyes on me, hm?"

Worry etched itself across her face, but she finally spoke. "Alright."

They walked through the corridors, Anne jumping at every sound and ducking into every alcove, worried someone would question them concerning the *princess'* presence. Agatha snorted, quite concealed from all eyes but Anne's, by magic.

"Are things dreadful here when Lord Wellington returns home?" Agatha asked as they strode down a particularly gaudy corridor lined with gold-framed portraits of sneering men. She wanted to inquire more about Miriam but didn't want to frighten her friend or cause her to fall into danger by knowing too much.

Anne waved her off. "No, no. They're fine. Miriam took ill before I came, but she was still up and about until a few days after I arrived. Since then, Wellington's been calling for me to dine with him in the evenings." Agatha stilled and Anne straightened a portrait, cheeks pink. "He's begun calling me by a pet name I am not fond of, but the food is excellent."

"Anne, that's not fine—"

She turned to her with a glowing smile Agatha could see right through. "Miriam will be better soon, and Lord Wellington will forget all about me."

Agatha hoped to Hespa she was right, for Anne's sake, but not for Miriam's.

"This is it." Anne pointed toward a door at the end of the hall, a sheepish smile on her face.

Agatha twirled in a small circle, taking in Anne's new room. "This is…quite an improvement from the dank underbelly of Castle Merveille." The room was stunning, with peony pink walls and silver adorning every nook and cranny. She looked down at the ornate rug beneath her boots, a frown deepening on her brow. In fact, it was concerning just how lovely the room was. No one treated servants so well.

"You didn't really come here just to see me, did you?" Anne asked as she closed the door. One that did not have a lock, Agatha noted.

"No, I did not." She walked to the lone window next to the bed, pushing aside a lacey cream curtain to find the view was little more than a brick wall, a gardening shed, it seemed.

Turning to face her friend once more, she asked, "Did you have any interaction with the Coronnocan Empress when she was in Merveille?"

"Not at all." Her braid shifted with a simple shake of her head. "I believe I only ever saw her at formal events and it was from afar."

Disappointment clouded Agatha's already muddled mind. She'd not expected a different answer, but they had so little to go on and an even smaller number of individuals they could trust. Was it only Mila who wanted Amira, or was she acting on behalf of The Order?

"Miriam did, though."

Agatha's attention snapped back to Anne. "How much?"

"She regularly brought the empress' food to her."

Agatha made a face. "In the castle? I thought she lived here with Lord Wellington and only came to Castle Merveille for events."

"That's correct. Empress Amira stayed here for a few days before returning to Coronocco."

"That doesn't make any sense… This was before you were here, yes?"

Anne nodded slowly, her forehead creasing. "Miriam told me about it when I first arrived. She was fascinated by the empress' wardrobe and the ink on her skin. She was already beginning to act differently than I remembered her, Miriam that is. Some things didn't make sense that she would say, but I definitely remember the conversations about Empress Amira being under this roof."

Agatha took up pacing, ignoring that her behaviour was clearly beginning to make Anne uncomfortable. "When was this, that the empress stayed here? I need a timeline."

"I–I suppose it would have been about a moon ago. A fortnight after the Eve of Hallows ball."

Exactly when Amira disappeared with Mila. The night she

stabbed Grimm. "Did Miriam mention how the empress was? Was there anyone else with her?"

Anne thought for a moment. "She didn't mention much. But she did say it was odd the empress arrived without guards and only one lady-in-waiting. I remember thinking that was strange when Miriam mentioned it."

Agatha stopped pacing abruptly. Amira had no ladies-in-waiting. It could only have been Mila. "I need you to take me to Miriam."

"But she's ill…"

"Anne, please."

The concern in her eyes bordered on fear, but Anne dipped her chin and led Agatha out into the hall. Two turns later, they crossed a covered balcony connecting Anne's wing of the castle to one much smaller, but no less grand.

"Miriam has this wing to herself when Lord Wellington is away," Anne whispered.

"Isn't Lord Wellington married?" Agatha knew full-well the aristocracy married for connections, not love. Mistresses and lovers were a fact in many of their lives, but they did not generally live within one's marital home and they were certainly not servants. Particularly ones physically punished by said lover.

Anne blushed. "I'm not certain Lord Wellington has spoken to Lady Penelope in years. She also has her own wing, on the opposite side of the estate. They only see one another when there is an event they must attend together."

Morons, the lot of them. "And how exactly did a servant become Lord Wellington's… What did you call it? *Favoured*?"

"That, I do not know. It's"—she grimaced—"peculiar, isn't it?"

"You can say that again," Agatha mumbled.

They approached a cherry wood door, the scent of medicinal chemicals assaulting Agatha's nose even with it closed. Anne offered her a wary smile before knocking lightly and opening the door a crack.

"Miriam?" she spoke softly into the dark room. When no one answered, she opened it further, tip-toeing in, Agatha behind her.

The air smelled stale beneath the layer of medicinal aroma, but the other scent was not that of sickness. Agatha couldn't quite put her finger on it. It was almost like the decay of a failed crop rather than that of illness.

"Miriam," Anne said again. "It's Anne. I've brought a friend to see you."

Agatha doubted the curtains had been opened in days. Nor had the fire been stoked in several hours, judging by the cinders and chill in the air. Three lone candles lit the space—one next to the bed, nearly burnt down, and two on side tables next to an empty chair. She couldn't tell how lavish the room was without any more light, but after seeing Anne's she assumed it would be grand.

The lump on the bed stirred, edges smudged in the dim light. They each took one side of the bed and Anne spoke. "Miriam. I know you're not feeling well, but there is someone here to see you."

When they were met with more silence, Agatha collected the other two candles and set them next to the one burning low on the bedside table. "Miriam." She pulled the covers back ever so slightly, just enough to reveal a clammy forehead and closed, restless eyes. "Miriam, it's Agatha."

At the sound of Agatha's name, Miriam's eyes flew open, a frenzied look in them. Anne took a step back at the sight and Agatha fought the urge to do the same. The young woman flung the covers off her sweat-soaked upper half, buttercream nightgown clinging to her skin. Her bloodless, cracked lips parted as if she might say something, but a violent shudder wracked her frail body, sending her into convulsions. Anne gasped as Miriam's eyes rolled back in her head. Agatha lunged forward, taking her bony arms in her hands. She was cold to the touch.

"*Merde*," she muttered. "Miriam! Can you hear me?" Miriam continued to shake and Agatha frantically looked around the room. "I need a cloth, a rag, something!"

Anne blinked rapidly a few times before her body registered that she needed to move. Flinging open the bedside drawer, she pulled out a small cloth and handed it to Agatha.

She cursed when a rivulet of blood oozed out the side of Miriam's mouth and down her chin. "She's already bitten her tongue." Agatha shoved the cloth in between Miriam's teeth and sank down onto the bed to hold the young woman in her arms. "What else is there?" she shouted at Anne. "Medicine? Anything?"

Anne fumbled in the drawer. "I—I don't see any. These are all empty!" She held up a handful of empty amber vials, the glass clinking together in her palm. Tossing them to the side, Anne fished in the drawer further, pulling out a needle and a glass vial full of a dark red substance.

Both women looked from the vial, to each other, to Miriam, still seizing in Agatha's grasp.

"*Fuck*," Agatha ground out, standing. "Anne. I'm so sorry. I —I don't have time to explain."

"Explain what?" she shrieked, staring at the vial of blood like it was going to come alive and devour her.

Agatha placed her hands on either side of Miriam's face.

"*Miriam, être immobile.*"

A faint, onyx glow lit Miriam's cheeks and Agatha prayed Anne couldn't see it. The young woman's body went still and calm, and Agatha relaxed a fraction.

"Guérir.

Guérir.

Guérir."

With each chant, Miriam's body soothed further and Anne's tensed across the bed.

"What are you doing?" she whispered, fear lacing her voice, her eyes wide and filling.

Agatha did not offer an answer until Miriam slipped into a deep, healing sleep. "I'll explain. I promise." But something caught her eye. She snatched a candle and held it close to Miriam's arm, careful not to drip wax on her. With a tender touch, she ran a gentle finger over strange marks on the inside of her elbow. Not the careful incisions of a healer. Was someone taking her blood, or giving her someone else's?

"What kind of illness does Miriam have?" she demanded of Anne.

"I haven't any idea..." Anne's eyes widened further and she rushed toward the door, peering out into the hall. "Someone's coming up the servants' stairs!"

Agatha flicked black sparks into Miriam's dying fire and hurried out after Anne. The two of them ran down the corridor, not slowing until they made it around the corner, and not halting for a moment until they made it back into Anne's room.

When they did, Anne whirled on her, huffing. "*What* is going on, Agatha?"

She'd never seen Anne angry, but that look was about as close as she thought possible for her sweet friend. This would be a cumbersome task, but she needed Anne. From the moment Grimm took the first sip of the draught, his eyes had darkened. The image of it, and his behaviour since, moved like a twisted play behind her eyelids. "Sit down."

Anne's frustration slipped into concern. "You're scaring me."

"I'm sorry." Agatha turned and sat next to Anne where she'd slumped onto the bed. "I have a lot to tell you."

"I know something is going on. Augustus has been strange. And then you do...whatever that was in there!"

"I know. I know. And I don't want you to blame Augustus for

any of what I'm about to tell you. He fought us at every turn for keeping things from you. I need you to understand he isn't trying to keep secrets and I need you to understand we've only kept you in the dark out of fear for your safety. I've wanted to tell you for so long. I can't keep it from you anymore—"

Anne softened and halted Agatha's words with a hand on hers. "Agatha. You are Princess of Seagovia and I am a maid. You will always have secrets from me. But *I* need *you* to know that it's your friendship, not your title, that tells me you will only do what you believe is best for me." Agatha sagged with relief. "However, it is also our friendship that I hope leads you to know that you can trust me. With anything. Including whatever it was you did back there with Miriam."

She knew in her marrow how true it was. "I don't know what I did to deserve you, Anne."

Her friend leaned in close, countenance as pure as sunshine. "No one *deserves* anything, Agatha. The right to be loved is intrinsic."

Agatha swallowed a lump in her throat.

"Out with it, then."

And she did. She spared nothing.

At the end of it, Agatha's palms were sweating. Anne had every right to take back everything she'd said. To fret, yell, recoil.

But, in true Anne fashion, she did none of those things. She simply took Agatha's hand again. "How can I help?"

WINNIE

One fingernail running across her bottom lip, back and forth, back and forth, her elbow propped on a sorry excuse for a table, Winnie contemplated snapping its neck—the little finch that was not deterred by mounds of snow and ice and sat chirping in a nearby tree. The Winter's unforgiving storm was only growing worse. There was no denying it was due to her proximity to Agatha. The slums were evidently not far enough from Castle Merveille. And yet, her Sisters still claimed they could overcome their demanded separation. Winnie scoffed to herself in the cold.

Even the slate-feathered finch's incessant chattering and the icicles dripping from her eyelashes were better than sitting in the shanty cottage at her back.

Winnie was certain her Sisters would disagree with her reasons for avoidance. *It's filled with the warmth of love*, Seleste would say. *Didn't you smell the mulled wine and Winter vegetables?* Sorscha would say. *She's a* witch, *Winnie, pick her brain*, Aggie would say.

Winnie found it suffocating. Eleanor was content bustling about, caring for her gran who refused to be cared for. She was a stubborn mule and ancient as dirt. Granted, she must have been a couple of hundred years Winnie's junior.

Aggie would have peppered her with questions, but Winnie just thought it rude. She didn't much care about this woman, witch or not. The woman didn't want Winnie around and she didn't care to be. There wasn't anything she could offer her, anyway, aside from a leaking roof and a filthy bed for Winnie to levitate over as she hardly slept.

Yuletide was a time Winnie usually spent gladly pouring herself into her newest Order from the Grimoire. Year after year, she took the sacred book from her ungrateful Sister's hand on the Solstice and dived headfirst into whatsoever she was Ordered to do. It wasn't rigidity as her Sisters so forcefully claimed, but a duty. One does their duty, or they face the consequences. Winnie did not find it a difficult creed to grasp.

Alas, the Book was ash long since scattered in the wind and Winnie was eating bonbons with a maid and her ancient crone of a gran. The Solstice would arrive in less than two days, and no Book would be placed in her hand. She would not be commanded by Hespa what to do with her Winter, but by her youngest Sister. Her *princess*, if Winnie was feeling disgusted enough.

Agatha had once been her greatest treasure. Now, they hardly even knew one another. They hadn't spoken a tender word to each other since the day Aggie was taken from her at the sweet and sticky age of eight. That was, aside from her wedding night when Winnie went to her Sister against her better judgement.

It was not that Winnie did not love her Sister. And it was not due to poor judgement that Winnie had gone into the Netherrealm to see her. It was simply that she and Aggie shared only blood now. Nothing else.

Sybil and Greta had made certain of that.

"Get in here and peel potatoes."

Winnie shifted her head and blinked at the old woman in the doorway behind her. "Pardon?"

"You might be pretty as a frost-covered lily, but you're under my roof and you'll pitch in."

They stared one another down and Winnie found she was entirely certain where all of Eleanor's bravado came from. "Very well," she relented through gritted teeth.

The aroma of a well-loved kitchen smacked Winnie in the face as much as the heat the moment they entered. Her stomach immediately soured when she laid eyes on the obscene amount of meat pies, seasoned vegetables, and a myriad of desserts. "Are we expecting an army?" It was far too much for a quiet evening just the three of them.

The woman levelled her with a stare. "Hearthmas is about

blessing our Goddess Three." She crossed her withered arms. "And how does one best do that?"

Winnie did not deign to answer what she surely thought was a moment to give a valuable lesson to a young woman.

Gran pointed a butter knife at her. "By caring for others." She set to slopping heaps of tart preserves onto flat biscuits. "Our dark knight might've paid our rent here in the slums for half the year, but most folk still don't have the means for a Yul–*Hearthmas* feast." She turned back to her biscuits and jam, gently setting another flat biscuit with a star cut out on top.

"And you have the means to do this for all?"

She wiped her hands on her apron, then handed Winnie a large bowl of potatoes and a knife. "Peel more. Talk less."

Winnie almost smirked and sat down. It was the most she'd liked a person in quite some time. For a moment, anyway.

"Ellie says you're a witch."

Winnie's knife slipped, the blade sliding across the slick potato and *thunking* into the scarred wooden table. "I thought you said peel more, talk less."

The old woman snorted a laugh. "I want you to teach my Ellie magic."

Leaving the knife abandoned, Winnie set the potato down and rose slowly. She walked with calculated steps to stand next to the woman, sharp-tipped fingers resting on the counter. "That isn't possible." It was. Halflings, or even those with less magic in their blood, often held some form of the gift, but if they did, they weren't oblivious to it for decades.

"Of course it is."

"One is born with magic, or they are not."

"My Ellie was."

Winnie fought a snarl. If that were true, how dare this woman keep Eleanor in the dark? "Does she know this?"

The old woman shook her head, a lock of her brittle grey hair falling loose from its confines.

"Then how do *you* know it?"

"I just know. Since she was a child, she's had an insight I could never explain."

That certainly did not signify *magic*, but Seleste's gift of cunning was something Winnie would describe in much the same manner.

"Then why not teach her yourself?" Winnie leaned in closer. "She's your responsibility, not mine."

The old woman shifted on her feet. "I promised her mother I would not."

Winnie huffed through her nose. "So, I teach her and you still get to claim you were loyal, then?"

"I taught her to *survive*." The woman stood taller, almost meeting Winnie's height. She was no crumbling thing, despite her weathered skin and gnarled fingers. "She is not high born. I taught her to claw her way up."

Winnie sneered. "She doesn't even know how to wield a knife, or have any other means of protecting herself, yet you put her in a castle to serve? You're daft if you think…"

"How dare you come into my home and disrespect—"

"*Enough*," Winnie growled, fury flashing white-hot across her vision. "Eleanor is with me for a short time, then she will live a long life within that castle. Isn't that right? She is safer if she knows how to *physically* protect herself, not walking about Castle Merveille with hidden magic." She looked away. "Only a *fool* would do that."

"Regardless of what you think of me, my Ellie is no fool."

"Where is her mother?" Winnie pushed a bowl of cabbage away from her vicinity, needing to do something in her exasperation. "A witch should live a long life."

The old woman's bravado fell away and she sank wearily into a chair. "She left her with me." Her gaze drifted off to some other time before she shook her head, her face clearing. "And then she died."

Winnie's icy heart cracked. "She just left her child with you one day? To be raised by someone else?"

Eleanor's gran took a deep, shuddering breath. "Sometimes the unthinkable must be done." Her attention drifted across Winnie's face, landing outside. She was still for a long moment, her words reverberating through Winnie's skull.

Three Hundred Years Ago

WINNIE

Summer heat, strange delicacies, and sweat-drenched bodies did not bode well for the senses. Winnie grimaced. Perhaps it had been a terrible lack of judgement to bring her Sisters to the dusty, crowded corner of Drifthollow occupied by a travelling troupe of performers.

Cirque du Barroque. The canvas banner flapped in the balmy breeze, the purple letters warbling.

As her Sisters chatted joyously, Winnie considered the packed bags beneath the bed back at their cottage. She could have had them halfway to the mountains already. Alas, once Aggie heard about the carnival, there was no getting out of it. They could spare a handful of hours, then they needed to return to the cottage.

A bead of sweat slipped down her back, no doubt soaking through her slip and white chiffon dress. It was wrong—to run. It was against the will of Hespa. The Goddess Three *blessed* the Sisters Solstice. It's what they'd always been taught. Their loving goddess set special tasks upon the Sisters to further Her will. It was an honour. But Winnie knew nothing beyond those doctrinal words preached to their coven by the magi. And she could not shake the feeling it was not a blessing, but a curse.

The thought sent a tremor down her arm, landing on her fingertips. A drip of frosted water beaded up, sizzling in the sun before it ever left her finger. Winnie shook her head firmly. Protecting her Sisters from this path until they were older did not make her a heretic like their mother. She chanted the notion in the back of her mind like a spell.

Aggie came up to tug at her sleeve and Winnie gathered the other two girls near as well. "There are many people here, Sisters. We must be vigilant and careful."

Aggie slid her fingers into Winnie's palm. "What is the most important rule?"

Winnie's breath caught in her chest as she looked down into her littlest Sister's sweet honey eyes. The phrase their parents had taught them so long ago. "Stay together," Winnie recited around the lump in her throat.

Aggie smiled up at her, carefree and innocent. "Stay together."

No. Protecting her Sisters did *not* make her a heretic like their mother.

Sorscha took Seleste's hand and the four of them wove through the crowd, under the banner promising them all things *fantastique*.

Every step beyond the entrance carried them past delicacies they'd never seen; colours and music they'd never experienced. The entire carnival was filled to the brim with the bizarre and incredible. A woman on stilts bent low to offer sugared and salted popped corn to children. An elephant shook the ground as it walked, with a majestic woman perched on its trunk, waving. Aggie shrieked joyously, jumping in the air. Seleste's eyes reflected all the wonder that was written on her face as she took it all in. Sorscha smiled at Winnie sidelong, taking her hand to pull her toward a booth.

As they skidded to a stop in front of the intricately painted box, Winnie read the letters and laughed outright. Sorscha's eyes shone mischievously as the first person behind the kissing booth came forward.

"This is a bit much for Aggie and Seleste to witness," Winnie said, her mouth still poised in a grin. "I'll stay with them and meet you over there."

"More for me, then." She giggled and kissed the handsome boy. Sorscha did not vacate her position and another young man came forward, his face twisted and one arm badly marred.

Seleste sidled up to Winnie. "What happened to him?"

She pulled the little ones aside as Sorscha bent in to kiss the boy without a second's pause, and Winnie's heart beat with pride at her Sister Spring's ability to see past a face. "Perhaps something terrible, or perhaps nothing happened to him at all. It doesn't matter. It's the inside we look for, Sisters. The beautiful can be grotesque and the beastly exquisite." She pointedly looked both of her young Sisters in the eye until they each nodded.

"Well, that was fun!" Sorscha bounced on her toes. She took Winnie by one hand and Seleste by the other, pulling them every which way while Aggie hung onto Winnie for dear life, giggling madly.

They visited stands with food that made their stomachs ache. They threw peach pits into jars to win flowers, raced each other around a maze of hay bales, and even visited a fortune teller. They were gulping in great breaths between their giggles over Seleste's *preposterous* fortune when a voice boomed across the carnival. The crowd's deafening volume died down and they all turned to see a line of men and women, all immaculately dressed. They looked as if they might be going to sup at Castle Merveille, not gallivanting around a dusty plot of land in midsummer heat.

As they fanned out, Winnie noticed some were so stunning

they were difficult to look in the eye. Others were deformed, like the boy from the kissing booth. When the last person stepped forward to complete the V-shape, she raised a large, elegant fan of feathers dyed violet. With one foot forward, she slowly lowered into a bow before the crowd. Behind her, there was a sudden crack of sound, so loud the crowd gasped in unison. A plume of purple smoke arose behind the woman and all the performers moved fluidly as one, circling behind her. They all hit their knees in the dirt, arms outstretched. Out of the smoke strode a man—the Cirque Master. A young man so captivating that no one could tear their eyes from him. His body was powerful, and he wore clothing befitting a prince, not a performer. Atop his head, he wore a peculiar hat. Tall, black, and flat on top. His head was tipped forward, and when he raised his chin, his mangled face held a lopsided grin and a mask of dark wood, almost black, concealing the upper half. Winnie took a compulsory step toward him.

"Welcome!" he boomed, arms out wide and an ornate cane dangling from one hand, its grip a silver fox head. The crowd cheered wildly and the Cirque Master bent into a deep bow. "Welcome, my beloveds, to"—his voice rang out, growing impossibly louder, enveloping the crowd from all around—"*Cirque du Barroque*!"

The people went mad with excitement. Aggie jumped and clapped, and Seleste twirled in place, her dress fanning out around her. Sorscha smiled from ear to ear, cheering. Winnie stood in rapt attention, her heart beating wildly.

The Cirque Master lowered his gloved hands, a hush permeating the grounds. "Before we begin, I must tell you all a little tale. A fairytale of a people once called"—he let his words dangle—"*the Druids*."

The crowd *oohed* and *ahhed* as the Cirque Master was suddenly lifted high into the air by two ropes tied around his waist. Winnie's neck strained to keep her eyes on him.

"You see," he shouted down over the crowd, "baroque's meaning might be known to many as extravagance." He swung over them, coming lower and lower. "Perhaps gilded, or magnificent. Finely detailed." He came so low that a portion of the crowd had to part, his voice still echoing all across the grounds. "But that is not baroque's *first* meaning." He landed deftly on his feet right in front of Winnie. She locked eyes with him, realising he was much younger than she'd thought. One corner of his twisted mouth twitched up and Winnie swallowed. "*Baroque*," he went on, eyes still fixed on her, "first meant irregularly shaped." He finally turned back to the crowd. "Deformed." He let his words settle in the air, a cognisance lodging in his captive audience's bones.

"You see, the Druids were descended from Elves." He began walking through the spectators, whose eyes were fever-bright with wonder. "Lost and alone here in this realm, they were destined to choose between their magic and their beauty. It was the curse of the Druids that brought their downfall. Every time their powers were used, their bodies contorted." He continued to meander through the crowd, all attention fixated on his charisma and charm. "It all began with small abnormalities—a blemish here, a crooked finger there. But it increasingly grew more severe as time went on. Eventually, using their magic at all was forbidden by the Druid Elders."

He knelt before a little girl and pulled a flower from behind her ear, sticking it in her hair as she smiled wide. "One day"—he stood and began walking amongst the crowd again—"a young man rose up to lead the Druids. A man who claimed the value of their race had nothing to do with their Elven beauty, or their Elven magic, or their Elven curse. He gave them back the *choice* to be who they were.

"When his people began bickering over who was right and who was wrong, this young Druid leader built a stage." The hot sun glinted off the fox head of his silver cane as he moved about.

"At first, the Druids were confused. What could a *stage* do for their people? The night it was completed, the Druid leader brought forth to his stage four new Elders. Two of great beauty, who had never used their magic. And two of great deformity, who used their magic regularly. The Druid leader bid them each to *perform*." He moved his cane in an arc above his head. "Their talents, power, and magnetism drew every Druid from their hut that night, gathering around their new leader's stage." The Cirque Master turned toward Winnie and her Sisters once more. "That night, under a blanket of stars, the *Cirque du Barroque* was born."

CHAPTER FOURTEEN

AGATHA

"Your hands are shaking, Highness."

Agatha finished adjusting the spelled brooch of the magus' sigil on Augustus' breast pocket and glared up at him. "So are yours."

The young guard swallowed hard and stepped back. "This is strange, isn't it?"

She reached into her pocket and clutched her blue lace agate crystal. Augustus fiddled with a stack of books Grimm left on their table days ago. When Agatha didn't respond, he moved to the balcony doors, shifting the burnished gold curtains to watch the snow fall out over Mer Noir.

"I don't like it," Augustus spoke to the sea. "Leaving him out."

Agatha blinked rapidly and cleared her throat. "You know I don't either, Augustus." It *was* strange, leaving Grimm behind while they planned how to spy on The Order. "We don't know how this works, though. We cannot risk von Fuchs or any member of The Order discovering we have any way of watching them. If they have some method they use to–to–"

She didn't know. They'd gone into this with too little gods damned information. Grimm had been right to hold off, but their studious search had been spent on the wrong details. He'd been so adamant about learning *why* The Order wanted him when they should have been concerned with learning *how* the draught worked. Now they knew none of it and their only chance was to let this nervous guard near with a spelled brooch and hope it provided any bit of information without him being caught.

"*Merde*," she cursed, turning her attention back to Augustus. "I don't think they can access his memories, but we don't know if the draught affords them the ability to hear or see through Grimm's eyes. There are many a dark spell that achieve such things to some degree."

"I know." Augustus' voice was quiet. "We can't risk it. It just feels like we're spying on *him*."

"We are." The young man's face fell at her words. "But we'll tell him everything the moment we can." He was such a good, honest man, Augustus. And they'd put him right in the thick of it all. Sometimes Agatha wondered if her sins would one day be paramount enough to swallow her whole. "You don't have to do this," she found herself saying. "I can do it."

Augustus scowled. "You know that isn't true, Highness. If they know what you are, all could be lost." He stood straighter, determination lighting his brown eyes. "I'll not say I'm unafraid, only fools claim that, but if Prince Grimm has taught me anything, it is that courage is not the absence of fear, but the fight through it and moving forward despite its presence."

Ah, that was why they'd chosen Augustus. Agatha offered him a small smile. "The brooch"—she pointed at it—"will use magic not entirely different from what I think the draught does as far as what it allows von Fuchs and The Order to see." Augustus' eyes widened slightly and she waved a hand. "It is not a dark spell upon the brooch. I selected one of revelation and sight. It will essentially function like the human eye. That does mean you must be in the room and I will not be able to hear much. What I do hear will be muffled. I'll rely on your memory of each conversation for details and specifics."

Augustus shifted on his feet. "I suppose that will help me look dumbfounded, trying to retain all that." He chuckled nervously and she smiled.

"You will have to be as innocuous as possible. There is a chance you will not be permitted into any inner chambers for a time. Von Fuchs is not a daft man, even if he is vile."

"I've done my best to blend in and appear as if I've been on the draught for ages. Here's hoping that fools him."

Gods, this was a bad idea. "Here's hoping."

"How will you er—" He wiggled his fingers in front of him. "See the happenings?"

Agatha strode to her armoire and pulled out a skeleton key to unlock it, the door creaking as she opened it. There at the back, behind the rod full of her dresses from her cottage nestled in the Forest of Tombs, rested a mirror of ornate bronze filigree and frosted, dark glass.

"Come look." Agatha pushed aside her garments.

Augustus stepped up to look over her shoulder. "Goddess, it looks like the depths of the sea within that mirror."

"*Voir*," she whispered, running one nail down the milky black glass.

With a shallow gasp, Augustus jolted backwards before coming forward again, eyes wide. "*Ce n'est pas possible…*" He stared, mouth agape, as his own image in the mirror looked back at him, distorted and stretched by the reflection within a reflection.

"It will be clearer when the brooch is viewing a real item, not a reflection. Turn toward me."

Augustus shifted his torso toward her, eyes still fixed on the mirror, Agatha's image blinking at him from its depths. "Madness," he breathed.

"Witchcraft." Agatha smirked.

With a glance at the time dial on the wall, Augustus wiped his palms on his uniform. "It's nearly tea time. It's now or never, I suppose."

Agatha put a hand on his arm. "You can do this."

He nodded once and left to find Grimm. Mabon flew down from the rafters sleepily and landed on her shoulder. He tittered and Agatha scratched behind his ears. "I'm nervous, too."

"GRIMM, AT LEAST SAY SOMETHING. PLEASE."

They sat in a snow-dusted carriage outside Dulci's *pâtisserie*, and Agatha had been attempting to get Grimm to speak since they'd climbed in. Several days on the draught and he'd become more than morose. He hardly spoke and when he did, it was almost as a foreign entity. She'd expected him to burn through it faster than a mortal, but the new dosage was incredibly potent—a massive oversight on their part. He'd downed an entire vial when they arose that morning, fell into a sickening stupor for the entirety of the day, and at nightfall, he remained lost to consciousness in every way that truly mattered.

Still, she clung to the hope of a few moments when the draught would release its vice on him and his gaze would clear just before he launched himself at her, embracing her and burying his face in her hair.

"Grimm," she said again, hating the plea in her voice. She'd pushed and prodded, more concerned about infiltrating The Order than for Grimm's safety and now here they were.

He blinked at her, never truly seeing.

"I told you not to take it today. What will Dulci say when you walk in there and you're not even...*you*?" It was useless. Words murmured into the void in a paltry attempt to soothe herself.

There was no witty retort. No referring to her as obstinate or telling her everything would be all right.

She shouldn't have said anything at all. Augustus had been spying for them for days and they still had no inclination of what the magus could glean from Grimm while he was under. Agatha crossed her arms to stave off the emotions threatening to assault her. She needed to remain hopeful that this endeavour would pay off. That the magus would soon be thoroughly convinced enough to let Grimm in, and Augustus by proxy. Thus far, Grimm had been vacant and detached with nothing to show for it.

Frustrated and glum, Agatha threw open the carriage door and stepped out into the snow. A moment later, Grimm numbly followed her up to the door of *Dulcibella's Pâtisserie*. It felt like an entirely different age ago that she'd first stood and looked up at the name that was now so dear to her. One they'd thought they would lose last Autumn.

Her recovery was well underway, and Dulci, in true form, demanded she be brought back to her home for Hearthmas—brought back to her Grimm. She was going to string Agatha up by her ears for Grimm's current state. Agatha shook her thoughts loose, her emotions scattering away like banshees screeching into the night. Now was not the time to falter. She knew Grimm. It didn't matter how he *seemed*, or what the magus or The Order would make him do, she would withstand it. *They* would withstand it. The two of them could not be so easily toppled, nor their plans so easily foiled.

It would work. It had to. She merely needed to hang on.

With one resolute nod and the steeling of her nerves against the vacant way Grimm regarded Dulci's, Agatha stepped forward and opened the door. The little bell over the door *tinked* and Agatha's jaw went slack.

"Anne..." Her friend stood across the shop laying out sugar plums. "This is—" Agatha's words trailed off, her chest tight as she closed the door behind Grimm. Dulci's *pâtisserie* was decorated with the wonders of Yule more intricately than the palace was. Thick garland was strung in tufts across the ceiling, draping over every surface and dripping with holly berries. Cinnamon, citrus, and cranberry mulled with cloves over in one corner, drifting along the air to land in the corner of her heart where nostalgia was buried. Winter Solstice did not often hold any warmth aside from a relief to be free of the Grimoire for another year, but there were snippets of Yule joy in her distant memory. Her mother baking sweet delicacies, and her father dancing with each of them as Winnie and their mother sang the ancient melodies of their coven.

Gloom drifted down to suffocate those precious memories, leaving only those of Sybil burning a gift Agatha had made her. *Gifts are for the weak.* Of Winnie taking the Grimoire and vanishing without a word to her Sisters. Of the man standing off in the corner, whom she loved dearly, his eyes clouded with thoughts not his own.

Anne walked forward and squeezed her hand gently. Agatha let her eyes fall away from Grimm and she smiled weakly at her friend. "It's beautiful, Anne. Dulci will be over the moon."

"I certainly hope so. I miss decorating the castle..." She risked a glance at Augustus. He'd taken up post next to Grimm the second they'd arrived. His brow was pulled low, shoulders tense. The guard was taking the change in Grimm almost as poorly as she was. He did, however, verbally express his appreciation at least four times a day for Anne now being informed of their secret faction's mischief.

"How did you slip away from Wellington's?"

She waved a hand flippantly. "He's still not been around

much and one of the nicer girls from the kitchens took over my duties for the day. I'll need to be back soon, though."

"Are things all right there? With you, and with Miriam?"

Anne looked down at her hands, fingers wringing together.

"Anne—"

"Agatha." Grimm's voice interrupted, squeezing her heart at the same moment it grated along her spine, the cadence of it entirely wrong. She turned, her attention firmly honed on him. He'd never spoken directly to her while on the draught, but it clearly hadn't worn off. She moved toward him like a moth to a flame, desperate for heat. The light between them sparked and she grasped at it, knowing what would meet her could only cause her demise.

"Grimm." She hated the hope that cracked through her voice. Augustus even looked away.

"I require tea." Agatha blinked at his brusque tone and he added, "Immediately."

She couldn't move. With the words—that simple, meaningless demand Grimm would never utter to her—the bond between them went slack. She took a step back and Augustus caught her arm.

Anne rushed forward. "I'll get the tea."

It felt as if ages were slipping through an hourglass like sand while Agatha waited for Grimm to take his tea and walk away to another corner of the *pâtisserie*. Not once, since that day in the sea cave last Autumn, had she ever wanted him to take one step away from her. Always, she only wished for him to come closer. Now, she wanted him as far away as possible. It was a creeping thing, that feeling crawling up her spine.

Wrong. Wrong. Wrong.

Augustus registered something on her face and waved Anne over before steering Grimm toward the stairs leading to Dulci's upstairs flat.

"How is he?" Anne whispered, turning Agatha toward a table

spread with fluffed cotton mimicking snow, and a platter full of gingerbread.

"He's not Grimm."

From the moment she'd told her about Grimm taking the draught—about everything—Anne had simply sat quietly with her. A steady stone in the sea of tumult.

The bell over the door gave its cheery ring, a vibrant voice immediately drowning out the sound. "This is marvellous!"

"*Dulci*," the women cried in unison, rushing for the old baker and crushing her in an embrace from either side.

She still smelled of Seleste's island and Agatha pulled back, anxious to find her Sister. Standing in the doorway, the perfect depiction of ease, Sister Summer brushed the snow from her cloak. "Aggie," she breathed, taking her hands. "It is so wonderful to see you this often. Her smile was as warm as her isle.

Anne bustled toward the stairs, arm in arm with Dulci, the two of them chatting fervently.

"Come in, come in. Just for a moment."

Seleste pulled her lip between her teeth, looking into the warm, inviting confectionary behind Agatha. "I don't know, Aggie. It sounds lovely, but the Solstice is still hours away, I worry…"

Snatching her hand, Agatha pulled her Sister Summer over the threshold. "We have to let our magic get to know one another with or without Sorscha and Winnie. You might as well enjoy some mulled wine and Yule confections while you're at it."

Seleste pressed her lips together, eyebrows raised and hands on her hips in censure, but there was mirth in her eyes. "The moment things go amok, I'm leaving."

"*Amok, amok*," Agatha mocked with a roll of her eyes. "Of course."

She threw the lock on the door and pulled her Sister upstairs to where Dulci was gesturing wildly, deep in energetic conversation with Anne over the Yule takeover in her home. It truly was impressive. The small apartment looked like something out of a Hearthmas fairytale with countless tapers twinkling and cedar branches draped throughout the sitting room.

"It is simply lovely, Anne." Dulci kissed the mousy-haired girl on the top of her head.

Grimm would have said it looked like a lovely *fire risk*. Agatha smiled sadly to herself at the thought and whispered a protection spell. Her smile turned genuine as she watched Augustus pull Anne underneath the mistletoe and steal a kiss when Dulci wasn't looking. Seleste wandered around, taking it all in and speaking comfortably with Dulci. Agatha found herself wondering how close they'd grown over the last weeks, holed up on Seleste's isle. In truth, she wasn't sure what Seleste did on her isle.

Agatha made for the cauldron of mulled wine, but her attention snagged on Grimm, poised in a chair in the corner, unblinking, gaze fixed on the flame of a candlestick draped in holly. Dulci stepped up next to her, face wary.

"That is not my boy, is it?"

Agatha let out a shaky breath. "No. It isn't."

With a smile that could warm the most frigid heart, Dulci turned, taking Agatha's cheeks in her hands. "He'll return, *mon chou*. Fret not and focus on what needs to be done. She moved her hands to Agatha's shoulders and kissed both cheeks. "He's a blasted fool for doing this, you know. If I would have been here…" She made a sound of disapproval and shook her head before her attention was drawn away. "Augustus! Hands!" Dulci darted off toward the young couple, muttering in Coronoccan as Anne blushed.

"Sister." Seleste glided over and put a hand on Agatha's lower back. "Are you all right?"

"Yes." She shook off the foreboding clouding her mind,

doing her best to paste on a small smile. "Certainly there are a few cakes we could frost together."

Seleste beamed. "Lemon, I hope."

Her excitement cheered Agatha, and she led her to Dulci's tiny kitchen where two lemon cakes were already cooled, awaiting that very moment. "Shall we?"

Seleste rubbed her hands together. "We shall."

The Sisters clasped hands, weaving their fingers together. Seleste's golden ray of magic gently wove through the air, flourishing as Agatha's onyx tendril coiled around it, the glimmer of them both setting their faces aglow.

"My goddess," Anne breathed, drawn in by the sight, the light glittering in her blue eyes.

"You can see this?" Agatha locked eyes with Seleste.

"So can I." Augustus came up next to Anne, draping an arm around her waist.

"Yep," Dulci confirmed from the other side of the small apartment. "Bright as day."

"Peculiar," Agatha mused. Perhaps that was another reason Hespa had commanded they be wrenched apart. Not only did their magic have the potential to be formidable and catastrophic together, but it was visible to the naked eye.

Together, their magic lifted a frosting spatula and dipped it into the bowl of icing. The movements were disjointed and sloppy as they began to frost the cakes, but it didn't take long for their powers to find a harmonious balance of give and take, push and pull. When the final touches were made to the first cake, Augustus took it right out from under them, his mouth watering. Seleste chuckled as Dulci cuffed him on the back of the head and Anne giggled.

As they began to use their magic to frost the second of the cakes, Dulci stood behind them giving orders to ensure it would be to her specifications. Agatha knew it must be grating on Seleste's nerves, considering she'd been baking hundreds of years longer than Dulci, but her face remained alight with contentment and she bid her magic do whatsoever Dulci insisted.

It wasn't much to look at, but they'd frosted the cakes together and no harm had befallen anyone. Yet.

Most likely thinking the very same thing, Seleste abruptly leaned in and kissed Agatha on both cheeks. "I'd better be going, Sister." She glanced at Grimm behind Agatha's shoulder, then offered her Sister a weak smile. "I'll return."

She bid them all farewell and vanished, leaving Agatha feeling chilled despite the others' presence. That eerie, slimy feeling emanating from Grimm felt as if it was climbing up their entanglement bond, threatening to choke her.

GRIMM

I can still feel her.

It's distant—*she* is distant—while I'm locked inside. She feels almost closer, yet forever out of reach. Her worry is tangled; an intricate web. That is the loudest of her emotions, by far. There is, off in the recesses of our bond, a minuscule burst of hope, and a grey cloud of…something.

Here, everything is silent except for her. It's such a torturous bliss. Masochistic or not, I cannot look away from her colours. That grey orb is bothersome, though. I don't know what it means. I gently reach for it and it shrinks. At first, I feared I'd scare it—her. But when I pull back, it grows larger, reaching a tendril for me.

Ah, she misses me. That awareness sends a crack of misery through my essence.

I suspect this is how I would experience Agatha if we were to be separated by some great distance. Apart, yet ever together.

Though this is worse than that. It's worse than when I wished to draw near to her, yet I had to play the bastard prince. This is worse because I know the intricacies of her now. I know the scope of her and what it is to love her; to be with her.

In truth, I must be sitting with her, but I can't see her. My eyes see nothing outside of this cavern. I see nothing but a void. I cannot even see my *wife*. I cannot hear her voice. I see nothing but this darkness and Agatha's kaleidoscope of emotion flitting about at times. I'm worried *they* can see her instead of me.

A flash of glowing light shoots by me and I reach out to grab it, but it's too swift. It fades and the cloud grows to an oppressive size. So overwhelming that I feel my mind staggering back.

Intent to taste her in even the smallest way, I watch, waiting for the thread of light to find me again. It does not come and I think of the feel of her in my hands, her body against mine, her voice husky in my ear… The light flares again.

She can still feel me, too. She can feel me think of her.

So I do. Without our bond as an anchor, I fear I would already be lost. Losing *her* is unfathomable and this decline into doing so is torture.

CHAPTER FIFTEEN

AGATHA

"Sweet Aggie." Seleste slipped into the bed next to Agatha, the Witching Hour on the Winter Solstice ringing out in cathedral bells across Merveille. "What ever is dragging your soul down to the pit?" She offered her a small smile, but Agatha couldn't bring herself to return it. She only let her weariness weigh her head down to rest on Sister Summer's shoulder. For a moment, Seleste simply ran her hand gently over Agatha's hair methodically.

"Grimm," Agatha finally said quietly.

Seleste's hand never broke from her soothing. "I know you likely thought his being a reaper would make this easier." Sister Autumn adjusted to peer at her Sister Summer. "But I fear it will only make it worse."

Sitting up, Agatha brought a portion of the downy covers up around her shoulders, twisting to face Seleste cross-legged. "Why do you say that? You don't think this will work?"

"I did not say anything of the sort. I believe it will grant him access into The Order, but not for the reason you want to hear."

She knew better than to ignore her Sister's words or the chill they sent up her arms. Seleste always saw more than the rest of them. More than anyone. It was part of the reason she marooned herself on her isle, away from the details that she couldn't ignore and would consume her mind. "What is it, Seleste?"

Sister Summer sat up and reclined against the headboard, the gold pieces wound through her braids clinking against the dark wood. "There is something amiss about Pierre and Mila. What occurred last Autumn."

"You mean when they tried to kill him? That's rather *amiss* in and of itself."

"*Mila* said The Order sent Pierre to kill Grimm." That telltale glint shot across Seleste's warm brown eyes and Agatha braced herself for her Sister's cunning. "I don't believe they want our Prince of Bone dead at all."

Acid roiled in Agatha's stomach. "You think we just sent Grimm right into their arms."

"Have you learned anything with the spelled brooch yet?"

The knot in Agatha's stomach tightened at her Sister's avoidance and she shook her head. "Von Fuchs was leery for a while, but he's finally let Grimm behind closed doors. Not Augustus, though. Moving the sigil to Grimm seems too risky."

"And your bond?"

Agatha fiddled with the seam of Grimm's pillowcase. "I can still feel him in our bond, but the outward person is"—she shook her head—"not Grimm."

"Is it worth it?"

Already, the magus was dropping his guard with Grimm. It would be a matter of days before he would reveal his hand. Still, she wasn't sure. All she could manage was a weak shrug.

Seleste reached out and clasped Agatha's hand. "Where is he?"

"He hasn't returned. Soon after you left Dulci's, he did as well. He just stood and walked out without a word. Augustus followed him, but I've no idea where they've gone. I wasn't near the mirror and by the time I returned to peer into it, it only showed Augustus facing a commonplace wall." She gestured to the open armoire. "It's been the same view since."

Seleste leaned in to kiss the top of her head. "Well then, we have until dusk to keep you occupied while you wait. That gives us a good long while. What should you like to do?"

Agatha's mouth formed a glum pout.

"Goddess' teeth." Sorscha appeared, sprawled on her stomach across the foot of Agatha's bed. "This day took ages to arrive."

"This day feels strange," Seleste added. "A peculiar Solstice indeed."

Agatha considered her statement and the truth in it. No Grimoire. No Orders.

"What is this new path we've chosen?" Seleste mused.

"You tell us, highly favoured one," Sorscha said to Agatha as she popped a candied walnut into her mouth from a tray at the bedside and reached for a glass bauble. "They certainly treat you well here, too." She examined the pointless trinket.

"I'm not highly favoured, Sorscha."

"The goddess hasn't visited any of *us*..."

"This path is freedom." Seleste drew them both back to the point and they regarded her solemnly.

Freedom was such a simple term for something so vital. Something every person intrinsically deserved. And yet, Agatha didn't think most people felt free at all. Whether they found themselves enslaved to ideals, stigmas, doctrine, culture, or responsibilities, they were all still enslaved. Weren't they?

"Freedom, hm?" Sorscha rolled over onto her back, staring up at the canopy. "I'm not so certain any of us know what that truly means after three hundred years of servitude."

Agatha was inclined to agree, but she would still fight tooth and nail to find it.

"Perhaps"—Seleste placed one of the throw pillows in her lap, legs crossed and fingertips toying with the tassels—"the Goddess Three simply wants us to be happy. To enjoy this life that is so fleeting, even for us in the grand scheme of things."

"I do know how to do that," Sorscha said through a snort. "Unlike you rigid whores."

Agatha smacked her hip.

"Did anyone tell Winnie we were meeting early?" Seleste inquired, frowning at Sorscha.

Sister Spring groaned, swatting one of the canopy's ties like a cat. "She's the reason there's a damned blizzard right now."

"It's Winter," Agatha said plainly.

Sorscha sat up on one elbow. "She's awfully snippy tonight," she told Seleste, who reached over and pinched her playfully. "The blizzard is because Winnie and Eleanor are across Merveille in the slums. They've been here a couple of days already."

Agatha's face scrunched up. She'd not received another letter from Eleanor since they left Sterdon. "But we haven't been in contact. Why would proximity like that cause such a large blizzard? Are you certain it's not just Winter?" She hadn't even considered that. Although, she hadn't spent a Winter outside of the Forest of Tombs in a hundred years.

"She sent Yula with a note. Said it happened as soon as she arrived and warned me not to be near you except on the Solstice."

Seleste eyed Sorscha carefully. "Was this before or after you came to practise with Aggie?"

"Definitely after."

Agatha kicked Sorscha. "Liar."

"Why didn't she write Aggie and me as well?"

"No idea."

"We should summon her…"

"Seleste, please. Can't we just have a moment without

Winnie ruining everything with her uptight rules? *Freedom*, remember?"

Agatha sighed. "We don't have time for all this division, Sister. And it is her day of birth, after all."

Sorscha blew a noisy breath past her lips. "Merde. Fine." She snapped her fingers and the three of them were standing in a kitchen that must belong to Eleanor's gran, facing Eleanor who was as white as a ghost at their sudden appearance. "Hello, pretty maid. Where is our Sister?"

Eleanor regained her composure and straightened. "Where is Gaius?"

Sorscha's eyes narrowed and she stalked forward. Eleanor stiffened, but, to her credit, she did not back away. "What if I told you he's lying tied to my bed?" She reached up and ran a sharp fingernail down Eleanor's cheek.

"Sorscha." Seleste censured.

Agatha blinked rapidly, steadying herself on a nearby shelf. The women in front of her were blurring at the edges, their voices far off, and her mind was abruptly growing muddled. There was a strange numbness seeping into the bond, leaving her feeling like she'd had too much wine. She shook her head to dislodge it and brought her fingers up to the cage of crystals encased at her neck.

"You wouldn't hurt him," Eleanor shot back at Sorscha, their voices sounding far off.

A low laugh bubbled up in Sorscha's chest, the sound of it almost disturbing. "Not anywhere you could see it."

"*Sorscha*," Seleste said again. "Stop toying with her."

She turned to Sister Summer, batting her eyelashes. "Who says I'm toying?"

In her haze, Agatha felt Seleste come up next to her and place a cool hand on her cheek. "Aggie?"

"I'm fine."

A voice wafted in from the hallway. "Eleanor, where did you

put that hideous dr–" Winnie stopped in her tracks as she entered the kitchen and crossed her arms. "What happened to meeting at a set time, hm? It's not dusk. It's the middle of the night. And the Solstice has hardly begun. And *what* are you doing in this poor woman's kitchen?"

"We've something to accomplish," Agatha broke in. "Get dressed."

Winnie settled her roving attention on Sister Autumn. "Not until I've had a proper night's sleep. Come back in the morning."

"Winnie, please." Agatha couldn't believe the pleading that slipped into her voice and neither could Winnie judging by the look on her face. "Can we just go now?"

"All you want to do is experiment with our magic," she said, her stern voice chilled. "The answer is no. Return in the morning when we've all had some sleep and we can discuss the venture at hand properly."

After a moment's pause, Winnie turned to Eleanor. "See them out."

"Winnie, please." Agatha watched as her tone hit her Sister Winter square in the chest. "Just try. Please." Tears pricked at the back of her eyes, vision still swimming with whatever was happening to her bond with Grimm. "What we face is too great for us to remain separated, Sister. We have no Orders, no Grimoire to keep us apart. We must fight forward, together."

"We still have Hespa, Aggie. Why does our doctrine mean so little to you?"

Agatha straightened her shoulders. "Why does it mean so *much* to you? Doctrine is *not* Hespa. When will you learn this?" Winnie's jaw tensed and Agatha softened. "Please. Please try, Winnie."

Sister Winter took in her Sisters, jaw clenched for a moment. "Let's get this over with, then."

The snow was nearly up to their thighs as Agatha walked with her Sisters, but the exertion felt exhilarating. The chill seeping into her bones was finally waking her mind from the peculiar slumber that had descended upon her. She couldn't help but think it meant Grimm was losing something. Or *they* were. Goddess, she felt losing even a portion of their entanglement would rip her in half. Worry gnawed at her insides like maggots feasting on a corpse.

It wasn't something they *had*; it was nothing to do with need or want. It wasn't something that had come between them. It was a tangle of themselves that had been woven together before they yet were. It defied logic, it defied nature. But it was undeniable.

"Explain why we had to be this far out here in the gods damned snow," Sorscha muttered between clenched and chattering teeth.

"You know why," Winnie ground out.

"Fine. Why did we have to *walk* the rest of the way after we transported?"

"To find a safe spot," Agatha jumped in.

"Just warm yourself," Seleste suggested, practically glowing with her own heated magic. They all stared at her with ire as she smiled up at the Yule moon.

"If we're going to do this"—Winnie shifted on her feet—"then let's get to it." She lifted her hand, an orb of magic glowing silver in her palm, so pristine and perfect that it looked like a glass globe.

Sorscha grinned wickedly, the crimson magic at the tips of her nails crackling like static as she wriggled her fingers, her face bathed in the red glow. Seleste took a deep breath, one arm out to the side. She closed her eyes, a sphere of golden light following her hand up and over as if she were drawing the sun from the horizon by sheer force. It settled in front of her, warming them all.

Aggie touched the tips of her fingers together, slowly pulling them apart, black wisps of her magic stringing like a spider web between her palms. She'd always thought her witchcraft must have been dark, for how macabre it appeared. Yet, it always encased itself in a silver glow.

Her web reached, of its own accord, toward its Sister magic. All four powers moved, dancing cautiously together in the centre of the four Sisters Solstice. Sorscha's magic crackled against Winnie's and blush snowflakes rose from her ball of ice and light. Amazed, they looked on in wonder. Seleste's amber light sidled up to Agatha's, the silver and black web winding around it until it looked like the moon draped in black lace. It was almost too beautiful to take in. A lump crowded Agatha's throat and she pushed her and Seleste's silvery orb toward Winnie and Sorscha's pink snow. As the magic drew near, Agatha could see tears in Winnie's eyes. Seleste's and Sorscha's as well.

Agatha doubled over, a searing pain suddenly shooting through her head. A piercing white light cracked through the centre of their magic like lightning and they all pulled back.

"I'm okay," Agatha said, holding her temple as Sorscha and Seleste rushed to her side. "Let's keep going." Whatever was happening to Grimm and their bond, she needed her Sisters.

"No," Winnie growled. "We're through."

"Winnie," Seleste spoke softly. "Our magic *needs* to commune. We have to find a way to be together outside the Solstice and Equinox." She splayed her hands. "All this, that's brewing across Midlerea…it's going to take all of us to fight it."

"You saw what just happened between us, Winnie," Sorscha pressed. "We need to do this."

Winnie's mouth went slack in disbelief. "Yes, I *did* see what happened!" She pointed a finger sharply in Agatha's direction. "And we're done."

Agatha attempted to remain calm, the searing pain in her temples receding. "Winnie…"

"No, Aggie. Look at you! Any number of things could go wrong."

"Any number of things could go *right*." At Agatha's tone,

Sorscha stepped closer to Seleste and wound their arms together. Silence fell, as dense as the snow around them, while they waited for Winnie to consider Agatha's words.

"Unbelievable. I'm not doing it."

"We all agree," Agatha said simply.

"*All*?" Winnie only spoke one word, but it was sharp enough to slice them into ribbons. "All except for me." Agatha blinked at her, but Winnie shook her head as if she could brush all of it away like a wayward moth. "This separation is something ordained by Hespa, or She wouldn't have told us not to be together."

"We don't know that *any* of this was ever Her! There is no more Grimoire, Winnie. People need us."

"*People* have survived before and they'll survive now."

Agatha baulked. "You cannot be serious."

"I think we should keep going, Winnie." They all looked at Seleste, her kind voice doing nothing to halt the flames two of her Sisters wished to hurl at one another.

Winnie nodded slowly, her stone-faced mask revealing nothing. "This is how it's going to continue to be, then? All of you against me?"

"Dammit, Winnie!" Agatha shouted again. "If you would just *stop* with your twisted morality code! You can't say a fucking curse word without punishing yourself, but you sure can look out only for yourself without batting an eye!"

Winnie recoiled. In three hundred years, Agatha had never seen her Sister do such a thing, no matter what insult she or anyone else had thrown at her. Sister Winter turned toward a thicket of trees and disappeared.

Seleste scowled at Agatha, but Sorscha simply shrugged, one elbow on Seleste's shoulder, examining her nails.

Agatha felt nothing. Except for the loud absence of their Sister Winter.

Three Hundred Years Ago

WINNIE

"Again."

Winnie bared her teeth at Greta. "Not until you let me see them. I want to see my Sisters."

Sister Winter, the elder, spread her stance and crossed her arms. "That's not possible."

"Yes, it is!"

"Again. You're sloppy with these spells and you're letting your emotions cloud your mind."

"I don't care about any of this. I want to know if my Sisters are okay. I want to see them."

"It is against our doctrine, Wendolyn."

"How can you tell me day after day that Hespa loves us if She has doctrines like this?" Winnie's voice cracked, ice coating her palms.

Greta snarled. "Watch your tongue, child."

Winnie only stood taller. "She sounds like my heretic mother who claimed love then set us all up to burn."

Her cheek was on fire before she knew what happened, Greta's slap reverberating through her skull. Winnie gasped and reached up to clutch her face, backing away as Greta inched closer.

"You listen here, you stupid girl. I only have a moon left to train you before I die *and you have to take up the mantle with my Sisters. You would do well to realise it is obedience that will keep* your *Sisters safe."*

Winnie paced outside the hovel Eleanor grew up in, her heart still beating frantically with adrenaline. How dare Aggie speak to her like that?

It was just more proof nothing would change. The absence of the Grimoire did not mean the realm would find peace at last. It did not mean she and her Sisters would find it between themselves, either.

Seleste appeared next to Winnie on the portico. "Aggie didn't mean you harm."

"Go away, Seleste."

"Sister, if you would let your guard down for one moment and let us in, things wouldn't be like this."

Winnie halted, turning on her so quickly that Seleste flinched. Good. Let her think she was the villain they all had her painted as. "Someone had to harden, Sister." The words were laced with poison and poised to deal a killing blow, each syllable slicing right where she wanted it to. "To keep the three of you from having to."

Seleste's lip trembled, but Winnie smiled coldly. "It doesn't matter, anyway. I don't need any of you. I've handled all of it on my own for this long."

A tear slid down Seleste's cheek and she vanished.

Winnie stalked off the porch and into the dark trees.

CHAPTER SIXTEEN

THREE HUNDRED YEARS AGO

WINNIE

Sorscha looked as if she might float away, or weep. Women dangled from silken ropes draped throughout the large cirque tent. Most eyes had moved on from the twirling trapeze dancers to the marvels brought forth by the Cirque Master, Barroque.

As they'd all filed into the tent, the master had changed his wardrobe into a—somehow—more magnificent ensemble. She wondered at the half-mask he wore and his tale of the Druids. Why hide himself away when he'd proclaimed the opposite?

There he stood, captivating the audience with illusions and grandeur. All except Sorscha, who continued to look up with a dreamlike glaze over her face. And Aggie, who sat pouting.

Winnie tore her eyes from the stage. "What is it, Aggie? Are you not having a good time?"

She crossed her little arms. "There was a man outside. A bird stole his treat."

Her words squeezed Winnie's heart. "Oh, Sister," she whispered. "Never lose your compassion." She took Aggie's chin in her hand and turned her so they were face to face. "No matter what."

Seleste leaned forward, engrossed in the magic of it all. Winnie smiled to herself. Witches that had seen countless spells, conjuring, and divination, were completely enamoured by parlour tricks and the distinct allure of *the show.* If she were being honest with herself, it had stolen her heart as well.

Her eyes grazed over the Cirque Master once more. Perhaps they could run away with the—

"Winnie." Sorscha elbowed her. "We need to go."

Detangled from their seats amongst the crowd and walking back toward the cottage, Aggie left Sorscha's side, coming up next to Winnie. "Are you upset we left the carnival?"

Winnie smiled down at her sadly. "You could say that." She still hadn't told her and they had only hours left, maybe less.

Aggie scrunched her face up and nodded, dragging her feet and kicking up clouds of dust. "Is it because the witch is coming to take me away?"

Winnie stopped dead in her tracks. "What?"

"The witch. She's coming to take me."

Sorscha and Seleste turned back toward them. "Were you eavesdropping last night?" Winnie asked.

She shook her head. "No. Mummy told me." Winnie exchanged a befuddled look with Sorscha. "Mummy told me often that four witches would come and one would take me away."

Yet she'd said nothing to the others. Bitterness flooded Winnie's veins.

"She said I'm special."

Winnie set her face stolid, veiling the conflicting emotions warring behind her ribs. She knelt on one knee. "Yes, Aggie. Do you remember what we were taught about the Sisters Solstice?" Aggie nodded mutely and Winnie tucked a strand of her wild hair behind her littlest Sister's ear. "You are Sister Autumn. *You* are a Sister Solstice." But it seemed Aggie knew that already as well. "What else did Mother tell you?"

"She said I'm special and not to be afraid, no matter what. That I will do great things for our realm someday."

Winnie couldn't help the tear that slipped out. She lifted Aggie's chin. "That is absolutely correct, sweet." She swallowed hard. "All of it."

Aggie nodded, her chin down and bottom lip quivering. "I'm still afraid."

Winnie felt the air rush out of her lungs and she swallowed back the tears crowding her throat, pulling Aggie into a fierce hug. "You're going to be all right, Aggie. Everything will be all right."

Aggie dug her fingers into Winnie's back, her face pressed against her eldest Sister's shoulder. When she pulled back, she reached to cup Winnie's cheek in her small hand. "We'll always have each other."

Sorscha and Seleste's eyes were misty as well, where they stood huddled together, observing. "We do need to get home." Sorscha's voice snagged on the last word and Winnie's thoughts drifted to the bags under the bed again. The mysterious Cirque Master.

The cottage was dark when they arrived. A small blessing that the witches had not yet come. On the stoop, as Seleste unlocked the door, Aggie spoke again.

"I think Mummy knew they were coming."

"The witches?" Sorscha asked, eyeing Winnie over their little Sister's head.

Aggie looked at her strangely. "No, the fires in Helsvar."

The wind shifted behind them and they all turned in unison to find Prue, her voluminous silver hair waving in the hot breeze.

Winnie instinctively pushed Seleste behind her. She'd expected Sorscha to be taken first.

Prue smiled warmly, her eyes burning with too much understanding and wisdom. "Wendolyn, I have never borne children, but I will care for Seleste as my own." She put her weathered hand to her chest. "I swear it."

An oath was nothing without a spell to bind it. Winnie rose to the challenge. "*Prêter serment.*"

Prue inclined her head. "*Je le jure.*" She reached within her pocket and withdrew a small crystal. She summoned a flame in her palm and dropped the crystal into it. A plume of glimmering smoke rose into the night sky. "It is done."

It did not ease Winnie's worries. Seleste pushed from behind her eldest Sister. She summoned a small bag to her shoulder and gave each of her Sisters a tearful hug. "It's going to be okay," she whispered, pulling them all forward into a huddle, arms linked together.

Seleste, ever the picture of grace. She walked down the steps with one last look over her shoulder at her Sisters. And then she was gone.

AGATHA

Agatha hissed at Mabon. He blinked his large, innocent eyes at her from where he perched on the door of her armoire. "You're not as wholesome as you look, you thief."

The bat tittered, wrapping his leathery wings around himself to hide the consumption of his stolen bite of *croissant*.

"Rotten little stink," Agatha muttered, popping what was left of her pastry into her mouth. Despite Grimm's state, she still grabbed four *croissants* every morning when she went down to the kitchens to retrieve their breakfast.

Grimm hadn't touched one in a fortnight.

Agatha had also begun going down to the kitchens well before dawn almost every morning. It began as a way to check in with Augustus' sister, Delilah, to ensure she wasn't enduring any hardship due to Grimm's demand that she control Agatha's food. To her relief, no one really cared much, and the magus hadn't been in the kitchens since a few days after Grimm began taking the draught.

At first, Agatha was relieved that at least one thing was going simply. Then…Seleste's words began to ring in her ears. *I don't believe The Order wants our Prince of Bone dead at all.* It was troubling how little the magus was paying mind to her, the thorn in his side, now that he had his hands on Grimm.

Mila had claimed The Order knew what Grimm was, but that couldn't be proven for certain, considering she'd also claimed they wanted him dead and that did not appear to be so.

The thoughts made her stomach roil.

Working her hands in the kitchen every morning until they were raw helped.

After the last of the fasts were broken and the kitchens were cleaned, awaiting the mad rush to provide lunch for the spoiled castle dwellers, Agatha would bid the kind crew of tired but thankful souls *adieu* and have tea with the queen. She told herself it was what Grimm would have wanted—someone checking in on his mum—but she partly did it for any reason to be away from their rooms until Grimm was dressed and gone.

That morning, as on all the others, the queen had beamed like a witless doe and missed her mouth with her teacup more times than not.

Augustus no longer met her for conditioning after her

morning tea, to keep up appearances, and she usually filled her time at Tindle's dress shop, convincing herself she was not useless.

"Get out of my way, darling. You're skulking and scaring off my customers. They want to dress like you until they see that scowl." He'd shooed her off and she'd returned to her armoire to stand and watch Augustus' pin give her another staggering view of a wall outside the Sanctuary as she munched on Grimm's cold *croissant.*

That was before Mabon swooped in and stole half of it right out of her hand.

She stuck her tongue out at the bat and he sniggered.

A movement from the mirror inside her armoire caught Agatha's eye. She watched with mild interest as her view shifted from a stone wall to the chest of a person in a black robe. "Mabon!" she whispered, but the bat couldn't have cared less. She leaned in as the image shifted, jostling. Augustus was walking somewhere behind the robed man. He had a peaked hood up, cast in all manner of shadows, but she was certain he belonged to The Order.

The bouncing, nauseating image revealed a doorway, the robed individual's silhouette outlined by a distant altar of countless candles, their light warm and inviting. She knew that was far from an accurate depiction of the Sanctuary as soon as the image stilled, a thick, stone slab altar looking out over rows of wooden pews, Grimm lounging in the front row.

Still, Agatha nearly jumped in triumph. Augustus was *in* the Sanctuary!

The sounds were all garbled and too muffled to make out, but the image was quite clear if she did say so herself. Augustus had been positioned near the back right, most likely too far back to make out any conversion that he could relay back to her, but he was in. It was now only a matter of time.

There were three others aside from Grimm, all speaking in

murmured voices and holding something she couldn't quite make out. Vials of some kind. Most likely vials of the draught. As she was pondering if they had changed the formula's potency *again*, she heard a dimmed shout. It sounded like it came from just behind Augustus and they all turned to locate the source.

Two individuals, both with hoods pulled low, looked to be arguing. One had a hand flying sharply through the air and Agatha watched carefully.

"*Gros plan.*"

The image expanded until the one shouting was much larger as if Agatha were holding up a magnifying glass. Her enlarging spell made everything blurred, but she could make out the faint lines of a mark on their forearm—a sideways eight. The same mark seen on both Pierre and the man Grimm saw with the magus the night he discovered the draught formula. There was also a scar there, just on the side of their wrist. Something about it struck Agatha as familiar, but she hadn't the chance to think on it. Magus von Fuchs rushed in through a door near the altar, his golden robes fanning out behind him and arms wide. Muffled sound or not, it was clear he shouted some version of, "*Everybody out*!" for Augustus left in a rush, as did two other glassy-eyed guards and everyone else except Grimm and the two arguing, robed individuals.

Agatha cursed when her view became another pointless wall. She slammed the armoire shut and closed her eyes.

It had been a while, but she could still envision the magus' study. In the next breath, she was there. While he was occupied with all that was happening in the sanctuary, she'd just search his private chamber again.

"*Èclairer*."

The dank space glowed with otherworldly light. All seemed as it had always been until Agatha's breath caught when she spied one shelf entirely changed.

Where chained books had once sat upon it, the shelf now had

several vials filled to the brim with liquid, and a scattering of menacing-looking tools.

She walked up to the row of vials and held one up. It was not the glowing amber of the draught at all, but a rusty, deep red. She popped the cork and sniffed, the copper scent nearly gagging her it was so strong. She snatched two, one of the others crashing to the floor in her haste. It shattered, blood splattering down the front of her olive dress.

"*Merde*."

She sent her magic to erase the evidence, then shoved the two vials of blood into her pocket. In a wisp of magic, she transported herself to the back of Tindle's dress shop and peeked through the curtain.

Per the usual, it was absolutely overrun with ladies and the occasional well-dressed man. Since being taken off the Blacklist, the old dressmaker had refused to move his shop, but the patrons flocked. He hardly had a moment to breathe, let alone spare for Agatha and Seagovia's dire circumstances. Agatha smiled to herself. He deserved every moment of his success.

Sneaking from the storeroom into the front of the shop, she had to sidestep all manner of women. Some aristocratic, waists tied up in unseen oppression, others in fashion pieces Agatha and Tindle had designed together, the beginnings of freedom etched on their faces. Despite the class difference, and the draught still in their veins, it was a wondrous sight to see.

"My beloved!" she heard Tindle shout from the far side of the shop, hand high in the air waving her over. She smiled wide and pushed through the throng, but they were all too preoccupied to notice who she was.

"Make way for Princess Agatha Peridot," Tindle screeched. Silence descended and the crowd of women parted down the middle.

"Ah, thank you," she said awkwardly. Then, "You didn't

have to do that," she whispered in Tindle's ear as she reached him, a faux smile plastered on her mouth.

"Carry on!" he shouted, and they did. Tindle pulled her into his office and slammed the door. "Why have you ruined this magnificent creation of mine with—my goddess, is that wine?" He sniffed and pulled back with a frown. "*Blood*? You walked into my shop like a rat crawling out of the sewage?"

"Gods, do I look that dreadful?"

He nodded tersely, arms crossed. "Change. Now."

Agatha obeyed. It certainly seemed like everyone was content to order her about lately and she was not enjoying it. Wardrobe successfully rectified with a deep peridot dress of fine velvet and black cuff sleeves, Agatha emerged from behind a changing curtain and held the vials out to Tindle. His forehead creased and he set his chained spectacles on the tip of his nose.

"What am I looking at here?"

"Blood."

He raised an eyebrow at her, then cast a forlorn look at her ruined dress crumpled off to the side. "From?"

"I don't know who, but it was in the magus' private study."

"Ah." He handed the vials back to Agatha. "You've also become a common thief, then?"

She ignored his question. "Why would the magus and The Order have vials of blood stored except for the purpose of dark magic?"

"You've confirmed The Order is exactly who is manufacturing the draught?"

She scoffed. "I think that's fairly obvious by now."

Tindle shrugged. "Then magic is most likely your answer. The bigger question is *whom* the blood came from and *why* they want it."

Her stomach roiled when realisation struck. "I have to get back."

"So soon?" Tindle uttered with saccharine disappointment.

She didn't bother with transporting herself. She needed the cold Winter air to calm her nerves and clear her head. She walked the entirety of the way back to the castle, cloaked in magic so no one would stop *the princess*. She wondered vaguely if that was how Amira had made it to Dulci's that night. It's what had first clued Agatha in that she might be a witch.

There had been no sign of Amira, still. Sorscha said they'd uncovered information, though she hadn't said what it was regarding. It struck Agatha as odd that the disappearance hadn't been made widely known. Clearly, no one wanted a ransom or negotiation. It was as if the occurrence didn't matter to the public at large. The Empress of Coronocco was taken, and no one batted an eye. Peculiar, along with everything else in their twisted web of chaos.

Near the castle, Agatha noticed the guards were more alert than usual, so she moved there quietly. Materialising in front of her fire, she was both elated and heartbroken to see Grimm lying on their bed, asleep.

In sleep, he looked just like himself. Her lover. Her husband. Her greatest friend. Her Grimm. It made her heart ache in a way that was becoming all too familiar.

She walked forward and gently ran a finger over his cheek, his lips, and his shoulder. She'd give anything to feel him against her, saying her name like an oath and loving her fiercely. The pain of him lying there and not *being* there was torturous.

In the last couple of days, as he burned through the drought an iota faster, he would make some sort of movement toward her when she missed him fiercely, like he could feel it down the bond. This was no different. As her heart ached, he began to shift under her hand, restless, like he was fighting to get to her. Grimm slid over to his back, an arm reaching out blindly. It connected with Agatha's hand and stilled. She nearly sobbed.

Clasping onto his hand, she leaned down to kiss his forehead. "Hello, reaper."

He did not stir or answer, but she held his hand to her lips and kissed his knuckles. It was then that she noticed the puncture wound at the crook of his elbow, a small bruise blooming around it. Identical to the ones on Miriam. With a gasp, she dropped Grimm's hand to the bed.

"*À ma sœur printemps.*"

Gaius jumped out of his skin at her sudden arrival. "Goddess, Agatha," he exclaimed, clutching his chest. "Where in Hades did you come from?"

"You should be used to this by now," Sorscha said, unruffled as she unfurled a bedroll.

"You're camping already?" Agatha looked around. "It's only mid-afternoon."

Gaius poked at a fire barely beginning. "*Your Sister* is hungry." He glared at her over his shoulder.

"Joubert women are always hungry." Agatha crouched next to Gaius and thrust two of the vials in his face. "The magus has Grimm's blood. And my guess is others' too. Miriam's almost certainly."

He threw his stick into the fire and stood, rolling the vials in his hand. "Isn't Miriam at Wellington's?"

The knot in Agatha's stomach wound tighter. "Yes."

She and Gaius shared a dark, silent moment between them. *Anne.*

"What does he want with blood?" Gaius said finally.

"My estimation is to use it for dark magic."

"Dark magic is archaic," Sorscha chimed in, stirring a pot over the fire.

"It's effective," Agatha countered. "Gods, are you cooking?" Sorscha waved her off.

"I agree." Gaius handed her back the vials and sat on a log.

"I would put nothing past the magus or The Order. Is Grimm any closer to leading you to them?"

Agatha shrugged and sat opposite him. "I don't know. Thus far, we've only discovered the magus holds strange meetings in the chapel at night on occasion, but he hasn't let Augustus in yet until today."

"We'll figure it out. This will all be worth it, in the end."

Agatha nodded, but she wasn't so sure anymore.

Gaius reached out and squeezed her hand. "Agatha, he's going to be fine."

"What did you two find out?" She changed the subject.

Sorscha came to join them, lowering herself languidly onto a boulder. "There seems to be a clan of grave robbers moving throughout the continent."

"But it's not jewels and treasures of death they're after," Gaius explained.

Sorscha shook her head and puckered her lips. "No, it is not."

Agatha looked between them. "What are they after, then?"

"Unclear."

Sorscha snorted. "It's unclear to him. I think it's rather evident they're after the *bodies*."

"Why would they want the bodies?" Agatha asked.

"Her theory is—"

Sorscha made an audible noise of frustration and they both looked at her, Gaius already rolling his eyes. "*Her*." She flopped her hand around mocking him. "Her, her, her." What is my name, *Gaius*?" Sister Spring locked eyes with him, filled with irritation.

"Now is hardly the time for this."

"What is my name?" she demanded again, crossing her arms.

With a sardonic smile laced with venom, Gaius reached over and grasped a piece of dried meat and took a bite of it, never breaking from eye contact with Sorscha. "*Mademoiselle Joubert,*" he crooned.

Sorscha growled and threw her hands in the air. "He refuses to say my name," she told Agatha and rose, walking into her tent.

"You won't say her name?"

Gaius shrugged, grinning as he took another bite.

Sorscha came storming out of the tent, a small journal in her hands that she tossed to Agatha. "Our notes on the consumed magi. As well as how I think it's connected to the grave robberies. This"—she tossed her hand around like a dead fish—"*name* debacle began as chivalry, and now it's just irritating."

"Well," Gaius spoke dramatically, "*demoiselle* here believes she can have whatsoever she wishes, or take it by force." He shot her a glare. "And that is simply not true."

Agatha rubbed her temples. "Please do not start bickering or I will lose my mind."

WINNIE

Winnie pulled her horse to a stop, reaching over to yank Eleanor's reins as well. "I swear on the ancestral dirt of my coven's mass grave, if you do not cease your *sighing*, I will claw out your throat with my nails."

Eleanor frowned but did not sigh again. The onslaught of thoughts peppering Winnie's mind left no room whatsoever for the maid's attitude. There was no way to predict how the Druids would react to seeing her again. She'd done her best to avoid them like the plague for nearly fifty years. It was likely they would welcome her with open arms, but it was just as likely they would cast her out with a foot to the rear. That possibility, and the uncertainty, were precisely why she'd not sent a letter ahead of them. She would have to take her chances and pray to the goddess that it would go in her favour. Surely, after half a century, they would not still be holding a grudge. Winnie frowned to herself.

She shook her head, cowl slipping with the movement and snow falling in her hair. No longer was she the hurt, vulnerable girl that stepped foot in the Druid troupe's camp. Time and life had ravaged her before them, and it ravaged her still.

"Are you all right?"

Winnie's attention darted to the girl, who recoiled slightly at the look on her face.

"You're even more morose than usual. Is it because of what happened with Aggie on the Solstice?"

Winnie blinked at her. She'd not told the maid an iota of what occurred. Nor had Winnie been there when her Sisters returned later that same day. Now she *knew* her traitorous Sister had been writing Eleanor and the maid had lied about it. "Why do you continue to think I will answer your invasive questions?"

With an eye roll to rule all eye rolls, Eleanor kicked her horse, trotting ahead. *Good riddance.* But the bird's words clanged around in her skull as they'd begun doing since she'd pecked her way into Winnie's life. This time, it was her assumption that Aggie had anything to do with Winnie's mood. She supposed the girl wasn't entirely wrong. Every encounter with Aggie stung a smidgen more than the prior one. Why, Winnie had never quite put her finger on.

However, in the girl's incessant prattling, she'd revealed several times how much she loathed Aggie for a time. Her impulsiveness and her stubborn, peculiar philosophy on… everything. Most of all, Eleanor seemed to have despised the way Aggie could convince—with very little effort—nearly anyone to follow her, with nothing more than a hat or a daring gown. All such mentions of this loathing were always spoken of in the past tense. What had changed for Eleanor?

The maid turned on her horse, slowing the steed. "What changed for me concerning Agatha?"

Winnie hid her jolt of unease. She had not meant to ask the question aloud, nor had she realised she did. She nodded once, then lifted her chin.

"Are you going to answer any of my questions?"

"No."

Eleanor's face drooped into a sullen frown. Winnie thought she would simply ride on and let silence befall them again, but she surprised her by speaking. "Grimm. That's what changed my thoughts about Agatha."

"The prince? How is that?"

Eleanor adjusted her position in the saddle and Winnie's horse pulled up next to hers. "When we were children, Grimm was my closest friend." She smiled, nostalgia radiating off of her in waves. "Grimm hated the castle. He always has. Not the structure itself, with its menacing gloom and all its old spires and mysterious nooks. The castle itself rather suits him, but the aristocracy does not.

"As a boy, Grimm had a guard with a soft spot for his antics. He would let Grimm dress in the garb of the common folk, and he would take him to the markets. At first, it was only on Gemme Road, but Grimm grew curious about Mer Row, and Christophe eventually gave in. That was the day I met him. I was assisting my gran at her stall in the square, selling soaps and things like that. I wasn't truly helping. I'd bartered a bar of fragrant rose soap for a tattered old book, *The History of Poetry*." She paused and smiled wistfully again.

"Gran said it was a rotten deal, but I'll never think so because a young boy strode purposefully up to me, finger pointed at my book, and said, *If there isn't any Berlusconi in that text, it's rubbish.*" Eleanor laughed. "I took his word for it. He snatched it right out of my hands and flipped through it. Satisfied he'd found at least one poem from Berlusconi, he handed the book back and walked away as if he'd just ensured I'd averted a major crisis.

"The next day, he showed up with a stack of books for me. Growing up in the slums, what my gran had time to teach me was all I had access to. Until Grimm." She shrugged. "At the time, he seemed like a blessing from the goddess, providing me with an immeasurable gift in the form of access to a world of knowledge I'd never have otherwise. I hadn't known what I was even doing with that poetry book, I only wanted to learn.

"Then, I met this ten-year-old boy who opened up the world to me. We became fast friends and I began to notice he didn't act like a child…ever. I don't think he'd really been around children except for Gaius, and he was just as stoic and studious as Grimm. We were thick as thieves, we three, and I introduced them to a few of my friends, Augustus, and Anne. Grimm taught me about literature, History, medicine, arithmetic… And I taught him how to live."

Winnie was struggling to picture the grumbling maid as anything but sober herself, while Prince Grimm appeared the picture of ease, languid, with his arms around her Sister. She would not soon forget the way he looked at Aggie with devotion and the smile that turned up the corners of his lips when he beheld her. Winnie's heart ached at the thought, for too many reasons to name.

"I used to be rather fun," Eleanor went on with a small chuckle, but it cracked and fell away. She looked down at her hands. "But the queen discovered where Grimm and his guard ran off to on most days. She forbade him from seeing us…me."

"And the guard?" Winnie wasn't certain she wanted to know the answer.

"He was hanged."

Winnie closed her eyes briefly. "The queen commanded this?" Eleanor nodded. It did not sound like Fleurina to punish her curious boy and the guard who let him be a child. Alas, a lot had changed since she'd last seen Fleurina, the young princess of Eridon.

"It was said that the ruling was the queen's doing, but I now wonder if it was the magus."

Not a witless dolt, then.

"It broke me," Eleanor confessed. "Not only did I lose my friend, but I also lost my access to knowledge. I lost my innocence to the way of the world. A prince could never live life with a peasant, let alone one descended from witches." She looked far off into the frosted treeline for a moment. "As he got older, Grimm learned to play the game. He learned to be cruel in front of the aristocracy, but anyone who truly knew him could tell it was all a means to an end—to keep them off his back. But, not many truly knew him.

"By the time I was employed in the castle, he'd openly refused to ever marry, and the court was in upheaval over it. Something happened around the time of his fifteenth birthday, but no one knew what. Time went on, and he became a stranger to me in all the ways that really matter. Only Gaius continued our friendship, and even that was dismal. A peasant is not suitable company for a lord, either, regardless of how kind Lady Manu was." She looked at her gloved hands. "Then, Agatha arrived."

Winnie watched Eleanor's face, the glow of the rising sun behind the snowy clouds setting her skin in golden hues. She had to grant that the girl was truly lovely.

"I hated her. Grimm tried to make everyone, even me, believe that he'd chosen her. Met her in some tavern in Rochbury or some nonsense. But I could see the misery in his eyes. He was still being controlled, like a child. I had more true freedom as an oppressed peasant than that man did as prince of his own damned country.

"I thought it was Agatha's fault. That she'd wormed her way in somehow. Then, I began to suspect her of witchcraft and I loathed her even more. I thought she was controlling him with dark magic. But the people just began eating out of her hand." Eleanor's face scrunched and she shook her head. "I worked so hard to leave the slums behind and she continually dragged me back there, thinking she could change things… Eventually, I saw the look in Grimm's eyes alter. Suddenly, her name sounded like a prayer on his lips. There was a heat coming off him when she was near.

"I even tried to tattle." She huffed a laugh. "I told the queen that Grimm was never in bed with Agatha when Anne and I went in during the early mornings. It wasn't long before I saw the same look in Agatha's eyes, too. But she wasn't thinking of *him*. Of what her presence in Castle Merveille could do to him. By then, I was chasing the draught across Seagovia with her. She still made no sense to me. I didn't trust her."

She halted her horse and Winnie did the same. "But I watched her break—this ancient witch. I saw the moment she thought she'd lost Grimm. I watched as all her hope fell away and it contorted her face. I saw her hit her knees, shove her bare hands against his gushing wound, and command him not to leave this life until they both would do so together. It…it was like watching the only lovers left in all the realms. And then I watched her save his life, very nearly ending her own in the process."

Winnie sat forward, head tilted to the side. "What do you mean, nearly ending her own?"

"He was doomed, Wendolyn. The blade had pierced his heart. Agatha almost burnt herself completely out to save him."

If a hand had thrust itself into her chest and squeezed her lungs, Winnie would not have felt it. Her youngest Sister, her Aggie, had found a love worth sacrificing herself for.

"That," Eleanor went on, "is someone I can rally behind." She let her words hang in the golden air kissed by snowflakes. "Agatha is a lot of things. And I disagree with her about almost everything, including how you were treated on the Solstice. But I do believe she is exactly what this realm needs. And I believe *she* needs *you*."

Winnie cleared her throat and urged her horse forward, a camp looming in the distance.

CHAPTER

SEVENTEEN

GRIMM

A continuous song. The same sombre liturgy plays endlessly here.

It's transfixed my attention to the point I no longer see the colourful knot of Agatha's emotions. They're now just a faint light off in the distance. I want to get to that light, but I can't. And I can't worry. All I can do is listen to the song and wonder distantly who is collecting the souls. They grow restless if they must wait for me. Perhaps Lady Death will come for me soon. Or, perhaps, She's as fooled as the rest.

I find myself lying down in this darkness. It's become difficult to sort through what is real and what is the magus. Or is this who I really am?

I wonder who is collecting the souls.

The darkness calls out again, this time it sounds sweet. Like relief.

I wonder who is collecting the souls.

I want that light, desperately. If I could just lie next to it…but I'm so tired. I know something was bothering me, but I forget now what it is. Was I collecting something? I see a flicker off in the shadowed abyss. Fireflies. I was collecting fireflies, was I not?

ELEANOR

A scantily clad woman slipped a sword down her throat.

A four-legged man juggled oranges.

A little girl with half her face drooping and a forked tongue twirled a baton with its ends on fire.

A man huddled on the ground, bent over double, his feet next to his ears.

These were the things that greeted them as Eleanor and Wendolyn passed through the heavily guarded entrance of the Druid clan's camp. Eleanor felt as if fingernails were slowly sliding down her back. She glanced at Wendolyn and found her…almost smiling.

Eleanor didn't like to think herself pompous, but the people surrounding them, with their abnormalities, were not exactly the sort that brought about any feeling of comfort. They passed a woman dressed in violet silk, so beautiful that she made Eleanor's heart constrict. It was the type of ethereal beauty that burns the soul and never leaves. Two men walked up to the woman, each draping an arm around her hips in unison. They were equally as stunning. So dazzling that Eleanor had to look away. Only to witness a man with two shrivelled arms spinning, kicking, and drawing his feet through the dirt in some sort of vicious dance with an invisible opponent.

Eleanor wanted to run. Or miss nothing. She didn't know which.

In truth, she felt a fair bit of shame for thinking any of it. It wasn't anyone's fault they were deformed or beautiful, but the juxtaposition made her uncomfortable. Where was she to look? It was like carnage you couldn't tear your eyes from or beauty you couldn't make yourself stop gawking at. What was she to do with her hands? Eleanor snuck another look at Wendolyn as a crumpled-faced guard led them deeper into the camp.

"Relax, Eleanor," she said in a hushed tone. "Remember that the soul looks nothing like the body." Wendolyn glanced sidelong at her. "Here, hearts and motives are what matter, for most."

Eleanor let the words settle into her like sediment at the bottom of the sea, but Wendolyn's last statement rang in her ears. "*For most.*"

The snow wasn't as thick in the camp just to the Sud of Merveille, but it was still clogging her boots. Though, her toes had become numb days ago, so she wasn't certain why she cared. Three large men walked by then, carrying mirrors. The glare of the sun glinting off the snow was intrusive enough, but the mirrors threw it in a different direction with each step they took. Eleanor caught glimpses of herself scrunched small, then pulled wide and distorted beyond recognition before the sun caught the third mirror and momentarily blinded her.

"Wait here while I speak to the Cirque Master." The old guard narrowed his eyes at Wendolyn.

"I know the drill, Quintin."

The man harrumphed and left them standing outside a black-and-white striped tent. If it weren't so small, Eleanor would have thought it a performance tent. Whoever resided inside must have a penchant for theatrics even off the stage.

"You seem awfully familiar with these—" A stunning woman strode by then, long skirts swishing along the snow and dark breasts entirely visible except for a tassel strategically placed on each side. Eleanor lowered her voice. "People." Surely she must be chilled to the bone.

The scantily clad woman's face lit with shock as she locked eyes with Wendolyn, her lips turning up seductively. "My, my. It's been ages, dove. If you're thrown out of that tent"—she flicked her eyes toward it—"find mine, will you?"

Wendolyn's gaze fell to the woman's full lips, then slid back up to her brown eyes. Eleanor could practically see the steam rising from the snow. Though she couldn't truly blame Wendolyn. The woman was part gazelle, surely. Every movement had poise unlike any she'd ever seen. Not to mention how very much of her *could* be seen. Her exposed body was begging for salivation, and judging by the tilt of her sultry lips—she knew it.

"*Tabitha*," Wendolyn murmured.

"Ah, so you've not forgotten me, then." Tabitha stopped only a handbreadth from Wendolyn and Eleanor found it a struggle to keep her eyes from going wide.

"How could one forget a mouth like that?"

Tabitha's eyelids fluttered shut briefly. Her captivating lips parted to say something, but the grumpy guard stuck his head through the opening of the canvas tent. "He'll see you now."

Tabitha stepped forward and pressed herself against Wendolyn in what *had* to constitute more than a simple embrace, whispering something in her ear Eleanor couldn't make out, and then she strode away.

"Close your mouth, Eleanor," Wendolyn whispered. Eleanor hadn't noticed she was watching the woman walk away. "*Heart*, not body. Remember that here."

"You certainly seem *familiar* with her body," Eleanor muttered.

Wendolyn only laughed. The sound felt foreign in her ears coming from the ice witch. She was still watching her with her brows furrowed when the striped tent flap peeled back to grant them entry.

One step inside and all unhurried romanticism or jovial behaviour fell to Wendolyn's feet like a corpse. Eleanor was so jarred by the sudden shift that she almost missed the creature Wendolyn's attention had landed on across the ornately decorated tent. For there was no other explanation of what stood before them behind an oak table, parchment and dripping candles scattered across it. No one, in all seven realms, had ever been more ravishing than this man with skin the most beautiful shade of brown that she wanted to reach out and touch him. His hair was so black it was almost blue, tied into a knot on top of his head. His forest-green eyes tipped up at the corners, accentuated by long, dark lashes. Chiselled cheekbones and an equally sharp jawline framed the most luscious lips she'd ever laid eyes on. For the life of her, Eleanor could not tear her eyes from him, or recall how to draw air into her lungs.

He, however, was seemingly having difficulty tearing his eyes away from Wendolyn, who stood like a block of ice, staring back.

"Wendolyn Joubert. As I live and breathe."

Oh, gods. Even his rich voice was divine.

"Laurent."

Wendolyn's coldness sent a shiver down Eleanor's spine, but the man before them only smiled wide. Eleanor looked between the two of them, silently urging them to speak so she could discover what lay between them, and hear his voice again.

"I must admit—" The man named Laurent rounded his small desk and Eleanor wanted to step backwards. His beauty was too much, too consuming. "I thought my men were playing at a cruel ruse." His eyes roved over Wendolyn and Eleanor squeezed her knees together. "How long has it been? Fifty years?"

Wendolyn remained as stoic as ever. "Something like that."

Eleanor squirmed. Dear goddess, if she didn't get out of this tent…

"You look well, Wendy."

"You're looking as hideous as ever."

He chuckled, the sound low and velvety. Eleanor almost whimpered, hating herself for it. She tried to recall if Druids had power over the senses in the hearth tales… Laurent sat on the edge of his desk, dwarfing it with his bulk. He crossed his ankles, folding his hands in his lap. A foggy glimmer shuddered over him and Eleanor stepped back, drawing a hand to her mouth.

Where the ethereal creature not of this world had just been, a hideous monster lounged. A face scarred and puckered on one side and drooping as if it had nearly melted off the bone. His mouth fell to one side in a macabre scowl that chilled her to the marrow. She could have sworn Wendolyn relaxed a fraction.

His eyes landed on Eleanor and she fought a wave of panic. "And who is this?" A mask appeared over the top portion of his face and he turned his attention back to Wendolyn.

"This is my travel companion, Eleanor."

"Apologies, demoiselle," he addressed her, eyes still pinned on Wendolyn. "My dear friend Wendy here prefers me in my deformed state." He winked, his mouth twisting into a distorted grin. "It reminds her of days gone by."

Wendolyn cleared her throat.

"Why do I have the feeling you did not come here for the reason I'd like?" he asked, the cadence of his voice still as alluring as before.

"Because I've not."

It was simply impossible that she couldn't sense his eyes on her, tracking her every movement as they meandered through the Druid camp. Eleanor could even feel them and they weren't trained on her. In fact, it was likely he hadn't noticed Wendolyn still had a companion with her at all.

"You do realise the Cirque Master's gaze hasn't strayed from you since the moment we walked out of his tent." It was not a question. Questions left room for debate. And there was no denying his attention.

"Let him look." Wendolyn shrugged one shoulder, her silvery hair shifting to fall like silk down her back. "Let him mourn his failures."

"What happened between the two of you?"

Wendolyn gave her a sardonic stare cold enough to send ice skittering across molten lava. Eleanor frowned. If the ice witch didn't want to give details, so be it. She would just have to dig them up herself. It would give her something to do while Wendolyn searched for the information they needed and left Eleanor to boredom.

Although, there was plenty to see to last a lifetime or two. A man with arms as thick as tree trunks and covered in designs of black ink nodded at her with a wink as they walked. A woman with one perfectly contoured body and two beautiful heads smiled kindly. They passed small fires with gnarled and ethereal alike tending cauldrons of food.

Wendolyn caught Eleanor staring open-mouthed at them all and she mumbled an apology. "It's all right," Wendolyn replied. "They're used to it. They're gawked at for a living."

Eleanor glanced behind them to find the Cirque Master peeling off into a tent, his attention finally falling away from Wendolyn. Her shoulders relaxed and Eleanor's curiosity about them inflamed again, distracting her from the wonders of the Druids.

They stopped abruptly in front of a tent thrice as large as the

Cirque Master's, and Wendolyn gestured toward it. "I'll need to converse with some of the performers before they set up for the night. You will go in here."

Eleanor blinked at her. "Go in there? You're just going to drop me off at a random tent?"

"Are you an infant?"

According to her, yes. "What if you have the wrong tent and I walk in on someone while they're indecent?"

Wendolyn looked vaguely amused. "What an interesting imagination you have."

"I'm serious, *Wendy*."

That shut her right up and her face fell. "Do not call me that."

"I'm not going into an unknown tent."

"It's not unknown, I know exactly what's in there."

"Care to fill me in?"

"That would be rather dull." Wendolyn turned and walked away, snow dusting the hem of her fur coat.

Eleanor muttered curses, turning to walk away, but a deep voice sounded just behind her, raking over her skin. "If Wendolyn Joubert told you to walk in that tent, I suggest you do so."

She spun around to face the intruder, her attention snagging on his wolfish grin and mellow posture.

"I'll take my chances with Her Highness, Queen of Ice and Misery."

His eyes flashed with humour and Eleanor pushed down a tremor in her abdomen. "You're braver than I am."

"You know Wendolyn, too, then?"

His head lulled from side to side. "Of her. Many stories in this clan begin with her." So she'd actually travelled with the Druids for a time? "My mother knows as much about Wendolyn as anyone can. She's not one to share."

Understatement of History. But that was one thing Eleanor

could understand. One's life was a private, precious thing not meant for just anyone. Sharing the intricacies of life with a crowd rendered the quiet moments loud, and unremarkable. She rather regretted telling Wendolyn about her friendship with Grimm, but there was nothing to do about it now.

"I take it you also know what lies within this tent." The man grinned at her and Eleanor crossed her arms.

He only smiled wider. "I do." The strange encounter ended as abruptly as it had begun when he strolled away whistling.

Eleanor shook her head, cold seeping into her bones. She thought she would have grown used to it. Alas, it was still as frigidly perturbing as on day one.

Just then, a gaggle of young adults came toward her, so engrossed in their boisterous conversation that they missed Eleanor completely. By the time they neared the tent she was attempting to flee from, they were so oblivious to her presence that they ended up corralling her forward like a lost sheep. Before she could extricate herself from their gangly limbs and deafening giggles, Eleanor found herself pushed through the tent opening and stumbling in.

The clambering noise hit her first. It was a deafening cacophony that sent her reeling, one she hadn't been able to hear even standing outside at the tent's opening. The next phenomenon to strike her was the enormity of the interior of the tent. There was no logical way something so large was housed in a tent that size, not naturally, anyway.

An elephant walked by then, the ground trembling beneath it and the woman atop shouting at Eleanor to move. She darted backwards, tripping over a tumbling group of small men until she landed in the dirt next to a large wooden circle painted with a target. A dagger whizzed past her ear and Eleanor yelped, scrambling to her feet.

A strong hand caught her arm, spinning her around to face them. "You look like a newborn foal. Who let you in here?"

Eleanor gaped at the Druid standing before her. Long and lean, she was etched out of pure night. Her ebony skin and coal-black eyes were startlingly beautiful, but part of her head, face, and neck were marbled with scars that looked like she might have been irrevocably burned. From the crown of her head, a multitude of tiny braids cascaded over one side to fall over the unmarred side of her face and down her back.

It struck Eleanor that this elder Druid woman bore her deformity like a badge of honour, rather than hiding it under her voluminous hair as she easily could have. Something about that fact made Eleanor stand straighter.

"I was instructed to come in here."

The woman's brow creased. "By whom?"

"Wendolyn Joubert."

Shock lit her eyes for the briefest of moments before bounding away. "I'd heard she was back." The woman stuck her hand out and Eleanor noticed the marbling marred her extremities as well. "I'm Lydia."

Unnerved by a woman extending her hand like a man, Eleanor gave a weak curtsy. Instead of returning it, the woman snorted and snatched Eleanor's wrist, forcing her hand around the woman's forearm, her other hand grasping Eleanor's as well, shaking them firmly once. "This is a Druid greeting."

The woman's grip fell away and Eleanor cleared her throat, smoothing her blonde hair. She forced her attention not to stray from this woman oozing powerful grace. "My apologies, madame. I haven't the slightest idea why Wendolyn sent me in here. Is this some sort of training area?" Eleanor looked around at all the people, each one vastly different from the last, in more ways than usual.

Lydia snorted again. "I have a few ideas why. And yes, this"—she spread one arm out wide—"is where we perfect our skills."

Off to the side and without the threat of imminent death in

the form of a misguided carnival trick, Eleanor let her gaze rove over the place. It truly was magnificent.

"Well," Lydia prodded. "Where will you begin?"

Eleanor's attention snapped back to the Druid's face. "Excuse me?"

Her teeth gleamed in the torchlight as she smiled. "Shall you want to fall from the air like the trapeze artists?" Eleanor followed her hand as she gestured up to the towering tent top and back down toward a man sticking his head in a lion's mouth. "Or perhaps teeth grazing your neck is more suited to your taste?" Eleanor squirmed and Lydia laughed. "Walk with me, and we'll see what catches your eye."

"It all catches my eye, madame, but that doesn't mean I wish to *partake* in any of it."

Lydia smiled in the knowing way only held by those significantly older than their present company. "I wouldn't want to face Wendolyn without making a selection, was I you."

Eleanor stopped in her tracks. "Wendolyn does not rule me. If I find something here that suits me, I will partake. Otherwise, I would appreciate it if you would all cease viewing Wendolyn through some fantastical image you've created of her. At the very least, let *me* not view her through it. She's not a deity, for goddess' sake."

One of Lydia's eyebrows rose halfway to her marred hairline. "And now it is clear why she sent you in here." Eleanor wrinkled her nose, opening her mouth to retort, but Lydia went on. "You're of a strong mind. So is she."

"She did more than travel with you all, didn't she?"

Lydia nodded. "She was much more to us all."

"And what part did the Queen of Ice play in your cirque?"

"Ah." She clapped Eleanor hard on the back. "Now that is her story to tell, not mine." Lydia began walking again and Eleanor struggled to keep up with her long strides. "There is much to choose from, and you might as well occupy your time while you're here. I don't know why Wendolyn has returned after so long, but I would bet it's not to join our ranks again."

Eleanor kept quiet, considering what she could mention to this woman. They needed to learn about the man in the mountain pass, but Eleanor was not the trusting type. Wendolyn knew these Druids, so it was she who was better suited to ferret out information.

Candlelight glinted off a blade soaring through the practise tent, and suddenly Eleanor was in the woods again, encased in an invisible bubble of magic, Agatha slinking away toward an assailant. She'd been helpless. A liability.

"The knives," she spoke before she could stop herself. "I'd like to know more about throwing knives." It was the only useful thing of the lot, anyway. She couldn't very well hang silks in her and Anne's rooms to dangle upside down from or ride an elephant into the castle. Some Druids were vocalising off to one side, and though Eleanor had a decent voice, she would not call herself a songstress, nor did she wish to be one.

"Very well." Lydia inclined her head, leading her toward four Druids with knives in hand and seemingly in some sort of heated debate.

"...beat you last time. It's your turn," the blonde man with one shrivelled arm spat as they walked up.

"Your mum's tit it is, Gio. It's Noreen's turn." The portly one pointed the tip of his knife at a lovely, copper-headed woman.

"I won't leave unscathed. I'm not doing it."

Lydia cleared her throat and they all snapped to attention as if she were a battle commander instead of a cirque performer.

"Tent Master," the portly one spoke up in greeting.

"Arguing over whose turn it is to stand beneath the apple?" The blonde's cheeks reddened at Lydia's words and Eleanor's face contorted in confusion. Lydia turned to her. "Whoever loses the day before, has to stand with an apple on his or her head, whilst the others throw their knives at it." She chuckled as

Eleanor's eyes widened before turning back to the others. "Where is Tomás?"

"Er. Late, Tent Master."

Lydia took in a long breath and exhaled slowly.

"Not that late." They all shifted to find the earlier man from outside the tent waltzing toward them, apple in hand. He brought it to his lips and took a big chunk out of it with his teeth before tossing it to the portly one. "'T's your turn, Oren." He leaned in and kissed Lydia on her marbled cheek. "Better late than never, yes?"

Lydia frowned. "Everything is always a jest with you. You think just because you're my son that the rules of this tent, this cirque, do not apply to you."

The three knife throwers busied themselves, but Eleanor kept rapt attention.

Tomás smiled, all teeth and a heartache waiting to happen to the next lonely girl. "Life is meant to be lived, Mami." He spread his arms out, head swivelling from one side of the tent to the other. "Look around. We are *cirque performers*." He took her by the shoulders with his broad hands, mirth dancing in his eyes. "*We* are what brings people joy. Don't forget, in all your commanding, to enjoy this adventure, Mami."

The corners of Lydia's mouth crawled upward and she cuffed her son on the back of the head. "You enjoy it enough for the both of us." He smiled somehow wider and Lydia shook her head. "Where were you?"

"Ah. Would you believe that three of your brutes never showed up to set up the tent for this evening?"

Lydia's lips pursed. "Again?"

"Again." His eyes darted to where Eleanor stood off to the side, an almost imperceptible lilt tilting his smile and her stomach flipped before his attention landed back on his mother. "I found them by the river. Two drunk and one well on his way."

His gaze wandered back toward Eleanor. The men in this troupe did not mind their eyes for one moment.

Lydia mumbled something and noticed where her son's attention landed. "Oh, yes. Tomás"—she turned with one hand splayed—"this is—"

"Eleanor Moreau," he finished for her, gliding forward. He gently took Eleanor's hand and brought it to his lips.

"You ran into Wendolyn, then, I see." Lydia's jaw was tight.

Tomás nodded to his mother, dropping Eleanor's hand. She hid it in the folds of her skirts. "I did."

"What else did she tell you?" Eleanor asked, with her lips pinched. If Wendolyn wanted to spew secrets, two could play at that game.

Tomás grinned and Eleanor looked away briefly. "She informed me that if you did not select knife throwing as your activity of choice, I was to do everything in my power to persuade you otherwise."

Eleanor's expression soured. "How wonderful. Now she dictates my life even more." She sighed, hating that Wendolyn knew what she'd select somehow. "You are the knife-throwing instructor, then?" She crossed her arms, one finger tapping her arm. He did not answer right away, so she let her eyes lazily climb up to meet his, unimpressed. He merely regarded her with lips turned up and humour on every plane of his face.

"Knife Master," Lydia corrected, interrupting their standoff. "Tomás will show you all you need to know." She walked away, leaving the pair of them alone next to a table full of knives.

"This shall be quite the treat." Tomás winked at her.

CHAPTER EIGHTEEN

AGATHA

Tindle let out a garbled screech, nearly choking on his bite of food. His fork clattered down onto the plate, chicken broth splattering the cream linen tablecloth.

"For the love of the goddess, Agatha!" She couldn't tell if he was more upset about her sudden intrusion or the stain he jumped to dab with a wet cloth. "Send a calling card or a—a raven next time *at least*," he spat.

Agatha leaned against the door jamb and snickered. "I did. You didn't answer the tapping on your damned window."

His attention darted to the raven silhouetted by moonlight as it hovered outside. He turned back, levelling Agatha with a classic Tindle glare, and her heart constricted with the familiarity. Everything was so chaotic at present that it all felt foreign. But Tindle? Same story, different audacious chapter.

She'd met with him at Dulci's the evening before to discuss what little they'd gleaned from Augustus' spying, but when the sun began to set on another disconcerting day, she'd found herself transporting to Tindle's before she realised what she was doing.

"Does Augustus know you're here alone?"

Agatha scowled. "Augustus is not my keeper, *monsieur*, and I'm not a captive."

Tindle regarded her with mocking disdain. "I was under the impression all royals were captives." He buffed his nails on the shoulder of his indigo evening coat. "My mistake." Agatha's lip curled and his sneer melted into a haughty grin. "Why are you here, then, darling?"

That was enough of an invitation, especially after his rude comments. Agatha took off her heeled boots and left them in the hall to spite him before strolling wordlessly to the small sitting room and falling back onto the wingback chair closest to the fire. A few breaths later, Tindle came in behind her, carrying her boots between thumb and forefinger like they were the dead carcass of a street rat.

Face contorted in disgust, he set them against the wall and dusted his contaminated hands on his pants with a shiver. "I might have helped you design those sinister things, but they've been on your *feet* and through *muck*. And you may be a princess, but you have the despicable manners of a feral cat."

Agatha snorted and Tindle frowned.

"Ah, that was retribution for the royalty hounding, wasn't it?" He rolled his eyes and sat across from her, still swiping his hands repeatedly on his pants. "Fine." He situated himself comfortably and folded his hands in his lap. "Now, why are you here?"

"Do I need a reason to visit a friend?" Tindle rubbed the bridge of his nose and Agatha smiled. It was too easy to exasperate him. "I've been thinking about something I saw belonging to the Grand Magus last Autumn." Tindle's brows rose. "It was a drawing of a young woman. At first, I thought it must have been his mother or sister, but the more I thought about it, that didn't seem right. The drawing was hidden inside his desk drawer, taped to the top."

Tindle rested his head against one fist, elbow poised on the arm of the chair. "And you just...*saw* this drawing there taped to the inside of the magus' private desk drawer? How interesting." Agatha glowered and he smiled, straightening in his seat. "Come now, I know by now that if there's an expectation such as a silly little thing called privacy, our dear princess will do the exact opposite." He adjusted his jacket and crossed one leg over the other. "I'm surprised Grimm hasn't told you this juicy detail."

The way the dressmaker said it made Agatha wonder what else he knew and how. But, Tindle somehow knew everything and very seldom explained the how of it.

Agatha glanced at the fire. "Grimm hasn't precisely been himself whilst taking the draught."

"Mm. No, I suppose he hasn't." A sadness crossed Tindle's eyes, but he pushed it away. "Magus Emile von Fuchs was married at one time."

Agatha baulked. "He *what*?" She shook her head, dark hair falling over her shoulders. "But magi don't marry."

"No, they do not."

"Meaning what? She died and he gave his life to The Order of Hespa as he aged?"

Tindle shrugged. "According to his records, von Fuchs entered a convent of The Order at thirteen like most young magi."

She twisted a lock of hair round and round her finger. "How did you discover this information?"

"*I*"—he put a hand to his chest—"did not. Your wicked prince is very skilled at uncovering secrets."

Agatha wished very much that they would uncover them all so this nightmare of twists could dissipate into the sunlight.

"My best guess is he also rooted through the magus' private

belongings at one time or another." Tindle *tsked.* "A match made in the depth of Hades, you two."

It made no sense unless von Fuchs wasn't truly an ordained magus of Hespa and he'd forged his papers. That, on the other hand, made a startling amount of sense. Agatha abruptly stood, prepared to transport herself back to her suite in the castle to tell Grimm, until she suddenly remembered his current state and stopped dead in her tracks. There was no husband there for her to tell her secrets to, only a puppet. She sat slowly back down, Tindle's curious attention fixated on her. "Would it be all right if I stayed here tonight?"

Concern filled his eyes, but the dressmaker didn't remark on whatever it was that he saw in her face. He watched her quietly for a moment before speaking. "Yes. However, if you stay here, we have something to discuss that you won't like."

Agatha deflated. "Only if you tell me whose morning coat is hanging by your front door."

He squinted and shook his head. "Not part of the deal. Stay and talk about what I have to say, or go back to the cold stone castle and your draught-filled prince."

Her lips formed a thin line. "Fine. Out with it, then."

Agatha expected him to look triumphant, but Tindle almost looked sanguine. "Let me preface this by pointing out that magic is clearly finding its way back to the daylight." Agatha tensed, but Tindle went on. "The Empress of Coronocco is a witch, as is the Princess of Seagovia." He splayed his hands out. "I'm convinced this is why you were stalked in the woods the night you and Gaius were attacked. I'm also convinced it's the reason Empress Amira was taken."

It was at the top of their list of possible reasons, to be sure. She still thought Mila wanting a body was a very clear motive if she thought Amira could give her one. But Agatha wasn't certain where Tindle was headed with this. "Magic never went anywhere, though. Not really."

"Of course it didn't. Yet, even the royal family, and just about every other soul in this kingdom, thought it was extinct. They've believed it for hundreds of years." He leaned forward, elbows on his knees and fingers steepled toward her. "Agatha, my point is we've been doing things the same way for a very long time and it has not worked." He pointed at her. "You, and your kind, witches and warlocks, even the *true* magi, have been ostracised just as the rest of us." He shook his head and leaned back in his chair. "It's time for magic to come out of the shadows and *lead.* And it is you who needs to do it." Tindle watched her with a fierce stare. "Let the kingdom, let the *realm* see a witch in power. Perhaps it's time to let magic reign."

But Agatha was already shaking her head. "No. I remember it, Tindle." She blinked rapidly. "I'd only just come into my powers, but I *remember* the Witch Trials. People were hunted down like rabid animals."

Tindle pushed to the edge of his seat. "But you are not just any witch. You're a Sister Solstice in a seat of power and influence. I understand you're not invincible, but who can really touch you? "

"It's not *me* I'm worried about, Tindle."

No, she was worried about all who would fall again for being different or misunderstood. The hedge witches who'd been quietly practising their sorcery in secret for centuries. The half-bloods who didn't even know they held magic in their veins, assuming they merely had an affinity for growing plants or nursing the sick back to health. The medically advanced, who were viewed as miscreants because they tinkered with alchemy or uncommon healing practices. The curious grave robbers who dug up cadavers in the name of progressive science and cut them open to learn how to heal. What would happen when these men and women were no longer seen as simply *peculiar* for being outcasts, the gifted, reformists, or corpse scholars?

"If you lead this," Tindle's words broke into her thoughts, "it can truly change this kingdom and this continent. Maybe even the entire realm."

"I don't want to be in a seat of power at all. The entire *point* of all of this is to give control back to the people, not to another set of royals who might destroy the continent in a later generation because they don't hold our values."

He clapped his hands together, the sharp sound cracking through the air. "*Exactly*. Take your place and set magic free. It will set the *people* free."

Agatha's mind swirled. It was possible, but there was a whole host of problems that could arise from that. There would always be those who hated magic, just as there would always be those who hated anyone different from them; anything they didn't understand.

What would happen when the Hallowed and the Hollow alike had magic, and everyone realised they had been equal all along? Pandemonium.

Agatha didn't respond and dived into her own thoughts, silence falling between them for some time. Eventually, her mind did what it had grown accustomed to doing in recent weeks. It began searching the entanglement for Grimm. The real him. Their bond felt nearly dormant, as it had for days, but there was the slightest sense of longing. A pang of sorrow echoed through her. Grimm missed her. Despite his actions of late. Despite the drowning out of his own mind and will, he still longed for her. Agatha swallowed the lump in her throat.

The fire had simmered down to glowing embers, and Tindle rose to stoke it, watching her out of the corner of his eye. "Things with the prince aren't going so well, then?" he asked quietly.

Agatha huffed a humourless laugh through her nose. "I don't think we have the time in all the realms for that discussion."

"Of course we do." Tindle winked at her. "I'll go put the kettle on."

WINNIE

Un, deux, trois... The chirping began right on time. Eleanor stomped into their tent, all frayed edges and crackling animosity. Lemon-lipped with accusation poised on her tongue.

"I am not some sullen child you need to displace," the bird spat. "I was not sent here to wait on you hand and foot. Nor was I sent here to fiddle with cirque freaks so you can keep all your secrets tucked away in your bosom behind your heart of ice." She stood there, hands balled into fists and chest heaving.

In truth, Wendolyn was impressed by her tirade. "Dear maid." Winnie examined her nails. "I've not once asked you to wait on me. Nor did I *displace* you. Those people are not *freaks*, and I did not want you to grow bored here."

Eleanor snapped her teeth like a rabid dog. "Therefore you send me into a tent full of cirque tricks and think it will pacify me? To select some pointless activity and leave you to do everything Agatha and Grimm asked of us?" Her back went ramrod straight. "I am more than what you make of me, and I'm done trying to convince you of it."

She slowly lifted her eyes to Eleanor's face. "I know you've a penchant for learning clandestine information. And I also know you've no idea how to protect yourself."

Eleanor's mouth snapped shut and she shifted on her feet before speaking again. "If you are going to use me, it would be nice to learn of it first."

"Call it what you wish." Winnie waved a hand and stood, striding to the vanity to prepare for her tea with the Masters before their performance that evening. "I'd stake my life on the estimation that you gained at least one secret this afternoon and that Tomás has already shown you three ways to better protect yourself in the form of"—she looked over her shoulder with disdain—"*cirque tricks*."

Winnie turned back to face the mirror, watching Eleanor's reflection as she looked away.

"What did you learn, then?"

Eleanor fidgeted, lifting her chin higher. "I'll keep that to myself, thank you." She turned on her heel, making to leave.

"Where are you going?"

She turned back, crossing her arms. "I'll tell you if you tell me."

Winnie smiled, her eyes narrowed. "I'm meeting with the Masters for tea. I'd like to see what they know."

"Then what were you doing all afternoon, if not that?"

"That was not part of this conversational agreement."

"Very well. I'm headed back to the practice tent until the performance tonight."

"Enjoyed yourself, did you?"

"It's satisfying to pretend it is your face upon that target and to throw a knife into your eye."

Winnie huffed a laugh, a genuine smile drawing her lips upward. "I'll be your target any time you'd like."

Eleanor frowned. "I'll hit the target eventually."

"Oh, I know. Magic, remember? I'll just be your muse."

Three Hundred Years Ago

Helda came next. Sorscha looked ready to fight. Or bolt. Winnie put her hand on Sorscha's bouncing leg.

"Let me say goodbye to Aggie," she finally said, the words barely audible.

"Hurry," Helda instructed. "It isn't safe to linger together any longer."

Sorscha's eyes widened, but she hurried down the hall to where Aggie was reading on the bed.

"Why is it not safe?" Winnie demanded as soon as Sorscha was out of earshot.

Helda pursed her lips, her kind eyes crestfallen. "Once a Sister comes of age and begins her training, her power can no longer mingle with the other Sisters outside of the Solstice or Equinox."

It took a moment to register why Helda looked so agonised, but then Winnie understood. "Y–you mean I won't be able to visit my Sisters? I won't be able to see them anymore?" Wherever they were being taken, she'd always thought they could learn to transport as their parents had and still be together when they could.

"I'm afraid not, outside of our designated times together."

Winnie struggled to breathe. The edges of her vision were dotted with black as she clutched her skirts in her fists, grappling with this news.

"Shh...shh." Helda came forward and sat, taking Winnie's hand. "You should have been prepared for this. Why do you know so little?"

"I–I know what the Sisters Solstice are, just as anyone else does, but that's it," she babbled. "The day of my first bleed, my father told me I was one of them, then Sorscha. And I told Seleste the day of her first bleed this past Spring. But beyond that, I don't think my parents knew." Except Mother had said things to Aggie…

"No. That isn't true." Winnie glanced at Helda for how firm her tone was. "Your parents knew perfectly well what was coming." She stood and cursed in an ancient tongue Winnie couldn't place. "The moment Sorscha was born, we suspected." She fiddled with one of her long necklaces. "The Order keeps a very close eye on any descendants of Lord Night or Lady Magic that come together."

"You're part of The Order?"

"No. No, no. Not like the magi. The Sisters are more than witches, but we are not quite mages, as far as ties to The Order are concerned. However, they like to keep watch over us. When Seleste was born, we paid your parents a visit that very day. When Aggie was born…" She threw one hand up in the air. "We returned to confirm what we all already knew. Four Sisters had been born of descendants of Lord and Lady Magie de la Nuit at the appointed time on a Solstice or Equinox. The new Sisters were finally among us." She paused. "Your mother threw us out."

Winnie baulked and Sorscha walked in then, her knapsack limp in her hand. "What's going on?"

"Mother knew," Winnie whispered. "She knew everything."

Hurt flashed across Sorscha's face. "And she didn't tell us?"

"You know by now that your mother was a heretic?" Both girls nodded. "She would not hear of it. Claimed this day would never come, that she would see to it. Then"—Helda flicked her wrist—"she just threw us out. Your father met with us secretly in their barn. We explained it all to him: In your fifteenth year, Wendolyn, we would each retrieve one of the four of you and train you. Hone your magic and teach you the ways of Hespa, the way of moulding History to Her will. When you turn sixteen, Greta will die. You will take up her mantle with Sybil, Prue, and me until Sorscha comes of age. So on and so forth."

Sorscha sat hard on a chair. "We can still visit one another at least…"

"No," Winnie choked out. "We can't."

Sorscha's lips parted and her eyes welled with tears. She

looked to Helda, but she only shook her head. "But Seleste…Aggie…"

"That's eight years for Aggie with that horrible woman," Winnie bit out. "Will she harm her?"

Helda's attention flicked away before landing back on Winnie. "Sybil will do what is best for our cause."

"Will she be kind?" Sorscha broke in.

"Sybil is powerful–"

"*Power*," Winnie interrupted, "does not give one the right to be unkind."

Helda sighed. "Try not to worry. There is nothing you can do, regardless."

Winnie clenched her jaw, looking down the hall at the luggage under the bed.

"Come along, Sorscha." Helda stood and beckoned Sister Spring. "We must be going."

PRESENT DAY

THE ROOM of too-familiar faces began to clear, too many sets of eyes on her. Winnie had elected not to speak. She hadn't ordered her thoughts enough to make any sort of declaration, or even ask questions at the Masters' tea time. To her utter surprise and equal relief, Laurent had brought no attention to her, other than his glance cutting her way all too often.

But that was the Druid clan. Her old troupe. Her once-found family. They were too much. Every last one of them stuck out like a sore thumb, whether from beauty or deformity.

They all lived a boisterous existence, knowing they had more than enough in one another. They took pains to ensure every last one of them found their worth in the unseen.

Winnie stared at her hands. It was one of the reasons she'd left. She was not a Druid. She did not hail from Elves and her magic did not alter her form. Yet, *she* was the fetid, rotted thing in the depths of the unseen. Wendolyn Joubert was not one of these stunning, hideous creatures of valour and virtue. She never would be.

Then Laurent had to turn out to be like her, instead of them—his own troupe.

Lost in her thoughts, she hadn't realised the tent had cleared. All the Masters off to command their faction of the troupe and prepare for the first night's show in Vorren.

The shuffle of stones skittering underfoot sounded behind her and Winnie fixed her countenance, preparing to face Laurent again with no show of emotion. *The ice queen*, Eleanor loved to call her. She was the queen of nothing now.

Thick fur boots the colour of congealed blood came into her periphery and Winnie's traitorous heart sank. She'd been wrong about the identity of the visitor.

"Wendolyn Joubert." Lydia sat hard on a bench across from Winnie, leaning over, elbows on her knees.

Gods, she was a vision. Most would only see the mottled skin she wore proudly. They might note the uneven shoulders and two different coloured eyes. Winnie knew that heart, though. The one of a warrior. A Druid woman who had scraped her way to Tent Master by the skin of her teeth and without the use of magic. No, Lydia Bonacieux was the real deal. Stronger, tougher, kinder than all the rest.

"Lydia."

"I have to admit, I never thought I'd see your pretty face again."

Winnie chose silence. If there weren't proper words, it was best to keep one's mouth shut.

"When shall I see you in my practice tent again, hm? Or, I suppose, behind the curtain in it?"

Winnie pursed her lips. "Ever the Tent Master."

Lydia's eyes hardened. "Ever the jilted friend."

Winnie looked away. "I'm sorry for that, I am."

The Tent Master merely held up her dark, disfigured hand. "There's no need for that," she said with one sharp shake of her head, braids falling in front of her good eye. "I understand why you did it. I do. But I must admit it did sting. So many years of friendship just"—she snapped—"gone."

Lydia had every right to say the words, but they cut deep within Winnie's belly. She'd held onto the foolish hope that Lydia would welcome her back, even after all the lost years.

"Liddy–"

"Are you going to tell me why you're really here?" She cut Winnie off. "It's clearly not for Laurent, the way he's been moping about like a sick hound."

Winnie snorted. "How much can I tell you?" Sharing had never been her strong suit.

And Lydia knew it. "Try all of it for once." A smile slipped, unbidden, to Winnie's mouth and Lydia reached out to smack her knee. "Out with it."

"There is a man in the Sacrèe Mountain Pass that is believed to have vital information regarding the safety of our realm."

Lydia tipped her head back and laughed. "Oh, is that all?"

Winnie shrugged. "Such is my life, you know." But Lydia didn't, not really. She knew Winnie was a witch—they all did. She knew there was a strange meeting of her *coven* four times a year, and she knew Winnie held onto her secrets like they were her life force. She supposed they were, in a way. "I thought perhaps the troupe might have heard word of such a man."

Lydia shook her head, leaning to crack her back. "Unlikely. We haven't travelled to perform near the Sacrèe Mountains in ages. Laurent refuses to go there." She looked pointedly at Winnie. "Too many memories."

Winnie let her gaze drift to the sunlight streaming into the tent, little flecks of dust dancing in it.

"I'm sure you could convince him, though." Winnie's attention snapped back to her face and Lydia laughed at the scowl Winnie made no attempt to cover. "You could stay. Travel with us, and we'll assist you in the hunt for information."

"Absolutely not."

"Shutting people out again, I see." She raised an eyebrow, welcoming the fight.

So Winnie swallowed it down. If Lydia wanted an argument, she'd have to try harder than that. "I don't want to involve you."

"Yet, here you are amongst our troupe again after fifty years." Lydia did not finish her thought, but Winnie knew where it would have been headed. Instead, the Tent Master stretched her long, lithe limbs. "Who is this Eleanor Moreau you travel with?"

"She"—Winnie closed her eyes against the irritation that arose with the girl's name—"is a friend of my Sister's."

"And not one of yours?" Lydia asked with narrowed eyes.

"We were not willingly paired."

"Since when does anyone have the power to make *the* Wendolyn Joubert do what they wish?"

There it was. That sliver of Lydia's light that had always crept into Winnie, making her believe she could trust. That she did not have to walk alone.

"Since my Sister became *Princess of Seagovia.*"

Winnie had never seen Lydia gasp, but she looked almost ready to. "Your Sister is the peasant princess?" Winnie nodded and Lydia leaned in, whispering, "Isn't she a witch?"

"She is, indeed. It's a nightmare."

"I'll say." Lydia blew out a breath. "She's making quite the difference in Seagovia—all of Midlerea if rumour is to be believed."

Winnie frowned. "Sure."

Silence befell them and Winnie let the sliver of trust shrivel up within it and retreat. She'd been too forthright. Too weak.

"That Eleanor has quite the throwing arm on her, I'll say."

A peculiar warmth bloomed in Winnie's bosom. "I thought she might."

"Tomás cannot stop talking about her."

Winnie's eyes flashed. "*Tomás* best keep his hands to himself. She is a young woman with no idea what Tomás is about."

Lydia smiled wide. "Oh, so she *does* care for her unlikely companion, then."

"If that is your assumption, Tent Master, what does it say about your son's reputation?"

A hearty laugh filled the space between them. "Tomás is harmless."

Not likely. He was a ravenous flirt with a penchant for mischief and good times. Sticky sweet at heart, but Eleanor did not need to be distracted by Druid seduction and jovial mayhem. "I came…when he was born," Winnie confessed.

Lydia only nodded. "I thought I felt you there. You've written Tomás over the years, too. Haven't you?"

Winnie didn't answer right away. She'd needed to know her friend's son. She'd needed him to know of her. It was the only connection she'd allowed herself to the Druids over the last five decades. Lydia had always dreamt of having a child… When she did, Winnie couldn't bear the thought of never knowing him. Finally meeting him today upon their arrival, a grown man… Winnie swallowed the lump in her throat. It was a meeting that felt like a reunion, just like the others. "A few times, yes."

"He never told me." Lydia grinned, running a hand up and down her thigh in the way Winnie knew meant she was fighting a swell of emotion. "I found the letters one day, and I wept for them. To know, despite everything, my boy would somehow know you, even a little." Winnie watched a tear fall to Lydia's knee. She swiped it away and cleared her throat. "You haven't seen a show in ages," she said looking up at Winnie. "Come tonight."

"I—I don't think I'm ready for that, Liddy."

She nodded once and stood, her hand reaching out to rest on top of Winnie's head briefly. "I'll make your excuses to everyone." She winked and strode out of the tent.

LAURENT

He heard the creak of the wooden ladder behind him but didn't bother turning. Only Lydia knew he came up there. Lydia and Wendy.

His Tent Master grunted as she dropped to the ground next to him, letting her feet dangle over the edge of the fly loft above the stage like his were. She draped her arms over the railing and nodded toward him, eyes trained on his masked forehead.

"What's goin' on in there?"

Laurent smirked, staring out across the tent's expanse. "Do you remember the night all the lights went out?"

"You mean the night Wendolyn came alive on stage for the first time?"

The Cirque Master's grin brightened his face. "Ye', that one. She glowed like the fucking moon." He saw Lydia watching him out of the corner of his eye.

"You know, I've always thought that night was a bit suspect.

How did all the lights in the performance tent go out one by one and no magic could relight them?"

Laurent shrugged. "Doesn't matter. The show must go on."

Lydia snorted and he turned to her with a smile a little dimmed at the edges. "Wendy couldn't find herself with all those eyes on her."

"Mm. So you made them go away."

He looked back over the railing to the stage below.

She squinted at him. "If memory serves, didn't the two of you disappear for days after that?"

His chest caved in the same moment his marred face broke into another grin. "We did."

Flashes of those few days assaulted him. The sun glinting off her pale hair. Her laugh as they balanced on fallen tree trunks in the river until they fell in and splashed to the shore. The warmth of her skin under his fingertips. A bouquet of flowers he'd picked for her, sticking one in her hair. The unmoored joy in her voice. The orange of the setting sun, blue of her eyes, violet of her dress, red of her lips. Her tapping on his shoulder then disappearing, his magic seeking her out. Tangled limbs in the tall grass.

"I don't even want to know with that look in your eyes." Lydia interrupted his reverie, nudging him.

He could still see her face so clearly. That was nothing she could take away.

"I've been thinking all evening," Lydia said, "about that night you met her, in the woods."

A night that played behind his eyes on a regular basis. "Ah, that was the night she first told me her name." He stood and Lydia eyed him curiously. "But that was not the first time I saw her."

"You saw Wendolyn before that night?"

He smiled wistfully. "Many, many times."

"How?"

Laurent squeezed his Tent Master's shoulder. "I'll see you at rehearsal."

CHAPTER NINETEEN

AGATHA

Agatha blinked back the tears threatening to spill out. He hadn't directly looked at her in five days. But she'd *felt* him think of her. It was almost worse than the vacancy.

It was working. The magus was so overjoyed that Grimm was a puppet, he wasn't even being careful anymore. If they could hang on just a little longer, she really believed the magus would use Grimm to lead her right to what The Order was doing.

Grimm's eyes snapped to hers and she startled forward, reaching toward him, but his gaze went straight through her. He stood, his movements too stiff, nothing of the casual, chaotic prince she'd married.

"If you'll excuse me," he spoke in a voice not his own, "I have a meeting I must attend."

Agatha cleared her throat. "Yes, of course." She had to be careful what she did or said around him. There was no way to tell if the magus had some twisted way of actually seeing through another's eyes.

He moved past her as she fiddled with the lace of her sleeve so as not to reach out and touch him. The door to their rooms closed, and she glanced at the time dial on the wall. If whatever the magus had just called him for lasted longer than sunset, Agatha would have to force Grimm to take another dose to keep him under. Then she wouldn't see the real him for another day, if not longer. They'd been doing this without much to show for it for far too long. She'd had to double-dose him for four days straight. Each time, he felt further away. Less and less like himself.

Agatha suppressed a shiver and counted the seconds until she'd likely be able to see him in her mirror via Augustus' spelled pin.

She set down her book and left the comfort of the fire. On the way to her armoire that housed the spying mirror, she picked up her crystal pouch from where she'd hidden it. Black tourmaline firmly clasped in her locket, Agatha opened the armoire and pushed the clothing out of the way.

"*Rèvèler.*"

Her anxious heart soothed minorly when she saw Grimm's back, Augustus trailing him through the corridors.

Thankfully, Augustus was so dutiful that the magus thought he had handled him with a simple—firm—suggestion that all guards take the draught. He had, of course, not, but the magus was none the wiser at present and he continued to allow him to guard Grimm. The magus was too cocky to think his plan would have flaws, too pompous to think Grimm would ever befriend someone lesser, and he believed his control to be so thorough that only one guard would suffice.

They moved through the corridors, past the magus' chambers, his study, and toward the Sanctuary. Two slack-jawed guards stepped out of the way to let them through, the bolt in the door sliding free with a groan. Why the chapel would need to be locked in the middle of the day was a sobering thought.

She had to credit Augustus for not visibly startling when they rounded the corner into the Sanctuary because even Agatha almost did.

There, on the altar, a woman was strapped down and stripped naked.

Her head was turned away from the pews, with her face toward the towering, golden statue of Hespa. Even in the warbled view through the looking glass, Agatha could tell by the tremble in the woman's limbs and the jolting of her breasts that she was in shock and sobbing.

As the doors behind the men slammed shut, the woman turned her attention toward them. A hand slowly came to Agatha's mouth, bile rising at the back of her throat as she beheld Mila. Prone. Naked. Her hair was matted to her head and a gag was fitted in her mouth.

"Ah, there you are," Grand Magus von Fuchs said, coming around the corner of the penance cage, his voice muffled by the magic of her mirror. He looked downright cheery and Agatha's hand shifted toward her knife. She cursed for being so far away, useless in her rooms.

"How lovely of you to come." He gestured toward Mila's sobbing form. "As it turns out, my little rat here decided to make plans of her own. It's a thing of comedy to employ a ghost. It's quite difficult to keep track of them, and even more difficult to ensure they do as they're told."

He sidled up to Grimm, who hadn't even glanced at Mila. Despite anything she'd done to him, Agatha knew he never would have left her there on that altar as she was, shamed and trembling. He would have covered her at the very least.

"Did you know"—he moved closer to Grimm's face—"that only another of Lady Death's court can truly touch one of the wraiths?"

His sickening smile sent Agatha's hand reaching for her dagger again. She needed to be there…

"It's a good thing I've kept some"—his hand flipped back and forth—"*things* around that can keep a subject of the Court of Achlys contained."

Agatha stepped forward. Augustus' hand twitched toward his sword at the silent threat to even Grimm's safety.

The magus tipped his head back and laughed, a soul-crumbling sound that echoed off the falsely Hallowed walls of the Sanctuary as if the place of worship was a Hollow tomb.

It was worth the risk.

"*Disparaître*."

Agatha materialised, unseen, in the back of the sanctuary just as the magus clapped a hand hard on Grimm's back. "Lucky for us both, you're rather dull now, and our Mila here has found herself a mortal body." He made an over-exaggerated frown. "Well, something of the sort, anyway. *Much* easier to torture." He turned and strode back to the altar, his robes billowing. "I, however, do not enjoy sullying my hands." He motioned to Grimm and he moved toward the magus stiffly. "You'll do that for me." He handed Grimm a knife and Augustus flinched.

Mila began to shout behind her gag, the sound hushed almost completely, and she struggled against the ropes binding her to the cold stone of the altar.

"You, dear prince, must teach this wayward wraith a lesson. Let her know exactly what happens when you defy my commands."

The magus yanked off the gag. "Any last words, ghost harlot?"

Mila threw her head back before launching a wad of spit at the magus' face. "I hope you choke on your own blood someday," Mila ground out.

Agatha slunk closer, so near that she could almost see the hairs on Mila's trembling arms.

"You promised me a body. And you lied." She choked on a sob tied up in the last word.

Von Fuchs laid a thin hand on her head and she flinched, his fingers landing on golden hair, where the edges of her form would have blurred into nothingness before. "Haven't you learned by now that patience is a virtue?"

"You took too long," she spat, attempting to scoot away from his touch.

"So you thought you could steal the empress for yourself and not get caught." He clucked his tongue against his teeth. "Foolish thing to do. Now you've gone and wasted this perfectly grand opportunity. It's a shame, really." He slid two fingers down her cheek, trailing further, over her exposed breast. "We could have had a lot of fun, you and I." She shifted, writhing, attempting to get away from his touch and Agatha itched to incinerate him right there.

The magus' hand lashed out like the head of a viper, latching onto Mila's chin so tightly that she cried out. "You wanted to *feel*, didn't you, ghost?" He lowered his sagging face to hers, still grasping her chin, and kissed her hard enough to hurt. When he pulled back, he thrust her head to the side, a small crack sounding from her neck.

"Boy," he addressed Grimm, "slice her up pretty. Let her *feel.* Make it slow and painful. If you need something more fun than that over-fed cow of a wife you're shackled to, feel free to taste this vixen." He sneered and Agatha's vision blurred with rage. "Then kill her. But leave her here, I'd like to look upon her broken body once it's done."

The magus turned on his heel and Grimm raised the knife. The door slammed with an ominous clank, the bolt sliding home.

Augustus was trembling. Agatha looked between him and Grimm, unsure of what to do. She couldn't reveal herself if the magus could glean information from what Grimm saw while he was under. All she could think to do was go up behind Augustus and somehow let him know she was there. But if she took the time to do that, Mila would die. Again.

He was supposed to torture her first. She could run to Augustus and maybe figure out someth—

Grimm's hand lifted high, his arm shaking violently as if he was fighting the command with everything he had. The knife came down to carve her and she began to beg, but Grimm slammed the knife down hard into her lung, pulled it out, then threw it against the wall and left out the back in a rush.

"Goddess above." Augustus ran for Mila, hand hovering over her, helpless as she sputtered on blood coming up her throat. Agatha appeared, shoving Augustus over as he sent up a hushed prayer of thanks to the goddess for her presence.

"*Agatha*," Mila croaked. "Please. Save…me."

"I don't think I can…" She ran her hands over her body, pressing gently around the wound. "This… This isn't a real body, Mila." Gods, she had to do *something*.

"Plea—" Her words choked off, her body convulsing.

"*Merde*." Agatha pushed up her ruffled sleeves. "Know that I'm doing this for Grimm and not for you." She held her palms against the wound and willed it to heal. It didn't feel like mortal flesh. It was a counterfeit. A well-designed copy, but still a copy. "Augustus," she commanded the green-faced guard. "I need clean linen and water. See if there are any communion supplies in the back where Grimm went out. He nodded and hurried off, steps too loud in the hushed sanctuary. Agatha continued to work on Mila, the wound sealing slowly, but it wasn't right. It was as if she was patching a hole in a boat with a bit of cloth shoved in. It wasn't going to hold.

Augustus brought a small pitcher half full of water and a gold propriety cloth, which was used to cover the bodies of Church goers who might cause *impure* thoughts in others during services. *Self-righteous lunatics*.

Without warning, Agatha doused Mila's face with the chill water and Augustus staggered backwards as she sputtered awake. "Why did you do that?" Augustus whispered loudly.

Agatha did not bother with an answer, there wasn't time. "Go check on Grimm. *Now.*" His lips formed a thin line, but he obeyed, hurrying the way Grimm had left.

"There's no door back here!" he shouted, running a hand over his head and looking around frantically.

"Fucking figure it out, Augustus!" she spat. The guard growled and ran out the main door and into the hall. "*Mila,*" Agatha leaned close to the wraith's face. "This will not hold. Your body isn't real. But you can still make this right. Tell me everything you know, and make it quick."

She struggled to rise, but she was still tied down. Agatha snapped the ropes with her magic and threw one of the cloths around her as she sat upright. "Hold this one against your wound. Press hard." Mila winced but did as she was told.

"I don't know much…"

"Amira gave you this body?" Her theory had been a stretch, but if it was true…

Mila nodded. "Yes." She sat on the bloody altar, propped up with one hand, the other holding the linen that was swiftly soaking through.

"What kind of power can accomplish that sort of thing?" Had Amira known about animancy?

"I truly don't know. I never discovered what kind of witch she is, or what power she wields. I only knew she could accomplish it. I overheard the others telling the magu—"

"The others?" Agatha interrupted.

"Yes. The Order." They'd known it had to be The Order, but a confirmation was still nauseating. "They told the magus they would create a distraction on the night of the Eve of Hallows ball and they would take the empress." Mila's breath was laboured and thick. Coated with rising blood.

"The explosion in the ballroom." Another confirmation ticked off the disturbing list.

Mila nodded, wincing. "They'd planned for her to be

wounded in the attack, and the magus' men would swoop in and carry her to the infirmary where she would be sedated and taken away. But when the explosion occurred, Amira wasn't there."

"She was headed to Dulci's because of Grimm's secret code."

"Exactly. They didn't know where she was, but I did. I wanted a body so badly. The magus had promised me but… And I'd heard them mention Amira could achieve such a thing. She came back to the castle, but there was no opportunity to retrieve her, for anyone. Then, Grimm got nervous. He kept claiming something was wrong and he wasn't sure if it was you or Amira, so he and Tindle took her to Dulci's again to hide her." Mila looked away. "I was the only one who knew. He trusted me… I just—"

"I have no time for your regrets, Mila. I need everything you have before that puncture in your lungs kills you. Because it's going to, and soon." Agatha crossed her arms, a pang of guilt shooting through her. Grimm would have found a way to save her, but Agatha was not inclined to forgive someone that stabbed her husband, her friend, and then stole a human being, forcing them to do her bidding.

"I developed a plan."

"How did you alter the Book of the Dead? How did you get Dulci's name in there? Pierre's even?"

"I didn't add Pierre's name. That was another in The Order."

"Who?"

"They never used names and their faces are always obscured." She shook her head, face too ashen, lips turning nearly white. "But they have a quill they use, they don't even need the actual Book in hand. It's how I knew to try it myself… I don't know where it came from, or how it works, but wars have been fought over it. Some we've never even heard of. Underground holy wars."

Agatha nearly staggered back. It was exactly what Tindle had said about the book she'd stolen from the magus, the one with the same phrase from her father's journal.

Afer mahn sur, coreg ah lur, olren fahn bre ankhur.

"They're not even documented, most of them, but the wars have gone on since the dawn of time, essentially."

"All over this quill?"

Mila nodded, eyes no longer focusing. "Or some form of it, yes. There were four separate factions that formed The Order of old, together. Something happened and they split, long ago. They've been at war ever sin—" Her words cut off and she sagged to the side. Agatha jumped to gently lay her down, blood bubbling up and dripping down the side of her mouth.

"You haven't much time," she whispered. "Where is Amira now?"

"I—I don't know. They found us. They took her."

"Why do they want her?"

"G—Grimm. They—" Her breathing was so laboured that her chest was rattling. She had moments, maybe less. "They want her to capture and wield his reaper form."

An eerie black shroud of smoke began to pour into the sanctuary from all sides. It leaked from the floor, bleeding from the ceiling and crawling toward them. Agatha stood protectively in front of Mila, knowing it was futile. She was as good as dead already. A voice came from the clouds, the faint scent of night jasmine tickling her nose. "*Agatha Joubert.*"

A gasp left her lips and she hit her knees. "Lady Death."

"Rise, child. You have nothing to fear from me, Daughter of Autumn. But you must find the quill and restore it to its rightful place." The clouds moved to hover over Mila.

"What will become of her?"

"My Daughter will return with me to the Court of Achlys to remain." A tendril came forth and caressed Mila's damp brow. "She has lived two painful lives, it would seem. I would like for her to have rest now."

Agatha's heart constricted. Such a merciful response, unlike her own.

"You do not lack mercy, Daughter of Autumn." Agatha was startled at Her insight. "You fiercely fight for my Son. I would have no one else by Thanasim's side. Ever."

Lady Death's smog encased Mila, a small breath of air, her last, escaping Mila's lips. The room cleared, the dark clouds evaporating, and Lady Death with them.

Agatha sagged against the altar, taking Mila's already chilling hand in hers. "Find peace, Mila," she whispered before transporting to her rooms.

She stripped off her bloodied clothing. Going to her Sisters was what they'd agreed upon. A council of equal parts. But all she wanted was to turn over in bed and run her hand through Grimm's hair as she recounted everything and he told her it would all be okay. That they could develop a plan and would figure it all out.

But the other side of the bed was cold.

Agatha dressed in riding pants and one of Grimm's shirts. Boots laced to her knees, she threw on her thickest cloak and pulled on the hat that changed the tide of Merveille those moons ago.

Her magic honed in on Winnie's location, and she was there in a blink, standing next to a worn tent in the middle of…a travelling troupe of performers?

Agatha looked around slowly, trying to make sense of what she was seeing. A disfigured woman walked by, twirling a baton, and a man that could have been a god fallen to earth sat mixing something over a fire. Off in the distance, the moon glowing behind it, was a large, striped tent and the faint sound of a crowd.

The cirque. Agatha could hardly believe her eyes. Had something happened to her magic? There was no way in all the realms Winnie was at a cir—

"*Agatha*?"

She spun around to find Eleanor, fresh-faced and *smiling* as she walked with a handsome young man. It was almost as alarming as Mila naked and bloody on an altar…

"What in Hades are you doing here?" she said as they approached.

"What in Hades are *you* doing here?" Agatha attempted to keep the shock from her face, but it was a lost effort.

"Winnie thought we might learn some information here, about the man in the mountain pass." Eleanor looked sidelong at the boy with her and Agatha had to blink and shake her head.

"I…alright, then. Where is Winnie?"

Eleanor pointed to a tent three over from where they stood. "She's in a mood."

"But when is she not?" The boy snorted before holding out his hand. "Tomás."

"Agatha. Winnie's Sister." Tomás' eyes bulged and he made to bow but Agatha still had his hand and yanked him up. "Please don't do that," she hissed.

"Apologies, Highn—" She glared and he smiled wide. "Right."

"If you'll excuse me, I need to face the Wrath of Winnie."

WINNIE

"Erm. Mademoiselle?"

Winnie lifted her head, too heavy for her shoulders, at the man that peeked through the opening of her tent. "What is it, Rufus?"

"There's someone here to see you. A visitor."

Winnie waved her hand flippantly and a form stepped into the shadows.

"The cirque?"

She took in her Sister Autumn, dressed like a man.

"They're well-travelled," she responded simply, voice tired. "I thought they might have information concerning the man in the Pass."

Aggie nodded, then pointed toward the camp with a bemused smile. "Are some of these the same people from when we were children?"

A sad smile formed on her lips. "Yes. They're Druids."

With a shake of her head, Aggie huffed a laugh. "I've been a fool not to realise all the folklore was grounded in truth."

Silence snuffed out the space between them, making the air stifled and uncomfortable.

"Winnie, I'm sorry…"

"Agatha, don't. It's fine. Just leave."

She watched her Sister Autumn sag, shoulders bent and a tangible weariness etched through the lines on her face. She watched as she reached for the tent flap to leave and Winnie saw the little eight-year-old girl she once knew. One morsel. She could offer one crumbling morsel of her life. A white flag. Couldn't she?

"I travelled with this cirque."

Agatha turned around slowly.

"For a very long time." Winnie could feel Agatha's anticipation in the silence, her confusion and intrigue. "It was..." She fumbled over the words. "It was my last memory. Of all of us together. So, when things became rough for me, I went to the cirque." Winnie shrugged one heavy shoulder. "One day, many, many years later, the Cirque Master from that last day together, he found me in the woods. And I left with the Druids."

Aggie regarded her with a heartache Winnie wasn't certain the source of. "Did you perform with them?"

"I did."

Aggie's lip wobbled. "I'm certain you were better than all the rest. I know you were to me."

Tears filled Winnie's eyes. "I was." She offered her a weak, damp smile.

"I'm sorry, Winnie. I'm so sorry that I didn't know."

There it was. The truth of them both. "You never tried to find me. And I didn't offer it up."

"Did Sorscha and Seleste know?"

Winnie shrugged. "Rules are rules. We weren't to be together."

Aggie shifted on her feet, the rocky dirt under her boots crunching.

"Eleanor is out there. You should have a look. You might enjoy it."

Knowing she'd been dismissed, Agatha moved to leave, but she turned back. "Winnie, when Ira died and I threw myself off that cliff, you came for me. Please, let us come for you if you need it."

The dam inside Winnie finally cracked, a tear sliding down her cheek. She nodded once to her youngest Sister and watched her leave.

Three Hundred Years Ago

This was her last chance.

Sorscha and Seleste were gone.

Any moment Sybil would arrive.

She would take Aggie.

If they ran. Right then. They might make it.

Winnie didn't know what facing an angry Goddess Three would look like. She didn't know what turning her back on being a Sister Solstice would mean. But for Aggie, she would do it. She would face it. And then she would rip the realm apart, thread by thread, until she got Sorscha and Seleste back, too.

Winnie bolted upright, running for the bags under the bed. "Aggie!" she exclaimed, skidding to a stop, nearly smacking her shins on the frame of the bed. "We're going to—"

"Run?" a bone-chilling voice sounded behind her and Winnie whirled, dropping the bags to the warped wooden floorboards.

Sybil had Aggie by a fistful of hair and one hand over her mouth. Winnie took one look at Agatha's terrified eyes and lunged. Before she made it a step, pain lanced through her chest, her limbs set aflame by an unseen force of unfathomable power and pain.

"Try it." Sybil's haggard face split into a grin made up of nightmares. "See what happens to your Sisters then." She ran her tongue across too-sharp teeth. "While you are forced to watch."

Winnie clutched her chest, clawing at the phantom beast squeezing her lungs.

Aggie tried to pull away, but Sybil yanked her hair harder and Sister Autumn cried out.

"*Take your hands off her!*" Winnie's grating cry was cut short by utter shock when Sybil disappeared, Aggie with her, crying out in terror.

Winnie crumpled to the ground in a heap, a guttural wail piercing the night.

A shadow appeared over her.

Greta had come to seal their fate like a tomb.

GRIMM

I used to collect fireflies.

In the Summer, when the days are hot and the only time it's tolerable to be out of doors, or do anything but lay around, is dusk. The breeze is still warm but it feels cool against your flushed skin. A great respite after the sweltering heat has wreaked havoc on you all day long.

The fireflies came out in the castle gardens, but they were ignored. Their twinkling brilliance was cast aside for promenades, match-making, and aristocratic connections.

It bothered me, as a boy. The disregard of glory, for the paltry.

I had made it my mission to collect as many of the fireflies as I could. To place them in a jar and watch. Give them the attention no one else gave them. Or me. And then I let them go.

Lady Death had come to me several times by then, instructing me to see the beauty of life and death. But that Summer night, it was different.

Seated cross-legged on the ground, my chin resting on my folded hands, I was entranced by the fireflies climbing an alchemy beaker I'd stolen from Professor Ludwig. Endlessly they blinked. I'd gone into the hedge maze to get away from the doe-eyed lies of the court and She met me there. Her voice bloomed like sweet nightshade against my ear.

"The time is coming, Thanasim." She wrapped a velvet-soft cloud of gloom around my hand as if holding it with Hers. "You'll soon see your true form and begin your training to collect souls."

The cloud squeezed my hand. I wasn't listening, not really, and She knew it.

"Thanasim." She followed my gaze, shifting between the flickering lights of the fireflies in my jar and those dancing out over the hedges and fountains. "What do you see?"

"I don't know. But it feels significant."

"Keep one," She whispered. And then She was gone, her dense black fog evaporating.

So I did.

My hand poised over the top of the beaker, I carried one back through the maze of hedges and then the maze of courtiers. I did not take it to my rooms. Instead, I ripped a strip of my shirt off and fitted it over the opening. I placed it alongside me in a boat at the marina, and I rowed to the lighthouse.

I watched the creature illuminate the jar, the desk, and a portion of the wall until I could no longer keep my eyes open.

Some time later, I awoke with a start. My soul somehow knew the firefly had perished. There, at the bottom of the beaker, it lay curled up on its back, never to blink its light again. Forlorn and moved beyond what I thought possible, I reached out to tap the jar, only to startle backwards at the sight of my hand. What little skin and sinew remained was rotted, my bones exposed.

I'd known it was coming; She'd said soon. But She calls all time *soon,* and I couldn't breathe. My hands trembled and one finger bone tapped the jar. The *tink* of it reverberated through the lighthouse and the firefly lit one final time. Tears welled in my eyes. And then I saw it move.

No, it was dead. Gone. I could see its lifeless form at the bottom of the glass.

A faint light blinked next to my head and I turned to see a shadow, a shade, a ghoul of the firefly. It hovered as if waiting for me. Tentatively, I reached up as its light illuminated my cheeks, and I caught my grotesque, cadaverous face in a nearby looking glass. I might have gasped, or perhaps screamed, but the firefly pulled my focus away as it landed on my skeletal finger. Waiting.

Waiting for me to collect it.

CHAPTER TWENTY

WINNIE

More than a week passed and the carnival was nearly over for the town of Vorren. Winnie had not attended, electing to keep her ear to the ground, observing and listening. She'd met with nearly every member of the troupe while Eleanor learned to wield a knife and sift secrets out of the gossip between Druids. Though Winnie had also learned interesting bits of information about the troupe she'd abandoned long ago, none of it pointed anywhere near a man in the mountain pass, and now they were preparing to pack up and head further away from the mountains altogether.

A decision to stay or leave had to be made before sunrise. Standing on the stage that used to be hers, she was no closer to the answer than the day Lydia had offered it. Like the moon orbiting their world, Laurent found her as he always did. She could sense him lingering beyond the curtain, that force of sunshine to her gloom.

Finally, he strode onto the stage, meeting her there in the middle. In their place at centre stage, as if no time had slipped by at all. He stopped a hair short of his mark, hands clasped behind his back. "We'll change course. Head Nord instead of Sud."

She did not meet his eyes, her pulse thundering at his implication. That they would change course for her.

After a moment of silence, he sighed, and all traces of his sunny disposition evaporated. "You know you will have to speak to me eventually."

"Do you have information concerning an illusive man in the mountain pass?" She watched his chest rise and fall.

"No."

"Then, no, I do not have to speak with you."

"Wendy, you've been with us nearly a fortnight. My troupe" —the words stung—"has fed you, put a tent over your head–"

Winnie laughed, cutting him off with a cold, cavernous sound. "That's where you're wrong. I've already paid Lydia for our lodging, food, and even the care of my horses. You have nothing to hold over my head."

He took one step closer. "You've snuck onto this stage every night. I've offered to change course—for *you.* The least you could do is *talk* to me."

"How many times must I declare that I have nothing to say to you?"

Hurt flashed across his face. "Do you truly hate me this much?"

Winnie barely stopped her feet from surging forward, but her lips parted before she could stop them. "I–"

"Cirque Master." They both turned toward the voice materialising from the shadows at stage left. "It's nearly time."

Laurent sent Winnie one last look of sorrow and pulled down his wooden mask to follow the boy out.

The evening had already begun in the field, with patrons frolicking, eating, and enjoying. They would have their fortunes told, marvel at the peculiar, and stand in rapt attention as Laurent Barroque led them to the grand finale—dinner in front of his stage. All the tables were already laid out and Druids rushed about, lighting candelabras and ensuring everything was perfect.

The final night of the cirque had always been her favourite. It had always been hers. Theirs.

Winnie turned and left the stage.

Alone in the tent she'd been sharing with Eleanor, bags already prepared to depart in the morn, Winnie sat on her pile of furs. Memories tugged at her left and right. Hot torches burning low at the edge of the stage, the hush of an expectant crowd, Laurent's wink just before they began, the roar of applause…

Unwittingly, her body rose and carried her to one of her packs. Before she realised what she was doing, she'd taken out her favourite gown. A luxurious thing of beauty. Forest green tulle cascading from her hips to the soles of her feet. Tight, delicate bodice patterned with reaching evergreen branches. Slender gold chains lacing up her bare chest to connect with a shoulder piece of sharp angles, a high collar, and romantic sleeves. The very gown she'd worn to every finale for seventy years. If it was to be her final finale, she wanted to do it justice by donning the gown one final time.

The camp was quiet as she walked back toward the performance tent, the sun dipping below the horizon. Everyone had already been ushered in, the sound of cutlery scraping plates and the din of excited conversation greeting her at the same time she stepped into the pool of candlelight spilling out onto fresh snow.

She was not prepared for the punch to her abdomen that came in the form of crippling nostalgia. The scent of Druid delicacies mixed with oil for the torches. The fevered anticipation of a crowd. Tangible nerves and stage fright wafting from behind the curtain from the performers, as if each finale was their first.

Winnie caught sight of Eleanor, blonde head bent close to Tomás, the boy dressed in stage makeup and the pinstripe suit he wore for his act. She was chatting with him, conversation flowing between them easily, as if she belonged there. Someone else at the table said something and they all laughed. As Winnie approached, Tomás stood and offered her his seat. "It's almost time for my act." He kissed Eleanor's hand and she blushed before he gestured to his seat for Winnie. "Please, take it."

As he scampered away backstage, warding off several swooning young ladies, Winnie reluctantly sat next to Eleanor.

"This is madness, isn't it?" She looked around the tent, wide-eyed and full of awe. So much like Winnie's Sisters that last night together. So much like Winnie for far, far too long.

A crackle and hiss sounded from the stage and the candles dimmed, several patrons crying out in surprise. To them, it was all just trickery. But Laurent was truly powerful. The stage filled with smoke and Winnie's pulse thundered in her ears.

The Cirque Master lowered his gloved hands, a hush permeating the grounds. "Before we begin, I must tell you all a little tale. A fairytale of a people once called"—he let the words dangle—"the Druids."

The smoke parted unnaturally to reveal Laurent, gloved hands splayed wide, mask in place, hat tilted to one side and a fox-headed cane dangling from his wrist.

"Baroque's meaning might be known to many as extravagance." He swung over them, coming lower and lower. "Perhaps gilded, or magnificent. Finely detailed." He came so low that a portion of the crowd had to part, his voice still echoing all around the grounds. "But that is not baroque's first meaning."

"Welcome!" he shouted, the crowd leaning forward in a synchronised wave. "Welcome to Cirque du Barroque. Where the mind is beguiled." Candles popped and sparkled all across the tent. "And wonders encroach upon you from all sides." Dancers appeared out of thin air around the tables, shrieks and stunned applause filling the tent.

He landed deftly on his feet right in front of Winnie. She locked eyes with him, realising he was much younger than she'd thought. One corner of his twisted mouth twitched up and Winnie swallowed. "Baroque," he went on, eyes fixed on her, "first meant irregularly shaped." He finally turned back to the crowd. "Deformed."

The crowd was crazed and giddy. Laurent's attention landed on Winnie. She sucked in a breath and pushed back her chair.

"Are you all right?" Eleanor reached out for her arm, but Winnie snatched it back and hurried out of the tent.

Chest tight, even the cold of the encroaching night couldn't soothe her or shake the memories loose. It was then that she remembered the hot springs near Vorren. The memories surrounding them were lush and sacred, dangerous. But she would be alone. She could think.

The stars were dusting the sky by the time she finally made it to the edge of camp. The springs were not far off, and she could still feel the crowd. Smell the cannons that had been fired. Still hear Laurent's booming voice as he charmed them all. She stayed in the treeline long enough to see the lights from afar, the fall of night her favourite moment of the cirque, and then Winnie slipped into the woods, out of her dress, and into the divine hot springs.

The frothy water seeped into her tired muscles, her worn and tattered soul. The warmth and the steam rising into the frigid air felt incomparable, but it did little to soothe her weariness. Lydia's words clattered around in her skull like a marble down the alabaster hall of her mountain home. *Stay*. Such a small word for the enormity of what it encompasses. Laurent's declaration of *change course for you*. Such an immense claim for a broken tie. Eleanor's claim that Aggie *needs you*.

Agatha was fond of reminding Winnie she was as immovable as a mountain. *Stubborn*, Sorscha would say. *Steady*, Seleste would say. *Stuck*, Aggie would say.

Aggie was right. Her version of *stay* had always meant staying the same. Stagnation.

Then, Lydia, with a simple slip of the tongue, offered up a different version. One with hope, and laced with love. Love a rotted soul like hers did not deserve. Love Laurent had squashed underfoot like the head of a serpent.

A soft hoot sounded in the snow-laden trees above her and Winnie looked up. Yula gracefully swooped down to meet her arm as it rose from the water, steam rising to greet her familiar as well. Magic wrapped around Winnie's forearm just before Yula's talons latched on.

"Hello, sweet," she cooed to the magnificent bird, running a hand down her pristinely white feathers. "What say you to the idea of travelling with the troupe again for a time?" Instead of responding, Yula flew away in a rush of wings. "That was rather rude…"

She heard the rumble of a low laugh and turned toward the sound. She would know that laugh anywhere. The one that curled her toes and set her skin on fire.

Sinking lower into the water to remain concealed, she watched Yula land on Laurent's outstretched arm, his mask gone and face beautiful. "She knows me in this form, too."

"She's always had poor taste in men."

He scratched under her beak and Yula leaned forward to nuzzle his face. "She missed me."

An ache knit together in Winnie's chest. Hot, cold, and tumultuous. "She can't miss what she never knew." It was a juvenile thing to say, but Winnie hated that mask. More than she hated the wooden one he hid behind.

Yula issued a contended hoot and flew off toward the moon. Laurent sighed, shifting into his true self. Winnie forced herself not to look away, despite the lump threatening to close her throat

"This is familiar." His lopsided face broke into a lopsided

smile and Winnie cleared her throat. "Isn't this hot spring where we—"

"Yes," Winnie cut him off. "Don't you have a cirque to go be Master of?"

Laurent looked up at the moon, then back at her, his gaze fiery. "Oh, I have a moment or two before I need to return and I don't believe we finished our discussion earlier."

The knot in her chest unfurled into a thousand fluttering moths, descending lower. She knew that look. Goddess, she'd missed that look. The only thing that ever made her cold soul burn. "Surely you haven't much time. The fire dancers will be done any moment and the trapeze will begin. Do you still return to the stage after them?"

"I do." His voice was so low, so velvety, her hips shifted beneath the water. He must have seen it, sensed it, for a spark shot across his eyes. Without warning, his magic stalked toward her through the steam, slipping beneath the calm water and wrapping around her waist. With no effort whatsoever, the magic pulled her through the hot springs toward him. The thought to stop him never fully formed within her. It couldn't. Not with that hunger in his eyes.

As she was pulled nearer the shore, the water shallow, her form was slowly revealed to him, the warm water sliding over her peaked breasts. The air was cold and Winnie made to heat herself, but Laurent was already there, his magic wrapping around her like a warm blanket. It even smelled like him and her eyes fluttered shut.

The magic set her gently down on the snow in front of him, loosening the hold, but not letting go.

"Fuck, I've missed you, Wendy," he said huskily as he drank her in.

She wanted to step forward, but she did not. "I'm sure in this many years without me, you've found plenty of bodies to keep you warm."

His magic tightened on her, wrapping around her waist like his hands, pulling her closer. She looked up at him, attempting to control her breathing. "None will ever feel as good as you."

Her throat went dry and she tried to step back, but his magic held her fast, snaking up to caress her cheek. She leaned into it, imagining the feel of his calloused hands on her.

"I meant what I said."

"And what is that?" she breathed, because her mind was growing fuzzy and she truly couldn't recall.

"I will change the course of this cirque for you. I'll change the course of everything, Wendy."

She reached up to run a finger down a coil of his power. A rumble sounded in Laurent's chest and his magic slipped down her neck, sliding down her breast. Winnie sucked in a breath and Laurent inched closer, his breath mingling with hers. The tendril of magic slid further, descending until it slipped between her legs and stroked, the feel of it so like his fingers that Winnie's knees nearly buckled.

Laurent put a hand on her waist, pulling her to him until her breasts were pushed against his chest, his magic still stroking. "Tell me you don't miss me. Miss *us*," he breathed. "And I'll walk away."

She was almost unable to stand. Any moment, she would collapse into his arms and let him ravage her the way no one else ever had. Winnie looked up into his face, her eyes heavy-lidded and his full of desire she could also feel pressing against her bare hip. She wanted him so badly. But he was her undoing. She wanted it so badly. This thing they'd had for so long. But it wasn't there anymore. Coals can burn hot long after a fire is dead.

Her lips were nearly brushing his when she said, "I don't."

His magic pulled away a blink before his hands did and he stepped back. She instantly felt cold. Hollow. Laurent said nothing as he walked away.

AGATHA

Agatha held up the freshly scrawled letters, blowing gently to dry the ink. It wasn't much information, but at least her Sisters would all know about Mila and perhaps one of them could learn what sort of peculiar power Amira had in order to give Mila a body. It was possible one of them would even know more about animancy and how it could all relate to Grimm.

She'd also seen the strange sideways numeral eight on more of the robed people the magus led Grimm toward. Not one of them spoke. She was beginning to wonder if they'd taken a vow of silence.

Her door crashed in then, and Agatha startled up, knocking the pot of ink all over her letters. "Augustus! What in the name of the goddess are you doing barging in here?"

"Have you seen her?" His chest was heaving, panic drenching every bit of his face.

"Have I seen who?" Her own heart was beginning to beat furiously.

"Anne." He ran a hand over his close-cropped hair. "I–I know I shouldn't have gone, but I had to see her."

Pulse roaring in her ears, she snapped at the guard, "You're babbling. *What happened*?"

"I don't know. She sent me a letter saying Miriam had gone missing and that Wellington had moved her into Miriam's old rooms."

Agatha's stomach soured. Miriam had been his favoured.

"I went to go check on her. It seemed odd that he would put her in such lavish rooms as she described. I didn't like it." As well he shouldn't... "But when I went, she wasn't there. I gave in and spoke to one of the servants and she told me no one had seen Wellington or Anne for a couple of days."

Agatha put a hand out toward him. "Let's not panic. Wellington is often away and it sounded to me like he often took Miriam with him. Perhaps he's now taking Anne." She heard herself say the words but they only made the sourness in her stomach worse.

"That doesn't sound any better, Agatha."

"No." She sagged. "It doesn't.

GRIMM

I cannot remember the last time I moved. This corner has a faint flicker of light. I feel that I'm supposed to know it. It's familiar, but I cannot place it. I used to collect something. I think it was fireflies, but something greater is missing. I was worried about something. What was it? That flicker looks at me, I'd swear it. I'm supposed to know it, but I don't.

WINNIE

"Again," Lydia commanded.

Eleanor threw her fist at Winnie with all her might, but it was laughable. And laugh, she did.

"Stop mocking me," the girl spat.

"Then stop being terrible. Use your hip, that is where the power lies, not your stick for an arm."

"Despite the fact that I am the one doing the training here"—Lydia shot Winnie a look before addressing Eleanor once more—"Wendolyn is correct. You need to pivot on the ball of your foot opposite your fist. Throw your weight into each jab by twisting from the hip."

Eleanor did her best to mimic Lydia's movements as she showed her, Winnie picking at the wrap wound around her hand.

"There you go." Lydia stepped back. "Again."

This time, when she threw her fist, Winnie knocked it out of the way and jabbed Eleanor in the gut. She doubled over, cursing colourfully. "Better," Winnie said, looking down at her.

"*How*?" Eleanor sputtered. "You just punched me."

Winnie shrugged. "You have to learn to take a hit, too." Lydia nodded her agreement and Eleanor spewed several more choice insults at them both.

"Oy, Joubert!" All three of them looked over at Narook striding toward them, his bulk straining against his riding leathers and apron. "Barroque says you decided to stay a bit longer." Winnie nodded. "So I made yer favourite."

A genuine smile tilted Winnie's lips. "And what is my *favourite*, Narook?"

"Lemon-herb chicken and roasted potatoes."

Winnie's stomach dropped. She had asked Narook to make that meal every year when she returned from seeing her Sisters on the Summer Solstice. "I can't believe you remember that..."

"Oy, it's nothin'. Druids live as long as your sorry witch arses." He tapped his temple with his wooden cooking spoon. "Gotta have a good memory. You three come eat first before the rest o' 'em scarf it all up." He turned to walk back toward the camp and the women followed. "Haven't had chicken in ages."

"Where did you find enough chicken to feed everyone?" Lydia asked. They hadn't been near a village in a few days.

The bulky cook shrugged. "When Cirque Master comes in with a wagon o' chickens I don' ask where he got 'em. I just start pluckin'."

Winnie looked at Lydia with a silent question and she shrugged. "Sounds like someone else wishes to celebrate your decision to stay."

She glowered at her old friend. "I didn't make this decision for him."

"Mmhmm."

ELEANOR

"Why does he want to see us?" Eleanor whispered as she followed Wendolyn to Laurent's tent. She'd been tense from the moment she'd interrupted Eleanor's knife-throwing practice with Tomás.

"I don't know."

"He probably only wants to see you–"

"You're staying with me," she ground out.

Eleanor recoiled, wondering if the Cirque Master had truly invited them both, or not. When they entered his tent and he looked confused by her presence, Eleanor had her answer. She squirmed, uncomfortable with the entire circumstance.

"What do you need?" Wendolyn crossed her arms as Laurent rose from his desk and came around to stand in front of them.

Lips in a thin line, Laurent's attention cut to Eleanor again where she stood just behind Wendolyn. "I wanted to have a word with *you*."

"Well." She flourished her hand. "Have at it."

Laurent sighed. "We'll talk later, then."

"We will talk *now*."

Laurent's jaw flexed and he shot another glance at Eleanor, discomfort sliding up her neck. "Fine." His lovely green eyes fixed on Wendolyn, Eleanor already lost to them both. "You came all this way. You've decided to stay–"

"For now."

Laurent's jaw tensed. "For now. You're even training again. Performing again."

Wendolyn's attention darted away. Performing? Was that where she snuck off to every night when Eleanor thought she was seeing Lydia or Laurent?

Laurent went on, a pained lilt to his silken voice. "We're still not even going to discuss what happened? Just pretend it never occurred?"

"There's nothing to discuss."

Eleanor moved back into the shadows, torn between enduring the awkward bite in the air to know what they were —*not*—discussing, and bolting to give them privacy. Alas, to escape through the tent's opening, she would have to walk in between them.

Laurent barked a laugh. "Nothing to discuss?" He folded his corded arms across his chest and raised his chin. "Like *fucking Hades*, Wendy. You've been here almost a moon and we've been dancing around this the entire time."

Her face remained blank, but Eleanor could see the challenge, feel the charge suspended in the air. "I will not discuss anything with you when you look like *that*." She spat the last word with enough venom that Eleanor slipped backwards another step.

Laurent's body shuddered, shifting into the deformed version. The pair of them squared off and Eleanor felt the tension crawl up her skin. "I'm just"—she pointed sheepishly at the tent opening—"going to g–"

"*Sit down*," they both commanded in unison without breaking their standoff.

"You left here in the dead of night," Laurent was saying as Eleanor folded herself into a corner of the tent, hoping to blend in, "without explanation. You just vanished."

"The fact that you need an explanation is reason enough for my leaving."

He ran a hand down the drooping side of his face. "I'm sorry, alright? I'm sorry you lost your position–"

A sharp laugh cracked out of Wendolyn, the sound so eerie it jarred Eleanor and seemed to have shaken Laurent, too. When her mocking countenance slammed shut, it twisted into something sinister. "I did not lose my position, Laurent. You gave it away." She stabbed a long fingernail into her own chest and Eleanor wondered idly how her nails never broke in travel or when she was practising combat. "I was the best this troupe had ever seen."

The best what?

"Of course you were." Laurent dared a step forward, but Wendolyn danced back and he splayed a hand—an offering. "You could make a grown man *weep*." His wistful smile sent a pang of sorrow through Eleanor.

Wendolyn nodded, her silvery-blonde head like a slow, mournful bell tolling her secret pain. "And you just gave it away," she whispered, finally breaking eye contact, her icy gaze fracturing as it landed on her toes. "All for what?" When she lifted her chin again, her eyes were clouded. "A pretty face?"

"Wendy–"

"Where is she now?" The fissures iced back over.

Eleanor swallowed a lump in her throat. She wanted to throttle this man—this beast—for what he'd done to Wendolyn.

Laurent's voice hardly carried. "Long gone."

"I told you." Wendolyn closed her eyes for a moment, then said the words again, louder, with a finger pointed at him. "*I told you*," she spat. "I told you she was dangerous. I *told you* she would lie to you. That it wouldn't last. You thought you'd give her my position and, in exchange, she'd give you everything."

"I had to, Wendy." The anguish in his eyes caught Eleanor off-guard. But not Wendolyn.

She crossed her arms, one finger *tap tapping* on her arm. "No. You didn't."

"Can't you see I did this for you? For *us*?" He shifted back into the god-like face.

Wendolyn backed up, fear crowding the planes of her face. "No," she shouted, Laurent flinching. "You did this for *you*."

Laurent bit his lip, teeth bared; shoulders rigid and one hand balled into a fist at his side. "You stand there, in your all-but-eternal beauty and you fault me for wanting mine back."

Eleanor recoiled into her pocket of shadow.

"You can't get it back, Laurent! This isn't real."

"Yes, it is," he growled, shifting in tandem. He put his hand to his broad chest, his exquisite face bent in sorrow. "Both of these forms are *me*."

Wendolyn surged forward and slapped his face so hard the sound rang in Eleanor's ears. She watched as the force garbled Laurent's glamour like a ripple through peaceful waters until it gave out entirely. "It–is–not–real. It doesn't even hold. It's not even *your* magic anymore. It's *hers*."

Eleanor looked away. Their faces were too bare. Their pain too raw. She couldn't look at it any longer.

"How can you fault me for this, Wendy?" His whisper sent a tear sliding down Eleanor's cheek and she hugged her knees. Daring a look at the ice witch, she only saw a woman whose façade had fractured irrevocably. Splintering. Melting.

"I have never known that man." Her voice was soft when she went on. "The price of your magic was your beauty, and the cost to get it back was me."

Wendolyn strode from the tent and Eleanor clambered after

her as Laurent sagged onto the edge of his desk, slumping forward.

Eleanor rushed from the tent on Wendolyn's heels.

"We're leaving," the ice witch snarled. "Now."

"Slow down, Wendolyn. You're upset."

She whirled on Eleanor, eyes mad with rage. "I'm not upset, maid. I'm *done*."

Wendolyn stormed toward their tent, Eleanor scrambling to catch up. "We need their help to find the man in the mountain pass."

"We'll find him ourselves." She threw back the tent flap and went in, the canvas slapping Eleanor in the face. "Get in here and pack your things."

Flailing with the blasted flap, Eleanor finally made it in, blood boiling. "I'm not going anywhere." Wendolyn halted, hands on her hips, and turned slowly toward her. "Grimm and Agatha sent me to find that man and I'm doing it with or without you. Our best chance is by travelling with this troupe, ears to the ground."

For a moment, she just stood there, immobile in that unnerving way of hers. Then she simply lifted one shoulder as if she could shrug Eleanor off, out of her life. "Fine. Then get out."

Teeth clenched so tightly they ached, Eleanor stormed out of the tent and set out to find Lydia. Perhaps she could talk some sense into Wendolyn.

She was halfway to the practice tent when Tomás skidded to a stop next to her, nearly slipping in the icy snow. "There you are. I've been looking everywhere for you." She scowled at him and he reared back with a huffing laugh. "What's got your knickers in a twist?"

"Wendolyn is leaving."

"What? Why?"

"Laurent."

Tomás blew out a breath and tugged at his ear. “Deep wounds there, I’m afraid. But she can’t leave. That’s why I was looking for you.” She tilted her head to the side and he went on. “One of the acrobats heard tell of a strange man who comes down the mountain every moon to set up a stall in the Lácdelle market.”

Eleanor’s eyes grew wide. “You don’t think…”

He shrugged. “She said his description was Coronoccan and some of his wares were…abnormal.”

Her eyes narrowed, nose scrunched. “Abnormal how?”

“Elixirs and alchemical conjurings. That sort of thing. He might just be your man.”

Eleanor made haste back to Wendolyn’s tent, barging in to find Lydia in a heated conversation with her. “We can’t leave,” she interrupted, not caring an iota for what Wendolyn would think about it. “We might have a chance at the man. Soon.”

Wendolyn snapped her teeth like a rabid wolf and wound her hair around one hand. She deposited it over one shoulder and it was the first time Eleanor had ever seen her look like her Sister. For an instant, she could see Agatha in her mannerisms. “What do you think you know?”

“One of the acrobats heard of a strange Coronoccan man that comes down from the mountains to Lácdelle. He sells peculiar elixirs at the market there.”

Her face suddenly soured further and Eleanor turned to see what Wendolyn’s attention had snagged on behind her. She just caught the sight of Laurent’s back as he disappeared through the tent flap and out into the night. Wendolyn tore after him, Eleanor on her heels and Lydia close behind.

Laurent, his wooden mask in place, brought a massive conch shell to his lips and Wendolyn shot forward. “What are you doing?”

His only reply was the low peal of the conch reverberating through the camp. By the time he took a breath and brought it back to his lips to blow again, all of the troupe had left their tents, coming forward.

"What are you doing?" Wendolyn whispered again, low and vicious next to him.

"Druids!" he shouted into the night. "Ready your tents. We leave at first light!"

"Where are we going?" Narook asked, nearest to him.

Laurent slid his attention to Wendolyn, his jaw tight. "Lácdelle."

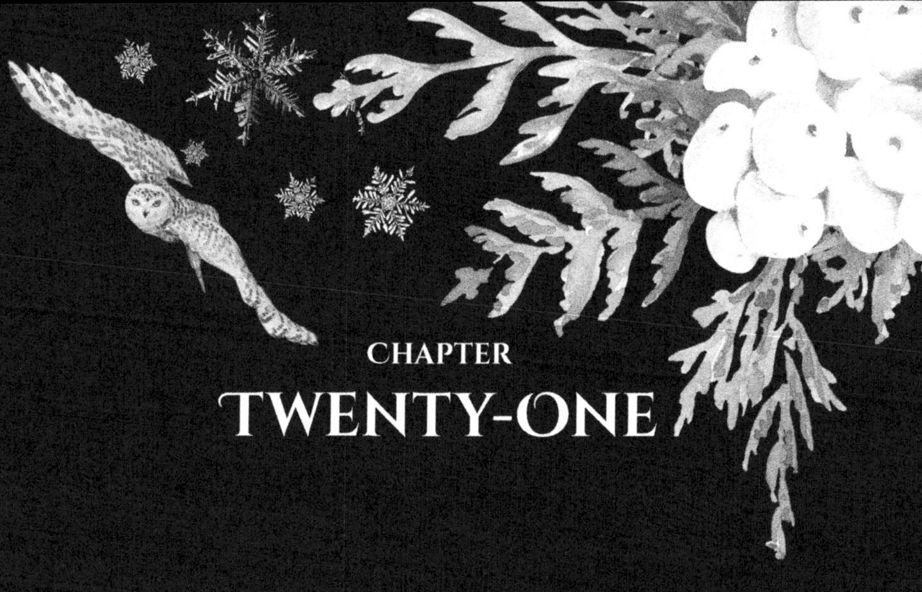

CHAPTER TWENTY-ONE

LAURENT

"I just think after changing course, we should take a night to rest."

Laurent considered Tomás' proposal as they wove through the bustling camp toward his tent. The young Knife Master was well on his way to being prepared to one day take over as Cirque Master. As the leader of the Druids. In truth, Laurent had lost count of the years he'd been leading his people and he'd long since stopped predicting when his last show would be. It could be any one of them.

In fact, that was most likely the very reason he'd instructed them all to set up for an impromptu show along their new route to Lácdelle.

But Tomás was right. The troupe needed rest.

"Alright," Laurent said, speaking up over the din of his troupe and the crunch of snow underfoot. "Tonight we rest. But tomorrow I expect messengers out spreading the word of a show in the area. We need to make coin, too."

The boy hopped up in the air and Laurent half expected him

to do a little jig. He laughed at his antics, still shaking his head as they entered his warm tent. A woman lounged on his table, and Laurent halted mid-step, a low growl forming deep in his chest. Tomás entered behind him, clearly startled by the sight of the woman, his mouth hanging open.

"Leave," Laurent hissed at Tomás.

"Laur–"

"*Leave*," he bellowed.

Thankfully, Tomás did as he was commanded, but Laurent knew he'd be waiting outside for him when this was over.

"Why are you here?"

The woman leaned back on her hands and Laurent's lip curled. He couldn't bear the thought of her scent being left on his belongings. In his tent.

She hopped down and sauntered over, looking up at him. "No charming smile for me? Why must I always receive the sour, sullen Cirque Master, while everyone else is greeted with the sun?"

"Because you're a liar and a fraud, Chresedia."

Not attractive in the common sense of the word, she was alluring and mysterious—the kind of beauty one couldn't quite place, with her dark hair and vivid green eyes, and wanted all the more for it. She shifted her hips, angling them toward his, and Laurent's fists clenched. In a movement as fluid as the sea, she reached up in an attempt to touch his contorted face. "Why wear this thing when you've been granted such beauty?"

He knew she didn't mean his mask. His magic darted forward, wrapping around her wrist just before she could lift the mask from his face.

"Oh, my," she breathed, pushing against his magic, determined to touch him.

Laurent tightened his grip on her wrist, to the point he knew was painful. She inhaled a sharp, seductive breath and he withdrew his magic in disgust, backing up. "Why are you here?"

"I missed you."

"You cannot miss that which you've never had." His pulse was too rapid. From her presence or the use of too much magic to hold her at bay, he wasn't sure.

"I heard someone very important to us both has returned."

Despite his swimming vision, Laurent took a step toward her and snarled. "Stay away from her."

She pouted. "You have always had such a soft spot for dear Wendy."

He leaned in. "That's because it will always *be* her. And never you," he ground out through clenched teeth.

Swift as a viper, her hand struck out, clamping her fingers around his wrist and pulling it toward her. "Oh, but I'll always have you in a way she never could." Laurent looked down to where she'd aligned their forearms, twin scars mocking him from their wrists. He pulled away.

"Get the fuck out of my camp."

She fluffed her hair, letting it fall down her back, hips swaying as she walked toward the entrance of his tent. "I do think I should pay her a visit," she said over her shoulder. "Don't you think?"

"If you so much as look at her, I will slaughter you in your sleep."

He hated that she looked pleased. "I'd adore seeing you try that."

Laurent ripped his mask free and smiled with none of the charm she'd been in search of. Vicious and cold, he stalked toward her, stopping close enough that she had to look up to keep eye contact where he towered over her. "It's *your* magic within me, remember?"

He just caught sight of the blood draining from her face before she bolted out of his tent.

As soon as the flap closed behind her, he turned and smashed his hand through the top of his desk. He was still cursing when

Tomás came in, eyes wide and gibberish falling out of his mouth. "Stop talking, Tomás."

"But—"

"Leave me be," he spat. His words visibly hit Tomás and he took a deep breath. "I'm sorry," he said, resting a hand on the Knife Master's shoulder. He often forgot how young the boy was. "She's a poisonous hag." Tomás snorted. "Go find a way to spend your night off, hm? I'll be fine." As soon as he made sure Wendy was fine, too.

Tomás left, blathering on about something Laurent paid no mind to. Once alone, he took three measured breaths and sent his magic out to find her.

AGATHA

Merde. For the love of the goddess, they needed to find some sort of signal Augustus could give her so she would stop having to witness him going into the lavatory through the spelled pin. Muttering curses, she looked away from the mirror, slamming the armoire shut.

A peculiar sound, like a distant waterfall, came from behind her and Agatha swung around. Her lips parted and magic danced along the lines of her palm when she was met with no less than a hundred glowing orbs of shimmering light. They blinked at her like shatters of crushed starlight and Agatha blinked right back at them in shock. Noticing her attention fixated on them in awe, the orbs swarmed around her, lifting her hair and her skirts, and brushing against her cheek. A laugh bubbled up in her chest and she couldn't bring herself to feel concerned over the strange magic, though she knew she should.

Just as she was beginning to convince herself she was under some peculiar spell, her rooms fell into shadow and smog. The lights, muffled by the fog, grew brighter—more insistent. They swarmed closer to Agatha, the sound like rushing water. When the room descended deeper into darkness, the cacophony fell away, only to be replaced by the faint chirping of birds.

"They grow restless without him," a voice, sweet as belladonna, came from the gloom.

Agatha dropped into a deep curtsy. "Lady Death."

She watched as a hand composed of shadow lifted out of the shroud of night, birds of fog and mist flitting toward the glowing orbs. "They do not wish to leave with me," She said, a few lights drifting around her fingers. Agatha could feel Her eyes on her. "They long to be with you, while they wait for my son."

There were so many… Far more than Grimm usually collected himself. This was the result of Mila's loss, then, too. "What am I to do with them?" She studied the one nearest her nose, floating peacefully as if it were merely a soap bubble. "I'm no reaper."

"You might feel that your bond has frayed, Autumn Witch, but you are tethered to my son for the ages." Lady Death cradled a light in her hand. "The souls know it."

"I still don't know what to do with them. I–I can't very well take them to the Afterlife." She searched the dark clouds for any sign of a face or body.

"I've reason to believe you have several hidden trunks in your possession."

Agatha baulked. "You want me to put souls into a steamer trunk?"

An ethereal laugh surrounded her, throaty and beautiful. "I only mean that you spell them into hiding, or they will follow you until Thanasim returns."

Agatha's heart thudded at her words as if he was gone—

away somewhere. "Is he lost, there?" she dared to ask, unsure if Lady Death even knew.

"Almost."

The smog thinned and Agatha's eyes filled with tears at the veiled sight of Her. A swath of deepest night come alive, elegance like Agatha had never witnessed. Supple, striking, and wholly feminine ferocity. Her violet eyes were impossible to look away from.

"You need only hold on, Agatha. You strive so very much. Slow down, grasp the truth, and do not let it go."

A brush of small wings touched her cheek and the fog roiled once more. "I will send a wraith for these. They seem to be soothed now that they've felt Thanasim through you. Hold onto your Prince of Bone."

Her rooms filled with warm light once more, the souls darting around wildly.

ELEANOR

"She's remarkable, isn't she?"

Eleanor startled backwards at Laurent's words as he came up behind her and she wiped a rogue tear from her cheek. "Yes." She stood upright from where she'd been leaning over the railing, hidden up in the scaffolding. "Yes, she is."

Never in her life had Eleanor heard such astounding beauty come forth from someone's voice. It was a wonder that Wendolyn wasn't famous throughout all of Midlerea for the music that issued from her lungs. It was the sort of voice that burrowed under your skin, soaked into your veins, and lived there until you took your last breath. Ethereal, otherworldly—a true *gift*.

Eleanor had discovered her the day before, so moved by her voice she'd followed her again. The comfort she felt…

"She told me she hadn't performed since she left here." Eleanor was surprised by the sadness creeping into her own voice with the words. When Wendolyn had told her that, it was nothing. A trite fact. Now…now that she knew what her performance *was*, it felt like a tragedy. A betrayal of herself.

He must have wounded Wendolyn greatly for her to leave such a voice behind. Laurent looked away and Eleanor noticed he did not wear his mask of beauty or the one that hid half of his face.

He caught her staring. "I have never listened to her sing with a mask. Not since the first time I heard her." He smiled sadly. "I didn't think I should start now."

"Lydia said you discovered her."

Laurent huffed a laugh, his eyes drifting to Wendolyn, longing etching a deep crease between his brows. "It seems that way. But it was she who discovered me. We'd just left Hiverterre, headed to Merveille. Deep in the woods one night after a show, I heard a song I just knew would end in my being devoured by a siren." He chuckled, his distorted face contorting further with a wistful smile. "I'd never heard anything like it. I pulled off my mask and let her lure me in.

"Goddess, when I saw Wendy by that stream, I thought I'd died and met Hespa Herself." He shook his head and smiled. "I was still just a boy, really, when I first saw her, and she was so young as well. We've both lived long, hard lives since then. Still, she was just as beautiful that day in the woods as the first time I'd laid eyes on her."

Eleanor started. "Wait, you'd seen her before that day?"

"Oh, yes. Many years earlier she'd come to my first show as

Cirque Master, in a small village called Drifthollow. I knew that day I was a goner."

"How did she come to travel with you?"

Laurent's eyes focused on a time far off and full of sweeter days. "As it turned out, she used to find us often and had our show memorised."

Eleanor smiled. That sounded like Winnie.

"I told her that we could use a voice like hers in our troupe. She was uh"—he shoved his hands in his pockets—"coming off a really hard time. So, she came."

"Just like that?"

His eyes crinkled at the edges. "Well, not exactly. Nothing with Wendy is ever quite so simple, is it?"

"Why did you do it, then? Give her part to someone else?"

Laurent looked down at the ground, all of his usual jovial demeanour a distant memory. "It was something I had to do."

Just then, there was a brush of sound behind them and strong hands clasped around Eleanor's waist. She shrieked and Tomás covered her mouth from behind, clutching her to his chest and chuckling. "Shhh!"

Laurent offered them both a sad smile and walked away, climbing down the ladder backstage.

Tomás released her, and Eleanor was surprised by how much her heart fell as he did so. His eyes danced with mirth. "You're spying on Wendolyn, then?"

"Not spying, really," she lied. "She'd been so damned secretive about her *performing* that I almost thought she was skinning patrons alive or something grotesque."

Tomás tipped his head back and laughed. "She'd never sully her dress for that."

"I've seen her do some horrifying things."

He climbed down the ladder first, holding up a hand to help Eleanor descend.

"Did you know she's the one who taught my father to throw knives when he was a boy?"

"She did not."

Tomás held both hands up. "On my honour. When Mami was learning every last cirque trick in the book to one day become Tent Master, I would get bored watching. She never let me participate." He smiled wide, boyish. "My father, however, received a sternly worded letter from my mum's long lost friend, when I was five, demanding he teach his boy what she'd taught him."

Eleanor snorted, disbelief etched across her face. "She wrote to the Druids over the years?"

"Only me. And that one letter to my father. She and Mami used to daydream about my parents having a child. Somehow, word reached her that the day had finally arrived, and Wendolyn was already gone." Tomás' dimple showed on his cheek as he led her away from the tent, snow crackling lightly underfoot. "I used to think of her as my fairy goddess matron. There's a right lot of wisdom in those letters she penned to me over the years."

Eleanor felt an ache bloom in her chest, the idea that the ice witch would, or even *could,* mentor a child, especially from afar...

"Come on." Tomás held out an arm and Eleanor settled her hand in the crook of his elbow. "I've not had a night off in days. What say we warm up next to the coals with Narook's famous mulled wine?"

She had to admit it sounded loads better than Wendolyn's cold presence in their tent when she was done rehearsing. The walk back through the camp was far less chilled and gruelling with Tomás heating her on one side. And inside. She felt her cheeks flush, grateful for the low light, and buried her nose in the fur of her collar. Most of the performers were already within their tents due to the cold, but more so for rest. They'd been training relentlessly as they approached the mountains. Wendolyn said they hadn't been there since she'd left the troupe fifty years prior, and Eleanor's estimation was that Laurent wanted to make a grandiose re-entry.

"How do patrons not realise you're all the same people from the cirque they saw as children and you haven't aged a day?"

Tomás nodded to a shrunken and shrivelled man huddled next to his dying fire as they passed. "Ah, well, those of us that do use our magic for performances—or life—do look quite different as time drags on. Those of us that don't"—he shrugged—"are either too hideous for the patrons to make eye contact with, or too beautiful."

Eleanor rolled her eyes and he laughed. "I thought you all prided yourself on inner worth and proving to the continent what is truly valuable about a person."

"Exactly. But that doesn't mean everyone else believes it."

"Why did Laurent do it? Why would he give up everything you all believe in, his beautiful message, for the restoration of his own beauty?"

Tomás stopped and Eleanor followed his lead. His brows were knit together in a way she'd never seen before. "I don't know what Wendolyn has told you, but Laurent is not a monster. He was dying."

Eleanor's lips parted. "Dying?"

"Yes. His magic was depleted. Gone. He used every ounce of himself to build this damned cirque and make it what it is today. By the time Wendolyn came along, he was a corpse walking. Once she began taking up with him"—he shook his head—"Laurent was as good as dead. His magic wouldn't replenish any longer. Before, it was slow, too slow, but then it just…stopped replenishing altogether."

"And his deal, with the songstress that took Winnie's place, it healed him?"

"Not exactly. His magic is still incredibly slow to replenish, but it does so now."

"She must not know…" Surely she didn't know that. How could she possibly fault the man?

Tomás shrugged. "Enough about them." He smoothed the lines from his face, slipping into his usual cheerfulness. "Wine, warmth, and good company." He took her hand and pulled her toward his tent.

LAURENT

He couldn't bring himself to leave.

Laurent made his way back toward her voice, hidden in the curtains, memories crashing in from all sides.

"LAU, THIS IS POINTLESS."

She wilted onto her chair in the middle of the stage and Laurent hopped up from house left, striding across centre stage to meet her.

"As soon as there are people in those seats, I won't be able to do this. I can't even do it with you sitting there." Wendy looked at her hands and he wasn't having it. Not this bowed woman alive with power and all the potential of a goddess.

He crouched in front of her. "Wendy, do you want *to do this?"*

Her head jolted up at that, her eyes full of ire and Laurent's pulse quickened at the sight.

"I was only making sure it is still what you want. You never have to do something you don't want to." Wendy's gaze dropped to her lap again and Laurent cursed himself for his careless

words. "With me. You never have to do something you don't want to, with me.*"*

One knuckle under her chin, he lifted her head. He let his attention search her eyes for a moment. The things she'd seen. Done. Been through. It was fucking madness. Yet, here she sat in front of him, this enigma. The most devout and the most pained, so much stolen from her.

He licked his lips and spoke. "Too many people live with their heads down and their light hidden. Your soul is too bright for that. It's entirely your own, your soul, but I'll help it any way I can."

She smiled and his heart swelled. "I'm not ordinarily so helpless."

"And you're not helpless now, nor will you ever be, Wendolyn Joubert." He stood and kissed her forehead. "I'll wait here all night, just to hear you for a moment."

AND HE TOOK his place back in her audience of one just as he had that night.

WINNIE

The last note rang out across the empty stage, whirling around the empty tent and filling her heart to overflowing. Singing the songs of her soul after being silent for so long made her wonder why she ever left.

With a deep, cleansing breath, she turned to leave the stage, only to find Laurent watching her, arms crossed and mask in hand.

"Apologies," she muttered. "I know you'll be rehearsing soon. I'm leaving."

He caught her arm as she passed, her eyes snapping to his fingers on her skin. "Stay," he said quietly, and she looked up to meet his gaze. "*You* sing tomorrow. At the next performance night."

"It's not enough time." She couldn't think of anything else to say.

Laurent smiled and her stomach fluttered. "Not enough time for you to fret about it, then."

She astounded herself by saying, "Alright."

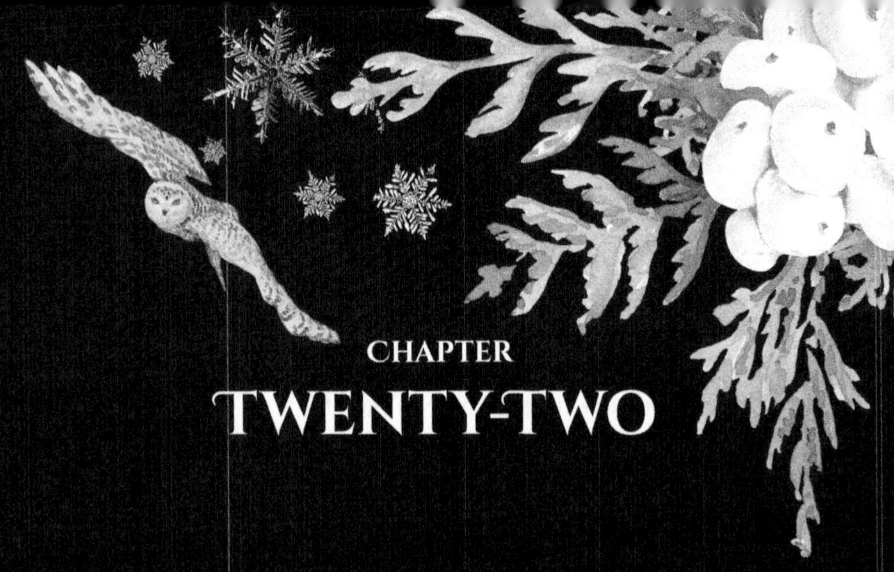

CHAPTER TWENTY-TWO

WINNIE

Winnie couldn't fathom why she'd agreed to this.

She could hear the gentle din of a crowd, anxiously awaiting the curtain to rise. She cleared her throat and smoothed her deep cobalt down, the velvet comforting. Her hair was unbound for the first time in weeks of travel and training to regain her strength as well as instilling some in Eleanor. Vaguely, she wondered where the girl would be sitting in the audience, and Winnie suddenly remembered she was on stage, about to perform for the first time in fifty years.

There was a ringing in her ears, but she just made out the sound of Laurent's voice, welcoming the audience to the finale of their performance. A dimmed cheer broke out and the curtain began to rise. With it, Winnie's nerves.

The stage lanterns came into view, the thick darkness beyond full of attentive eyes she could not see, but feel.

She couldn't do this.

Somewhere behind her, Laurent's fingers glided over the strings of his lute, encouraging her, and Winnie's breath caught.

But the melody began to set fire to her lungs and her lips parted.

She couldn't help the sway of her hips.

The melody teased her hair, it wound around her, intoxicating. The audience sat in rapt attention, a smudge of shadow beyond the glimmering edge of the stage.

Tomás beat the drums somewhere off to her side, Winnie's knees trembling against the pull of the music. She was supposed to be here alone, on this stage. Her return to the cirque. Her farewell.

She turned, against her own will, and caught Laurent's eyes. They glittered in the fire of the stage lanterns and he nodded. He knew. He knew she would walk out of this tent and soon disappear again.

Let him remember her like this. Awash in the glow of music —their music.

Winnie opened her mouth, the drums pounding in time with her thudding heartbeat. Everything else disappeared, but the notes—collecting in her chest until it burned.

One slow step forward and her voice burst forth.

She used to be wild.

Vibrant and free. A flower swaying in the wind.

Winnie could feel the crowd's awe—their collective intake of her voice—and Laurent's steadiness. His presence, his melody filling every empty space around her, drawing her voice out like a moth to a flame.

She used to dance.

Reckless abandon. A flower swaying in the wind.

Winnie moved, caught in the waves of synaesthesia. A sensation she hadn't felt in decades.

She used to be cold.

Wandering alone. Right in the midst of them all.

Laurent's music surged, the drums kicking up speed. Winnie's voice rang out.

She set fire to her meadow.

She watched it burn.

All for a shadow that wasn't real.

A lie dressed up as truth.

Winnie could feel the audience descending with her, into the depths of the lyrics. Let them wander with her. Let her voice reveal her ghosts. Laurent moved, slipping to stand next to her.

To breathe is to live. To bleed is to feel.

And she is nothing.

A ghoul in the shadow of a willow weeping.

Pillaging the wreckage, sifting for her soul.

The drums slowed, the lute's notes drawn out and melancholic. Laurent's mask shifted as he opened his mouth, his voice calling out to chase hers.

Awaken, he sang. *Rise, wild one.*

Winnie closed her eyes.

Awaken, he sang. *Rise, wild one.*

Winnie lifted her eyes to his—audience forgotten. Drums pounding.

Awaken, he sang, his gaze burning. *Rise, wild one.*

He turned to face her, one note ringing out as he removed his mask. When his hand returned to the strings, he played so beautifully it hurt. It crushed her chest and felt like the sun.

The music hit a crescendo and Winnie lifted her face to the tent's zenith.

Her voice called out from the depths of her soul—no lyrics, no words, only the sensation of breaking free. A dawn crashing through the twilight.

Laurent and Tomás felt the shift in her song, playing to meet it, the tempo rising with hope.

Lost in the dark no more, she sang. *She is found.*

There she is home. There the darkness is as light.

Winnie spread her arms wide, her notes drawn out. Laurent stamped his foot with the beat of the drums, his playing feverish, the audience stomping in unison with him. Her voice filled the tent to bursting.

She is risen. She is the light.

A fallen star. Life in the night.

The music slowed, sweet and tender.

She is wild.

She is free.

Winnie's last note rang out until well after the lute and drums stopped. A hush permeated the tent in its wake. Laurent regarded her with glistening eyes, years of ghosts etched in the lines of his face. The intoxication of the moment slipped out of her veins as quickly as it had come. The audience stood as one and roared her praise, drawing her back to reality, snapping the magic of the moment like the owl snaps up its prey.

"I'm sorry," she whispered before rushing off stage.

The crowd was still shouting her praises as she ran off into the woods. Everything within her felt raw and open, too deep and too shallow all at once. That song…he'd never sung like that. *She*'d never sung like that.

Winnie sat on a felled tree trunk, welcoming the snow beneath her. She let a coating of frost form along her palms and held them to her burning cheeks. A slow smile spread across her face. Fifty years had gone by since she'd performed publicly. And tonight had felt like coming home.

Too much like coming home.

After sitting for a good, long while, she stood and walked back toward her tent. Though she knew it was pure folly, a flicker of hope made its home inside her bosom. Perhaps things truly could be different. Perhaps she truly could be free. Perhaps she wouldn't need to run… Despite the warning bells in her head, Winnie let the idea linger, her smile along with it.

The camp was mostly deserted, everyone still cleaning up

after the finale, or passed out in their tents after another long day of performing. Fatigue was beginning to weigh on Winnie as well, especially when her tent came into view, its hot coals and mulled wine calling to her.

But inside, sitting on her bed of furs of all places, was Laurent. His wooden mask slid upward as he smiled and all Winnie's joy fell right off her face. "What are you doing in here?"

"I thought we could talk." He sat up and gestured toward a tray of hard cheeses and dried meats he must have planned ahead for. The show couldn't have ended long ago. "It isn't much, but it's our tradition, right?"

Yes, their tradition for… A jolt shot through her.

"It's our anniversary," he said, voice soft as the furs he was lounging on. Her furs.

"We don't have an anniversary anymore, Lau."

His eyes sparked at her slip of the tongue and she clamped her mouth shut. He rose and prowled toward her. "Is that so?" Slowly, he approached, all swagger and heady aura. "We'll see about that." He looked down into her face, eyes flicking to her lips.

She licked them involuntarily, her fingers itching to remove his wooden mask. To run her fingers over the blemished face of the man that meant everything to her so long ago.

He leaned in, lips grazing her ear. "I'll pour the wine," he whispered, his breath sending a shiver down her spine. Laurent stepped back and she instantly missed him. She was going to sleep like the dead after the emotional storm that had raged through her in a single night.

Winnie watched as he picked up the jug of wine, then held it in the air, looking around as if confused. "Well, fuck," he said, breaking the spell he'd held over her with his seduction, and she snorted. "I forgot wine glasses."

Before he could even open his mouth to ask, she handed him two water skins. "Will these work?"

"You doubt me?" he teased and she regarded him haughtily. "Watch and learn, non-Druid."

He held them in one hand, drawing a circle around them in the air. The water skins began to morph into stunning crystal wine glasses and he held up his fingers, then blew, a spray of magic sent out into the space around them. The fire in the brazier sent a twinkle of light reflecting onto the top of the tent like stars. Laurent followed her line of sight and spoke something to the candles. They began to dim, but then they flickered, their fire licking up abnormally high. Winnie was watching them, confused, when Laurent let out a strangled groan. She turned just as the glasses hit the ground in a shatter, and he doubled over, clutching his abdomen.

"Lau!" She lunged for him. "What's happened?"

He waved her off, trying to laugh, but his face was twisted with pain. He staggered forward and she wrapped an arm around him, using her magic like a crutch to get him to the pallet of furs. Easing him down, he groaned again. "My magic is a bit testy these days."

Winnie froze, her hands going still on the fur she was pulling up around him. "Still?" He tried to sit up more, agony sending his face into a grimace and she ripped his wooden mask off. "Laurent. How long has this been going on? Isn't this *her* magic?"

"No, no. I mean—" He broke off with another groan of pain. "I don't know how it all works. It will be fine. I just have to—" He doubled over again, lurching to one side. "Wait it out."

"It's been like this all this time?" Winnie's mind reeled. Why had she left if—

"No. It's gotten worse."

Her heart leapt into her throat. "When?"

"I suppose it's been nearly a moon."

Oh, goddess. Winnie stood, the tent spinning and Laurent's voice drowned out by a crashing wave of emotion. She knew he was shouting after her but she had to get away. She had to. Nearly tripping every other step, she made her way as quickly as possible in her current state to the outskirts of the camp, where no one would see her slip into the woods and never return.

She was almost to the hot springs when he found her.

"Dammit, Wendy!" he shouted, words halting her like a knife to the back. "You can't fucking leave every time something becomes difficult." He growled the words and she couldn't bring herself to turn around. To see the pain on his face. "*Look at me.*"

She closed her eyes. Willed herself to fill with steel and ice; to remain strong.

"*Please*," he breathed and she broke, shifting through the snow to face him. He was still clutching his side, sweat on his brow. "What about the life you have here, with the troupe?"

She let bitterness, hot and sticky—safe—fill her veins. A sneer slipped onto her lips and she saw it hit Laurent in the gut. "That life was taken from me the moment you made that deal." She had to make him believe it. She had to.

His lips parted and he moved back a step, shaking his head. "No. *No*." He pointed an accusatory finger at her across the snowy brush and broken past between them. "No, Wendolyn. You know none of this is about me, or the deal, or any of it." His words were full of so much venom, so much hate. She knew because it was clogging her senses, too. "This is all because you hate yourself."

Winnie blinked.

"You hate yourself for your heretic mother. You hate yourself for losing your Sisters. And you hate yourself for what you goddess damned *did* before I found you in those woods."

Winnie's vision was blurring. Too much. It was too much.

His voice lost its harshness, face weary with sadness and the pain that must still be plaguing him. "You think if you push away happiness, if you find a reason to leave and keep leaving, then you won't have to face it." But those words hurt worse. "One day you'll have to face it, Wendy. And all I wanted"—he put a hand to his broad chest, breathing still shallow—"was to face it with you."

But he didn't understand.

Eleanor came running through the woods toward them, shouting her name. "I heard raised voices." Laurent shook his head and turned to walk away, Eleanor huffing and looking between them.

"At least go get your things," he said over his shoulder, all bitterness dissolved into weariness. "I know you've dresses and baubles you'll not want to lose."

The last unbroken sliver of her heart cracked.

When he was out of sight, Winnie went the last few steps to the hot springs she'd planned to vanish from. Instead, she took off her clothes and waded in, Eleanor quietly waiting at the edge. The bird never waited. She always spoke her mind and made demands and stuck her nose where it didn't belong. Waiting was worse. Winnie feared it meant she was worried about her.

"Eleanor," she spoke out over the foggy water. "Be a dear and go pack our things. We're going to the mountains alone."

"Why are you doing this?" Her voice was so quiet, it almost didn't carry.

"You have no idea what you're talking about. Leave it be."

"No."

"Will you not learn?" Winnie hurled the words at her. "How many times must I tell you that I do not wish to discuss my life with an infant?"

Eleanor's lip curled. "To you, yes I am an infant. But that does not mean I have not lived and it does not mean my friendship does not matter!"

Winnie let the barb bounce right off her frigid, marble skin. "Friendship?" She tipped her head back and cackled at the moon, a deep and unsettling sound filling the fog. "I'm afraid friendship is not a luxury I am afforded, *maid*."

"Only because you're terrified."

Attention clawing its way up to Eleanor's face, Winnie considered gutting her right there. "*Of what*?"

"Everything. Everyone. Of love most of all."

Winnie smiled, cruel and unusual. "You don't know me at all."

She threw an arm out in the direction Laurent had left toward. "I know that calibre of pain and *this* calibre of bitterness can only be inflicted by a love so deep most would butcher for it."

"Why do you care, Eleanor?" She tried to sound bored.

"Because you are a different person here, with them. You can *breathe*. You sing. You'll leave all this because Laurent didn't want to be seen as a monster anymore?"

Winnie rose from the water and summoned a dry, champagne-coloured gown, far too elegant for the forest.

"You're both *fools* to think this is something as trite as what his face looks like. Laurent turned his back on everything he stood for the second he made that deal. He spent his life and mine with him proving that it is the inner workings of a man that make him worth looking at." Saying it all out loud made her nauseous. It was so childish and shallow. But it was what they needed to think. All of them.

"He loves you."

"And yet he still wears the face of the man I do not know." Goddess, she didn't *fucking* care about his face. She couldn't hold onto the charade much longer. "I told you, Eleanor, people are what they are. Even the ones who look like they're fighting for a better tomorrow will fail. They will always choose themselves. It's the banality of evil."

At least the last part was true.

"He was *dying*, Winnie." Eleanor shifted on her feet, hands splayed and eyes glossy. "He had to replenish his magic or he would die."

Something in Winnie crumbled. The broken ice of her heart tumbling down. "Do you think I don't know that?" The words barely had any sound at all. Like snow falling in a hush to the ground.

"How can you possibly be so angry with him, then? Wouldn't you rather he appear different than be dead?"

Winnie swallowed hard. Her resolve dissipating. "Laurent was dying because of me."

Eleanor baulked. "*What*?"

"He doesn't know that, Eleanor, and you can't tell him. I thought—" She ran a hand over her wet hair. But she didn't know what she thought.

"I—I don't understand. Did you hex him or something?"

Her lips pursed. "Don't be ridiculous." Everything within Winnie wilted. "The last day my Sisters and I were together, I took them to this very cirque. Once they were gone, wrenched from me forever aside from the Solstice or Equinox, I would often find the troupe every chance I got. Hide in the back and watch. It…it was a reprieve.

"I didn't know they were truly Druids for a time. Then, I began to notice they were always the same people, show after show, year after year. The Witch Trials were rampant, but I was beginning to hope the cirque troupe was a lost coven. Perhaps mine hadn't been the last full coven."

Winnie summoned her magic to dry her hair. Eleanor buried her nose in the fur lining of her coat, listening, and Winnie sent a careless wisp of magic to warm the girl.

"One Winter, when I'd already been stealing away to the cirque for over thirty years, the Grimoire Ordered me to never see the Druids again. That's how I learned what they truly were—that the tale was true. But I'd developed a particular interest in the Cirque Master. I learned it was his first show, the night my

Sisters and I went, and I couldn't stop thinking about him. I obeyed, at first. I spent a few years in a small village, but, eventually, I came back. Soon after, I had to face my Sanction. It is the highest fathomable punishment for a Sister Solstice. Issued for disobedience.

Eleanor's intense gaze was pitying, and Winnie looked away.

"It was excruciating. When it was over, I had no will to live. But I heard at a market that the cirque was coming, and I thought—the worst has happened to me, I will go. That night, after, Laurent found me in the woods. I travelled with them for seventy years, only leaving to meet with my Sisters and execute my Orders.

"One day, the Grimoire said something else disturbing. That Laurent would die, because of me. I tried to leave, but I loved him too much." Winnie turned away, shame painting her cheeks. "Then, he began getting sick. His magic was depleting…."

"Because you defied your Orders not to return to the Cirque."

Winnie nodded. "He's worsening. It's happening again because I'm here."

Eleanor was silent for a long moment. "Well, then. Let's go pack our things."

LAURENT

It came out of nowhere.

Narook was saying something about a bowl of soup, holding it in Laurent's face, but it was drowned out, blurred by the sound consuming his senses.

"Oy, Barroque, take the damn bowl. There's more men behind ye'"

Laurent pushed the food away from him, some of it slopping onto the ground, and bumped into the tired performer behind him.

"Ay!" Narook looked down at his toils wasted, seeping into the grass.

"Silence." Laurent's husky voice hardly carried, but everyone nearby the campfire fell silent, watching him. But they were the furthest thing from his mind. As still as he could possibly be, he listened, eyes roving the treeline in the distance.

"Barroque." Lydia came up next to him, voice quiet. "What is it?"

He didn't answer. There was a coolness lacing the warm Summer breeze. Familiar. It was so familiar.

He was moving toward the trees before he realised his feet had carried him away from the fireside. Behind him, Lydia was shouting his name, Narook and a few others in a frenzy. If he sensed a threat, they would go into near madness to protect the camp. He should've turned to tell them it was all right, but he couldn't stop.

The dying light was even murkier in the woods, fog clinging to the trees. Still, he let it lead him—the sound. Deeper into the woods he ventured like a captive. Somewhere in the back of his mind, he knew he'd meet his end when he found the source of the sound. A melody, a voice so beautiful that it seeped within him, down to his marrow.

Deeper, deeper it led him.

Lost, lost in the woods.

But it felt like a journey impossible to refuse.

The moon glinted silver off the lake and his breath caught, ragged in his throat. He ripped his mask free, desperate to miss nothing.

Her hair was the hue of the moon, her voice the sweetest

nectar. He watched in awe as her back stiffened, his presence registering, and her melody fell away. Slowly, she turned to face him.

The face he'd thought of every night since the first he'd laid eyes upon it.

"It's you." He moved toward her, unable to stop himself.

"And who might that be?"

Proud, proud. He knew she'd be proud, with the cut of her jaw and the gleam of purity and pain in her eyes. How long had he waited to hear her speak?

He leaned against the trunk of a nearby tree, letting the mask of nonchalance take the place of his wooden one. "You tell me. You're the one who's attended three hundred and thirteen performances over the last hundred and fifty-some-odd years." Her eyes softened and he smiled.

She looked away, but he didn't let his face falter. When her attention landed on him again, her chin was lifted once more. "You've not aged."

"Neither have you."

"You're truly Druids."

Laurent nodded, amused.

"It's fascinating you're real."

Shifting his weight, he crossed his arms, shoulders squared and grin wholly genuine. "We've been nothing more than a mode of study for you these years, then?"

Her lips curved, just enough. "More or less."

Fuck, he was doomed.

"What is your name?" The words flew out of his mouth unbidden. His heart pounded, pulse loud in his ears.

"Wendolyn."

It was like a kick to the teeth, hearing her name. Every night for over a century and a half, when he looked out into the crowd for her, he'd thought of this moment. Of learning her name.

His imagination had well and truly failed him. His fantasies had been nothing compared to this.

He pushed off the tree. "Stay," he said before he knew he was speaking again.

One of her eyebrows lifted. She looked like a damned goddess in that flowing white gown. An apparition. A dream. "That's rather presumptuous of you."

"Stay the night in our camp." Her eyes were still on him, but her face had turned away, ever so slightly. He stepped toward her. "The grande finale is tomorrow night and, if I'm not mistaken, you've somehow managed never to see a grande finale before."

A beat of silence. Two. Three.

"Alright."

CHAPTER TWENTY-THREE

AGATHA

A flute of champagne halfway to her mouth, Agatha felt more than heard someone come up behind them. Grimm stiffened next to her, clueing her in that it was the magus or some minion of his. Not that he'd seen anyone approaching, either, but the disgusting draught coursing through his veins had him eerily in tune with the magus.

"Good evening," von Fuchs' snide voice sounded at her ear, in between her and her imposter of a husband. At present, she was numb to him.

"And to you, Grand Magus."

Grimm sat rod straight until the magus turned to him. Then, his body melted into a languid state, reclining with an easy smile on his face. It was so close to the mask he used to wear when she'd first arrived in Merveille that the champagne curdled in her stomach.

"Isn't it just lovely to have our old Prince Grimm back?"

The magus walked away, and Tindle leaned into her side, opposite Grimm. "Chin up, darling. It's almost over."

She didn't know if he meant the dinner or this dreadful plan they'd enacted, but it didn't matter. None of it was ending soon enough. They weren't any closer to uncovering *who* anyone else within The Order was aside from the magus, and no more information about Amira had turned up whatsoever. And the mysterious quill of immeasurable power? Forget it.

In truth, Agatha didn't give two screaming banshees about any of it and loathed herself for it. She needed her tumult emotions to go to Hades because the classism and oppression hadn't stopped, and she was too damn old to let her personal issues cloud her judgement.

The empress of an entire nation was missing. Some fractured group of narcissistic control mongers were starting underground wars over a goddess damned *quill*.

But, the fading of her bond with Grimm was fracturing *her*. She didn't know how much more she could take. Each day he was farther away, but his face, his voice…they remained the same and it made the wound cut that much deeper.

All evening, she'd chanted the same thing in her head. *Get this over with, go hide in your rooms. Get this over with, go hide in your rooms.* She hadn't even cared when Tindle brought in three new gowns for her to choose from—ones that he planned to put up in his shop. What did a dress matter when she'd all but lost Grimm and she still had no idea where Anne was?

Grass is green. Marble, sturdy and strong, is beneath my boots. But Agatha couldn't stop the descent. It was too steep. She needed Mabon. Or an elixir. She shoved her hand into her pocket, thumbing her lepidolite crystal. Servants walked in, beginning to pass out plates of dessert—a *meringue* by the looks of it. It would be over soon and she could lock herself in her rooms. Or go to Tindle's, perhaps. It was harder and harder to be with Grimm at all.

"Could I stay with you again tonight?" she whispered to the dressmaker.

His mouth turned down at the corners, eyes forlorn, but he nodded. "Of course."

"Princess Agatha," a voice across the table drew her attention. A woman she'd seen several times before but had never caught her name. She must have seen the lack of recognition on her face, because she looked down at her plate quickly, a blush colouring her cheeks. "Lady Eldridge, Your Highness."

"It's a pleasure to properly make your acquaintance at long last, Lady Eldridge."

"And yours, Your Grace." She smiled prettily, those around them pretending to be enjoying their dessert and not eavesdropping. Every conversation at court was an open carcass to pick clean and then feed to the rumour mill—and they all knew it.

"I wanted to personally offer my thanks for the work you're doing in our kingdom." Lady Eldridge gestured to her gown. It was the expensive version of Agatha's deep evergreen dress she wore to the Hearthmas dinner a fortnight prior. "I am not fond of bright colours, you see, and I'm even less fond of the mistreatment of others."

Agatha began to respond, a flicker of hope finally sparking inside of her after such a void as of late, but a laugh bubbled up out of Grimm, mocking and cold. It cracked through the air, the entire dining hall turning in their direction.

"As if," he spoke loudly, clearly, "a line of dresses could change the course of a kingdom." He looked sidelong at Agatha, down his nose at her and she gritted her teeth. She wasn't sure if it was rage or hurt flooding her, but she was close to snapping. He kept his voice loud, too loud. "This is precisely why a *king* sits on the throne, ruling a kingdom. Pretty dresses and frivolity should be kept where they belong—a pointless means of prettying up a dull mind."

Hands overheating, Agatha pushed back her chair, relishing

the horrendous screech it made across the marble. She threw her napkin down onto the table in front of Grimm and stormed out of the silent, gawking room.

Out in the hall, she gathered her skirts in her hands and bolted for her rooms, Tindle close on her heels and Augustus calling after her, nearly breaking his cover.

WINNIE

They'd been gone from the troupe for two days' time, but the snow was becoming too thick to see through as they rode. The girl had been nearly silent the entire time. No demands. No irritating chatter. No arguing with Winnie over pointless things. She'd finally given Winnie what she wanted, but it wasn't peaceful silence at all. It was unnerving and full of sorrow that Winnie didn't understand.

They'd holed up in a small cave off the road and the delay had Winnie anxious. She pulled her hood low over her brow and headed for the cave mouth.

Eleanor stirred from her nap, rising with her eyes squinted against the light of the fire. "Where are you going?" she croaked.

"I need some air."

"We're outdoors."

"We're in a dank cave."

She walked out into the night, ice and snow stinging her face. Even that did little to calm her nerves.

You're always anxious, Sorscha would say. *Try and relax*, Seleste would say. Winnie stopped in her tracks. She realised she had no idea what *Aggie* would say to her at present. Standing there, dumbfounded in the middle of a blizzard, eyes blurring from the cold, Winnie decided she wanted to ask Aggie. In person.

But she couldn't. It was wrong. She would be punished.

Her heart hammered against her ribs, more than it did when she took a life, or Laurent's lips neared hers. No, this was the lung-crushing, cold, chilling terror seeping into her veins kind. The fear that entered her blood at the thought of disobedience.

Struggling to breathe, Winnie staggered further from the cave and into the tree line. Gulping great breaths that did nothing to properly fill her, she sank onto her knees, the cold biting through her wool skirts. She clutched at her chest, memories of Sybil's painful magic coating her lungs like smoke. Her Orders shifting from simple—helpful—to heinous in Talan's hand and back to peaceful, but in Belfry or Monarch or Hissa's.

The horrifying, soul-wrenching thing she'd been Ordered to do as her Sanction…

Winnie pressed her palms hard into her eyes, willing the hot tears collecting there not to spill.

"There is no more Grimoire," she whispered to herself in the moonlight. But the Grimoire had been Hespa's Book. Who was to say She would not enact vengeance for any disobedience, just like Greta had taught as doctrine? Just like the goddess had that day.

A sob erupted from her chest.

That day. *That day*.

Winnie vomited into the swirling snow.

All the contents in her stomach retched up, she tried to stand, but her limbs were too hollow. Too heavy. Too unsteady. She told herself she'd already faced her Sanction. It was the worst the goddess could do to her. The ultimate punishment for disobedience. *That day*. That day she faced the greatest pain she could ever fathom. That day, the goddess ripped her heart from her chest and left a rotted corpse to walk the realm.

There was no logic in this terror coursing through her—she

knew that. Nothing could ever compare to that day. No disobedience or rule broken could cause a pain worse than the one she'd already faced.

She'd already been with her Sisters outside the Solstice. They'd been together and let their magic work together. But she knew it was not the act itself causing her terror.

It was the fear of punishment.

None of the thoughts, no matter how truthful, calmed the waves crashing over her as they filled her lungs where air should be.

Like the time she pulled Aggie, dead, from the sea.

Winnie ripped at her hair, sweat breaking out across her forehead and sliding down her back despite the glacial wind. Still gasping for breath, she clawed forward. Like she'd clawed at Greta that day the First Sisters took hers away.

Her vision began to blur at the edges, blacken. Like the walls of their home as her father shoved journals in her hands, her Sisters weeping, clutching her skirt, and fire consumed everything, everything.

"*Be brave, my lily rose*," he'd whispered before he transported them to Drifthollow. Without him. Without anyone.

The world was closing in on her and she slumped forward, her cheek in the snow. As her lids closed, she felt a glowing presence next to her. It whispered something and she woke, gasping in Agatha's rooms within Castle Merveille.

"Breathe!" Aggie commanded, crouching over her with wild, fearful eyes. "Dammit! *Breathe*, Winnie!"

She was trying, she was trying. But the air wouldn't go in.

"Are you injured?" Aggie was searching her, frantic hands touching her face, her chest, and every inch of her. Winnie managed a shake of her head, her own eyes wide, breast heaving, the ache so deep. *So deep.* It had never been this bad before, the spiral.

Aggie's face registered something and her mouth fell open.

"Oh, Winnie." Her eyes filled with tears and she settled. She suddenly looked so calm, like when she was four and Winnie used to sing to her.

But now Winnie was making horrifying, garbled sounds because her chest was caving in.

Aggie took her trembling, cold hands into her strong, warm ones. "Winnie." Her voice was so tender. She hadn't spoken to Winnie with tenderness since the day Sybil took her.

The ache went somehow deeper. She was going to die. Right there on her Sister's floor in a castle full of strangers. She couldn't die with Aggie as a stranger, too.

"Winnie," she said again, even sweeter. "Breathe. Like this."

She lifted Winnie's hands, cupping them together like she would dip them into a pool of water for a drink. Carefully, she held them together and brought them to Winnie's face, covering her mouth and nose with them. Eyes wide, Winnie tried to scoot away.

"Shh, shh. You're safe," she cooed. "Breathe." She held Winnie's own hands over her face, keeping them flush against her skin. "Ride the wave. It will end. Just breathe."

Slowly, her breaths began to even out, the air finally making its way into her lungs and her body's convulsions slowly ceasing.

"Think of something green." Aggie waited for a beat. "Wiggle your feet and focus on the feel of the movement." She waited for another beat as Winnie obeyed. "Fix your eyes on a spot on the ceiling and feel the firm ground beneath your back."

The cold sweat dried on her skin, her eyes clear and crisp again.

Aggie let go of her hands and smiled weakly. "They happen to me, too." Mabon flew in then, headed for Agatha's shoulder. Instead, he changed course and landed on Winnie's chest. "Mabon can sense panic attacks." The slight pressure sent the rest of the episode skittering away.

"I'm sorry," Winnie croaked. Agatha waved her off and stood to pour a glass of water. As she did, Winnie stood shakily, holding Mabon against her. "Can I train Yula to do this?"

"Of course. I can help you if you'd like." She handed Winnie the glass of water.

Winnie took a small sip, watching her Sister. No brimstone was falling over their heads. No tidal wave crashing through the castle walls.

No, her Sister simply stood there, flesh and blood and magic wrapped up in an elegant evening gown. "Oh! You were going somewhere." Winnie urged Mabon to fly away and set the glass of water down. "I'll go."

"No, please don't." Agatha sat on the chaise, the fire glinting in her honey eyes. "I actually just left somewhere."

Something was wrong. "Aggie, are you all right?"

She looked at her hands, fiddling with her thumbnail. "No." As she closed her eyes, a tear slid down her cheek, kissing her freckles. "I know we need Grimm to take this draught, but he's —" Aggie broke off and Winnie came forward.

"Has he hurt you?"

"No." Aggie huffed a tearful laugh. "Nothing like that. He's gone further and further away in our bond, lost to the draught's effects, and he's so cold. Unfeeling. I know the things he says to me are the magus talking, or The Order, or whoever blasted started this damned mess, but it still stings."

Winnie took her chin in her hand and made Aggie look at her. "Do you remember your wedding night, when I came to see you?"

"When you were almost ripped apart by Lady Death's birds in the Netherrealm?"

Winnie glowered at her. "You are tougher stock than this, Aggie."

Her Sister's brows knit in the middle. "Eleanor told me the very same thing on the night of the Eve of Hallows ball when the castle was attacked. I hate this." She threw her hands up in the air like a child, letting them fall to her lap limply.

Winnie looked impressed. "That maid isn't quite as daft as I thought, then. My point is that you know your reaper prince. You know this is not him. You still have the bond in some manner, yes?"

Aggie nodded. "It's so faint, though. Too faint. That's what worries me. I'm terrified Grimm is almost gone. Nearly snuffed out by the power of this magic. It's consuming him."

Winnie thought hard. They did need to know what the reaper could find out, but there had to be a limit. Aggie was too stubborn to pull the plug, though. "Who is collecting souls while Grimm is…away?"

"Lady Death has sent handmaidens to replace Mila, but many of the souls have flocked to me. I've been coordinating with the wraiths the best I can."

"Shouldn't the proper hand deliver them unto Lady Death? Perhaps it's time to return him to his duties and find another way to flush out The Order."

Agatha scowled at her. "You're just trying to protect me."

Her words hit them both square in the jaw at the same moment. Perhaps they would not remain strangers after all. How odd it was that someone could say a few simple words and change the course of everything. "Can you blame me? I don't like to see you hurt."

Agatha smiled weakly. "He'll be in soon. I hope."

Winnie stood and kissed the top of her Sister's head as she did when Aggie was a child. "Pull the plug, Aggie. Let all of this drain away. Your bond is more important than anything he could uncover."

In a blink, Winnie was back in the frozen woods outside a cave.

It's all right to not be all right, Aggie would say.

Winnie's eyes narrowed, studying Eleanor as she splattered

blood all over the floor of the cave and her powder blue dress attempting to skin a squirrel. "You're mutilating it. There won't be any meat left."

Eleanor ignored her, concentrating on her task with clenched teeth.

"I can take care of that for you," Winnie said, voice bored.

"No," Eleanor ground out. "I want to learn how to do this."

For several more moments, Winnie watched her. It had been a very long time since she'd attempted to decipher another's emotions with effort. If it wasn't obvious, she didn't have time for it. People were such a tangle of things they *felt*. That was precisely why Winnie shoved everything away.

Boring, Sorscha would say. *Not healthy*, Seleste would say. Winnie paused, watching Eleanor and thinking about her youngest Sister. *Face your feelings,* Aggie would say.

Winnie sighed. The girl was sad. She continued to observe her for some time, trying to decipher why. She'd formed a sort of friendship with Tomás, but Eleanor didn't seem the type to mope over a boy. Winnie snorted to herself. A grown Druid who *acts* like a boy.

She hadn't wanted to leave any of them, had she? Yet she did. For Winnie. Perhaps only for the reaper and Aggie. But it didn't matter why she'd done it. She had, and now the girl was morose.

"Put the knife down."

"No."

Closing her eyes, Winnie took a deep breath. "Eleanor, put the knife down. I'm going to show you something."

She regarded Winnie warily, but she set the knife and the mutilated squirrel corpse on the bloody ground and stood. Winnie summoned a clean cloth and tossed it at her. "What is it?" she asked, wiping her hands with little to show for it. It was no matter, the lifeblood would help in this case. A piece of nature.

"Hold out your hand."

Eleanor blinked at her.

"Hold out your hand, you stubborn mule."

With an over-dramatic sigh, she did.

"Repeat after me. *Faire apparaître*."

"What is this? What are you doing?"

"My goddess, would you just cooperate? *Faire apparaître."*

"Faire apparaître." Nothing happened.

"Again."

"Faire apparaître." Still nothing.

"You don't need to try so hard, dove."

Winnie looked up at her mother, frustration coating her vision. They'd spent days trying to coax her magic into revealing itself. Still, her hand sat empty.

"Let down your battlements, Winnie." Her mother was so beautiful. Everyone said she was her spitting image, but Winnie couldn't see it. Her mother was like a goddess compared to her. She had the patience of a saint, whereas Winnie was always angry and easily irritated.

Her belly was swollen. It would be a matter of days before another babe joined Winnie and Sorscha, and Winnie reached up to place her hand there. Her mother smiled down at her. Winnie closed her eyes and focused, hoping the babe would kick her hand. The world stilled, her frustration cast off in the wind.

"Try it now," her mother whispered.

"Faire apparaître."

Her mother's belly glowed white, the light shining through Winnie's hand, making it turn pink. She gasped and pulled away, afraid she'd hurt her mother, but she was smiling from ear to ear. "You've done it, dove. Look."

Winnie followed her mother's gaze to her hand. A glowing orb of magic shone like the full moon in her palm, bits of ice crystals floating off to melt in the sunlight.

"Well done, my sweet." There were tears in her mother's eyes as she crouched in front of Winnie. "I am so proud of you, my precious snow witch."

"Lorelai."

Both their attention was drawn away to her father's voice and the magic dissipated. Her mother's face fell when she took in her husband's stricken countenance. "What is it, Ambrose? Is Sorscha hurt?"

"Your missing journals... It appears someone stole them."

Winnie watched her fair mother go cadaver pale. "What do you mean?"

"They've ended up in the hands of The Order. One of them has come to see you."

Something sharp passed over her mother's face before it altered, slipping back into the one Winnie knew. Her source of comfort, love, and peace. "Winnie"—she knelt to her eye level once more—"take Sorscha to play in the stream, will you?" She smiled, but her eyes looked...wrong. Afraid. "Run along, dove."

"RELAX, Eleanor. Think of the most peaceful moment in your life."

"Is this magic?"

Winnie frowned. "You're not *this* daft, maid. Keep up."

"I don't understand."

"Your gran promised your mother she wouldn't teach you

magic. I made no such promise. Now *seek peace* and say it again."

"My mother what? But I'm not a witch."

"The same blood runs in your veins, does it not?"

Eleanor huffed, eyes darting around before she started to fidget. Winnie crossed her arms, finger tapping, waiting. Finally, Eleanor shook herself like a dog coming out of the water. "Alright." She held out one hand, breathing in through her nose and out her mouth. A gentle, serene air descended upon her.

"*Faire apparaître.*"

Eleanor gasped as a pale, glowing blue bird, the colour of her eyes, fluttered in her palm.

Winnie smiled to herself. "Fitting."

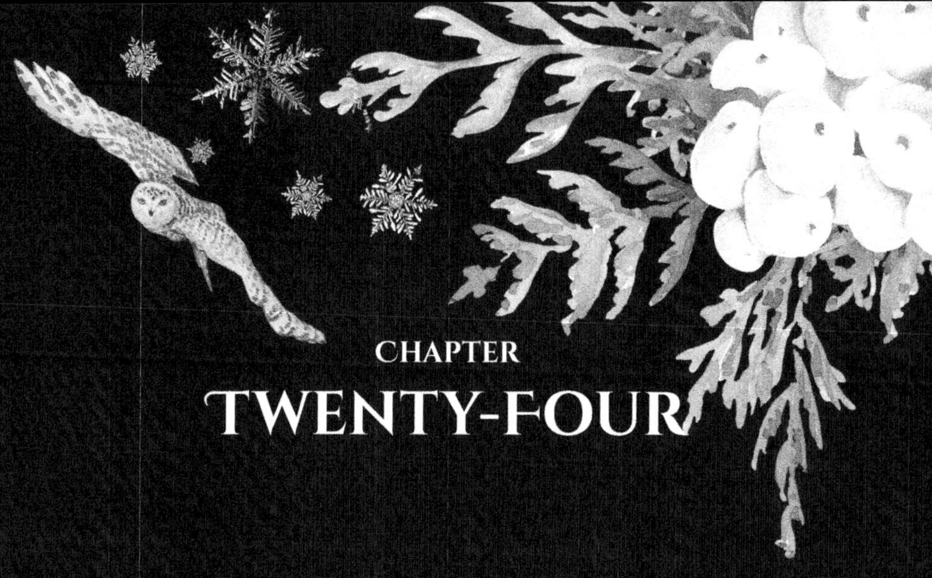

CHAPTER TWENTY-FOUR

AGATHA

Castle Merveille was a flurry of chaos. Guards ran rampant around the corridors, barking orders and warning hysterical courtiers to stay in their rooms. At first, Agatha thought there had been another attack on the castle as there had been on the Eve of Hallows, but she soon learned through their hurried shouts that their terror stemmed from something else.

"*Princess*." Someone came up behind her and she turned to find Augustus, his face stern. "What are you doing in the halls?"

"I heard shouting…"

"Get back to your rooms immediately, Highness. It's not safe." He began herding her back to her rooms and she smacked at him.

"Slow down. I don't understand what's happened."

Two servants passed by them, one dabbing at her eyes with her crisp linen apron and the other giving Agatha a half-hearted bow, his brow pulled low in anger.

"*Augustus*," she whispered.

"Get in your rooms." He opened her door, looking up and down the corridor as he shoved her inside.

"What's happened?" she snapped. His face paled and she knew. "It's Grimm, isn't it?"

Augustus shot one more glance down the corridor and rushed into her rooms, slamming the door behind him. "The magus is trying Grimm for treason."

Heat shot across her palms. "He *what*?" she snarled through clenched teeth. It didn't make sense. The magus was so proud of his puppet not two hours prior at dinner.

"It all happened so fast…" Augustus began pacing, rubbing at the back of his neck. "When the dinner ended, Grimm was asked to go with the magus to a meeting of the elders," he stuttered. "One of them in the Sanctuary—a woman—the one that was arguing with another that first day I was allowed in… She's not been at the meetings for a while, but when she came tonight, she was irate that Grimm had disobeyed his orders. She said it's not possible on the draught, to push back like that. Not since they changed the formula after the defiances you insisted on last Autumn."

"I still don't understand. What order did Grimm defy?" She hadn't seen everything that happened with him whilst on the draught, of course, but Augustus had been there for most of it and she'd seen nothing through the spelled brooch that was treasonous of him.

"Mila," Augustus stammered.

Agatha shook her head. "He killed Mila a fortnight ago…"

"But he did not torture her."

Her heart lodged in her throat. The magus had indeed given him specific instructions to do so. "*Merde*. He did resist, didn't he?" *Gods*, they were in trouble. "When is the trial?"

"Tomorrow." The guard took up pacing again. "If he's found guilty, they'll hang him."

And the king and queen were fucking useless at present.

"*Merde*!" Agatha growled again. "Augustus, find him. Make sure he's okay. I need to go to my Sisters."

With a curt nod, he grabbed the doorknob and made to pull the door open, but Agatha pushed against it, locking eyes with him. "Be careful what you say, but please let him know we won't let this happen."

"You have my word."

"WHAT'S THE PLAN HERE, AGGIE?"

She didn't answer Seleste. Agatha just stood there, hidden in a bubble of magic, staring at the glum building and the barren, snowy land. It was unnerving, that something as innocuous as a shack of a storeroom could house a thing so damning as the draught. Looking at it, toes long grown numb in her boots and little puffs of breath clouding her view, Agatha could only see the vacancy in Grimm's eyes. Feel it, digging out a corner of her soul, scraping away at their bond like the inside of a pumpkin meant for a lantern.

The malevolence she'd first encountered, standing alongside Sorscha and battling the sinister thread of magic, was worming its way into Grimm, despite his ability to fight against it for a moment. Agatha could almost taste the diseased magic on the back of her tongue. And it was only tangible because of her entanglement with Grimm. What he was facing, in the recesses of his mind—what this vile thing was corrupting in him.... A dull roar began at the back of her skull, seeping forward and blooming across her eye sockets in a sea of red.

"We burn it to the ground."

"Yes!" Sorscha cheered at the same moment Seleste censured, "No."

Agatha's murderous attention snapped to Sister Summer, her ears ringing with the siren song of violence. "He's facing a trial for *treason*, Seleste. We need a distraction. What better one than this? Killing two birds with one stone."

"Aggie..."

Agatha put a hand to her bosom, heart thundering underneath her palm. "I can *feel* what it's doing. And he's a *reaper* for goddess' sake. Imagine what it's doing to the others. To the helpless. They're just going to continue to invade—lands, minds, and willpower—until they have it all. And try anyone for treason who stands in their way."

"That is true. My qualm is not with the distraction itself but with the timing. We need to understand why they're doing this and who this mysterious woman is. They answer to her, it sounds like."

"The Order wants Grimm dead." Sorscha flourished a hand as if it were the most obvious thing in the realm. "And hanging him is the perfect excuse."

"We don't know that they want him dead."

Sorscha made a face and Agatha jumped back in. "What *do* we know then, Seleste?"

"That The Order has Grimm's blood." She ticked it off on a finger, raising another. "We know they want to harness his reaper form. And we know Grimm *is* powerful. It's likely your study on animancy and the scope of Grimm's capabilities was not fruitless if he's fought back enough to defy even a portion of a draught-induced command. I'm certain they do not want him dead." Seleste's didactic tone melted into that of compassion. "I know this is frightening, Aggie. But we must learn what it is they want to use his reaper form *for*. Sorscha is partially right, finding him guilty of treason and hanging him will provide the perfect alibi. But what if The Order merely plans to make it *look* like he's hanged, so they can make him disappear for their own reasons?"

"Fuck." Sorscha blew out a breath.

Agatha met her Sister Summer's eyes, her own filling with hot tears of anger. "Even if that's true, I have to do *something*, Sister. I have to do something to keep him from that noose, a ploy or not."

Seleste's tender attention settled on Agatha for a long moment before she sighed. "Alright."

Sorscha bounced next to them, magic already crackling off of her fingers in red sparks.

"Wait." Seleste lashed a hand out to shove Sorscha's down. "There are people in there."

"Yes." Sorscha put a hand on her hip, magic swirling around her. "The *enemy*."

"They're still people." Agatha's voice sounded spent, even to her own ears. "They could be just as controlled as Grimm is."

Sorscha looked up at the night sky and groaned. "Fine. At least let me have the fun, then."

"There won't be many of them. It's the middle of the night," Agatha said.

"I'll handle them," Sorscha declared.

"What are you going to do?"

But Agatha already knew the answer by the sly glint in Sorscha's eye. When a grin came to match it, Seleste frowned.

"Come now, they're magi or temple clerics, they're not *dead*." She shrugged one shoulder. "They might just thank me." Before either of them could respond, Sorscha was gone.

"What do you think she'll do?"

Seleste adjusted her cloak. "Lure them out is my estimation."

Agatha made a face at her Sister. "You know as well as I that holy men cannot be *tempted*."

Seleste snorted. "We should have summoned Winnie."

"I did. She ignored it again." The ache in Agatha's chest as she said the words penetrated much deeper than she thought it could. After Winnie came to her, Agatha thought things would be different. She supposed it wasn't that people couldn't change, it was that *Winnie* couldn't. But she still found herself wanting to believe Winnie was merely still dealing with the after-effects of her anxiety. Agatha knew all too well the bone-deep exhaustion that followed a wave that forceful.

Sorscha appeared again in their invisible portion of the snow, her stomach covered in blood and something furry dangling from her hand.

"Did you kill that innocent fox?" Agatha accused.

"Foxes are sly, devious, and quite cruel to one another." Sorscha pointed her bloodied fingernail at the storehouse. "Just like those bastards in there." She handed the dead fox to Seleste. "Hold this." Shirking her elaborate red coat, she tossed it at Agatha before ripping her dress from collar to stomach and smearing some of the blood up onto her cleavage.

"*Merde*, Sorscha," Seleste muttered.

The magic around them rippled like a soap bubble as Sorscha pushed through, clutching her abdomen and stumbling in the snow. As she neared the front entrance, she began to cry out for help.

"Do you think this will really work?" Seleste's face was torn halfway between wonder and horror as she watched Sorscha pound on the door.

It opened and three cloaked men spilled out with the light. "Won't they just take her *inside*?"

But then Sorscha started shouting something incoherent and pointing off down the road. A few more men filed out, running through the snow toward nothing. One stopped to help her, running his hand down her body and Sorscha pulled out her dagger. Agatha cursed and threw her magic toward Sorscha as she ran, still cloaked in invisibility. The knife tumbled from Sorscha's hand and she growled at Agatha before pushing the man back and begging him to please find her attacker. Chest puffed up, the man ran off toward the others and Agatha shot Sorscha a glare.

“Behave yourself.” And then Sister Autumn slipped into the storehouse to ensure it was vacant.

Content that it was, Agatha let her killing calm descend upon her, draping over her shoulders like a mantle. Black flames lit in her palms, licking the air as she walked slowly around. When Seleste walked in, golden flames dancing in her own palms, Agatha lifted her face to the rafters and sent her onyx fire to rain down from above.

Seleste let her flames take the far wall and Sorscha sauntered in, a cunning grin plastered on her blood-smeared face. Red sparks popped and crackled against the black and gold, catching and trailing, small explosions going off like shooting stars.

“That will suffice, Sisters.” Seleste turned and they followed her out.

The snow had begun to fall again, and Sorscha tugged on Agatha’s arm. “Let’s get back to the castle. We’ll need to be ready to swoop in when they learn of this.”

Numbly, Agatha stood there, watching the fire take the roof, reaching out a window, glass shattered and flames hungry. “I need to watch it. Just for a moment.”

Sorscha slid her hand down to Agatha’s and wove their fingers together. Seleste took her other hand, and together the three Sisters watched the draught storehouse burn, lighting up the Winter sky in fireworks and plumes of smoke.

…DEUX, *trois, quatre, cinq…*

Finally, the robed individuals ceased filing out of the Sanctuary, where Sisters Autumn and Spring waited around a corner in the hall.

"I still think he'll be held in a dungeon," Sorscha whispered in Agatha's ear.

Ignoring her, Agatha checked the ward around them and slipped a tendril of her magic in, just before the door would click shut. The dungeon had been her first thought as well, but Seleste had made a valid point before parting from them to return to Dulci's—there had to have been a place other than the common castle dungeon to hold Mila, and Grimm was likely to be held there as well.

On the night of Mila's death, Grimm had run out through a door at the back of the Sanctuary, but the chamber was fully interior with no obvious outside access or even a visible door. It was as good a place to begin as any.

Sisters Autumn and Spring slipped in, their invisibility hardly necessary in the Sanctuary lit only by a lone candelabra, its flames flickering over the altar. The air was musty, the pungent smell of smoke lingering from where magi and guards alike had blown out all the sconces and candles in a rush once word had spread that the draught storehouse had gone up in mysterious flames.

Satisfied they were indeed alone, Agatha lifted the cloaking spell. "There." She pointed behind the golden rendering of Hespa. "Augustus couldn't find a door that night, but a passageway must lay behind that curtain."

"Even so, I'm not so certain he would be there, Aggie. He's the prince for goddess' sake. Wouldn't they have him more heavily guarded? There's no one here."

They cautiously moved down the aisle between the pews, flashes of Agatha and Grimm's wedding day, only twisted and dark, assaulting her mind. "Not if this hidden chamber is a secret and not if he's sufficiently…" Her words stumbled over the bile in her throat. "Subdued."

There was still a great chance they would run into guards. If The Order, or at least the magus, was so concerned with

Grimm's abilities that they wished to feign his execution, they would probably still have him watched.

"A few guards is nothing we can't handle, anyway," Sorscha drawled, echoing Agatha's thoughts. "Could be fun." She winked.

Once they reached the back, Agatha spotted a small alcove. Upon inspection, it seemed unremarkable. Just a stone nook that might have once held a wash basin for cleaning oneself after a sacrifice. "There must be some sort of hidden door," she muttered, running her hands along the rough stones. "There has to be."

Sorscha stepped up to inspect the alcove until the end of her skirts snagged on something near the floor. "Drat! It's going to rip."

"Well stop pulling at it." Agatha bent down to untangle the soft, scarlet fabric. When she did, she realised what Sorscha had been caught on wasn't any old nail or a jagged bit of stone, but a mechanism, right at foot level.

"Lumière."

Light blossomed in her hand, a star that had come down from the sky, illuminating a minuscule peddle of sorts. Almost like one would see at the foot of a piano.

"What in Hades…" Sorscha knelt too, to inspect it.

Heart pounding and dread curling in her abdomen, Agatha pushed the mechanism. A soft whoosh of air sucked at the edges of their skirts, the stones shifting in on themselves to reveal a hidden passageway.

"Well, I'll be damned." Sorscha looked at Agatha. "After you, Highness."

"Coward."

"He's your husband, not mine."

The Sisters rose in unison, Sorscha calling a red flame to her palm, and they stepped into the corridor. The moment they did so, the stones knit themselves back together at an alarming speed and with great silence, sealing them inside. Agatha held up her orb of light to view Sorscha's face, disturbed to find her self-assured Sister a bit pale. Nothing good could lie at the end of a dank passageway. "You're stronger than anything down here, Sorscha."

She snorted. "Not Grimm."

Apprehension coated Agatha's veins. "You think he's dangerous."

A faint drip of water echoed off the stones in a rhythm. "I'm saying we haven't any idea what they've done to him, Aggie."

They continued on in silence, no sign of light except for their own, flickering gently with each step. Abruptly, the passage widened, a shallow pool of water on the tunnel floor. A chaotic chittering filled the musty air just before the deafening rustle of too many pumping wings. Sorscha barely bit off her scream, throwing her hands over her head and crouching as hundreds of bats swooped down, swarming around the witches.

"Aggie, make them stop!" Sorscha growled, her head between her knees.

Agatha smiled. She reached her arms out and let the night stalkers envelop her. Their playful chittering turned ominous, a warning she could not ignore. Their wings brushed against her, lifting her hair and her skirts, and they flew off in a rush down the corridor.

"There is danger ahead, Sister."

Sorscha stood, cursing and brushing her hair back into place. "Of course there is. Let's get it over with."

A few moments of walking later, a warm glow shone around a curve in the tunnel. The silence, however, remained—thick and unnerving.

"*Trouver*."

Agatha sent a bead of her magic ahead, nearly invisible for its translucent blackness blending into the stones. When it returned to her, it enlarged to reveal the image of two guards in the orb's depths. One sat in a chair, his head lulled to the side, resting against the wall, and the other standing stock-still. In front of a prison cell.

"*Agrandir.*"

The image enlarged further, the edge of a filthy mattress just visible within the cell, one hand draped over the side, a glint of gold on a finger. *Grimm's wedding ring.*

"It's him."

Sorscha dipped her chin once, magic already crackling around her in crimson sparks.

Agatha stalked forward, drawing her magic from the depths of her, its power multiplied by how deep below the earth's surface they walked. Turning the corner into the torchlight, she thrust countless threads of black tendrils out, encasing the standing guard before he had a moment to conceive what was upon him. At his garbled shout, the other guard awoke, only to find Sorscha standing over him, smiling wickedly.

"Hello, dearie." She sat on his lap, his eyes wide—entranced—and she pushed back his hair to rest her fingers on his temples. "This might hurt," she cooed, then sent shocks of her magic into him.

Agatha wrapped her webs of black, silken magic around and around the guard until he was entombed in a cocoon. "Sorscha, go tell Seleste and Dulci we've found him. I'll transport him to the *pâtisserie*. Sorscha blew her a kiss and was gone. Threat sufficiently dealt with, Agatha rushed to the rusted iron bars, whispering Grimm's name. When he didn't answer, or even stir, she began to panic.

"*Ouvrir.*"

Metal ground against stone as the cell door crunched with the power of her fretful magic before it twisted and flew against the far wall. Ignoring the lack of control over her magic stemming from her dread, Agatha ran for the soiled cot, her hands on Grimm before she could stop to consider it.

"Grimm, I'm here. Wake up. You have to get up." Her throat felt thick.

His eyes peeled open, settling on her, and she let out a small sob. But his face hardened. Slowly, he sat up, rage radiating off of him in waves.

WINNIE

Just outside Blanc Côte, Eleanor stretched in her saddle, letting her little finch of magic dance around her horse's mane. She hadn't managed to do much more than conjure the bird, but Winnie could already tell the magic she possessed was much stronger than anticipated for a half-witch long descended.

"Where did you run off to tonight?"

Despite the frigid temperatures, Winnie felt an urgency to continue on their trek, even in the dark. It wasn't something Eleanor agreed to quickly, but she'd had a nap and Winnie spelled a lantern to hover over them so she could practise her magic beneath the Yule Moon's aiding power. She'd eventually agreed to keep moving.

"Do you mean when you were decorating the cave with the viscera of a squirrel?"

Eleanor made a disgusted face. "Don't be crass."

"I went to Aggie," Winnie said before she could stop herself. *Went to* was a generous term. More like her magic betrayed her.

"Is everything all right there?" Eleanor looked as shocked as Winnie had been.

"You tell me."

"What is that supposed to mean?" The finch in Eleanor's

hand dissipated, shards of magic shooting up into the snowy evergreens looming over them on the trail.

For once, Winnie hadn't meant to argue. Her soul was far too weary. "Why has Aggie been writing to you and not to me?"

Eleanor looked down at the reins in her hands. "I think you know the answer to that."

"You don't seem surprised I knew."

"I don't know why I would be." A wisp of blonde hair fell from her braid, landing against her cheek, golden with the lantern's light. "But I don't know why *you're* surprised she wrote to me and not to you."

The maid had a point. Winnie looked off into the trees, wondering where Yula was. She wished the owl could comfort her the way Mabon had. "Things weren't always like this," she said quietly. "We used to be thick as thieves, the four of us."

Eleanor regarded her for a moment before speaking. "Love does not just go away, Winnie."

Sister Winter closed her eyes.

WINNIE SNIFFLED, her small hands holding the pieces of her mother's locket. "Do you still love me?" she asked, big blue eyes filled with glacial tears.

Her mother dropped to her knees and placed a tender hand on her eldest daughter's cheek. "Love is not so very fragile, my sweet." She swiped a tear and smiled serenely. "Love is tender, but it is strong. Capable of enduring far more than you can imagine." She kissed Winnie's forehead. "I will always love you. No matter what. Just the way you are."

Winnie's tears kept coming, and little Yula nuzzled her cheek from where she perched on her shoulder before flying off into the trees. "But I broke it. That is your favourite locket."

Her mother smiled. "Let me see." Winnie uncurled her small fingers and her mother whispered a spell, the four pieces coming together with a golden gleam of magic before sealing. "Good as new."

Winnie leapt into her mother's arms, burying her face in her neck.

"Love does not disappear, dove. Even if you feel you no longer know it." She pulled her daughter back to look into her eyes. "If ever you feel lost, return to where love knows you*."*

AGATHA

She was trembling. With rage. With heartbreak.

"Get out of my sight, *now*," he spat again.

Grimm, not-Grimm, the vile creature lurking inside of his skin, stalked toward her, rage plastered across his face. It hurt. It hurt to look at him. Never, *never* would he look at her like that. She knew it, deep down. But she couldn't shake it—the images, the fear that she was losing him for good.

"They've locked you away down here, I've come to help y—"

"This dungeon is mine, you filthy whore. This whole fucking castle is mine. This *country*. Do you really think you can command me to leave? Do you really think I go anywhere I don't want to be?"

"Fine," she said through gritted teeth. "Then I will leave."

"No." He stepped in front of the cell door, blocking it. "I've changed my mind. *Stay*."

The cadence of his voice made her stomach churn. Her heart was beating uncontrollably. Her palms were on fire. She didn't want to hurt him, but she was terrified she was going to have to.

"This isn't you, Grimm. Just calm down."

His face contorted and she instinctively took a step backwards at the sight. "Command me one more time." His voice was so low, so grating, she shivered.

GRIMM

The light grew brighter.

Just for an instant, it lit the darkness. Do I know you, little light? It flashes again and I feel its fear. It is so afraid. What should a light fear but darkness? It flashes again and I can taste its fear. The only thing I've felt in ages. I reach for it, with my hand that is not a hand, just a wisp of gloom, and I grasp it. In my shadow palm it looks like a firefly, flashing fear, fear, fear.

Agatha.

Her memory flows from the light, melding with me. Reminding me. And *she* is afraid. I lift the light to my ghoulish mouth and I swallow it whole. Letting it push, press against the shadows of this place. They hiss, receding, petrified of the light.

I blink and she's there. Truly there, right in front of me. My little witch. And *she is terrified.* She's looking at me. Not at my face, but at my raised hand. *She's so afraid.* Why is my hand raised?

Oh, gods…

CHAPTER TWENTY-FIVE

AGATHA

For half a breath he froze. He looked from his hand to her, his chest rising and falling rapidly as he pieced it together. His eyes were wild, frenzied, horrified.

"Did I hurt you?" he breathed. Her heart tore in two. It was him. He was *him*. Somehow he'd ripped free.

"No," she bolted forward, taking his raised hand. "No, you didn't." Not physically.

His chest heaved once and something akin to a snarl tore from him, a manic, unhinged sound. "You're lying."

A mask she'd never seen on him, one built of wrath and a lust for blood, slipped down over his face. He was radiating violence, head to heel. In a flash, he was moving toward the cell door, stalking down the corridors of the underground tunnel, a monster to be unleashed on his kingdom.

"Grimm," she called after him, spelling a light to follow him. "Stop!"

Like an untamed beast, he moved through the dark, Agatha's light casting his shadow against the stone walls. She could feel their bond untangling itself from the draught being pushed away, but he was still acting as if he couldn't hear her, blinded by his rage.

"Grimm, please!" She reached him and pulled at his sleeve, but he shook her off.

When he reached the end of the tunnels, the passageway into the Sanctuary was sealed. For a breath, she thought he'd stop—collect himself. She watched as he bowed his head, a hush permeating from him. When he lifted his chin to look at the wall, he disappeared into a cloud of black vapour, seeping into the stones.

Agatha gasped, momentarily stunned. When she recovered, her mind spun, but she whispered.

"Fantôme."

She materialised near the altar of the Sanctuary, Grimm already vanishing through the doors into the castle corridors. His edges flickered to reveal the reaper and Agatha ran after him, shouting for him to stop, pleading. If he didn't keep it together, he would shift right in front of the entire castle. Her shouts continued to fall on deaf ears. He moved like a man possessed.

Augustus came alongside her, but she didn't know when he'd gotten there. "What's happened?" he asked urgently. "What is he doing?"

"I don't know! He broke free of the draught, but he's gone mad!"

They were nearing the populated corridors of the castle and Augustus rushed forward, pulling at Grimm's arm, but he shoved the guard back so hard Augustus slammed into the wall, plaster cracking.

"Grimm, *please*!" Agatha shouted, the few midnight courtiers in the halls looking on with mouths covered and eyes wide.

He continued his hunt, no amount of her begging even

registering to his ears. Augustus came up next to her again. "You have to do something, he's coming undone!"

"I can fucking see that!" she shouted.

They rounded a corner toward the magus' chambers, the corridor mercifully empty, and Agatha knew what she must do. A string of curses flying from her mouth, she reached into the deep well of her magic and pulled the thread that was forbidden. The one they were never to touch. It was born of darkness, Lord Night's malevolence, His power to wreak havoc. And Agatha's was the strongest of her four Sisters. Coaxing, pulling, she withdrew it, up, up, up, her equal light delving deep to get out of the way. The sinister magic wound around Grimm, and his step halted in mid-air. He tried to break free, writhing and snarling against the binding, but it held him fast. His crazed eyes locked with hers and they did not soften, but she could see him. *Him*, her Grimm, in them. He would not hurt her. Never.

Augustus skidded to a stop next to her, attention darting between them and up and down the corridor.

An emotion she could not place tore across Grimm's face and down their bond, nearly making her double over, and he stilled, eyes locked on hers.

"I love you," he whispered, just before the reaper broke fully free, throwing off her magic as if it were nothing more than a bed sheet. She staggered back, her magic beginning to deplete, and Grimm kicked in the magus' door.

A muffled scream sounded as she rushed in after Grimm, Augustus on her heels. "Guard the door, no matter what you hear."

The guard gritted his teeth but nodded tersely just before she slammed what was left of the door in his face.

She saw Grimm pause in the entryway of what must be the magus' bedchamber for a split breath before he charged in roaring. The high-pitched scream sounded again and Agatha ran in after him.

Anne.

She lay prone, much—too much—like Mila had on the altar, tied to the magus' bed and skirts pushed up to reveal her lower half. A gag was fitted into her mouth and he was scrambling off of her, pants barely up by the time Grimm's skeletal fist connected with his chin. He flew back across the bed, head smashing against the headboard before Grimm yanked him up by his hair and slammed him up against the wall.

Agatha scrabbled at the ties binding Anne's wrists, afraid to use her magic and make this all somehow far worse by revealing her power to the magus or draining herself to uselessness. Tears and snot coated Anne's face and she kept sobbing, Agatha shushing her with too much stressed force to truly provide comfort. She saw Grimm slam the magus against the far wall again, hissing something too low for her to hear. A strange light flared from the magus just before Agatha felt a searing pain at her side and hit the railing of the bed with a howl. Grimm whirled toward her at her outcry and it was just enough. The magus shoved his hand into Grimm's exposed rib and he went slack, dropping the magus to his feet, his reaper form dissolving into Thackery Peridot.

"Grimm!" Agatha shouted, and Anne wept, scooting back against the headboard as if she could get away. The magus was not as defenceless as they thought. Grimm stood as still as a statue, eyes glazed over and face slack. All traces of his fury and revenge had dissipated, hands loose at his sides. Agatha pushed to her feet, palms hot and prepared to display her own set of powers.

The magus, with his thin, sagging chest heaving, took up a handkerchief and wiped blood off his hands. It was too much to be the blood leaking from his nose… That's when Agatha noticed shards of glass on the floor and a jagged piece hanging from a chain around his neck. He'd kept a vial of Grimm's blood for such an instance as this, should he somehow defect.

Agatha shifted her feet, teeth bared. How could he do this with blood?

"You know"—he continued to wipe at the smears of precious blood coating him—"I really prefer him as a puppet. Much more enjoyable than that pompous arse who thinks he can change the realm." He *tsked* and turned toward Agatha. "Ah, she's finally ready to show me her magic. Let's have it, then."

Agatha wasted no time giving him what he wanted. She threw a searing shard of power at him, sharp as a dagger. With no effort whatsoever, he knocked it away, the magic landing on the carpet with a hiss. He chuckled darkly and Agatha sent two more—one he would move to block and another to veer off and slice him. He blocked both with ease.

"Do you truly think I've accomplished all that I have by being so weak? So defenceless?" He tutted again. "My, my. You hopeless romantics are so blind. You witches who think the good in your magic will win."

"You," Agatha bit out, "are nothing but a pawn. You realise if I don't kill you The Order will, yes? When they've used you up like the old, useless rag you are." It was then that she noticed he had the same extraction marks as Grimm. As Anne and Miriam.

Oh, gods…

They were linked, somehow, he and Grimm.

A bolt of magic shot toward her, far faster than her own waning power, and she barely dodged it, the wall singed where her head had been.

They moved around each other in a slow dance, sending out slivers of their magic. Agatha had never, in all her years, been equally matched. A dagger of his power sliced through her shoulder and Agatha winced. She dug deep into her well of dark magic, uncaring if it was wrong. Anne was hurt and terrified. Grimm stood staring at the blasted wall. But she'd used so much of her magic to try and hold him back. She should have let him rage.

She would have to rage herself.

Agatha let it feed the well. Anne's fearful eyes, Mila's last breath, Grimm's eerily silent bond. She could feel her magic feast on the agony, the fury. She would very much enjoy killing this magus. She'd dreamt about it for moons. How she would slit his throat, reciting the names of all their fallen, all their broken, all their oppressed, as he bled out on the boots that made the kingdom turn their back on him. Full circle. She would bring the last hundred years full fucking circle.

Agatha stalked forward, raining her power down on him in sparks of black magic. Bits and pieces broke through his shield, leaving singed marks on his skin. A bolt of magic slipped past her barrier, lodging deep within her gut. Still, she advanced. A deep gash opened up on his leg, revealing bone. He staggered to the side with a cry of pain and Agatha unsheathed her dagger from her thigh. She was so close, one more step—then a searing pain shot through her shoulder, her hand dropping the dagger on instinct. She heard Anne cry out, but it was muffled and she couldn't make sense of it. Something thudded against her temple and the world began to fade, but not before she uttered one word. A name.

Winnie.

GRIMM

Trapped.

I am encased within the recesses of my own mind and the monsters here are infinite.

This is the place where terror resides. Where it thrives; opens its maw and roars because it, too, is afraid. Here, fear simply *is*. It is everything. It is the air, the ground, the walls, the light.

This is the place where shadows don't exist because it's made up of eternal night.

There are no corners. No place for the villain to lurk, or the boy to hide. No, here, in the recesses of the mind, exists a void filled with pain. A monster that is the boy and the boy that is the monster. Here, they are synonymous.

They're not memories, or fears, the ghouls that haunt here. No, they're more than that. They're less than that. They're everything.

They fill up your mouth, seeping down into your chest, running down your veins until they've consumed you. A ghoul comprised of torture because it is truly…hope.

Here, Agatha smiles, her joy unmoored, a hand on her swollen belly where she stands at her darkened cottage. *Our* darkened cottage. In our gloomy field of pumpkins and alder trees. The shadows are light, really. Light that knows the beauty found in the mysteries of the dark. Not like here, where the black suffocates with its vile, false hope.

Here, I am no prince; no king. Here, Agatha takes my hand and pulls me toward a rushing river, her auburn hair flying wildly behind her. Here, we discard our clothing and let the cool water wash over us, not a care in all the realms for our nakedness. We're finally free of our noose.

Here, a ghoul of tattered skin and rough bone juts out of my soul. It—he—me—takes Agatha by the neck, bones crunching. Her eyes go wide, and I watch the light leave her honey irises. She feels limp in my grip, little more than a rag doll and I cast her off, a gift to the shallow water, running inky with the threads of my loose soul.

Here, I discard her, as if she is nothing. The ghoul that is me leaves the river, without a care in all the realms for his nakedness. He's finally free of his mortal cage.

Here, I am the destroyer who wreaks havoc.

Here, the terror melts and reshapes. This time, into killing her softly. Sweetly. Tenderly. A gift to her. A mercy. A slow poison I feed her as we lie naked, wrapped in each other's arms.

Here, I am the destroyer who wreaks havoc.

Here, my fears are not fears at all. They are truths.

A release. A retribution. A gift to me. A penance.

Locked within my own mind, I am forced to face the incarnate evil that I am.

Here, I am the destroyer who wreaks havoc.

A lover. A killer. A gift to no one.

I am the monster.

AGATHA

Agatha's eyes opened to fire. The room was set ablaze, one curtain scorched and the canopy of the bed catching. A candle was tipped on its side and Anne was screeching behind her gag, kicking uselessly at the flames nearing her.

Blinking to clear her vision, Agatha saw a glowing form in the middle of the room, the magus suspended in the air in front of her.

Winnie.

"Aggie!" she was screaming. "*Get up*!"

She made to stand but a bout of nausea knocked her back down, the room spinning beneath her.

"Aggie, *get up*! I can't hold him!"

She made it to her feet, swaying, and Winnie threw everything she had at the magus. He cried out, turning mottled shades of purple and red beneath her magic, but it wasn't enough. Her stores were running out. "Winnie," Agatha breathed. "Wait."

"Have you gone mad?" she snarled. "End this. *Now.*"

"I think Grimm's life is tied to him, the blood binding them!"

Winnie shot her a panicked look. "Aggie, he's going to kill all of us!"

Agatha picked up her dagger, unsteady on her feet. Slowly, she moved toward the magus. *Grimm*, she spoke through their entanglement as she moved. *Grimm, wake up. Find me. It's what you do. You* always *find me. You have always found me.* She stood, looking up at the man that had caused so much pain. He struggled against Winnie's magic and she was pushed back a step.

"Aggie, you can do this," she said through gritted teeth. "End this monster."

Grimm, wake up.

He had to push back from this control, or he wouldn't survive without the magus.

Wake up, my love.

Agatha pressed the tip of her knife to the magus' heart, Winnie lowering him just enough.

Grimm, wake up.

The magus fought against Winnie's magic and she cried out in pain. "I can't hold him, Aggie! Do it!"

Tears streaming down her face, Agatha pushed the tip of the knife deeper, piercing flesh. The magus snarled at her, spewing insults, half-mad.

"Grimm, *please*," she breathed.

Winnie's power gave out and the magus fell to his knees. Agatha gasped as her bond with Grimm flooded her very soul, rushing in where it had lain so cold. There was a sudden flurry of movement next to her and Grimm was upon the magus, his hand striking straight through flesh, sinew, and bone, down to the viscera in his abdomen. He roared, Agatha's very bones rattling with the sound, and yanked the soul of the magus straight from his body. Effervescent gold floated within Grimm's grasp. The vague shape of a man. All Agatha could think was that she'd expected his soul to be black. Burnt.

Grimm gnashed his teeth and the sack of flesh thudded to the floor. He brought the strange shimmer of a form to his skeletal face and snarled, "You should have known better than to trifle with my wife." He lifted the magus' soul high above his head and slammed it down so hard it burst into innumerable flecks of dust before coalescing into a body-shaped gimmer again. Grabbing the soul by the ruff, he turned his decrepit countenance on Agatha, exposed, decayed muscle pulled taut for holding the restless soul. "Do we have what we need from him?"

Before she could respond, the returned bond must have betrayed her because the bones of his jaw clacked together, teeth grinding. "No," she said simply to confirm what he already knew.

With another roar he slammed the magus' soul back on the floor, fireflies of essence bursting out again. This time, when the bits of melted life were reforming their shape, Grimm shoved his hand into it until they swirled around his skeletal arm. With a growl, he thrust his arm into the magus' lifeless body. When he pulled it back, the body contracted and the magus sat up, gasping, clutching at his chest. Grimm's boot connected with the side of his face and the magus' head cracked against the floorboards.

He knelt down next to him, a menacing creature of the night. "If you touch Agatha—or Anne—again, I will make the torture before your eternal damnation long and immeasurably painful."

The magus sneered up at him, barely conscious, but Agatha could see the tremble in his limbs. "Yet here I live. You will one day regret that, boy."

"You live because I still have need of you, maggot." He

struck him in the temple with the sharp bone of his elbow, the magus falling slack against the bottom of the bed.

Grimm shifted back into Thackery, locking eyes with Agatha for a breath before she dashed to untie Anne and Grimm moved toward the door to find Augustus.

"Wait." Winnie halted them both, breathing heavily. "Get to my home immediately. All of you."

"No," Grimm countered. "That filth needs to be bait. We tie him up in the dungeon and wait for The Order to sniff him out."

Winnie lifted her chin. "There will be a reckoning coming for this."

"She's right," Agatha agreed, lifting a glass of water to Anne's mouth and rubbing small circles on her back.

"*Fuck.*" He ran his hand through his hair. "I did not put him back to show him mercy," he ground out. "He will give us what we need or he dies for good."

"Then take him to my home, too." Winnie looked at Agatha and then back to Grimm. "Between Agatha and Vera's magic, then the rest of us combined, we can hold him. Lure them in."

"Winnie, it's your home…"

She waved Agatha off. "That doesn't matter. Get there, all of you."

"Our magic isn't ready to be fully together yet."

"Then get it ready," Winnie snapped.

"*Merde*, my mother." Grimm worried his lip between his teeth.

Winnie turned toward him and stood very still. "Your mother?"

"She's on the draught as well." He turned to Agatha. "Isn't she still?"

Agatha nodded. "I've managed to make her doses lower, she's almost off, but not yet."

"I can't leave her, not now."

"Leave it to me." They both stared at Winnie.

"You can't abduct the queen, Winnie."

She pinned Agatha with a sardonic stare. "I won't abduct her, she'll leave of her own accord. Who can be trusted in this court?"

"Dulci and Tindle," Agatha answered.

Grimm shook his head. "This is a bad, *bad* idea…"

"It's not safe here. Get the girl and the magus to the mountains. I'll meet you there with Eleanor once we have the empress' man in hand."

"What are you planning to do with my moth–"

But Winnie was already gone.

WINNIE

It was despicable how easy it was to locate the queen and slip into her rooms without magic. The guards were senseless twits and there was only one maid in the rooms with the queen.

"Oh!" An older maid jumped at the sight of Winnie when she sauntered in like she owned the place. "Who let you in here?"

The queen sat motionless, staring out the window at what was most likely a lovely garden in Spring. "Grand Magus von Fuchs sent me to summon you to his study," she addressed the maid. The woman went ghostly pale and Winnie had to fight a grimace. The evidence of his vileness was damning. "I'm to sit with Her Majesty until you are through."

The maid swallowed hard, tears pooling in her eyes, but she nodded once and left. Winnie prayed there would be no one in the magus' study that was of like mind with him. The door clicked shut and Winnie observed the queen. She had only moments before someone who had their wits about them realised something was amiss.

It had been a very long time since she'd seen Princess Fleurina, but the young girl's countenance was still there, wonder peeking through the cracks of age and a draught-induced stupor. Winnie hadn't exactly formulated a plan before she embarked on this endeavour. If this was the queen on a lessened dosage of the draught, she might be in for a challenge.

Aggie and Sorscha had fought off the draught's malevolence together when it wasn't nearly as formidable, but in a larger quantity. Perhaps she could drive it from the queen's blood.

"Do I know you?" The queen's words pulled Winnie from her thoughts with a start. She sat, head cocked to one side and dreamy eyes set on Winnie.

"Your Majesty." She lowered her head. "I'm a friend of your son's. He sent me to ensure you're safe."

"Has something happened to him?" Queen Fleurina blinked, childlike, but a mother's concern was pushing past it.

"He and Princess Agatha needed to leave for a time, and Prince Grimm asked me to ensure your safety." Winnie moved forward slowly. "In order to do that, I need you to be well again."

Her brows contorted. "Am I ill?"

"You are. But I can help you." Winnie reached out slowly and offered the queen her hand. "I need you to trust me."

"Are you a healer?" Her curiosity remained, but there was no mistrust there.

"I am." She had been. Long, long ago. Queen Fleurina rested her elegant hand on Winnie's. "This might hurt a little, Your Grace." But she was regarding Winnie strangely all of a sudden. Anxious the queen would cry foul, Winnie sent her magic plummeting through her veins. She winced but kept steady.

"I do know you," she whispered as Winnie worked, sifting through blood and water.

"I don't believe that is possible, Your Grace." A slick, oily coil rubbed up against her magic and she nearly startled backwards, sucking a breath through her teeth. She pushed to drive it out, bits of it flaking off like charred wood.

The queen's face began to clear, brows still pulled together. "No, I do know you."

"You've been very ill, Majesty. Things might appear a bit hazy at present." But her pulse was thudding in her ears. Perhaps she'd made a grave mistake offering to do this. Her magic was weak after battling the magus, but the draught's power was still shrinking away from her light.

"Friend of my son, you say?" Her voice was clear, all traces of wonder replaced with bright lucidity.

Winnie nodded, the last of the draught skittering away beneath her magic. She patted the queen's hand with the cloth. "There we have it. A topical ointment soaked into the skin."

Queen Fleurina withdrew her hand, folding it in her lap beneath the other, shrewd eyes trained on Winnie. "The songstress."

Winnie stilled. "You must be mistaken, Your Gr–"

"Wendy." Her heart stopped. "That is what the Cirque Master called you."

"It is not safe here and Prince Grimm has asked me to relocate you."

"You've not aged a day," the queen ignored Winnie's statement. "It must have been over fifty years ago you visited my home in Eridon."

"Majesty, we need to get mov–"

"You said," she spoke forcefully, "that you needed me to trust you. I am a queen, not a fool. Now make me trust you, or I am going nowhere."

She fully understood why the magus had drugged the woman, she was no idle threat. "Fifty-three years. You were eight when I sang for your court in Eridon."

"You are indeed Druids, then, the cirque troupe?"

"Something like that. We really do not have tim–"

"What's happened to my son? Has the magus harmed him?"

Winnie sighed. "Yes and no."

"I'm not stepping one foot out of this room with you until you tell me everything." She raised her chin and Winnie couldn't help but admire the woman.

"The magus is not what he seems."

Queen Fleurina pursed her lips. "I know that much. Again, I am no fool. Start further forward."

"You know the draught is not what it seems as well, then?"

The queen blinked at her cynically.

Winnie sat in a chair across from her. "Prince Grimm has been on the draught." The queen paled. "When he came off of it, he discovered it had caused him to do some undesirable things to Agatha."

"*Princess* Agatha," the queen corrected with great offence.

"Right."

"Is she all right?"

Winnie's heart constricted. She'd never expected the royals to love her Aggie, not for any fault of Aggie's, but because she'd assumed them cruel. All except for Fleurina, up until Eleanor had told her the ugly truth. "She is. But Prince Grimm captured the magus."

"And he fears I'm unsafe while The Order comes looking for their puppet."

Winnie nodded. "He'd like for you to go stay with Monsieur Tindle and Madame Dulci."

The queen stood and began milling about, packing a few belongings. "It would take Grimm a lot to capture the magus." She paused and looked at Winnie. "Did anyone see him?"

She considered the woman for a moment. "See him do what exactly?"

The queen's eyes narrowed. "How well do you know my son?"

"Agatha is my Sister."

Surprise flashed across her features before calculated thought clouded her brow and she looked much like her son for a moment. "No wonder." She shook her head and sat, a dressing gown bunched in her hands. "Our Daughter of Autumn. Agatha of Helsvar. The Burned City. The place of the last witch coven." Her far-off gaze turned to Winnie. "You're not a Druid."

"I am not."

"Goddess, they do make a perfect pair, don't they…" Her eyes moved off again and Winnie didn't bother agreeing.

"You know what your son is, then?"

"Of course I do. I'm his mother."

Winnie held no doubt, looking at the fierce cut of this queen's brow, that she had done great and terrible things to protect her son. And he might never know it. The thought of a strong and selfless mother nearly bent Winnie over double. She swallowed hard. "We need to get moving, Your Grace."

"WHAT IN HADES!" Monsieur Tindle shouted as the back door of his home flew open, crashing against the wall. Winnie entered through it, her invisibility falling away. "What in all the realms!" he screeched, clutching his chest with one hand and reaching for a fire poker with the other. "Get out of my house, you whor–" He gasped until he choked when his back door slammed open again and the queen strode in to stand next to Winnie. "Your Majesty. What… What is happening?"

"The queen needs sanctuary. Can you provide it

sufficiently?" Winnie had her doubts after witnessing the small man come at her with nothing but a fire poker.

"I can." He looked between them both.

Winnie turned to the queen. "I'm not sure about this."

"If Grimm said Tindle and Ducibella, then it is them."

Winnie sighed before turning and snatching Tindle's chin, sharp nails digging into his cheeks. "I don't care what affection my Sister and her husband hold for you. I will rip your entrails out with my bare hands if the queen sees harm under your care."

Tindle straightened, a sneer on his face, and Winnie saw why he'd been selected. "On my life, *Winter Witch*."

Laying her secret out before a queen he didn't know already had the information was a strategic move and Winnie almost smiled at his boldness. She patted his cheek hard. "Good boy. Send my Sister Summer to my home when she arrives with Dulci."

Just before she made to transport herself back to Blanc Côte and Eleanor, a gnawing thought ran its claws down her back. They did not know this queen, not truly. If what Eleanor told her was true about her having Grimm's old guard hanged for taking him into the markets, Winnie had long been mistaken about what she thought she knew concerning the former Princess of Eridon.

She turned slowly to the queen and spoke, not mincing her words. "The guard. The one that allowed your son into the city as a boy." Winnie let the words dangle. "Did you truly have him hanged for it?"

Queen Fleurina's stoic face slipped into a smirk, making her look years younger—like the young princess she and Laurent had sung for. "No," she said. "It made me seem ruthless at a time when I needed the magus' attention away from my son." She sat in a chair near the fire and folded her hands primly in her lap, Tindle looking on with wide eyes. "That guard is quite happy on a farm in the Sud."

She regarded the queen for a moment. Then, Winnie bowed low. Something she had never, ever done. "Your Majesty."

CHAPTER TWENTY-SIX

GRIMM

They'd travelled through the night. The early morning, he supposed, since the sky grew pink at the Estern seam soon after they left Merveille. It was quite a feat to get himself and Agatha out of the castle with an unconscious magus and a beaten girl, only one guard in tow. One who spent the first leg of the journey muttering all the ways he wished to kill the magus.

Grimm couldn't blame him. In fact, he *had* killed the vile bastard for what he'd made him do to Agatha and what he'd done to Anne. Grimm shuddered at the thought. The only thing that kept his sword in its scabbard and his reaper at bay was the knowledge he would get to kill the magus again once he was finished extracting the necessary information.

When the sun was beginning to rise in full, they made camp. That was when they'd told him what he'd done to Mila. Without a word of response, he'd walked into the frigid woods alone. There he stood, a frozen stream at his feet and all his regret for cold company. He should've found a way to break free of the draught sooner. A way to learn the information he gleaned and *remember* it. He couldn't remember a damned thing.

They told him he'd defied its clutches when he killed Mila, that was why he'd been accused of treason and The Order wanted him locked up, but it was still a failure. He'd managed to kill a fucking ghost.

Gods, all she'd wanted was to *live*. He didn't care that she'd tried to kill him. She was a scared, broken girl, fighting for life the only way she knew how. And he'd ended it with finality. Then, he'd raised a hand to Agatha…

His stomach roiled. He still couldn't think about that one.

She'd already healed her wounds inflicted by the magus, but Grimm would never forget exactly where they'd been on her skin, each one his fault.

He felt her call out for him through the bond for the third time since he'd walked away. Her worry gnawed at him and he shoved his hands into his pockets and ambled back to their humble camp.

When he returned, she was sitting by the fire, waiting for him. "Why do I get the feeling you're avoiding me, reaper?"

Because he was.

"I need to handle the magus." He moved toward the tent von Fuchs was chained up in, but Agatha was in front of him in a flash of magic. He stepped back.

"Grimm."

The pleading in her eyes made him look away. He wanted to reach out for her, pull her into his arms. But he did not. "We'll talk," he murmured. "I promise."

She nodded, a pang of sorrow shooting through the bond, and stepped out of his way.

As he was lifting the flap to the magus' tent, Agatha called after him. "Lady Death came for Mila Herself. She said she would be at peace now."

Grimm stilled, his back to her, and he squeezed his eyes shut. He swallowed the lump in his throat and walked into the tent.

The magus was still as stone in the shadows. Augustus stood on the other side of the tent, hanging by a thread. He shouldn't have left the guard alone with him.

"Go see Anne," Grimm commanded quietly.

"Gri—"

"Go see Anne." There was no mistaking his tone and Augustus left with one more look of pure hatred over his shoulder at the sneering magus.

As soon as the tent was in darkness again, Grimm shuffled forward and planted a solid kick to the magus' chest where he kneeled. The old man coughed a laugh, righting himself the best he could with his arms bound behind his back.

"Keep that look off your face."

"Yes, Your Highness," he scoffed.

Grimm grabbed him by the shirt and hauled him up until his sagging face was in front of him. "You must know by now that I have every power to end you." He ground his teeth together and threw the man back down into the mud. "What does The Order want with me?"

"Come now." The magus' cough rattled in his chest as he scooted backwards despite the bravado in his voice. "You're not daft, are you? They want your reaper."

"I *am* the reaper, you prick. *Why* do they want me?"

Von Fuchs laughed, low and cruel. "They'll find you now. You've no chance."

He was counting on it. Grimm stalked forward, crouching down in front of the man. "Mark my words, von Fuchs. I will enjoy, nay, *delight in* killing you and taking you to rot in the Underworld. What you tell me determines if my joy will be drawn out and slow, or quick and clean."

"And what if it's more than you that they want?"

Grimm stilled.

"Now you've gone and made them angry. And drawn your little witch out like a lamb to the slaughter."

Grimm sunk his fist into the man's jaw. The magus began to cackle, his broken and bloodied teeth shining crimson in the dim lamplight, and Grimm walked out.

AGATHA

Anne hadn't spoken the entire first leg on the road to Winnie's mountain home. In truth, none of them had much. Once they'd told Grimm about Mila…none of them were ready to speak of the other horrors they'd each faced. Augustus had come into the tent to speak with her, but she remained vacant. When tears began to pool in the guard's pleading eyes, Agatha walked him out.

Back out in the snow, his remaining composure broke and he began to pace. "I'll never get the image out of my head, Agatha." His breath clouded in front of him, eyes rimmed with red and cheeks chapped.

"Neither will she."

"You should've let me in there." His voice cracked on the last word and he sat hard in the snow, arms clasped around his knees. "I'm sorry," he breathed before she could respond. "You didn't know."

And yet Agatha had placed just as much blame on herself, anyway. "There is much I wish would have gone differently." She crouched to place a hand on his shoulder.

"She shouldn't be alone right now."

Agatha nodded and stood. "Neither should you. You should find Grimm."

"He's not much better," Augustus muttered. "Go." He caught his tone and looked at the toes of his boots. "Please. Go be with her."

Agatha returned to the tent to find Anne in the same position she'd been in since they left the wagon—curled on her side on a mound of furs, staring at the canvas.

"Anne, I'm going to conjure a nice bath for you, alright?"

Silence.

"*Bain moussant.*"

A small copper tub fit for a queen materialised in the centre of the tent, a splash of milky water escaping the lip and landing on the muddy ground. Steam that smelled of lavender and rosemary wafted to fill the atmosphere. Agatha moved to crouch down next to the pallet Anne laid upon. "Let's get you cleaned up, hm?"

Anne moved woodenly, her eyes never truly focusing as Agatha pulled her up, gently undressed her, and helped her into the tub. The marks on the insides of her arms were identical to Grimm's, and Miriam's. She also had bruises around her thighs and wrists, as well as her ribs.

Swallowing down her nausea, Agatha poured hot water over Anne's hair, her heart constricting with the twisted mirror it was of her first night with Anne last Autumn. The light had gone out of her sunshine. There she sat, hands around her knees, eyes far away and lost in the dark corners of her mind.

"I can give you something," Agatha spoke softly, "to make you forget."

Anne moved her head, almost looking at her. "Did you take it, to forget what happened to you, after Ira?"

Her eyes ticked up to Agatha's and her heart sank. She shook her head. "No."

Anne's attention moved back to the bubbled water lapping at her knees. "Neither will I."

"I should have tried harder to protect you." Agatha couldn't keep the quiver from her voice.

"No. I should have tried harder to protect myself." Anne paused for a moment and Agatha thought she'd lost her, but she spoke again. "The weak, timid part of me died last night."

Agatha's hand stilled, the jug of water poised over her back.

"And she will not rise again."

GRIMM

He felt her come into their measly tent before he heard her. Never, *never* again would he lose sight of her within him. Not for a breath. He'd kept himself from touching her, though he wanted to desperately. He couldn't erase that memory of her face, terrified of him—of what he'd become. Every time he closed his eyes, it haunted him.

"Come here," she said softly, and he turned to find her sitting on the furs piled to make up their travel bed.

"Agatha—"

"Come here," she said again, more firmly.

He sighed and rose from a log, surprised at how hard his heart was hammering against his ribcage. The closer he moved toward her, the more he could feel her in their entanglement, heady and intoxicating. Despite how much he wanted to close the distance between them, he refrained, keeping a step back. "I hurt you."

She looked up at him. "*The Order* hurt me."

"Agatha, you were terrified. Of *me*." He put a hand to his chest, heartbeat thudding against his palm.

"No." She rose and stood in front of him. "No. I was afraid I would have to stop you."

"Because I had my gods damned hand raised to you," he growled, stepping back and pushing his fingers through his hair. "How am I supposed to live with that, Agatha?"

She came forward and reached up, placing her hands on either side of his face. The scent of her made his head swim. "You don't have to, because it wasn't you. I trust you, Grimm."

His attention darted away and he tried to step back, but she grabbed the unbuttoned collar of his shirt and pulled him toward her.

"*I trust you*, Grimm." He let himself look into her honey eyes and his heart cracked. She was so peaceful in the bond. So gods damned peaceful and perfect. "Tell me where you were, in your mind."

"With you."

Her head cocked to the side and he couldn't stop his hands from moving to her waist, pulling her the rest of the way to him.

"I was lost. Gone. It was just…a void of darkness. But I knew I was searching for something. I found a tiny flicker of light and I held on with all my might."

"I was afraid I'd lost you," she said quietly, fiddling with the corner of his collar.

He gently lifted her chin until she looked into his eyes. "I will *always* find you."

"I know."

"I would never harm you, Agatha."

She ran her finger over one of his dark eyebrows, the familiar touch calming him as she searched his gaze. "I know that, too."

She rose up on her toes and pressed her lips to his, tender and loving. He brought his hand to the nape of her neck, thumb gently caressing her cheek. The taste of her reminded him of the sweetest wine and even sweeter promises, more delectable than it had ever been before.

Agatha parted her lips and Grimm's tongue found hers, their kisses growing more ravenous with each ragged breath. The desperate need to prove to themselves that the other was really there drove them even closer together, seeking all that had been stolen from them over the last moon.

Grimm pushed his fingers into Agatha's unruly hair, his other hand grasping her hip. She pulled back just long enough for him to see the desire in her eyes. With a hand to his chest, she pushed him toward their bed of furs until he sat. Slowly, she slid onto his lap, her proximity almost more than he could handle.

Holding his gaze, Agatha shifted on him, and he went hard as stone beneath her. His body's response drew a stuttering breath from her that unhinged his decrepit soul.

Desperate to coax more sounds from her, he made quick work of unfastening the stays of her travel gown. Without care for the delicate fabric, he pulled the bodice down until she was revealed to him. Her breasts shifted with the movement and he groaned, twisting to lay her down on the furs, her breaths coming in hungry bursts as he closed his mouth around her nipple.

Grimm pulled back and looked deep into her eyes, his love for her overwhelming. No, he would *never* lose her again. Not for a moment.

He lowered himself to kiss her gently and she smiled against his lips. "Is that all you've got, reaper?" she teased.

He arched a brow as unquenchable desire shot through him like lightning. "You should know better, little witch," he answered. Then he rolled, pulling her back on top of him.

The sharpest glint of wickedness shimmered in her eyes before she whispered, and their clothing vanished. With nothing left between them, the slick warmth of her body grazed him. She was already so wet with need that it made him throb.

Grimm gripped her backside with the force of all his pent-up passion. He wanted to taste all of her, slowly. But it was not a moment for taking their time. This was a moment for turning one another mindless with bliss. A moment to think of nothing but this—*of each other*. Of every stolen breath they'd been apart. Grimm meant to leave Agatha satiated and yet still starved, relieved and yet still so very desperate. A reawakening of their bond.

Agatha didn't hesitate. She lifted her hips and slipped onto his cock, a moan escaping her as she slid down and down, taking him to the hilt. He cupped her breast in one hand and dug his fingers into her hip with the other, urging her as she began riding him in their fluid rhythm that set his blood on fire. She was so beautiful, wanton and glorious atop him, her head tipped back as ecstasy painted her face. He wanted to see her like this again and again, driven toward utter annihilation.

By *him*.

With his climax rising, Grimm moved his hips in time with hers, thrusting, desperate to feel the torturous clench of her release. He teased her nipple one last time before lowering his hand to stroke the tender place between her legs. Her sharp nails bit into his shoulders, and he relished it because the whimper that left her belonged to *him*.

Never again would he lose sight of her. Never again would he let anyone touch her. He would rip their soul straight from their body before he would let that happen.

"Grimm," she breathed, pawing at his chest as she leaned forward, bearing down on him and against his stroking thumb, right where she needed it. He once vowed to learn what brought her the most pleasure and to do it repeatedly. He was a man of his word. He knew what she wanted and he gave it to her.

And there it was, what *he* desired more than anything. She tightened around him, her pleasure threatening—*brimming*—so close.

Intent on answering her need, Grimm pulled Agatha forward

and ground his hips into hers, pressing so deeply that the delicious friction ripped a ragged moan from his chest.

"*Agatha.*" Her name was an oath. A plea.

"*Oh, gods,*" she cried, melting onto him, tangling her fingers in his hair.

Her constriction around his cock was so intense it pulled him to the brink with every pulsing wave. Agatha's eyes opened and locked with his, the love and passion in her gaze enough to force him over the edge with her.

"*Fuck,*" he breathed, thrusting into her until his vision darkened at the fringes. In those moments, the only thing he knew existed for certain outside of himself was her. *Them.*

She collapsed onto his chest, trembling, her breasts pressed against him. He let her lie there, caressing a long line up and down her spine until he sensed her drifting toward sleep. Carefully, he rolled their bodies, remaining inside her as he kissed her neck.

"No, no, little witch," he whispered against her hair as he hardened once again for the woman he loved. "I'm not done with you yet. We've lost time to make up for."

WINNIE

Eleanor had been asleep for the entirety of the previous night's mayhem. When she awoke to Winnie staring at her, she immediately panicked, asking what happened. She did deserve to know. They were her prince and princess, her queen, after all. Her friends. But, Winnie wanted to be on the road first. There was still much to sort out in her mind before she could articulate it all. Find a…diplomatic way to tell the maid her friends had faced such trauma.

"*What happened*," Eleanor asked for the fourth time since they set back out on the trail toward Làcdelle.

"The magus is what happened. That snivelling, sorry excuse for a rodent had Anne—" So much for diplomacy.

"*He what*?" Eleanor shouted so loudly that a flurry of birds rushed out of a nearby tree and sparks of magic flew out of her hand.

"She's fine. Physically. Your reaper prince ripped the magus' soul right out of his saggy sack of bones and Agatha got Anne out."

"And you waited to tell me this?" Thankfully, the question seemed to be rhetorical, because Eleanor cursed bitterly and murmured something about ripping the magus' soul out herself. "Is he dead?"

"No. He's on his way to be detained in my home for Grimm to question, but I don't think he'll get to."

"Your home? Why would you ever do that?"

"I knew we'd have the man from the mountain pass soon and with things as tenuous and dire as they are, we need to convene quickly once we have him. My home is not that far from here."

"Alright, but why couldn't Grimm just return to the castle in a fortnight and question him then?"

Winnie grimaced. "I think part of his plan is to lure The Order into coming to retrieve their old puppet."

"And you think they will succeed, even hidden in your home?"

"That is my fear, yes."

"It will all work out, somehow."

Winnie eyed her sidelong. "Look at the pessimistic bird being positive."

She barked a laugh and Winnie smiled.

It was a strange thing, having someone by her side again after so long that she could talk with. A friend.

But she could not have that. Especially after what Anne's association with Aggie gained her.

"I need you to understand something." Eleanor's head cocked to one side at Winnie's tone. "I will teach you the basics of magic on our journey. But, once we locate this illusive man and deliver you back to Merveille, you and I are through, and our time together will be complete." Winnie stopped herself from fidgeting upon her steed as dejection bloomed on Eleanor's cheeks and her magical bird burst into a spray of blue.

She pushed its fragmented magic away and sat straighter in the saddle. "Is that really what you want?"

"A long time ago, I vowed to be alone, in life. When this task for my Sister is complete, I will return to that vow."

Eleanor's face was unreadable. "I don't care what you *vowed*. Is it what you want?"

"What I want does not matter, Eleanor."

"Like Hades." This stubborn mortal never minced words and, goddess help Winnie, it held her steady. It made her face her feelings just as Aggie would say she needed to do. "You're just scared to be happy. As Laurent said."

"Laurent doesn't know I was *killing* him. My presence is *wolfsbane*. I've made my vow and it is final. It's what is best."

"Vows need to be re-evaluated on a regular basis. One might very well vow to protect their magus until they learn he is a vile rapist and murderer. Should that vow still stand?"

Curse her for being correct. But Eleanor gave Winnie no time to respond.

"Is it what you *want*, Winnie?"

She let the words sink into her. A crack splintering through her frozen walls. Eleanor's forehead creased in a challenge, her frosty blue eyes looking within Winnie. The fracture deepened.

"Or do you want a companion? An equal. Someone you can

trust. Someone who will press you from all sides to be the greatest version of yourself, but who will *never* push you to be anything you are not?" Eleanor sat straighter, tears pooling in Winnie's eyes, despite her best efforts. "Because I believe you have that. In Agatha. In Laurent. And in *me*." Her face softened, but only slightly and her words continued to cut through the frigid air, landing blows against Winnie's walls. "If you don't want to go back because you think you're killing Laurent, or you're being punished because of some crock of shite thing an abusive witch taught you, then *fine*."

Winnie pulled her horse to a stop and sat very still, a glacial tear slipping down her cheek.

Eleanor turned her steed so they were face to face. "You will not be alone with *me*. But you will always be given the room to be alone when you need to be, and you will never lose yourself or be less of who you are. I will not trap you, or hold you back. I don't want to go back to Merveille. And I don't want this bickering, maddening friendship to end, Winnie."

The crack spread, fissuring into a spider web, cleaving the ice of Winnie's fortress until it sat on the cusp of shattering, perilously close to falling away entirely. She dipped her chin once, it was all she could do with a torrent of emotion consuming her.

"If you loathe me still in a fortnight, we'll re-evaluate." Eleanor smiled and Winnie couldn't help but genuinely return it.

She blew out a breath and Eleanor opened her mouth to speak again, but the sound of pounding hooves shot through the woodlands toward them.

"Get off the road," Winnie hissed. She snapped the hitch hooking their wagon to the horse and kicked the beast into motion, veering off the path.

Eleanor followed her into the thick trees. "What's wrong?"

"Anyone moving that quickly means trouble."

"What about our cart? Won't they ransack it?"

"They might. Shut your mouth and keep quiet!"

The thundering and shouting of voices urging their horses faster came closer. Winnie dismounted and crouched low in the snow, Eleanor following her lead. She prayed to Hespa their tracks would soon be covered by fresh powder and that the men wouldn't stop to investigate the cart. They should've moved further away from it, but there hadn't been time. Perhaps they would ride right past thinking it was a trap.

The sound of pounding hooves abruptly stopped and Eleanor looked at her, eyes wide.

"This is it," came a faint voice. "It's their cart."

Eleanor's face contorted and Winnie snarled. She stood and stalked forward through the woods, her hands balled into fists at her sides because she knew that voice.

"*Laurent*!" Winnie shouted when she broke free of the trees. "What in all the realms are you doing here?" She stared daggers at the Cirque Master and Tomás as they dismounted.

Laurent never slowed, striding toward her, stopping only a handbreadth from her face.

"*What do you want*?" she spat.

"I want you to stop running." He shifted on his feet, crossing his thick arms across his chest. "I thought I could let you go. But I don't *want* to, Wendy." His skin was pulled tight across his brow, countenance more serious than she'd ever seen him. "We were together for longer than most mortals even *live*. And over the last fifty years, I've never stopped thinking about you, never stopped hoping you'd come back. I've never stopped hoping you would be in the audience one night. Every show, every fucking one since you left all those years ago, my final thought before I take the stage has always been that it could be the night. The show I finally see you again." The depth of his words shone in his eyes. "Then you *did* come back. You're *real*. With me in living colour and breathing and taking every ounce of my concentration because you drive me *mad*, Wendy."

"You can go on without me," she breathed. A foolish, trite thing to say.

"Dammit, I don't *want* to go on without you is what I'm saying."

Winnie backed up, shaking her head, hands trembling. "You have to, Lau. You must find a way."

A tear fell down her cheek and Laurent reached out a hand, but she was already gone in an icy spray of magic.

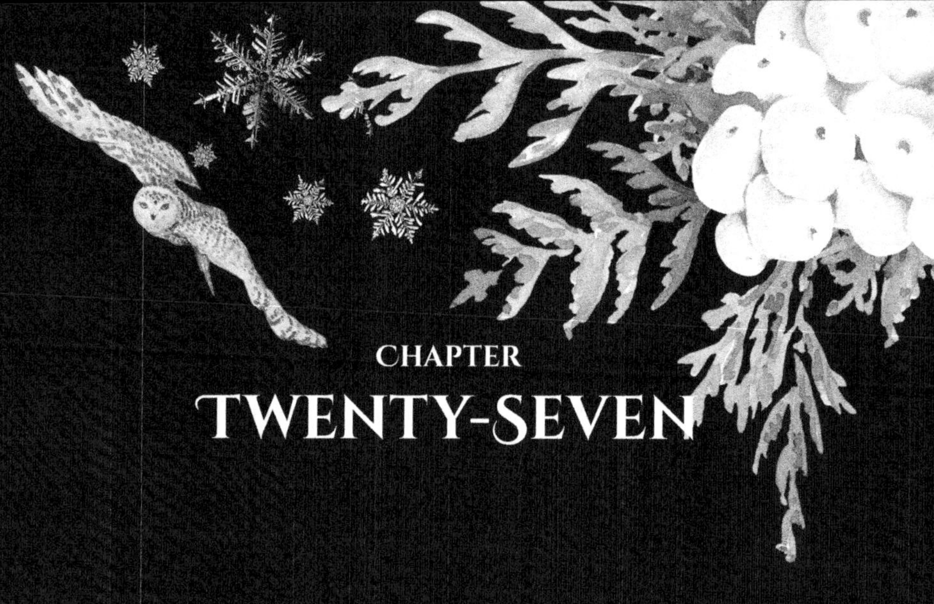

CHAPTER TWENTY-SEVEN

AGATHA

"I ought to string you up by your ears and slap you senseless!"

Agatha and Seleste watched with no small amount of amusement as Dulci tugged Grimm around by the ear, berating him for taking the draught.

"You could have gotten yourself bloody well killed and then where would we be? Huh?" She cuffed him on the back of the head for the fourth time and shoved him down onto a white settee in Winnie's common room.

To his credit, or perhaps detriment, Grimm was barely concealing a grin of his own. "I missed you as well, Dulci."

"Like Hades, you damned fool." The old baker threw her hands on her hips. "No closer to finding the empress, either, are you?" Grimm opened his mouth to answer, but Dulci swatted the air toward him and stormed off spewing a litany of curses in Coronnocan.

"That went better than I thought it would," Grimm muttered, tugging at his bruised ear.

"She was quite terrified," Seleste informed him placidly. "She loves you dearly."

Grimm scrubbed at his jaw, guilt flooding the bond. "I suppose I should go assist her with whatever pastry havoc she is about to wreak on Vera's kitchen to deal with her fury."

Just then a loud crash came from the direction of Winnie's kitchen and Vera came hobbling out and screeching, "What in the goblin's arse is that woman doing in my kitchen!"

Grimm winced. "I'll take care of it, Vera."

"You best, Fancy Pants!" She looked at Seleste, her face and tone softening. "You never said you was bringing plus one, girl." She shooed Sister Summer toward the gilded corridor. "Go on. Your room is ready. I need some air."

Vera disappeared and Agatha went to check on Anne.

WINNIE

The wind was ravenous at the top of the goliath mountain behind her home. She willed the air around her to still, the ice cracking where it plummeted from the mouth of a waterfall, down into the frozen lake. Winnie took three steadying breaths, focusing on the feel of the snow beneath her boots, the crisp mountain air, and the sway of the evergreens dusted in white. The sky was turning deep blue at the top, the sun just beginning to sink behind the horizon. She closed her eyes.

"I CAN'T."

"That is merely a lie you've told yourself, dove."

Winnie scowled up at her mother, who only smiled gently in return. "I cannot halt a waterfall."

Her mother bent to clasp her hands. "Ah, but you can. Let down your battlements, Winnie. The limitations you have are placed there by you and you alone. The walls around you are not real. Let them down. Knock *them down. Never shrink, dove. You are wild. Free. There is no cage unless you lock yourself in."*

Winnie closed her eyes tight, squeezing her small hands into fists. Never shrink. I am wild. Free.

She gasped and opened her eyes. "I could freeze it!"

Lorelai Joubert beamed. "You will *freeze it."*

"WHATCHA DOIN' way out here?"

Winnie inhaled sharply, her eyes flying open to find Vera watching her. "I needed some air."

Vera snorted and sat on a frosted, fallen tree. "You'n me both. Aren't yer supposed to be finding that mountain pass man?"

"I needed a moment to collect myself and this is where I often do that." It was why she'd selected to build her home nearby.

"I know."

Winnie scowled at her stewardess, who smiled knowingly and patted the log next to her. She sat with a huff.

"Trouble at the cirque?"

Mouth agape, she turned on Vera. "What did you just say?"

"Relax." The old crone nudged Winnie's shoulder with hers. "I've kept yer secret. Even told Aggie I dun' know a thing."

"You *don't* know a thing…"

Vera's wrinkled face quirked to the side. "Don't I?" She looked out over the frozen waterfall and smiled. "Nah, guess I don' know about the seventy years yer spent at the cirque as the best-damned singer the continent's ever seen." Winnie blanched. "Guess I don' know 'bout the cirque master, or that loneliness is really why yer put the advert in The Spectre fifty years ago."

Winnie was no longer breathing. "H–how?"

"Doesn' matter. But it doesn't take a genius to know why you went back to the cirque."

"I needed information about the man in the mountain pass," Winnie defended.

"Nothin' at all to do with one Laurent Barroque, then?" Winnie sneered and Vera nodded, gaze still out over the snow, sky speckled with pink. "What I *don'* know, is why yer left in the first place."

A knot formed in Winnie's stomach, tears stinging the back of her eyes. "I–I hurt him. My magic, my presence, it's killing him."

"I never heard such a thing as all that. Druid magic is damn near stronger than a witch's, mind you."

"But I am a Sister Solstice. And–" The words caught in her throat, suddenly feeling like parchment. "I defied an Order." She looked at her trembling fingers. "I was Sanctioned."

Vera rested her gnarled hand on Winnie's. "Now that's a bunch o' hogwash. Yer telling me, as a Sister Solstice who's been hauntin' this realm for three hundred and sixteen years you still can't see the goddess for who She is? Ain't no loving mother that's ever lived would put her child through such punishment and call it love."

Winnie's vision swam with her tears, the heat of them turning ice cold as they slid down her cheeks. "She never claimed the Sanction was love," Winnie whispered, "only punishment. She took my greatest love from me."

Vera grasped both Winnie's shoulders so hard it hurt, turning her toward her. "Now you listen here, Wendolyn Joubert, and you listen well. If you let one thing within that stubborn fortress of yours, let it be this. If it ain't loving, it ain't the Goddess Three. You hear me?"

Winnie let out a sob.

"Dove, whatsoever you've lost, remember that family can be made. *Chosen*." Vera tucked a strand of hair behind her ear. "You must continue forward. You've only just begun."

Winnie almost forgot whom she was sitting with, so like her mother Vera sounded. "But Laurent... He's dying because of me."

"*Fooie*!" She spat. "Yer a healer, ain't ya?"

"I was, long ago, but–"

"But nothin'. Heal him."

"I can't–"

Vera's eyes sharpened, her face stern. "You will. Let down your battlements, dove."

Winnie's lips parted at her words, a golden light she'd never seen flickering to life in her palm.

"The only walls you got are of yer own makin'." Vera stood and ran a tender hand down Winnie's cheek before leaning in and whispering fiercely, "*Burn them to the ground*."

She snapped and was gone.

Fingers gilded and trembling, Winnie closed her eyes and thought of Laurent.

"*Wendy*."

She opened her eyes, shocked to see she was still on the mountaintop, and he was there standing before her. She'd never transported another person that wasn't her Sister. Certainly, it had to have come as a surprise to him as well, but his eyes never left hers. Unwavering.

"Wendy, are you all right?"

Stepping forward, she outstretched her palm toward him. His

face glowed in the light of it, but still, he did not break eye contact with her. "Do you trust me?" she whispered, her hand hovering in front of his heart.

"With everything I am."

She pushed her palm forward, connecting with his chest. Winnie watched in awe as the golden magic poured from her, seeping into Laurent. Still, his gaze did not leave her face. The molten power spread beneath his skin, consuming his chest, and his shoulders, crawling up his neck and flowing down his arms. When it filled him completely, a brilliant light burst forth as if incinerating him. Winnie was pushed back into the snow by its power, her arm over her eyes against the blinding light. When the world went nightshade again, she lowered her arm, terrified she'd just killed him.

Laurent stood, staring in disbelief at his hands. They were smoother. Unscarred. He locked eyes with Winnie, mouth agape, and lifted tentative, trembling fingers to his face. Smooth and free of blemish or disfigurement. "You healed me."

"Restored."

He marvelled at her for a moment before speaking, voice gruff with emotion. "Take the beauty back, Wendy. I don't want it."

Tears filled her eyes to the brim. She stepped forward, resting her palm against his cheek. "You're certain?"

Laurent smiled, full of warmth. "I don't need it," he repeated.

Winnie blinked to clear the gathering tears, letting them fall unabashed. She summoned the deep well of her magic and banished the outward show of Laurent's beauty. No amount of magic could ever steal who he was. Not even death could have done such a thing as robbing him of it.

Beneath her hand, the disfigured face of the man she fell in love with returned. He smiled down at her, wrapping his hands around her waist. She caught the glint in his eye, the very one that stole her heart on her last day with her Sisters, as a Cirque

Master wooed his crowd. Winnie ran a thumb over his cheek, moving down to trace his lips.

He leaned into her touch. "I've only ever wanted you, from that first moment I laid eyes on you."

A sob choked out of her as she looked up into his eyes. "I'm so sorry, Lau. I thought I was what destroyed you. I thought *I* was killing you because the Grimoire forbade me from seeing you and I did it anyway."

Laurent shook his head. "Even if it had been you, I wouldn't have walked away."

"I know. And that's why I had to. Once I was Sanctioned, I thought–I thought it would be different, that I could see you. But then you became so sick… I–"

Laurent silenced her with a kiss. It began tenderly, a reacquainting. But then they both remembered. The century they spent eyeing one another across a cirque. The seventy years they spend tangled in each other's arms, travelling the continent, growing, healing, learning—together. The fifty years they spent missing one another. Laurent's fingers dug into the small of her back and she parted her lips, his tongue slipping in to meet hers. She melted into his body, grasping at his waist.

He pulled back, huffing, his chest rising and falling rapidly. She reached to run her fingers along the muscles there. "I missed you, Wendy," he breathed, his breath clouding the air. "I can't even begin to explain how much."

"Then show me just how much."

His eyes flashed and he had her by the waist, pulling her toward him. He kissed her fervently, desperation and released sorrow coating his lips.

AGATHA

Sipping the coffee Vera so graciously made, Agatha wandered out onto the veranda overlooking Winnie's snowy expanse. For the first time in far too long, she felt serene. Even with the vast unknowns. Even with the magus chained in a room down the hall and The Order likely to knock on the door.

Grimm came up behind her, wrapping his arms around her waist and attempted to slip his fingers under her robe. She laughed and swatted his hand away, setting her coffee down. "Gaius and Sorscha will be here soon. You need to get dressed."

He buried his face in her neck, kissing her until she felt heat pool between her legs. "Mmm. Tell me that delicious feeling I just tasted from you is a lie and I'll go meet them in the woods."

She turned in his arms, wrapping hers around the back of his neck. "Well, the bond can't lie."

Before she could register it, his hand slipped up her robe, fingers sliding between her legs. She could feel his response against her hip and his sharp intake of breath made her shiver. "Neither can that."

A grunt and the clang of metal sounded behind her and they pulled apart to look out over the balcony, Grimm adjusting himself. "Damn you," he teased as she laughed.

Peering over the railing, they caught sight of Augustus positioning a sword in Anne's hand, then moving to hit it with his own. Agatha couldn't hear their words, but he shifted his grip, showing her how to stand firmly, and she copied him. He motioned for her to go again and she did, her arms too weak to accomplish much.

"Why didn't I think of that?" Grimm mused and she reached up to run her hand over his messy, close-cropped beard.

"Grimm, I adore you, but you cannot live your life blaming yourself for everything."

His eyes met hers and she could feel his sadness. That was

not something he would easily give up, but she would spend the rest of their ancient lives helping him to do so.

"I do need to go meet Gaius and Sorscha." He leaned down to kiss her gently, but she brought her hands around the back of his neck again and pressed her hips into his. His fingers dug into her backside and he pulled back, growling. "Do not tempt me so, witch." He kissed her forehead and left to dress.

Once she'd done the same, Agatha went outside, but only Augustus was still there, his shoulders slumped and head lowered where he sat on a stone garden wall.

"Please don't ask me to stop training her," he spoke as Agatha sat next to him. The sorrow in his voice was nearly unbearable.

"Quite the contrary."

He looked over at her.

"Teach her all the ways you know to slaughter a man and I will do the same."

A ghost of a smile crossed his lips and she stood, holding out a hand to help him up. "Come on. Vera makes the most astounding *crêpes*."

GRIMM

He could get lost in Wendolyn's library for days. The space was filled to the brim with the sort of books he normally had to hunt for. There were innumerable things he adored about being married to a witch, but her, and her Sisters', collection of literature had to be at the top of his list.

He felt her coming nearer as he thumbed through the old

texts. "What have you found now?" she teased as she closed the library door behind her and a shiver went down his spine.

If he could guarantee no one would barge in on them, he'd take her amongst the stacks of books and see how many they could knock from the shelves. That would be a delightful way to select which to choose next. Alas, they had the new development of learning there used to be *four* factions of The Order and a magus to eventually interrogate...again. Von Fuchs had been uncooperative at best, and he was beginning to act as if he were falling ill.

"Busying my mind with old maps of Midlerea."

"Still nothing on the factions?"

Grimm shrugged. "If your Sister had something of the sort, she would have known about them, yes?"

Agatha made a noncommittal noise. "Perhaps."

"I did find this." He shuffled through the many maps spread out before him, brow pulled low and muttering curses. "Now I can't find the damned thing."

Agatha watched him move to another table, smiling to herself. He felt a pang of heart-warming wistfulness from her. She'd always said he *was* chaos incarnate, but he knew she adored it.

"Perhaps Vera came in and picked up after you. You are rather destructive." She picked up a half-eaten *croissant* that was hard as a rock.

Grimm waved a hand dismissively. "She's been in a mood since Dulci and Seleste arrived. Ah, here it is." He withdrew a torn piece of parchment from underneath an empty tea cup and handed it to Agatha.

"Did you *rip* this out of a book?"

He snorted at the irate look on her face. "I didn't fancy lugging the whole book around." Her frown deepened. "Just look at it."

The page crinkled as she flattened it on the table. "It has a tea stain," she grumbled. "Goddess above…" She leaned closer. "Is that– No, it can't be. What are these?" She fixed her attention on Grimm, brow scrunched.

"They're some kind of sigils. It struck me that there were four of them with only minor differences."

"Where did you find this?"

"Oddly enough, in a book detailing different maps of the continents. At first, I thought they were some sort of cartographical key, but I'd never seen anything like them before. Then it dawned on me that each one was on a separate page, detailing a separate continent. This one"—he pointed at the page in front of Agatha—"is just a blank page of them, side by side." He studied the rendering for a moment. "This is more of a sketch, as well, while the rest of the text is much more detailed."

"Could we look back further? If these are sigils for the four factions, there must be a combination of them fully together as one, right?"

"I'm not certain. Even separately they remind me of the drawing I found on Pierre last Autumn."

Agatha nodded. "I thought the same, but about my mother's locket."

"I'm glad it wasn't just my overactive imagination."

Augustus burst through the door of the library then, huffing. "It's the magus. He's started foaming at the mouth."

Grimm exchanged a look with Agatha. "Go retrieve your mother's locket. I'll handle this."

WINNIE

Laurent ran a tender finger across Winnie's forehead, down her cheek and traced her lips. He leaned to brush his lips against hers. "I refuse to wake from this dream."

She smiled up at him, eyelids heavy with a sense of freedom and bliss she hadn't felt in centuries. "You never turn off your showman charm, do you?" she teased.

"Never." He hauled her closer and she moulded her body to his where they sat cuddled in a warm cocoon on the mountain. "We must, however, return to wherever you whisked us from. Tomás and Eleanor might worry."

"I don't think the bird has *worry* in her. Only complaints and stubbornness."

"The bird?" he chuckled, the scruff of his chin tickling her cheek.

"She follows me around like all the other birds and chirps twice as much as any of them."

She felt Laurent smile against her head. "Mm. She reminds me a bit of you when we were younger."

Winnie sat up, aghast. "How dare you!" But her face cracked and she sputtered a laugh.

"I just call it how I see it. Blonde, opinionated, stubborn…" She dug her nails into his bicep and he laughed, standing and pulling her up with him. "Come on. We still have a strange man to locate." He grinned manically. "And some catching up to do."

Winnie smiled back, summoning a deep indigo coat. They'd spent hours talking in each other's arms, the simmering fire between them building. Winnie sighed, sobering. "I have something I need to do first."

Laurent's brow furrowed, the otherworldly warmth around them folding into him with his power. "What's that?"

"I need to show my Sisters what happened."

He stilled, hand adjusting the dagger at his side. "Do you mean…?" She nodded. "Wendy… You're certain?"

"It's time."

"Would you like for me to come?"

Oh, how she'd missed this man. "It's something I must do on my own." She walked forward and kissed him. "I'll find you all on the road after."

"Wh– You can't just leave me here!" Laurent shouted after her.

Winnie turned back and smiled wickedly. "Your magic is *fully* restored, Lau."

His eyes sparked with possibility. At the edge of the tree line, she turned back again, just in time to see him somersault off the side of the frozen waterfall.

CHAPTER TWENTY-EIGHT

AGATHA

The air in the library dropped in temperature, ever so slightly, just before Winnie appeared next to Agatha.

She addressed Grimm first. "If you'll excuse us, I have something I need to show my Sister."

He looked sidelong at Agatha, an ankle crossed over his knee and a tome open in his lap. He hadn't been this relaxed in almost a moon, and the sight made her heart ache. Grimm shrugged and returned his attention back to whatever Historical text he'd selected this time to learn more about the four factions of The Order. "You've an incomparable library, Wendolyn," he said.

"Enjoy it."

Her tone sounded sincere and they both regarded her quizzically before exchanging a befuddled look.

"I mean it," she said, looking between them.

Agatha huffed a laugh. "All right… What's going on?"

"If you would, be a dear and get Sorscha. I need to summon Seleste."

"Can this possibly take place out of this room?" They both

stared daggers at Grimm. "What? I'm rather enjoying this study on how the Coronoccan culture has evolved."

Agatha rolled her eyes and Winnie glowered. "Fine, *Your Highness*."

"Thank you kindly, *Winnie*," he cooed.

"He's a spoiled prat," she murmured to her Sister Autumn. Grimm snorted, eyes roving over the pages, one hand already reaching for his quill.

The two of them went out into the hall and each summoned one of their other Sisters. Sorscha appeared in the marbled hallway barefoot with a silk wrapping around her head. "I finally had a chance at a proper bed," she whined.

"It's important," was Winnie's only reply.

"I was three doors down the hall, you buffoons. You could have just knocked."

Seleste arrived holding a muffin, one bite in her mouth. "Aggie, you truly under-presented Dulci's confections. I must have eaten my weight in them by now." She came forward and kissed each of them on the cheek. "I was just down in the kitchens, why've you summoned me?"

"Winnie, what's going on?" Agatha echoed.

A heavy weight seemed to drag her shoulders down. "I have something I need to show you. Take hands." She held hers out and Aggie took one, Seleste the other, Sorscha closing their circle. Sorscha glanced out the corner of her eye at Agatha, then Seleste, before all three of them fixed their attention on their eldest Sister.

"Before we go any further, with this I'm showing you... Or with our plans, our life, our Sisterhood..." Winnie shifted her weight, gown brushing against the marble under her feet. "I need to know that, no matter what you see, you—" She broke off, and Agatha saw her throat bob as she swallowed. She dropped Sorscha's hand and clasped Winnie's with both of hers.

"What is it, Winnie?"

"I need to know that you won't let me go."

Seleste broke free and stepped to run her hand up and down Winnie's back. "Never. We would never let you go."

Agatha nodded. "Seleste is right. Whatever it may be, we will not be broken, the four of us."

Winnie looked at her elegant boots. "You say that now…"

"Winnie," Sorscha's scratchy voice broke in, "we might hate you for a moment, I won't deny that possibility. But, they're right, we'd never let you go."

Agatha smiled reassuringly. "What's the most important rule?"

"Stay together," Winnie whispered. She cleared her throat, blinking rapidly. "Right then." She straightened and held out her arm. When she nodded once, they clasped her hands. "Close your eyes."

When they opened them, they were standing in a meadow, the Spring sunshine peering through the trees, a quaint cottage in its centre.

"Where are we?" Sorscha asked, taking it all in.

"Where's Winnie?" Seleste looked around anxiously.

Agatha couldn't tear her eyes from the cottage, an ominous feeling coursing through her. "I think she's in there."

Her Sisters followed her pointed finger. "I've never seen this place before," Sorscha said. "Have you?" Agatha and Seleste both shook their heads.

A wail of pain pierced the serene meadow and they all took off at a run for the cottage.

Sorscha slammed through the door first, shouting Winnie's name.

"I don't think she can hear us, Sorscha. I think it's a memory." The edges of the world seemed foggy, iridescent like a dream. Sharing memories was incredibly complex and powerful magic.

"I think Aggie's right." Seleste agreed, slinking through the place, searching.

It was a simple home but decorated in a style very fitting of a younger Winnie. Much younger. Not finery, but beautiful and purposeful. Yula rested on a perch in the corner next to a bookcase, but she was antsy, her feathers ruffled. Worried.

"Shh, Yula." Agatha moved to smooth her feathers, but her hand went through her like a ghoul. "She's worried. We have to find Winnie. Something terrible has happened to her."

"Oh, gods." Sorscha put a hand to her mouth, staring down at the wooden floor in the hallway.

"Is that–"

"Blood," Sorscha whispered. Agatha's heart pounded, lodging itself deep in her throat.

They followed the trail down the hall, another guttural scream coming to meet them. Seleste pushed past her Sisters, calling Winnie's name regardless of the fact she wouldn't be able to hear them. Her foot slipped just as she rounded the corner into a bedroom and Agatha vaguely wondered *how*.

"Goddess above." But Seleste was staring into the room, hardly registering what bodily fluid she stood in.

Agatha and Sorscha came up on either side of her in the doorway, gasping in unison.

On the bed was Winnie writhing in pain, blood soaking the sheets and a swollen belly protruding. Agatha covered her mouth, tears pouring down her cheeks at the sight.

Seleste brought a shaking hand to her mouth. "She's all alone."

They moved closer to the bed. Arms clasped and huddled together, they watched, crying as Winnie laboured, sweat sticking her white-blonde hair to her head. She screamed again and the Sisters' tears multiplied.

"*She's all alone*," Seleste repeated.

"Sisters," Sorscha breathed. "It's too much blood. I think this has taken too long. Look how weak she is. She can't even hold her head up. We have to do something."

"We know she lives," Seleste answered, clutching them both on either side. "Hold onto that."

Agatha burst out a sob. "But the babe."

Seleste snapped into focus, a strange calm washing over her as she gently pushed her Sisters away and rounded the bed, studying Winnie's belly. "It's breech," she said, almost to herself. Her hands lit with light.

"Seleste, you can't alter the past," Agatha warned, worried she would somehow harm Winnie if she tried.

"Maybe we were always here," Sorscha whispered, going around to where Winnie was dilating. "Do it, Seleste."

Another sob choked out of Agatha and she moved next to Winnie's ear. "Sister. We're here. Shh… We would never let you do this alone." Her vision blurred behind the tears, but Agatha put her hand to Winnie's forehead, paying no mind to it disappearing against her skin. "Shh. I'm so sorry you thought you were alone."

Seleste began to chant, her hands glowing over Winnie's belly. "*Tourner. Naître. Vivre.*" Winnie's belly began to move. "The babe is moving! *Tourner. Naître. Vivre.*"

A desperate cry of agony came forth out of Winnie and she grabbed onto the headboard, writhing.

"It's not working! The babe turned back!" Seleste shouted over the pained screams. She dropped her hands and moved to watch the hollow of Winnie's neck. "Her pulse is too low, she's dying, too."

Sorscha and Agatha rushed to join hands with Seleste, encircling their Sister and the babe.

"Tourner. Naître. Vivre. Tourner. Naître. Vivre."

Another scream tore from Winnie's throat and her stomach shifted violently.

"Tourner. Naître. Vivre. Tourner. Naître. Vivre."

"Go, Sorscha!" Agatha shouted.

She ran for the foot of the bed. "It's working! I see the head!"

Agatha moved back to Winnie's ear. "You have to push now, Sister. You can do this." She glanced at the low pulse in her Sister's neck, her eyes rolling back in her head, and another sob tore from her. "Winnie. *Please*." She knew in her heart that Winnie would make it, she was the one that brought them there, but this was torture. To watch her Sister dying, to not know if her babe would make it. "Winnie, gods dammit, *push*!" she screamed. Winnie's eyes opened, unfocused, and Agatha shouted it again. "*Push*, Winnie!"

She watched as her eldest Sister grit her teeth and pushed with everything she had, crying out with the roar of a lioness.

"Push!"

"She's crowning!" Sorscha shouted, Seleste still chanting through her tears.

"Winnie. Come on, Sister. You can do this."

With another primal cry, Winnie pushed, the babe's head slipping free.

"One more," Agatha whispered. "One more."

With a final push, the shoulders broke free of Winnie and she reached down to gently pull the babe the rest of the way out, its squalling the most beautiful sound any of them had ever heard. *Life*.

"It's a girl," Sorscha sobbed as Winnie cuddled the babe to her chest.

"Shh, little one," Winnie whispered, using linen to clean her. "Oh, you are my heart's greatest love. My *daughter*." She kissed her head of dark hair. "Lilette."

Agatha, Sorscha, and Seleste fell to the floor together, a heap of limbs and snot and laughs, holding one another and sobbing. Once they'd recovered enough to stand, Winnie was nursing Lilette and they gathered around her.

"Oh, Aggie," Seleste breathed. "She looks like you."

"And Mother," Sorscha added.

The babe opened her eyes and they all made various sounds of awe. "Oh, her eyes," Agatha cooed.

Lilette's attention shifted from her mother to them and they all three gasped. Winnie smiled down at her daughter, then followed her attention. "What do you see, little one?" She looked around, through her Sisters. "Lilette Proctor," she mused, kissing her daughter again.

Agatha's stomach curled into a knot. She suddenly remembered exactly where she'd heard that surname before.

The scene folded in on itself in a roiling fog, unfurling into all four Sisters surrounding a large fire, somewhere in the mountains. The present-day versions of themselves looked between each other as they slowly circled their former selves.

"*Aggie*," Winnie was saying as if she'd already said it several times.

Agatha was staring into the fire, face solemn, almost in shock. "I remember this," Agatha whispered. "I'd just been sent to poison a dignitary, but he caught me and things turned… bloody. He was my first close kill."

"*Aggie*," Winnie said again and young Agatha finally looked up. "How was it? How did your Order go?"

"*It was fine*." Current Agatha flinched at her past self's tone. She had been a broken shell of herself and would remain that way for a very long time.

"How old were you?" Seleste asked.

"Around a century, I believe."

"I don't recall anything significant around that time, do you?"

Sorscha and Agatha shook their heads. "Do you think she already had Lilette?" Sorscha asked. "She seems around the same age."

"She's looked this age for three hundred years, Sorscha."

Sister Spring glared at Agatha. "She does seem anxious to hurry this Solstice along."

"*Give me the Book, Aggie*," she was saying.

The scene shifted into Winnie rocking Lilette, nursing her, in the same dress they'd just seen her in at the Solstice. The babe looked older, perhaps six moons of age. Winnie was singing to her in that ethereal voice Agatha had always admired but grew to resent. She'd sung like that to her at one time, when things were simpler and they'd not yet known the Grimoire, or pain. Hearing her like this, singing to her own daughter, Agatha once again found it the loveliest voice she'd ever heard. A restoration of something lost.

Winnie kissed the babe's forehead and laid her in a bassinet. The Sisters followed her out of the small room and down the hallway. She hummed to herself, stopping to sip from a small vial. Winnie set it down and Sorscha bustled over to sniff it.

"Chamomile and rose hips. Good for nursing mothers."

They watched from a dimly lit corner as Winnie sat in a comfortable chair and took up the Grimoire, still humming, and opened it.

"Goddess, she looks so happy…" Sorscha whispered.

As if her musing broke a spell, Winnie's face drained of colour and melted into horror. "*No*." She went slack, staring down at her Order in the Grimoire. Then bolted upright. "NO!" she screamed, throwing the Book and running down the hall.

"Oh, gods," Seleste shouted as they rushed after her. "The nursery."

They burst through the door on Winnie's heels, just in time to see her hit her knees, an ominous, ghastly shadow lurking in the corner. "Please," she begged. "Not my child. Please, take anything else," she sobbed, "*anything*."

The ghoul shifted toward the sleeping child, an extension of the shade slipping forward and turning razor-sharp before the babe's face.

"No!" Winnie screamed, launching herself toward the bassinet and pulling Lilette up into her arms. The babe fussed and began to cry, Winnie rocking her on instinct. "I will do it," she cried. "Just leave! Leave my daughter!" she screeched at the ghoul, flinging her hand out until a white dagger of magic shot forth, sending the shadows slithering away.

She dropped to her knees again, clutching her child and sobbing. After a long moment, an unnerving calm slid over her like a second skin. She lost no tenderness for her daughter, but she moved like the undead. Winnie dressed Lilette in a precious ivory dress and did her short hair up in a blue ribbon. Winnie donned a cloak, then gently laid her babe in a basket, wrapping her in a blanket. "All snug as a bug, my sweet." She leaned in close and Agatha thought her heart would shatter as she knew Winnie's must be, but she didn't understand what was happening. "I love you more than all the stars in all the realms, my Lilette. I hope you never forget that." The child smiled and cooed, reaching up to take Winnie's cheeks in her chubby little hands. A tear fell down to meet her fingers and Winnie moved to kiss her palm. "Precious girl. You are fierce. You are strong. You are kind. May you live and shake this realm."

Winnie stood and lifted the basket to her arm. She donned her hood and carried the babe out into the snow, her Sisters following silently, invisibly behind. She walked down the path that led to her cottage, into the village proper. Three turns through the city centre and she veered down a dark lane with one lone house at the end. Small, with a dilapidated porch and a lopsided barn. She knocked on the door until the young lady of the house opened it, robed and candle in hand.

"Hester." She squinted out into the dark night. "Goodness me, are you all right? It's the middle of the night."

Winnie straightened her back and held out the basket. "Her name must remain Lilette Proctor. You will raise her as your own." The woman gaped openly and began shaking her head, but

Winnie shushed her. "Do not go easy on her, but never withhold love. She carries magic in her veins, as we do. Her History lies within the town of Hiverterre."

"Hester, stop. What's going on?"

"I have to go, Amalia. I will not return. Love my daughter."

Winnie walked away, the young woman's shouts muffled by the sudden snowfall. A babe's cry pierced through the distance and Winnie closed her eyes, set her hood back in place, and vanished.

When the fog rolled away to reveal the present, Winnie was on the floor against the wall of her hallway, with her head in her hands.

"*Winnie*." At Agatha's voice, she looked up, face full of sorrow.

"*How could you*?" Sorscha spat, all rage and unfettered edges. "How could you just leave Lilette like that?"

"I had no choice, Sorscha. I was Sanctioned."

"How could you let us blindly follow the Grimoire after something like that? You *made* us follow it." One of her hands sliced through the air. "You should have fucking said *no*! You're just like Mother!"

"*Sorscha*!" Agatha shouted, her voice cracking off the walls. "Take a walk."

Sister Spring's face contorted with fury and a slash of hurt before she disappeared.

The remaining Sisters Solstice settled onto the floor of their eldest Sister's mountain home, holding one another until Winnie finally spoke.

"She's right," Winnie said softly, looking at her hands.

"Perhaps," Agatha offered. "But I did not say no to the Grimoire, either."

Winnie looked up at her sadly.

Seleste rested a gentle hand on her back. "None of us did. What happened, Winnie?"

"The Grimoire forbade me to see the Druid troupe." She looked at Seleste. "The cirque I took you to, on our last day together, it's a troupe of Druids." She shook her head, face hidden behind the curtain of her blonde hair. "I kept finding them. Every time I thought I couldn't bear the separation from you three, I would find the cirque. I fell for the Cirque Master, Laurent. But I kept to the shadows, the back of the shows. I never conversed with him or the others. When an Order came to never see them again, I obeyed, for a while. I met a man in a village just outside Hiverterre. He was a magus and the Witch Trials were rampant and—" Her words choked off.

But Aggie knew the rest. "Jéan Proctor."

Winnie's attention startled to her. "Yes. How did you—"

"Grimm saw his name on an old letter in a book of yours Vera brought us. He had heard the story of him and Hester Perrault—you, I imagine."

Winnie nodded, Seleste speechless, taking it all in. "I don't understand how he knew the story. It was all but wiped from the record by the elders. Even his grave was unmarked."

"Grimm said as much, that there was little record of it except some letters written by an unknown person. They were sold to a professor of his, Ludwig in Merveille."

"How could it have gotten in my books?" Winnie rubbed her temples as if trying to dislodge cobwebs. "I don't know who would have written about it, or known... I fled the night they found me guilty. I hadn't even told Jéan I was with child yet. And he was dead by the time I returned. When I discovered that… I don't know. All I wanted was to find the cirque troupe, the Druids. I wanted to see the Cirque Master's face and forget. So, I did. Only once. Then I returned to my duties and prepared for Lilette. But that Winter… The Sanction came."

"Perhaps Lilette lives," Seleste suggested with a wilted smile.

"It's been far too long for a half-witch to survive. She would have been extraordinary to see two centuries."

"Some tea, then." Seleste pulled her up and Agatha followed. "Let's get you some rest before you need to be back on the road, hm?"

"They're not far from here, Eleanor and the others that are with me."

"Perhaps I'll send a raven to them, and you may all stop off here to have a good night's rest, or two. I have a feeling there is more you need to tell us about your life, Sister."

CHAPTER TWENTY-NINE

SORSCHA

"Touch my plate again and I will slice off every one of your fingers."

Tomás' hand was poised over Sorscha's plate, her dagger up against his index finger. The fiend smiled handsomely and plucked a bite of bread from her plate, popping it into his mouth. Anger flashed through her and she made to stab her dagger down into the table, just to scare him, but she blinked and he held a dagger next to her cheek, a wide grin on his face as he chewed his bread.

Seleste had insisted the two Druids convene for a couple of nights at Glacé Manor before venturing further into the mountains with Winnie and Eleanor to find the man in the mountain pass. Thus far, sunflowers had popped through the snow out front and all the snow in the back had melted. Otherwise, nothing tumultuous had occurred, except when she and Winnie were in too close of proximity. That had caused the manor to shake violently all three times.

"Knife Master," Laurent clarified from the far side of the

table, filling his own plate to the brim and slopping food on the tablecloth.

"*Gods*. Are all Druids this"—she waved the tip of her knife between them—"uncivilised?"

Gaius snorted across from her. "Says the woman who threatens people with her dagger at every turn."

"And never wears clothing," Agatha chimed in.

"Now this has gone a bridge too far," Sorscha snapped.

Seleste came up behind her and planted a kiss on the top of her head. "Tell me you're working things out with Winnie," she whispered.

Sorscha snorted.

"They're all just teasing you," Seleste said loud enough for all of them to hear.

Working things out with Winnie was doubtful. But the realm needed them and that meant *all* of them, magic working together, not causing mayhem. It would take time for that to happen, and for her to even begin *considering* forgiving Winnie. One does not *give up* their child just like their fucking mother before them did.

Alas, Sorscha was here, with her family and her new friends. Good food, good drink, and—mostly—pleasant conversation. She could put almost anything aside for a night, in circumstances like these.

"Well," Grimm spoke quietly to Agatha, the look in his eyes making Sorscha ache to be seen like that. "Shall we go check on Winnie and the magus?"

"Oh, give it a moment," Sorscha interrupted them. "Winnie will return." She lifted her glass of wine and Agatha watched Grimm closely, something silent passing between them.

With a sigh, he raised his glass, eyes on his wife. "To tonight."

"To tonight!" Sorscha echoed boisterously, and the others followed with fervour.

They spent the evening trading stories, laughing, eating… forgetting and avoiding. Sorscha watched them all.

Agatha wore a hint of a true smile. Eleanor had rosy cheeks every time the Knife Master spoke. Laurent kept watching the door for Winnie, even getting up once to go check on her. Grimm was absolutely lost to Agatha. Seleste laughed with Dulci and Augustus. The quiet, sweet maid, Anne—she held deep sorrow in her, broken up only by half-smiles when the guard ran a tender finger over her cheek or poured her more wine.

Sorscha's observant gaze moved to Gaius, only to find he was watching her, stoic and sombre. "Are you all right?" he mouthed. She nodded once before the door opened and Winnie finally entered. The room fell silent, expectant.

"There is nothing medically wrong with the man," she said as she sat in the empty seat next to Laurent, a cold plate of food in front of her. "I'll check again first thing tomorrow, but at present, there is no indication as to why he's been foaming at the mouth. It's almost as if his body is ridding itself of something that doesn't even exist."

"Perhaps he's merely faking it," Tomás offered, biting off a piece of roasted turkey.

"Then *perhaps* I'll try less medicinal methods in my next examination," Winnie murmured.

Agatha shrugged and they all looked at her. "You can try it. But he's as stubborn as you are."

"*I'm* stubborn?" Winnie put a hand to her bosom. "You're the stubborn mule."

From then, it was raucous laughter, wild stories, and Vera scolding them all until they each began to yawn and eventually padded off to bed.

When the house was quiet and still, Sorscha continued to sit at the table, staring out at the moon-bathed mountains in the distance, Ostara wound around her forearm.

"It's a lot"—Gaius' deep voice startled her—"for you, isn't it?"

"What is?"

"This family thing. Everyone together."

"I don't know." And she didn't. She couldn't place what was gnawing at her. Sorscha had always trusted her gut, but she wasn't sure what it was saying at the moment.

Gaius took a seat next to her and poured them each a goblet of mulled wine. "Care for my opinion?"

Sorscha snorted. "Be my guest."

Leaning back in his seat, Gaius unbuttoned his collar. He was growing more comfortable with her and far less rigid. He still refused to call her by her name, but it was more a game than anything now. In fact, he'd developed no fewer than fourteen other names for her to avoid slipping up, three of which were downright salacious for him. "Well, *petit serpent*, did you notice there were no tremors here until Wendolyn arrived?"

Obviously, she knew that quite well. "And?"

Gaius frowned, head tilted to the side. His evergreen eyes were tinged with sadness and she wasn't sure why. "I don't know what happened between you and Wendolyn the other night, but it would seem the longer the rest of you are together, the less destruction it causes."

"It's not my fault she's a selfish whore," Sorscha spat. "We've summoned her plenty of times to work out how to be together and she refused. You know that."

With his brows pulled low and lips pressed tight, Gaius leaned his elbows on his knees and took Sorscha's hand. "You need to talk to her, *gamine*."

Sorscha suppressed a smirk. "You know you're the *gamin* in this scenario, yes?"

Gaius smiled wide. "Hardly." He squeezed her hand and dropped it. "Go. Get it over with."

"Give me one more night to wallow in my rage."

He pushed her shoulder and stood. "Fine. But if this manor crumbles down on my head, there will be Hades to pay for you."

"All bark and no bite, Lord Gaius Asholm."

He waved her off and retired to his room.

WINNIE

"This is your room, then?" Laurent prowled across the space without even looking around at the marble floors and gilded walls.

The light on his face brought tears to Winnie's eyes. A man of all smiles, but the true light had gone out long ago. Here he was, restored and glorious. And hers.

The curtains drew shut, closing off the view of the mountains. The gleam in his eyes turned hungry and the multitude of candles lit upon her book-lined shelves. He took the last step toward her, taking her face gently in his strong hands. His lips found hers in a kiss fevered and desperate.

The stays of her dress and corset came undone by his power and he pushed her up against the wall next to the roaring fireplace, slipping his hands under her corset. The warmth of his touch through her chemise pushed the heat building between her legs to nearly unbearable. She let out a heady gasp as he pulled the restricting garments down to her waist, and Laurent chuckled against her neck.

Winnie arched her back as his lips trailed her collarbone and her breasts swelled within the thin fabric still separating her from him. She reached for his shirt, but he chuckled again and pulled back. He clicked his tongue.

"I'm afraid not, demoiselle." Gently, he took her wrists in

one large hand and pinned them against the wall above her head. "You wanted me to show you how much I missed you. Now, let me do just that." He released his grip, but her arms remained pinned by his magic. A thrill shot through her and Laurent grinned wickedly. "I believe I will enjoy this."

He stood before her, taking one teasing step away. "*Un*." Her dress vanished. "*Deux*." Her chemise fell to the plush fur rug at her feet. He looked her up and down and licked his lips, the bulge in his pants making her ache. He looked into her eyes and grinned. "*Trois*." Her underthings disintegrated. Laurent sucked in a breath, eyes roving, drinking. She could almost feel his lips on her body again and she needed it so badly.

"So help me, if you don't get over here I will break free from this magic."

"Wait your turn, you demanding thing."

He closed the distance between them slowly, too slowly, and Winnie shifted her hips, a small whimper escaping. "Patience is a virtue, you know." Laurent took her face in his hands again and kissed her deeply. She needed to feel him against her and he knew it. Which was precisely why he refused. A showman to his utter core.

He pulled back, running a finger down her neck, letting it slip lower until he traced the curve of her breast, the peak of her nipple. Her mind was growing muddled. Foggy with desperation. He saw it in her eyes, a carnal desire reflected in his own. He took her hips in his hands, and just that simple, possessive touch drew a gasp from her. Fifty years had passed since she last felt that pull. Her body had not forgotten what he could do to her.

Laurent slid one hand back, grasping the curve of her backside, almost, *almost* bringing his hips toward hers. He leaned down and kissed her neck in the spot only he had ever found. The one that drove her mad. Her back arched, the wainscoting biting into her skin and his grasp on her backside tightened. His lips moved to her breasts, tasting, exploring. His tongue trailed around her nipple before he pulled it into his mouth and Winnie thought she would explode right there.

"Oh, gods," she moaned and Laurent's chest rumbled in response.

He slowly knelt before her, hands roving. Sweet kisses he dealt along her abdomen, her hips. When he reached the curled hair at her pelvis, he pulled back and looked up at her, a grin spreading across his face. Her lips parted and he slipped his tongue between her legs with short, teasing strokes at first. He reached up with his fingers to pull her apart, his tongue stroking methodically.

Winnie moaned, writhing against the wall and his magic, desperate to run her hands through his hair. She pushed her hips forward in time with his stroking and one of his hands came up to cup her breast. Everything within her was coiled for release. Laurent must have felt her tighten beneath his tongue, his hot, sucking lips, because he growled and spread her legs further apart with his shoulder. The world exploded from within her and she moaned his name as he drove his fingers within her to magnify the ecstasy.

When she was done and he stood, Winnie was mad with need. Her wrists ripped free of his power and her magic clawed at his clothing. She stalked forward, vicious with desire. She grabbed his back with one arm and wrapped one hand around his hard length, stroking him once.

"*Fuck.*" He put an arm out and leaned on it against the wall.

"Payback," she whispered against his lips.

She knelt in front of him, stroking hard and slow, enjoying the look of pure animalistic male pleasure on his face. "Gods, Wendy."

"Oh," she purred. "That's nothing." She took him into her mouth until she could feel the tip at the back of her throat and then she sucked, pulling him in and out of her mouth in a rhythm.

"*Fuck*!" He grew harder in her mouth and she could taste he was close. She backed away, her tongue tracing the tip of him. He looked down at her with a hunger she'd never seen. It was wild in his eyes and he growled through gritted teeth, pulling her up. He pushed her up against the wall, spreading her legs and lifting one to fit around his waist, burying himself so deep within her that she gasped. He held her leg fast, pulling out and thrusting himself back in, her breasts bouncing. Pleasured exclamations burst out of her in quick succession as he pressed into her over and over, his thumb coming between them to stroke her. They came in unison, both proclaiming an oath with their pleasure.

WINNIE OPENED ONE EYELID, sensing an intruder in the dark, the fire low. Laurent tensed beside her on the white fur rug but also feigned sleep.

The scent of Spring rain and floral blooms filled the air and Winnie sighed. "It's just Sorscha," she said quietly.

Laurent groaned and three lanterns flicked on. He pulled a thick blanket off a chair near them and stood, wrapping it around his waist. "I'm going to sleep in the tub," he mumbled and walked blearily toward Winnie's lavish lavatory.

Naked under the thin blanket she'd shared with Laurent and not quite as comfortable as her Sister Spring as such, she summoned a champagne silk nightgown and rose to sit on the bed.

"The Cirque Master after all these years, huh?" Sorscha's tone pulled at Winnie's heart.

She nodded and climbed beneath the duvet, lifting the edge in invitation. Sorscha's bottom lip quivered and she slipped into the bed, nestling her head against Winnie's shoulder, just as they had done so long ago as children.

"I'm glad to see you happy, Sister," Sorscha whispered.

So many years apart. So little did they truly know about one another. Yet, even with all of Sorscha's anger toward her, Winnie knew her Sisters loved her, as she loved them.

"I'm sorry that I failed you, Sorscha." The words felt thick in her throat. "I've failed so much. I wanted to protect you all. Once I failed—once I faced my Sanction and I lost Lilette…" Her voice broke off and Sorscha snaked her arm around Winnie's middle. "Fear became my dearest friend," she finally finished.

"Anger is mine."

"No more, then, Sister. Let us venture forward. Together."

Sorscha let out a hiccupped sob. "May love be what binds us," she spoke through her tears.

The last fragment of Winnie's walls came tumbling to the ground, burnt to ash. She kissed the top of Sorscha's head. Her precious little Sister. "May love be what binds us," she echoed.

Winnie blinked, stunned by a sudden flare of light illuminating the duvet. Sorscha abruptly sat up. "Do you see that?" she whispered.

Winnie threw back the blanket and let out a sharp gasp.

Her icy magic had woven around the crimson serpentine threads of Sorscha's, glowing brighter and brighter until the entire room was bathed in blinding fuchsia. Squinting against the light, Sorscha laughed and Winnie put a hand up to block the fiery rose luminance.

"Gods!" Laurent exclaimed, flinging open the lavatory door. "Can't a man slee— What in Hades is all this?" He threw an arm around his eyes and stumbled back into the lavatory, slamming the door shut.

The light bounced playfully off the cream walls until it came to hover in front of the door, almost beckoning them.

"I think it wants us to follow it…" Sorscha rose from the bed, her blood-red nightgown cascading down to her ankles.

Winnie followed and they opened the bedroom door to let the light free. Once in the corridor, it sped off in a frenzy, the Sisters rushing to keep up, giggling madly at the lunacy of it all. The magic lit the marble hall in a shade of pink that would nauseate Agatha, then promptly banged upon her and Seleste's doors simultaneously until both their doors opened.

Seleste was alert but confused, wrapping a cobalt dressing robe around her middle. Aggie emerged ready to wage war, her auburn hair and stormy nightgown wild, a dangerous orb of onyx magic at her palm poised to strike. When she saw it was only Winnie and Sorscha, she cursed colourfully.

Aggie registered the smiles on Winnie and Sorscha's faces and her eyebrows rose. "Are you drunk?"

"Why is the hall…pink?" Seleste mused, wandering out of her room. "Goddess above, is that your magic?"

Aggie's lips parted, hope in her eyes. "Is it?"

Without warning, her orb escaped her control and dived into the fray, muting the light's hue to a dusty rose. They watched in awe as Seleste's magic shot from her hand unbidden and tangled itself in the knot of magic, turning it into an extraordinary glow of rose gold.

Sorscha reached out to touch it. Seleste followed.

Winnie looked at Aggie, the last three hundred years a distant nightmare. "*May love be what binds us.*"

Aggie's eyes filled with tears and she stepped forward in tandem with Winnie.

"May love be what binds us," they all four said in unison, Winnie and Aggie reaching forth to join Sorscha and Seleste.

As soon as their hands made contact with the brilliant glow, it burst, diving into each of them until they themselves were aglow. Regarding each other in awe and wonder, Aggie's locket broke free from her neck, floating toward the middle of the Sisters Solstice.

"What's happening?" Sorscha said.

The locket—their mother's locket—cracked, just like it had in Winnie's hand all those years ago. The four pieces broke apart, one gliding through the air to each Sister. They reached out to take them, their combined magic also breaking apart and shooting into each piece until they lay cold and normal in their trembling palms.

"What just happened?" Sorscha breathed.

Winnie closed her fingers around her piece. "I think we just ended our forced separation, Sisters."

Seleste jumped forward, wrapping an arm around Winnie on her left and Sorscha on her right. Sorscha pulled Aggie in and they fell to the ground in a heap of limbs and tears—just as they'd told Winnie they had the night Lilette was born. Only, on this night, Winnie was not alone.

She'd never truly been alone.

AGATHA

"Have you found anything?" Agatha came up behind where Grimm was sitting and slid her hands over his shoulders and down his chest, nuzzling his neck.

"No, and I won't if you come in here distracting me like that." He turned his head and kissed her hard. He pulled back and smiled against her lips. "What am I looking for again?"

Eleanor came in then, a tray of steaming coffee and some of Dulci's *croissants*. "Don't get used to this," she said, setting the tray down. "I no longer serve anyone."

Agatha smiled and Grimm said, "*Good*," before snatching a pastry.

Eleanor laughed. "We're preparing to leave before luncheon."

"Do you have everything you need?" Grimm asked.

She nodded, her attention snagging on the papers spread across the desk in front of him. "What are you researching now?" She leaned in, then darted back a fraction, turning toward Grimm. "Lilette Proctor? How strange. That was my mother's name."

Grimm and Agatha turned abruptly to each other. "Your mother?" Agatha asked slowly. "Was it a name passed down in your family?"

Eleanor straightened, her brow furrowed. "No. Actually, my mother had a name unlike the rest of her family. It was an homage to something her parents never explained. She died when I was a child, and my gran brought me to Merveille."

Agatha's heart hammered against her ribs and Grimm's face was stern.

They all turned in unison at the sound of Winnie's cool voice as she leaned in the doorway from the hall. "Where did she hail from, your mother?"

"Gran always said Hiverterre."

Winnie's eyes fluttered shut for a moment. "If you'll excuse me, I have somewhere I need to go. Please keep our guests comfortable."

She disappeared and Agatha exchanged shocked glances with Grimm.

WINNIE

It couldn't be.

The old woman stood in her kitchen, humming a sea shanty and stirring a pot.

"Eleanor is not your granddaughter."

The woman jumped half out of her skin, slamming a hand against her chest. "For the love of the goddess, child. You startled me. Use a damned door next time."

Winnie did not so much as blink. "*Eleanor is not your granddaughter.*"

With a sigh, the woman wiped her hands on the towel hanging from her apron and beckoned Winnie to sit. She did not, but the old woman did.

"Ellie is my granddaughter in all the ways that matter."

Winnie stood very still.

"How did you piece such a thing together? Ellie hasn't a clue. She thinks I'm her father's mum." Winnie still did not move or speak, and the old woman stared her down. After a long, heavy moment, her head cocked to the side, eyes squinted, and realisation dawned on her face. "Ah, is this why you sought Eleanor out, then?"

"I sought no one out."

"You look like her, you know. Lilette. Are you her daughter as well?"

Winnie's lips parted and she finally sank into a chair. "Lilette was my daughter."

She baulked. "I'm afraid to know what sort of power you wield to still be alive." The woman shivered. "Lilette was raised by another. Amalia."

Winnie nodded solemnly. "Yes." She lifted tear-laden eyes to her. "You knew Lilette well, then?"

"She was my greatest friend. Raised well by the people her mo—*you* left her with. Kind and gentle souls. We grew up just a stone's throw from one another, keeping to our own kind and practising very little. The Trials were still rampant at that time. Lily was different from the rest of us, though. She aged slower and her magic was formidable. More powerful than anyone I've seen to this day." The old woman smiled. "Lily always said she wanted to set foot on every continent in the realm, and she did. She sailed the high seas and trekked across mountains. The entire realm was her oyster. Her great lover, the wide open expanse of life."

"She was happy, then?"

The woman nodded. "She was. Her family never kept the truth about you from her. She knew her mother was powerful, brave, and loved her fiercely. They taught her that sometimes the right thing is the hardest to do, but what you did, you did for reasons unknown and only out of love. They always knew that. It was hard for Lilette, at times. She often had moments of hating you, but she always came around. Not much could keep her down for long. Until…"

Winnie hung her head, tears slipping free and sliding down her nose. "What happened to her?"

"Well, I was no Lily. Content to piddle around in my garden and kitchen, my big adventure was moving here to Merveille with Ellie. Lily returned from one of her wild adventures one day and came to visit. I was already looking well on in years by then, that was just over three decades ago. But Lily was still fresh-faced and beautiful, Some power she had, her magic. She'd met a mortal man in Merveille whom she fell in love with. A widower. Lilette finally put down roots after lifetimes as a nomad."

The woman smiled, shaking her head. "They were happy. He had youngins that needed a mother, and Lily was the most amazing kind. The years passed by and the children grew up. I warned her against conceiving a babe of her own at her age, at *his* age, but Lily was stubborn as an old ox." She laughed, but it choked off and her face fell. "One day, just before Ellie was born, George's heart gave out as he was riding. He fell off his horse and never woke.

"When Ellie came, Lilette loved her, she did. But she couldn't think. Couldn't breathe. The other children were grown, off living their own lives. She had no one in the house with her and she was mad with grief over George." She looked away, then ran a finger down the length of a scar on the table. "Lily came and left Ellie with me one day—"

"And just never came back."

She nodded mutely.

"Just like her mother before her." And Winnie's mother before her. Her lip pulled back. Sorscha was right. She should have said no that day.

"She did come back, a few years after I'd moved Ellie to Merveille. She was haggard and still half-mad, aged a hundred years. I don't know if she was sick, or her grief had dried her magic up… Lily kissed me and Ellie and said her goodbyes. I knew we'd never see her again. It was the deep sort of goodbye one gives as they depart this life."

"And you're certain she's dead?"

The woman nodded and the hope blooming in Winnie's chest crashed to the ground. "Buried her myself. I don't know how she did it, but I felt it when she passed. Something in Ellie broke, too, out of nowhere."

Winnie gasped. She'd had a moment like that as well. Sitting on the veranda of her mountain, looking out over the falls one Summer day, she'd doubled over in sudden pain. Not physical, but a deep sense of loss that lingered for days. "The fourth of Août," she breathed.

The woman's brows rose. "Yes. I located her and brought her here to be buried."

Winnie placed a hand on her chest, the pain almost too much to bear. "Can I see her?"

She followed the woman through the slums, down into a small valley and into the woods. It felt so eerily similar to the last walk she took her daughter on, nearly on the same date, all those years prior. She supposed, in a way, this was truly the last. They approached a small plot of land with a frozen stream and the woman stopped.

"This here is my land. No one knows it is mine, not even Ellie, because I want her to have it when I'm gone." Her eyes met Winnie's. "You'll ensure that happens?"

"I will." It felt so foreign, the idea that Eleanor was her *granddaughter*. Her flesh and blood. Her *family*. Just days prior she'd chosen her. Chosen to take a chance on the infuriating little bird as her friend. Vera's words flashed in her soul. *Family can be found. Chosen.*

"Lily is just there." She pointed to a small, simple headstone peeking out of the snow.

Winnie slowly made her way to it, each step purposeful and healing. She knelt before the grave and rested her hand on the name. *Lilette Proctor*. "You *lived*, my sweet. Long and full. One day, we will meet again, and I will never give you up for anything. I will love your daughter," she vowed, her voice breaking. "I will protect her. And I will never let her go, either." She stayed like that until the streams of tears on her cheeks began to freeze.

Then, she stood and strode back to the old woman. "What is your name, Eleanor's gran?"

"Louisa."

"Well, Louisa. You and I must visit with our Eleanor *toute suite*."

CHAPTER THIRTY

WINNIE

"If you do not stop staring at me, I will cut off all your pretty hair."

Eleanor scoffed. "Like Hades. Now I can say whatever I'd like to you and you can't threaten me properly."

Winnie sighed atop her horse, Eleanor grinning like a mad woman atop hers. In fact, Laurent was smirking as well and Tomás coughed a laugh behind his fist. "Is this how it will be, then? You'll take on the role of a spoiled little child? Louisa may have you back, then."

"Oh, *Gran*, get your knickers out of a twist."

Winnie threw a dagger past Eleanor, sinking it into a tree. Her eyes went wide and she looked thoroughly offended, but Laurent threw his head back and laughed, Tomás snickering as well.

"How dare you!"

"Call me Gran one more time."

"This is how you treat family?"

"Yes."

Winnie kicked her horse up a speed. Her witch hearing just caught the sound of Laurent behind her, bringing his steed up next to Eleanor's. "She never misses, you know. She won't really hurt you."

Poised to turn and throw a dagger at *Laurent*, Eleanor's answer halted Winnie. "Oh, I know. She's just still so damned cranky."

Laurent laughed and Winnie smiled to herself. "That's just Wendy."

"How far left now?" Tomás called. "I don't think I've ever been this far Nord."

Winnie pulled the reins and let them catch up. "Not far now."

"Not far at all," Laurent confirmed. "I'd say we'll make it by nightfall. With any luck, we'll be there before the market closes up for the day."

Anxious to have their journey over and potentially, finally, find the elusive man from the mountain pass, the travelling party urged their horses faster, making it to Lácdelle before the sun had truly begun her descent.

It was a fine village, guarded by the Sacrée Mountains on one side and Silver Lake on the other. Winnie marvelled at the boats, frozen in place, their edges curved up toward the sky. Bobbing in the water of Silver Lake on one of those watercrafts one chilly morning sounded divine. Laurent followed her line of sight and planted a kiss on her cheek. "Perhaps we'll hole up here come Spring," he murmured against her hair.

"Love birds," Eleanor snapped from behind them. "Can we get a move on? I've never been so cold in my life."

Tomás took her gloved hands in his, rubbing them and blowing his warm breath on them. Winnie snorted at the colour staining the girl's cheeks that had nothing to do with the frigid wind.

"Perhaps if you would move past the little magic finch and attempt to heat yourself, you wouldn't be quite so cold."

"As if it's that simple."

"It is."

"Ladies, ladies," Laurent stepped between them. "There is a cosy inn just there at the foot of the mountain and I would really enjoy a good night's"—he looked sidelong at Winnie—"*sleep*. So, yes. Let's move along."

They meandered through the thick mud, doing their best to spot any peculiar stall of wares underneath a poorly constructed wooden covering. At least the snow wasn't falling on them relentlessly, but it still made its way under the shelter, dusting everything in white.

Several stalls boasted roasted nuts or meats, their fires guttering every time the wind blew. Others had wool stockings and sheepskin moccasins; jarred fruit—from goddess knew where in a place as frozen as Lácdelle. Soon, the sun was sinking behind the mountains and many of the stalls were closing down.

"Is it time to call it a night?" Eleanor groaned, swiping at her muddy boots uselessly.

"No." Winnie pointed at Eleanor. "You're with me. Tomás, go with Laurent. It will be dark soon."

It was most likely a mistake to choose the girl…*Eleanor*, she corrected herself, but she and Tomás would accomplish nothing. Truth be told, Laurent would probably convince her it was a better idea to procure rooms at the inn before the rest of the market-goers did. In fact, she would likely find him and Tomás there before too long.

"Winnie, it's getting late. He's probably already gone. Can't we just ask someone?"

"No one needs to know anything about this." They dodged a wily child running after a loose hound, and a woman shouting that she was closing and her roasted walnuts were discounted.

"It's a simple question."

"Not if he truly sells strange wares. Anyone that inquires about him will be noted by someone."

Eleanor began to grumble again, but Winnie halted, throwing an arm out so hard that Eleanor ran into it with a grunt. "What in Hades?"

"Just there," Winnie whispered, pointing discreetly. A man, dark as night and covered head to toe in white, fiddled about with bottles, the *tink* of them gliding down the market aisle to meet Winnie's ears.

"Is that him?"

"Let's find out."

"Ah, good evening, mademoiselles." He smiled brightly. "It is quite late for a pair of beautiful women to haunt a mountainside market alone, is it not?"

Eleanor tensed next to her, but Winnie detected no threat. Curiosity concerning what might be in the rows of bottles lining his stall *almost* distracted her from the task at hand. "You come down from the mountain pass?"

The man's eyes creased at the edges as he smiled, more calculating than warm. "I don't see how that has anything to do with my wares, demoiselle. I assure you, they are worth your coin."

"What do you have to offer?" Winnie chastised herself for her curiosity, but it was gnawing at her.

"What do you have need of?"

Winnie's eyes narrowed. He was *that* kind of man, with *that* kind of wares. It could only mean he dealt in things mortals cannot, or he had access to underground markets Winnie did not even want to consider.

"Poison," Eleanor blurted.

Subtle.

"And what would a pretty thing like you need poison for, anyhow?" He kept his voice light, his mouth curved and eyes kind, for Eleanor. This man already knew Winnie was the threat.

"My father beats me." Winnie's attention fell on Eleanor. "I haven't prospects for marriage and no means to run. I need a way out."

The man softened, almost buying her story. He hobbled over to a row of amber vials. Winnie had thought him advanced in years, but she hadn't realised quite how far until he began walking. He took one up, leaning heavily on a cane with his other hand, and shuffled back over. "This'll melt the insides right out of him." He handed Eleanor the vial and she paled.

Winnie hoped it was true. She handed the man a coin pouch. He smiled kindly and made to turn away.

"You will come with us to Merveille," Winnie stated plainly.

He turned back slowly. "Pardon?"

ELEANOR

"You are needed in Merveille. It is urgent and of the utmost importance." Winnie did not so much as blink and Eleanor almost rolled her eyes. They weren't going to get anywhere with her making demands like that.

"Forgive me." He put a hand to his chest, brown eyes twinkling. "You are immensely beautiful, the both of you, but you are not my type and I am not overly fond of being commanded what to do, even by beautiful women who wish to kill their father."

Winnie opened her mouth, but Eleanor blurted, "Your prince and princess need you."

With the slowness of a predatory snow leopard, Winnie turned her head to glare at Eleanor with enough ire to make her visibly fidget. The man's forehead creased, a smile playing at the corners of his mouth. "*Princess*, you say? I was under the impression our dear prince refused to marry."

"He did. But, Princess Agatha is different."

"*Eleanor*," Winnie warned, her voice low and menacing. Fingers of magic came up and pinched Eleanor hard at the back of her neck. She tried not to wince, satisfied that she had at least gained the man's interest and pissed Winnie off for extra points.

He regarded them with shrewd eyes and Eleanor's palms began to sweat inside her thick gloves. "Princes *Agatha*," he mused. "The Autumn Daughter has finally come." Winnie and Eleanor exchanged a panicked glance as he stared off into the distance.

His thoughtful demeanour vanished and he smiled wide, spreading his hands out. "Well, who am I to deny my prince and princess, then?" He shuffled out the side of his stall, gathering a few things into a satchel around his body, and slammed a large wooden gate over it, turning a key in the lock. Shoving the key into his pocket, he turned to them. "Follow me to my tent to gather my belongings."

When he turned and began hobbling away, Winnie elbowed Eleanor in the side. "*What* were you thinking?"

"He wasn't budging," she whisper-shouted out the side of her mouth as she rubbed her ribs.

"These things take time. That was *far* too easy after you spouted confidential information."

"You were acting as the ice queen!" Winnie made a face and Eleanor sighed. "You know, when you act so peculiar people think you've gone mad."

"I don't care how I was acting. This is a delicate situation and now you've implicated my Sister. What if he's not even the right man? Anyone can sell you what you *think* is poison."

"Your *Sister* is the only reason he's coming with us. He knew about the Autumn Daughter. And Amira specifically said the man would know about Agatha. About the Daughter of

Autumn. If you'd *listened* for one moment, you would've known that."

Winnie pulled her to a stop, a finger in her face and the last few straggling patrons watching. "I know *exactly* what my Sister said. I also know we have no *leverage* now. That man knows our information and we know none of his. We have nothing to bargain with now, you fool. What if he wishes to do harm to my Sister and Grimm? What if the *empress* wishes them harm? What if she's been working with the magus this entire time and this was all a trap?"

Eleanor blinked, turning white as the snow.

"We haven't any choice now. Let's find the men and return home as swiftly as possible."

AGATHA

"And we really know nothing?" Agatha whispered, looking toward the hall where, behind the third door on the left, Rah sat waiting.

"We know he knew Amira personally," Winnie said, "her entire royal line, actually. And he has some secret knowledge concerning the two of you"—she pointed a fingernail between Agatha and Grimm—"and us, as Sisters."

Grimm frowned. "*Hidden knowledge* is simply a pompous arse's ploy to con innocent people out of money and life."

Eleanor blinked at him and Sorscha smirked. Seleste and Dulci sat calmly on the bench built into the bay window of Winnie's parlour.

"Wisdom of an ancient reaper," Laurent muttered, running a coin absently over his knuckles, back and forth. Tomás watched the coin like a cat before snatching it. The Cirque Master cuffed him on the back of the head.

"Does he even know where Amira is?" Gaius asked.

"He refused to speak with us, without Aggie and Grimm."

Agatha took a calming sip of her coffee just as Grimm shoved in another bite of *croissant*.

"Let's get on with it," she said, setting down her cup.

Vera hobbled away to retrieve the man, returning a few moments later. In the space between the shuffle of feet against the floor and this unknown man entering the parlour, Agatha exchanged an anxious glance with Grimm, mirrored in their entanglement, but also in the faces of all in attendance—which was everyone, sans Augustus keeping watch over the magus and Anne lingering in the hall nearby.

"Ah, good morning, Your Highnesses." Rah bowed at the waist. "Everyone." He gave a general, small bow to the others.

His white robes were rather tidy, as was his cane—something Agatha wasn't sure why she noted. Shaking her head to dislodge her trepidation, she handed Rah a cup of coffee and his eyes widened in surprise. "That is rather generous of you, Highness. Our Peasant Princess, indeed." The smile accompanying his words seemed genuine, no insult to be found, but ire shot through the bond from Grimm.

"We haven't a lot of time," Agatha said. "It's imperative that you tell us why Empress Amira would send us to retrieve you."

Rah took a sip of coffee and set the cup on a side table before the fire, eyebrows high and glancing around at all the sets of eyes watching him. "I must admit, I'm not certain myself." He shifted his weight on his cane.

"You're lying."

Agatha shot Grimm a look, but he didn't even register it.

Rah chuckled. "I'm afraid you're only seeing what you want to, Prince Thackery."

Grimm's jaw flexed. She didn't know what he was thinking,

but there was calculation coming from him. "Then why come?" he challenged. "Why come all this way?"

He shifted on his feet again. "I was told my prince and princess needed me. I was not told why."

"You agreed to come when you heard my name," Agatha broke in. "Tell us why Amira sent us to you. We do not have time for these games while she is missing."

Rah's face went slack and his cane slipped across the ground. "Missing? Empress Amira is *missing*?"

Agatha nodded, crossing her arms to hide her own shock at Rah not knowing this information.

Scooting back to sink into the lone empty chair in the room, Rah scrubbed a hand down his face. "I truthfully do not know why she sent me to you." He shrugged. "You already know you're the Daughter of Autumn and the Prince of Bone."

"You have to know more than that," Grimm interjected. "What does it *mean* that we are them?"

Rah's brow furrowed. "You don't know?"

Agatha glanced anxiously at Grimm, then shook her head, catching Winnie's piercing blue gaze before turning her attention back on Rah.

Face contorted with confusion, Rah mused, "But your mother's journals…"

The air caught in Agatha's throat and she heard Sorscha shift behind her. "My mother's journals? What do you know of my mother?" She hadn't a single journal of her mother's…

Rah splayed a hand as if it were obvious. As if he hadn't said something that would cause her heart to hammer against her ribs and her ears to ring. "Your mother was the High Priestess of the Fourth Order before the Second Order waged war and took control, creating what is known today as the one, singular Order."

Agatha staggered back a step and Grimm put a hand on the small of her back to steady her.

"The four factions," Winnie interjected.

Rah nodded in her direction, turning back to Agatha. "How could you not know this?" Rah shook his head, befuddled. "Your father spent the rest of his days, after Helsvar and your mother burned, furthering her work."

"*No*," Agatha said numbly. "My father died that day. They both did."

Rah's face twisted in what she vaguely thought could be anguish. "No, Princess Agatha. He did not."

Sorscha stormed up to Agatha's side. "You're a liar!" She lobbed the insult at him with spittle flying and Gaius was on his feet, dragging her backwards, whispering in her ear.

Winnie came up in her place and Seleste next to her. When Sorscha calmed after a few breaths, she stood on Seleste's other side.

"Explain yourself," Seleste demanded in a way Agatha had never heard from her sweet Sister Summer.

Rah looked nervous, but he did not step backwards. A mark to his credit, if Agatha were keeping score. She noted that Laurent had moved to stand behind Winnie and Tomás had taken Eleanor's hand across the room. A faint tapping came from behind Agatha, drawing her attention away until she realised without turning it was Dulci tapping her finger relentlessly on a table.

"Brother Ambrose returned to *Araignée*, where your mother hailed from, after Helsvar burned. He spent the remainder of his days convincing the four factions that the Sisters Solstice died that fateful day. That you four were no more."

"*Why*?" Sorscha demanded. Her magic was crackling at her fingertips, uncontrollable in her fury. Likewise, Agatha's hands felt hot, but her mind was reeling. Their father had lived?

Rah adjusted his stance, leaning more heavily on his cane. "Why, because of—"

His words were cut off by a blood-curdling scream.

Everyone looked confused, but Grimm dashed out of the room, Gaius and Agatha on his heels.

Augustus rounded a corner, nearly slipping in his haste. "It's the magus. He's unhinged."

Anne came up behind him, panting and pale. Grimm gently took her shoulders in his hands and slowed. "You're all right, Anne. It's going to be all right." She nodded too many times, tears pooling in her eyes, and Grimm handed her off to Agatha.

GRIMM

The screams did not cease as he made his way through Wendolyn's house, toward the wine cellar that served as the magus' dungeon. When von Fuchs had grown ill, they'd moved him deeper within the manor to keep the others safe. He'd worried The Order wouldn't be as apt to find his beacon if he were hidden under a manor surrounded by mounds of snow, but it was for the best.

The cries of terror morphed into uneven sobbing as Grimm descended the stairs into the cellar, Gaius at his back. He turned to gauge his comrade's reaction, surprised to find the comfort it lent him to have his friend back with him, especially in dire times such as these.

Curled up in a foetal position against the far stone wall, the magus trembled. His hands and feet were bound together, a rope leading from his ankles to a load-bearing beam in the wall. At the sound of their approach, he gasped, startling backwards against the stones, his eyes wild and filled with fear so thick Grimm could almost smell it.

"Where am I?" the magus pleaded. "Who are you?" He

looked around frantically. "Where is my wife!" His guttural shout broke off into a convulsive cry.

Grimm locked eyes with Gaius, unnerved to the bone. A chill ran down his spine, but he stepped forward. The magus darted backwards against the wall once more, looking at his palms as if they belonged to someone else. Grimm put out a placating hand, searching the magus' face. It was different. Something was different… His eyes had a striking clarity he'd never seen on the man, one he never realised had been missing.

Had they somehow managed to place someone else in his body? "Who are you?" Grimm asked, fighting to keep his voice even.

The man before him looked between his own hands and Grimm, chest rising and falling rapidly. "E-Emile von Fuchs." He pressed his back harder against the wall. "My wife," he pleaded. "Adrina. Where is she?"

Emile von Fuchs… What in Hades had happened to him down here?

"Grimm!"

Augustus was shouting his name up in the manor and he spun around to face the stairs.

"Grimm! Hurry!"

Without a second's hesitation he was flying up the stairs three at a time, Gaius close behind. He flung open the cellar door with enough force to hit the wall behind it, wood splintering. "Augustus. What's going on?"

He could feel tension, turmoil… Agatha was scared. And furious.

"Someone's coming," Augustus breathed. "Coming up the mountain. There are several of them, all in black cloaks. We can see them from the window."

Grimm cursed and began shouting orders, demanding everyone arm themselves. Gaius peeled off to do the same, ensuring everyone knew their exit point and when to use it.

Laurent slid to a stop next to him, magic thrumming. "Go with Gaius," Grimm demanded of the Cirque Master.

When Grimm made it to the parlour window, his heart fell to his knees. Out in the snow, front and centre, was his little witch, black magic cascading around her in the twilight.

The Order had answered his call.

CHAPTER THIRTY-ONE

AGATHA

They'd come. The Order had truly come to her Sister's *home* and Agatha knew exactly what they wanted. It was not the magus, but Grimm. And they would only get to him over her dead body.

Winnie stepped up next to her, glacial wind wrapping around her arms, awaiting the chance to be deployed.

Seleste came to Winnie's side, hands aglow and more fury than Agatha had ever seen her wear.

Sorscha stepped up to Agatha's other side, red lightning darting out in front of her and singing the snow. "Who's ready to play?"

Agatha's killing calm slipped over her like a fine gown and she smiled wickedly. "Let's go."

Winnie took the first step forward, spinning her arm above her head, a cyclone of snow building.

The robed individuals halted, faces obscured beneath their hoods and standing in a V shape. "We only want to talk."

"Like fucking Hades," Sorscha shouted. "Leave!"

"You have something of ours." The one at the tip of the V stepped forward, hands splaying when Winnie sent her cyclone closer. "We simply want it back."

"You forfeited the life of the magus when he abused my friend." Agatha came to the front, desperate to coax more from this person. It was the voice she'd recognised in the mirror back in Merveille, but she still could not place it.

A flash of teeth came from under the hood. "We care not what happens to von Fuchs, Daughter of Autumn."

Agatha's skin crawled, her magic surging around her in wisps of deadly nightshade. "What is it you want, then?" She jutted her chin out to keep from shaking.

"You know very well what we want."

Those teeth again. And Agatha felt Grimm behind her. *No.*

"Ah, see, that wasn't so hard, poppet."

GRIMM

Grimm clenched his jaw, fragmented memories assaulting him at the sound of that voice. He blinked them away, focusing on the power flowing through his veins, should he need to use it, as he stalked toward them all.

"What do you want with me?" he snarled.

"Oh, now, that is terribly obtuse of you to not already know, Marchand de Mort." She flicked her wrist and the others fanned out, surrounding Agatha and her Sisters before Grimm could get close enough. He let out a growl and pushed at one of them, but a shock of pain lit his abdomen on fire and he doubled over.

Agatha and her Sisters went back to back, hands out and magic at the ready.

"The Sisters Solstice," the woman crooned, her voice disembodied. "How very long the realm has thought you a myth. But I"—she danced forward a step, her cronies letting her into the circle—"I've always known."

Grimm straightened and pushed forward again, an invisible jab striking him in the jaw. He tasted blood on his lip and he gnashed his teeth at her.

"Just like I've always known that you, dear Prince of Bone, would be the key."

He blinked and the woman was right in front of him.

AGATHA

As soon as she landed in front of Grimm, Agatha sent her magic plummeting into the robed souls nearest her. Her Sisters did the same, Sorscha disabling one with a strike of lightning to the chest, the cloaked man falling to the snow in a smoking heap. Seleste's magic struck down two, their screams filling the dusk as they clutched at their eyes, melting from the light of the sun. Winnie sent shards of ice into a woman cutting her until she stumbled back enough for her to freeze her solid. Agatha's victims writhed on the ground, tormented by nightmares that had come alive behind their eyes.

It was magic she had not used in a very long time, but she would do anything to protect Grimm. To protect her Sisters.

"My, my." The woman clapped slowly, walking in an easy circle around the Sisters. "You are astounding, the four of you." She turned sharply back to Grimm. "If only the reaper would do what he's told." She tutted, stalking forward, what was left of her minions creating a tighter circle around Agatha and her Sisters.

Grimm squared his shoulders as the woman approached and Agatha raised her hand to send her magic into her, when a debilitating pain shot through her ears. Her magic fell away as she covered her ears, landing hard on one knee.

"What have you done?" she heard Sorscha shout over the deafening noise in her ears.

She opened her eyes in time to see Winnie spray the two in front of her with ice, only to have it shot back at her. With a cry of pain, she stumbled forward and Seleste knelt to help her up.

"We need to join together," Sorscha spewed, hauling Agatha to her feet. Her head was still spinning with the strange noise and she lost her footing, stumbling to the side again, just in time to feel a searing pain shoot up her leg and pool in her abdomen. She screamed and hit the snow again.

Grimm was snarling like a rabid dog, held down by two of the robed men. "Stop!" he shouted. "Whatever you're doing to her, stop!"

The snow felt so cool against Agatha's cheek. She wanted to close her eyes, but Grimm was still pulling, shouting, trying to get to her. His edges were beginning to flicker and a deep cloud of smoke was billowing from him. Her triumph quickly changed to horror when she saw the leader of the pack smile beneath her cowl at his transformation.

Agatha rallied herself, Sorscha tugging her up while Seleste did the same to Winnie. Battered, Sisters Winter and Autumn joined their magic with Seleste and Sorscha, their powerful orb of rose gold growing until it erupted into sparks that descended upon the robed individuals and incinerated them on the spot.

Seleste gasped for breath and Winnie dropped back down to one knee. Sorscha cursed. "Aggie, it's using too much. Something isn't right."

Agatha watched as Grimm shifted fully into his reaper form, his skeleton roaring, stalking forward toward the woman whose hood had fallen away. Her back was to the others, but

Grimm's step never faltered, no sense of recognition coming from him.

Laurent sprinted from the manor then, a shield of magic radiating around him, rippling the air. His step faltered briefly when he got close, shock dancing across his eyes. The woman pushed one arm out toward Grimm and the other out at Laurent. His shield disintegrated and both men froze in mid-step. The woman tipped her head back and laughed into the falling night. "Even the two of you, powerful as you are, are no match for me. What has happened to you, Cirque Master?"

Agatha's vision went white with rage. Winnie ran for Laurent while Sorscha and Seleste went to battle the remaining three men in robes.

Agatha magicked herself from where she stood, landing directly behind the woman and wrapping a tendril of magic around her neck. Sister Autumn's eyes went wide as the woman cackled, throwing off her magic as if it were child's play, sending it back to choke Agatha.

She writhed, gasping for air and tearing at her magic. What kind of sorceress could turn her own magic on her?

Agatha was lifted up into the air, feet dangling like the Witch Trial women buried in her Forest of Tombs. Clawing at her neck, spots began dotting her vision.

The woman righted her hood and turned to face Agatha. Winnie let out a war cry and transported to stand between them. Within a blink, there was a sickening snap and Winnie was crumpled on the ground whimpering. Agatha tried to scream, but she had no air and her vision was going dark.

Sorscha shouted, but everything was beginning to sound like Agatha had water in her ears. Sorscha stomped the ground and lightning shot up through the cloaked woman's feet, jolting her. Seleste magicked forward, sending a plume of blinding power into the woman's chest. She stumbled back a step and the noose around Agatha's neck loosened its grip slightly.

She could feel Grimm straining in the bond to break free of the hold she had on him. Laurent was squirming, his mouth sealed shut with magic. He was finding more success than Grimm, but they were both helpless.

The woman lashed out, her razor-sharp nails catching Seleste's eye, running down the side of her face, flaying flesh. Seleste screamed, clutching her face, and Sorscha unleashed a torrent of lightning, screaming as she did, pushing the woman back and back with snow spraying up around her. The woman dug her heels in and bared her teeth, face still lost in shadow.

She pushed her hand forward and Sorscha flew through the air, landing hard with her head smashing against a rock.

Agatha managed a garbled sound and it was all the woman needed to remember she was still alive and gaining back control of her power. She sent her own magic to bind Agatha's throat once more, sending her higher into the air.

A flash of white caught her eye and Vera came out of nowhere, wielding a spelled frying pan. She held her own, walloping the woman for an instant before she dropped her pan and clutched her heart. When she pulled back her hand, there was blood on it and Seleste screamed, rushing forward, blood marring her own face. She fell to the ground next to Vera and pulled her onto her lap.

Agatha's vision was only wide enough for a pin, unconsciousness dragging her under. What she could see was muddled by tears, but she could still make out Grimm in their bond. His thread was brighter than hers. Stronger. Pulsing and fighting. Hers was surrendering and with every slowing of her heartbeat, he pushed harder.

"Let's see if your Prince of Bone can break free now to save you," the woman drawled, pulling out a vial that was tied around her neck by a string.

As Agatha gagged, she pulled at her magic, begging it to be stronger. To break Grimm free.

Still, she was held fast.

A ball of golden light hit the woman in the back, Seleste clutching Vera to her chest, her arm extended. It singed the woman's cloak but did little else. Irritated, she whipped around and sent her own ball of magic into Seleste. A grunt escaped her and she collapsed on top of Vera.

"Where was I?" She ran a finger down Grimm's exposed cheekbone and Agatha found another iota of fight left in her. She kicked wildly, her limbs only half responding.

The woman pulled out the stopper on the vial and poured its contents onto her palms.

Grimm's blood.

Agatha managed to press against her magic enough to take one gasping breath, the woman's attention drawn foolishly back to her. "Why won't you simply stay *down*," she shouted, tightening the magic again.

Agatha felt the surge just before Grimm roared, breaking free of her confines and sending his skeletal hand deep into her chest. The woman dropped the vial into the snow, Grimm's blood coating it in droplets of red. "Let her go," he growled, pulling the woman's essence out just enough for her body to teeter.

"Oh," she laughed, menacing and eerie, "I would be careful, poppet. If I go, so does she." Her eyes flicked to someone behind Grimm and he turned, seeing at the same time Agatha did.

Anne, standing in the snow without a cloak as Augustus chased after her with his sword drawn and terror on his face. Her eyes were vacant. Devoid of life.

Oh, gods. It wasn't Grimm's blood. It was Anne's.

"Let them go. Let them *all* go," Grimm demanded.

"Every bit the gallant prince, aren't we? And what do I get in return?" she taunted.

"*Me*," he spat, shoving her essence back into her body.

No. Agatha pushed with all her might, her magic hardly responding at all, as if it were injured itself. Weak. Missing.

A slow smile crept through the shadows cast by the woman's hood and she snapped. Agatha and Laurent both fell to the snow. Augustus made it just in time to catch Anne as she collapsed.

Agatha reached up a hand to Grimm and she could see the glisten in his eyes. "*I will always find you*," he mouthed before the vile witch snapped again and his body went slack. In another breath, they were both gone, and Agatha screamed.

To be continued.

FROM THE AUTHOR

Dearest Reader,

It is my sincerest hope that you find yourself within these pages and know that the time has come. YOUR time has come. Rise, wild one. Let nothing and no one hold you back. Break off the limits, tear down the box. You've never been yourself in the corner, love.

I adore connecting with my readers. I do so mostly through TikTok, Instagram, and my Patreon—JL Vampa. I have a cozy group, JL's Vamplings on Facebook. Please do follow me on social media and join email list, which you can sign up for at jlvampa.com. There are also lovely art pieces, special editions, and fun merch at wickedwhimsyboutique.com

I hope to see you on the rest of this journey with the Sisters Solstice continuing in SPRING OF RUIN.

Best Wishes & Dark Tidings,

J.L.

facebook.com/jllvampa
instagram.com/jlvampa
patreon.com/jlvampa
tiktok.com/@jlvampabooks

MORE FROM J.L. VAMPA:

ACKNOWLEDGMENTS

Mama–You know every book I write is for you. You know my love of reading is thanks to you. And you know every tiny part of me that shows up in Winnie or Aggie, or any character better than anyone else. I love you.

Manon—Thank you for adding such helpful pages of kitty gibberish to my manuscript. And for all the late night snuggles as I write.

Mr. Tramel—You'll be in every Acknowledgements section until I die. Without that encouragement in the produce aisle of a market that I doubt you remember, I might never have penned another word.

A.E. Kincaid—My Write or Die. Welp, I'm crying. Without you trading words with me in the middle of a damn pandemic, I would have given up. I'll never, ever forget that.

KayleighAnne—If it's not too late for coffee, I'll be at your place in ten.

Jac—"If I'm alive, so are you. Our grave will be dug as one, and we'll climb in *together*." Thanks for being the only lovers left alive with me and for never reading the acknowledgments so I don't have to find something new and mushy to say.

My babies—Thank you for loving Mabon as much as I do. Thank you for teaching me every second of every day with your precious souls. I love you forever, just the way you are. No matter what.

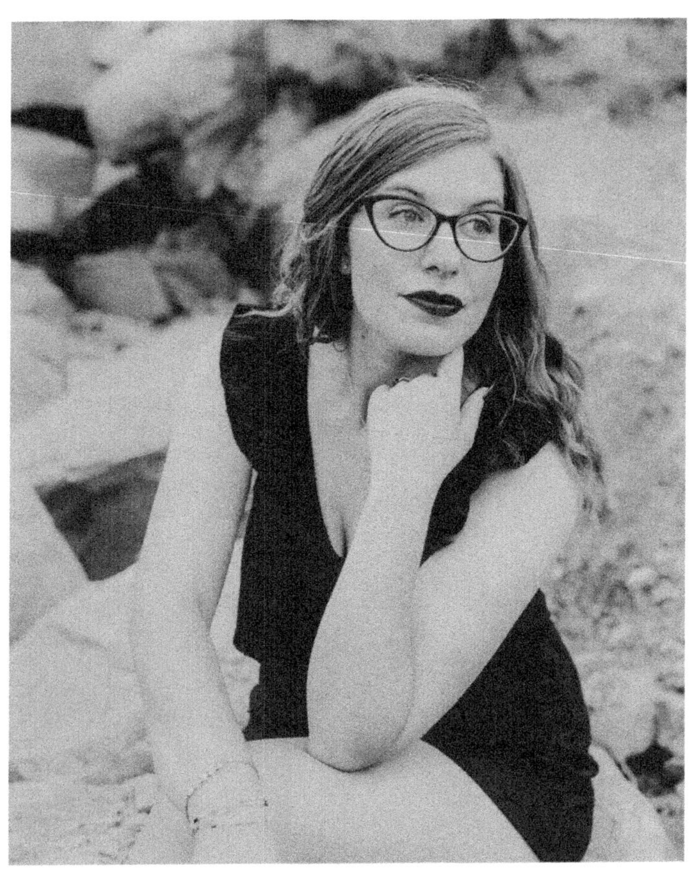

J.L. VAMPA

Jane Lenore (J.L.) Vampa is an author of Fantasy and Victorian Gothic fiction. She also owns a macabre-style bookish shop, Wicked Whimsy Boutique, and teaches writing courses via the Vampa Writing Academy. She lives in Texas with her musician husband and their two littles who are just as peculiar as they are.

Be sure to follow JL on social media.
@JLVampa

Printed in Great Britain
by Amazon